BOBE MAYSE
A Tale of Washington Square

BOBE MAYSE

A TALE OF

WASHINGTON

ʃQUARE

BY

NANCY BOGEN

THE TWICKENHAM PRESS
NEW YORK

Chapter Four appeared as
"Hippolyte Havel, An Imaginary Life" in
Anarchy, A Journal of Desire Armed, Spring, 1992.

First published in 1993 by
The Twickenham Press
31 Jane Street, Suite 17B
New York, New York 10014

COPYRIGHT ©1993 NANCY BOGEN

All rights reserved. No part of this book may be used or reproduced in any manner whatsoever without written permission, except in the case of brief quotations embodied in critical articles and reviews.

Library of Congress Cataloguing-in-Publication Data

Bogen, Nancy, 1932–
  Bobe Mayse : a tale of Washington Square / by Nancy Bogen.
    p. cm.
  ISBN 0-936726-03-2. — ISBN 0-936726-04-9 (pbk)
  1. Strikes and lockouts—Clothing trade—New York (N.Y.)—History—20th century—Fiction. 2. Greenwich Village (New York, N.Y.)—History—fiction. 3. Triangle Shirtwaist Company—fire, 1911—Fiction. 4. Women clothing workers—New York (N.Y.)—Fiction. 5. Mothers and daughters—New York (N.Y.)—Fiction. 6. Havel, Hippolyte—Fiction. I. Title.
PS3552.0434B6 1993   92–63378
813'.54—dc20   CIP

FIRST EDITION
Printed in the United States of America

For
ARNOLD GREISSLE-SCHOENBERG,
without whom this book could not have been written.

CONTENTS

Prologue
1

Four Lives
15

The Strike
103

The Fire
247

Epilogue
317

BOBE MAYSE
A Tale of Washington Square

PROLOGUE

PROLOGUE

       What makes Washington Square the special place that it is? Most people who are familiar with it would answer at once: Washington Arch and the circular fountain nearby, and possibly include pale pastel-green Garibaldi on his pedestal with sword half drawn. To complete the picture, they would doubtless add Judson Church's light orange-yellow hulk and its graceful companion tower, and the north side's faded red-brick townhouses with their immaculate white doors flanked by Grecian columns.

 There it is, Washington Square—only not quite. To a long-time traverser of its walkways like myself—from my apartment on nearby West 4th and Perry clear across to New York University's English Department—there is something more to the Square, a certain charm that's greater than the sum total of those parts. But, alas, in recent years with so much of the old gone and so many new features that are out of keeping—like the blockish World Trade Center towers dominating the southern horizon—that charm is now more to be imagined than perceived.

 How far back in time would one have to go then to find the "real" Washington Square? At least to the first decade of our century, I'd say—that is, when the townhouses, which graced three of the sides, were strictly for living in, not given over to university doings, and the grassy places in between, instead of being the Quad, formed a part of everyone's front lawn, with the Arch and fountain, wafting up a mist onto a surrounding lily pond, as the centerpieces. Towering structures there were of course, on the Square's fourth side: NYU's Main Building together with those named Celluloid and Lees for commercial purposes. But they were towering within reason—no higher than ten stories—and their facades, of off-white stone, were adorned with pediments and columns so as to be in harmony with the townhouses.

In those days there was a clearly discernible class division among the residents of the Square. In the particularly fine houses on the north side lived the swells—people named Livingston, Rhinelander, and Stewart, whose roots went back to the Revolution and before—along with Johnny-come-lately's like John B. Claflin of H.B. Claflin's Department Store. And in Number 10, the mayors of New York made their homes, George B. McClellan, son of the Civil War general, being the last to do so in 1906. The Square's west side, which was less grand, housed others not quite so prominent—the merchants Hugh Kelly and Celestino Piva, for example—and a whole host of clerks, saleswomen, and the like in flats and single rooms. To be avoided at all costs by anyone decent and self-respecting was Washington Square South, whose houses were roosting places for all kinds of artistic riff-raff, especially Number 61, which was presided over by a German-Swiss widow named Catherine Branchard and eventually came to be known as the House of Genius because of the number of famous ones who stayed there. Saloons, with the usual hangers-on, were not uncommon on that notorious south side; one in particular seems to have flourished for ever so long on the corner of Thompson opposite Judson Church, where now stands an ultra-modern Roman Catholic chapel.

Every weekday morning there was a great flurry of departure from the residences, with the menfolk of the north side, wearing top hats and frock coats, being whisked away to brokerages, banks, and law firms in horse-drawn carriages or impeccably polished automobiles,

Prologue

while the less fortunate, in meaner garb, either hopped a trolley, or else hoofed it over to the Sixth Avenue El or the new subway on Astor Place.

In the midst of this general leave-taking, crowds of poor young women appeared on the scene, all dolled up to the extent that scanty pocketbooks would allow. Mostly Jewish and recently arrived from Russia, Poland, and the Austro-Hungarian Empire, or else Italian, they swept across the Square busily chattering—in their own tongues, of course—and oblivious, or seemingly so, to everything else. Where were they heading, those unseemly foreigners? Toward what the genteel residents deplored as another blot on the neighborhood—the side streets behind Washington Square East, which were lined with factory buildings where all manner of stuff to wear was made, including those new-fangled garments for ladies called shirtwaists.

There the immigrant horde labored until after dark, when the factories disgorged them and the scene on the Square was repeated in reverse—with buggies and motorcars rolling up and trolley bells clanging.

Meanwhile, the streetlights had blinked on with an electric crackle, and were glowing purplish. Then, as people all around the Square settled in for the evening, the windows in the houses began brightening—to bluish tones on the Patrician side and to yellow from gas across the way among the Bohemians.

Sundays were another matter, with hardly anyone about at first save for a few souls walking their dogs. But then, shortly before eleven, respectable doors began to open, and with hails of "Good Morning" back and forth, men and women in subdued Sunday colors went trooping over to the Church of the Ascension or First Presbyterian a few blocks up from the old Brevoort Hotel on Fifth Avenue—to troop back before very long and venture forth no more, except perhaps for a brief after-lunch trot or spin through The Central Park.

On Sunday afternoons in good weather, the Square and its benches became the province of the workaday folk who lived thereabouts. Gowned and cravated in cheap imitation of their betters, they had for entertain-

ment the fellow with the crushed black fedora, red bandanna, and a pert monkey on his shoulder—the hurdy-gurdy man, inevitably trailed by a band of Italian slum kids looking to strut around for a penny.

The tunes that he cranked out were generally easy ones—like "Sweet Rosie O'Grady." But now and then one's ear picked up something rare and intricate, which his box-with-the-handle sounded out as if the maker of its mechanism had caught the harmonies straight from the lips, the throat, the very soul of Caruso or Melba in one of the aeries of the Metropolitan Opera House of an evening...

One year for a month of Sundays, the Square echoed and re-echoed with a lover's final avowal—"I will never let you go! Never!"

Or so the quivering strains seemed to say.

There's a bronze plaque hanging beside the entrance to NYU's Brown Building that commemorates a sad event. It reads:

> On this site, on March 25, 1911, there died in a fire at the Triangle Shirtwaist Company, 145 people, most of whom were young women between the ages of 16 and 25.

One day some years ago—as it happens, close to the anniversary of that event—my eyes chanced to linger on the plaque for a moment as I was about to step into Brown, and all at once reality struck home. I suddenly realized that the tragedy had indeed occurred there, on the eighth, ninth, and tenth floors where classes were being held, and gazing upward, I began to imagine the smoke and heat from the flames...people, trapped, screaming...the females, some of them mere children, in the long cumbersome dresses they wore in those days...

The vision of utter chaos and agony was still hauntingly in mind the following Sunday, when I went to pay my weekly visit to my mother, Fanny. As she was in her early eighties, I wondered if she remembered that terrible day; if nothing else, she, so full of anecdotes usually, was sure to know something about it from hearsay,

Prologue

having been a machine operator in a dress factory after World War I and an active member of David Dubinsky's very vocal ladies garment workers union, the ILGWU.

It was warm and crisp out, so Fanny was seated on her terrace, which overlooked Eighth Avenue from the eighteenth floor of one of those pink ILG buildings in the West Twenties. Greeting her, I marveled at how fit she seemed—considering all. Her face, a formidably Sephardic one, with an "olive" complexion and sparkling black eyes, positively glowed in that light; her hair, also black and pulled tightly back into a bun, glistened. Always a snappy dresser (to borrow one of her generation's expressions), she looked exquisite in a blouse of Betsy Ross red set off by a string of white beads and a large white button on each earlobe, and a navy skirt with matching hose and pumps.

I should explain a little more about Fanny. A victim of crippling arthritis, she had recently been confined to a wheelchair, presumably for good—a hard fact to reckon with for someone whose whole life had been spent in hustle and bustle—second only to such a one's having to resign herself to being "under the thumb" of a nurse-companion.

A ritual of my plying her with questions about the chair, the companion (discreetly withdrawn inside), the food, her medication, and so on had to be gone through first before anything else. I waited until Fanny had grasped my hand and pulled it into her lap, which she had taken to doing of late after the cross-examination was over. Then I told her about the commemorative plaque and put the new question to her—did she have any memory of that conflagration at Triangle which had claimed so many young lives?

"Oh—yes," she answered rather slowly and deliberately, "I was only a little girl then, but I do remember it—very well—vividly, in fact."

And then the oddest thing: her eyes, those shining black eyes, lowered, and she added very softly, "I lost a sister there."

I looked at her, startled—a sister? This was news to me. My mother had only two sisters that I knew of, Dinah and Pauline, both of them older. Aunt Pauline, closer to her in age, had passed away about a year ago. Aunt Dinah was still going strong at eighty-seven.

"My oldest sister—Martha," Fanny explained, in a wistful way. "She was only eighteen—a wonderful girl—and in love too."

"Well, I—I'm sorry," I stammered, though mystified as to why I'd never heard any mention of that Martha before.

I waited for something more to be forthcoming, but nothing was. Fanny's mind had drifted off somewhere—to a happier place—and I decided to let the matter be for the moment, pursuing it no further.

Still, it certainly is strange, I couldn't help thinking. Had that oldest sister's loss been so profoundly felt as to plunge the whole family including Fanny's parents, my grandma and grandpa Ferber, into utter silence all those years? Or what?

After supper—our favorite noodle dish, *lokshn*, *kez*, and *puter*, with lots and lots of pot cheese and oodles of butter—I began strolling home along Eighth Avenue as was my wont. However, instead of turning in at my place, my feet somehow led me further to Washington Square.

It was getting on toward six o'clock, and with evening shadows gathering, only one spot in all that space still had sun—crazily, the very spot, Brown Building's upper stories!

Again I found myself picturing how it must have looked then, with flames shooting out the windows and young women leaping from them as they frantically sought escape from the heat, smoke, and burning…

An aunt of mine was there, died there that day, I said to myself, finally and reverently.

Several days later, I went to have lunch with my Aunt Dinah, and there was greeted with a fresh surprise—a real shock.

As get-togethers between Aunt Dinah and me have always been few-and-far-between, requiring some good reason on one of our

Prologue

parts, again let me explain. During their childhood, she and Pauline, who was only a year or so younger, were constant companions, usually to the exclusion of my mother. Later on in their teens and twenties the gap widened when Dinah and Pauline married two ambitious young furriers, while Fanny began sewing away in the factory. The furriers soon made it big, enough for them to bid farewell to the Lower East Side, where they'd all grown up, and eventually to install themselves and their families in costly homes in Forest Hills with adjoining summer hideaways in Rockland County. Fanny, in the meanwhile, had met and married my father Murray Greenberg, a cutter, and the two of them had set up housekeeping in a snug but comfortable apartment in Brooklyn, where they continued to live until his death ten years ago.

Recently, Dinah's world had suffered a kind of eclipse, with the passing away not only of her dear Pauline, but also the two partners, their husbands. Suddenly, in advanced age—with her children settled in far-off Chicago and California, and involved with families of their own—she had found herself very much alone. While down in Florida that past winter, she had contacted Fanny and tried more than once to get them to do something together—only to no avail, my mother politely but flatly declined each time. And that was what had prompted Dinah to phone and invite me up: having just re-opened the country house after brief stays with the kids out west, she wanted to sound me out as to how to "break the ice" with Fanny and make up for all those years of neglect.

Turning into Dinah's driveway, I became aware of a general hush all over—quite a difference from the pleasant activity that I recalled from past visits. The house, a refurbished Victorian, seemed as desolate as Pauline's next door, all shut up and waiting to be disposed of by her children.

As for Dinah herself—well, she was still the same old Aunt Dinah, I saw, as she unlatched the door to the screened-in back porch: as fair of face as Fanny was dark, with startling blue eyes, and hair, kept closely cropped, dyed to a light reddish-brown. Never having shown a knack for dressing up despite her affluence, she had on what can only be described as an expensive housedress, its print of tiny pink tulips on a pale blue background.

First things first, over frosted glasses of iced tea, Aunt Dinah wanted to know about my mother's condition, since Fanny had disclosed only the barest details. As I filled her in, she listened with slow nods, realizing that most of the good times she'd envisioned for the two of them—like a round-the-world cruise and even season tickets to the opera, which Fanny so enjoyed—were now out of the question.

When it came time for lunch—blintzes immersed in sour cream—the subject was exhausted, so I decided to chance bringing up possibly another difficult one, the mysterious Martha, who had been in my thoughts constantly.

No sooner done than Dinah was staring at me wide-eyed—"I'm sorry to have to tell you this. I have no idea of whom you're speaking, I've never heard of your Martha. There were only three of us—myself, Pauline, and your mother."

"But—but—" I didn't know what to say—or think.

To drive her point home, Dinah got a black hand-tooled leather case from somewhere inside, and opening it, set it before me—"This was taken around 1907."

It was a glass-enclosed photo of her father and mother, my grandpa and grandma Ferber, as a young couple with their family; I'd seen it before, of course, and now remembered it. In a fashion typical of the time, grandpa, in a dark suit with a white wing collar and dark tie, was seated with the baby on his knee—Fanny, aged two, with her raven tresses—and on his right was six-year-old Dinah in calf-length ruffles. Grandma the *balebos*—hard worker—stood on his other side, stuffed in dark lace-trimmed taffeta, with Pauline, a near-blonde of five, also in frills, beside her on the left.

Clearly, nothing further needed to be said; if there had been another child of fourteen or thereabouts, she would have been among them, and that was that.

Prologue

It took a long while of silence for the true state of affairs to sink in: that Martha had never existed; my mother had made her up.

"I'm sorry about this, Barbara," Dinah said, after going and putting the picture away, and patted my arm.

But I didn't understand. It was so unlike Fanny to do something like that; in all my life I never remembered her saying the least little thing that wasn't an actual fact. Why even in my pre-school days, it was Daddy who always spun the yarns at bedtime, with Fanny always marveling at how clever he was.

Just as puzzling if not more so, why had Fanny invented that fourth sister? What was it that she'd hoped to accomplish by so doing?

Dinah seemed to read my mind—"I must confess, Pauline and I always felt that your mother was—a little touched."

What! But what a thing to say! "What do you mean?" I demanded, almost beside myself.

Dinah threw me a foxy look. "You k-n-o-w," she answered.

"No, I don't, I don't know," I said.

"Well, the way she lived."

I still couldn't follow her drift—"Lived? Lived how?"

"Her going to work in that factory for one thing."

"What was wrong with that?"

Dinah's look grew sharp—"Wrong? She was swimming against the tide, that's what. Your father too. Everyone else in those days was trying their darndest to lay their hands on some cash to start a business with and get ahead in the world."

"So?" I said. "They chose just to work for a living, so what?"

Dinah's eyes squeezed together menacingly. "There was also the crowd they ran with—A PACK OF DYED-IN-THE-WOOL REDS!" She finally spat it out—"YOUR PARENTS TOO!"

What! My parents? Communists? But was she serious? "Why my folks were the biggest bourgeois homebodies that ever walked the face of the earth," I argued back, as anyone who was at all acquainted with them knew. "And if they walked a picket line now and then, it was strictly for what they felt they or their fellow workers were entitled to, believe me."

"Oh, come on!" Dinah shot back. "They belonged to Dubinsky's union, didn't they? He was a socialist, no?"

"Well, yes, of course, but—"

"Communist, socialist, it's all the same," Dinah dismissed with a wave.

But how could she be so obtuse? I was all for giving her a good piece of my mind and treating her to a lesson in political philosophy to boot—however, only for a moment. Best simply to change the subject, I decided.

Her children and grandchildren were safe bets, so we chatted about them for a while. But then, Dinah, always one for sticking the knife in deeper and giving it a twirl, switched to me. Hadn't I, at age fifty-five, gotten tired of living alone yet, and wouldn't I have been better off if, instead of becoming a professor*keh*, I'd gone to work in an office, where I could have met someone?...

Happily, it was soon time to leave.

"Don't forget to say hello to your mother," Dinah reminded me at the screen-door, then shook her head and frowned with concern. "I only hope for your sake that's the end of it, Barbara."

Needless to say, I was plenty worried. What could this fabrication by my mother signify? Was she indeed beginning to lose her wits? And if so, was the lapse some further manifestation of her illness, or was she simply growing old?

The first thing to do obviously was to get hold of her doctor, which I did as soon as I arrived home.

A fortyish nuts-and-bolts type but also a mensch, he re-checked her medications in his directory, and then finding nothing amiss there, recommended a number of tests, including a CAT scan—which, to make a long story short, were duly performed.

Prologue

But, of all things, they didn't turn up anything.

"So where do we go from here?" I asked, after hearing the news from him on the phone. I was still deeply troubled: in my calls to Fanny, which were now daily, she persisted in believing in the reality of her Martha.

"Well, normally in such cases, the next step would be to refer the patient to a psychiatrist," he answered. However, in view of my mother's age and physical condition, he just didn't see the point.

"Meaning?" I pressed.

Meaning that the sessions would drag on and on with nothing much being accomplished. "I suggest that you try and live with it," he advised. After all, Mother functioned satisfactorily in other respects, didn't she, so what difference would it make really?

"Is that it then?" I wanted to know.

No, he had a further piece of advice for me. "Go over there and spend more time with her. And above all, draw her out and listen to her about Martha." I pictured him smiling slightly at this juncture, and poking up his glasses, slipped down on his nose a little in the process. "One can never tell what the upshot might be. Martha's story might in some curious way turn out to be a mirroring of her own—"

"Like an *apologia*, a justification?"

"Something like that"...

So be it; I lost no time in following through. The next day, as soon as my last class was over, there I was hastening up Eighth Avenue.

It being quite warm, Fanny was out on the terrace again—in a dress of dainty white cotton pinched together at the waist by a red leather belt, whose accent was reflected in her earrings and shoes.

In her lap was a ball of white thread and a crochet needle, with a doily in the shape of a many-prismed snowflake well under way.

"So how'd we make out?" she asked, meaning with the medical tests.

"Everything's fine," I said—the truth, after all.

She smiled with a twinkle in her eyes, those bright black eyes.

So, now, let's begin, I prompted myself, after taking a seat beside her. "You know, you keep on mentioning your sister Martha, but I'm sorry, for the life of me, I can't picture her."

The smile did not diminish by so much as a hair. "Would you like to hear about her first—or Jerrold or Hippolyte?"

I suddenly became conscious of the homeward-bound traffic below on the avenue. By sitting up straight and craning my neck, I could see people, freshly released from jobs, scurrying along. A breeze had arisen; dust was flying: it would rain soon. Above ground, in our line of vision, a white plastic bag was floating, like a jellyfish.

"Were Jerrold and Hippolyte her beaux?" I asked.

"No, just admirers," the stranger, my mother, answered very sweetly. "Her beau was someone else—if you can call him that."

"It sounds as if you have quite a story there."

"Yes," she said with quiet assurance. "Yes, I do."

This is the story—or rather, these are the stories—as she related them. "Wove" would perhaps be a better way of putting it.

Here and there I have taken the liberty of adding embellishments from reading and from a long list of people consulted too numerous to mention.

Let them receive thanks here collectively in her behalf.

FOUR LIVES

CHAPTER

I

But first, before we turn to Martha and the others, it is necessary to say something about Fanny's folks, especially her mother, because they figure importantly at the end of our story; also because it is interesting to see where the family originated and how they got here.

Her name was Bertha, and she came from Berdichev, a small city not far from Kiev in the Ukraine. What her true family name was nobody knew, for she was a foundling...had been left as a new-born infant in a basket in the women's section of the Merchant's Synagogue. The year was 1870.

At first little Bertha seemed destined for more misfortune, as the young woman into whose hands the Ladies Auxiliary of the synagogue put her had recently lost a husband and an only child to the dreaded cholera, and scarcely paid any attention to the baby that was Bertha. But fortunately, the Ladies learned of this neglect from the neighbors, and they found a new home for her with Pincus and Brucha Rabinovich, an older childless couple who turned out to be kindness itself.

Uncle Pincus, as little Bertha came to call him, was short and heavy-set, and had a bald spot in the middle of his head. He was in dry goods, with a modestly thriving business in Berdichev's commercial district, and ambitious but not overly so. Tante Brucha, his wife, was stout like him and afflicted with weak eyes and a perpetually runny nose that left her nostrils permanently red. She shared Uncle's mild temperament and enjoyed a reputation for keeping a good house. Their dwelling, of sturdy stone, was situated on one of the better residential streets, in Berdichev's Jewish quarter of course.

Bertha's chief delight as a little girl was the parlor, as she was fond of telling her youngest daughter Fanny in after years. There one found all manner of tantalizing rare things, such as a gilt-legged sofa and chairs covered in pale blue, lemon, and pink satin brocade, thick velvet drapes the color of ripe olives, a deep-piled Persian rug of salmon and leaf-green with threads of gold running through it, and most precious of all, a glass-enclosed cabinet reaching almost to the ceiling, on whose mirror shelves were arrayed a dainty china tea service, a silver samovar with a matching pair of candlesticks, and a collection of incredibly thin crystal goblets with the most delicate tracings of flowers and birds on them. Here of a Sunday afternoon would gather members of the Rabinovich's circle, which included some of Uncle's colleagues in the cloth business, a few other tradespeople, a lawyer or two, a doctor, and their families.

Bertha's second favorite room was the dining room, where there was a magnificent crystal chandelier overhead, whose candles were set ablaze on special occasions. Built into one of the walls was a brown-enameled peat stove for keeping toes toasty in winter, and in the center of the room, occupying its whole length, stood a mahogany table and chairs, each of which had a dark red velvet cushion with a tassel. There at mealtime, with Uncle and Tante sitting grandly on either end, Bertha eventually took her place.

The Rabinovich's prided themselves on being what the Russian Jews of those days called "enlightened," meaning that Uncle wore long sideburns reaching almost to his chin instead of a beard and

Tante dared to show herself in public with her own hair—alas, a very thin fuzzy brown with the scalp showing. But in order to live at peace with their more religious neighbors and also "so as not to be a shame before the gentiles"—the *goyim*—they introduced no forbidden food into the house—*treyf*—and put in an appearance at synagogue on Saturdays and the High Holy Days. Tante, despite her aversion to wigs, was not quite so advanced in thinking as Uncle, dutifully lighting the candles every Friday night and actually praying over them like her mother before her. "Who knows" and "It doesn't do any harm," she would explain with a shrug and a slight smile to anyone who raised an eyebrow.

Bertha grew into a charming girl—a *meydl*—so everyone pronounced her, with a head of fine black hair and a very fair complexion, in which were set light bluish-green eyes, a small wide nose flanked by chubby cheeks, and a sweet little mouth. Uncle and his friends had very strong views about the education of females, a topic much under discussion in those days, so from early on Bertha sat with a tutor learning to read and write in Yiddish, which they all spoke, and not long after started going to classes given by a rabbi's wife to read a little Hebrew in the Bible so that "she would know what it was to be a Jew." Later on, Uncle added tutors in Russian, German, and arithmetic among other subjects—and in all of them Bertha demonstrated herself not without talent and unostentatiously eager to please.

Tante, who still harbored old-fashioned notions about what a woman should know, had her way with the girl too. Beginning in her seventh year, Bertha began spending her spare time in the kitchen, and by her mid-teens she had helped Bella the hired woman prepare just about everything delicious that one could think of—from gefilte fish, stuffed cabbage, and pea soup with *flanken* to carrot *tsimes*, potato *latkes*, and matzoh *bray*. To this was added instruction in sewing, on the treadle machine as well as by hand. And Bertha being nimble of finger, it wasn't long before she could take an old rag of a dress and transform it into something else—which was quite a knack according to Tante, for one never knew "what might happen in this world." Eventually the two of them turned to knitting, crocheting, and embroidery as well.

About boys, Bertha began to think around the time when everyone normally does, with a pleasantly full feeling in her chest and a fine warmth below, especially around that time of the month. What went on between grown-ups in the privacy of their bedrooms she seems to have known when fairly young; Tante must have seen to that part of her education too.

On reaching the age of sixteen, Bertha gathered from remarks dropped by Uncle and Tante, as well as from what was going on with other girls her age, that it was time to think about getting married, and possible candidates were indeed there among sons of their friends. But it wasn't until three years later that someone truly struck her fancy, the younger of a pair of brothers named Ferber, recent arrivals from Vilna who had started up a small dye works in Berdichev's outskirts. The one Bertha liked was called Elya, and he had a face even fairer than hers, topped by a shock of dark brown hair, with a foxy little beard that wagged when he smiled. Her heart immediately went out to him when she heard that he had lost his parents as a boy, and had been cared for by his brother Avrem, who was older by a dozen years. Whether this Elya had a like affinity for her, Bertha had no way of telling, as he seldom spoke, and when he did, it was never to her. But the whole world knew better.

Everything came to a head one Sunday six months after the Ferbers began frequenting the Rabinovich house. It was a lovely summer day, and Elya showed up earlier than anyone else, alone, in his dark blue jacket with gold buttons that so became him. At a hint from Tante that something was afoot, Bertha too had taken pains with her appearance, putting on her maroon dress with the cream-colored collar, which made the light bluish-green of her eyes stand boldly out and heightened her hair's blackness. After a brief hello and a curious stare, Elya went to the little garden they had behind the house, and Bertha, urged by Tante, followed, joining him on a stone bench beneath a magnolia tree. There they remained for several minutes scarcely breathing, until Elya, gathering his courage, reached up and plucked a magnolia blossom and slipped it in her hair, then smiled his twinkly smile uncertainly. Bertha took it in her hands, pretty pink flower-ears, and held it close to her bosom—and then they both went back inside, without having exchanged so much as a single word.

The following Saturday, older brother Avrem—who had his own shock of dark hair and pointy beard—came to dinner with his small round-faced wife, Dora Leah, and Elya. And there beneath the crystal chandelier sparkling with candlelight, Bertha's true love placed on her finger a petite silver ring with a twinkling diamond in it, and solemnized the moment by pressing his lips to her cheek. But what a pressing! With only Uncle's woolly whiskers to judge by, Bertha had never dreamed that a man's mouth could be so...melting. Something like a streak of lightning flashed through her.

After that, the young bride-to-be and her fiancé met regularly under the magnolia tree, where everyone more or less left them alone, and where they held hands and even spoke a little now and then. Once Elya went into a pout when her attention momentarily strayed to a young workman mending something nearby.

The wedding took place several months later right there in the garden, and for this event the Rabinoviches outdid themselves, sparing no expense. There were weeping violins and a groaning clarinet, and everyone danced a lot. Then finally, in the wee hours of the morning, with the whole company a little tipsy or *farshikert* as one said—why it was time for the young couple to go. So off they drove in Uncle's droshky to a cottage that Elya and his brother had built practically with their own hands, as indeed they had Avrem's cottage next door and the modest factory building, a short distance away. There in the days that followed, Bertha and Elya worked matters out to their mutual satisfaction—which Bertha, in supplying this account to her daughter Fanny years later, said was owing ninety percent to luck and a sense of humor, the other ten to caring and understanding.

And there in Berdichev, were it not for something unforeseen happening, they probably would have ended their days, in time moving to a good stone house like Uncle's and Tante's, for the brothers knew a thing or two about business. Yes, something happened one day that was so out-of-the-ordinary as to change their lives forever beyond anyone's wildest imagining.

It was early in the afternoon on the second day of Passover the following spring, and Bertha had just returned from cuddling Dora Leah's baby, born a few months before. All at once, glancing out the window, she caught sight of Avrem and Elya lurching along the road toward home as if they were drunk. What could it be? As they drew closer, she saw that their faces were dark as if covered with soot!

Immediately Bertha rushed out the door. Sister-in-law, who had noticed too, was right behind her, with little Josef in her arms.

"What happened?" they both cried out, on reaching the husbands.

"There was—a fire," Elya haltingly explained—their dye works. The whole place was a smoldering heap of ruins, with everything gone, their machinery, available stock of dyes, and chemicals to make more with.

How the fire had begun was a mystery, but because it was close to the goyim's Easter, Avrem could not help wondering later, when they had calmed down, if it had not been set deliberately by some of them thereabouts—some low-life—with the connivance of the envious among their help and the support of local priests. Certainly, as all four knew only too well, incidents like this had been occurring with increasing frequency in Jewish communities all over Russia. In one instance, Avrem reminded them, a holy man was supposed to have worked his congregation up to fever pitch with some nonsense about Jews drinking the blood of Christian children on Passover, and then led them on himself to burn and pillage, bearing before him a ceremonial gold cross on a rod.

Bertha herself had a faint memory of something like that happening when she was very young—of being taken away by the Rabinoviches in the middle of the night (to visit relatives up north, they said), and then of returning to find the lovely house and the others on the street all smashed up inside. Also dimly remembered by her were whisperings about some of the people who had stayed behind...about their wishing themselves dead because of bad things done to them.

But she held her peace because there was the here-and-now to consider, which was more important. What were the four of them going to do, how were they ever going to manage with not enough money saved up for them to start over again, let alone to live on for very long?

The Rabinoviches came riding over posthaste as soon as they heard, and without further ado Uncle generously offered to provide whatever was needed. "After all, it's not as if I didn't have a personal interest in this matter," he chose to justify the gift with a protective arm around Bertha.

A long night followed in which the two brothers and sisters-in-law sat in silence in Avrem's kitchen.

It was he, finally, who spoke up, with a new proposal—that the four of them should go to America. Clearly, they wouldn't be the first to do that, he argued. Everyone able to seemed to be heading there, and if things continued as they were—with the Czar allowing more and more restrictive laws to be enacted against the Jews, and with fake accidents like this one taking place, almost for a certainty, now that he thought about it—they wouldn't be the last to go by any means. Avrem's voice boomed out—"Let's make a really fresh start!"

Bertha looked toward Elya, bewildered.

Husband's cheeks were burning with the prospect.

So there we are, Bertha sadly thought. I'll have to leave them, the only family I've ever known. Then indignation rose up in her—It's not fair! Especially since life in that America was also far from perfect, to judge from what some people had to say. Only, only—she felt a pang—if I insist on staying, he could go without me—and then what? I don't think that I could bear it...flesh of my flesh.

When the Rabinoviches learned of the decision, Tante began to cry softly and Uncle, blinking himself, heaved a sigh—"What can I say, children—*kinderlekh*. Go in good health—*gey gezunterheyt*."

There were assurances from the young people that they would be returning for a visit before very long, and the old ones spoke of themselves coming over to see them. But in her heart of hearts Bertha knew better: once gone, she would never set eyes on them again.

A month later, after much sorting and packing, the two couples were on their way, indeed following an already well-worn path—to the Austrian border by horse and wagon...across it on foot in the dead of night, schlepping baby and bundles...overland to Germany by train, plopped on all their goods in fourth class...a whole night of chasing bedbugs in a pier-side hotel in Hamburg...two weeks of being buried alive in the ship's belly, in a huge room crammed with straw-filled bunkbeds that stank to high heaven.

At long last came the Statue of Liberty and on the lower end of Manhattan a seeming solid mass of tall buildings—five stories high at least—with the enormous hulk of the Brooklyn Bridge towering over them...which Elya and Avrem kibitzed about with chins shaved clean, the beards of custom gone!

The odyssey continued in long lines on Ellis Island, with all sorts of puzzling questions and medical probings...and later, on the ferry landing at the Battery, where amidst an uproar of clanging horsecars a young fellow with an unhealthy red face named Yossel, cousin to Dora Leah on her mother's side, was waiting to haul them away to the East Side in a rickety old wagon drawn by a broken-down nag, both of them borrowed...first to a dank cellar room lit by a single smoky lamp, his home, and a supper of watery cabbage soup served up from an ancient pot-bellied stove by Minna his wife, who also had a sickly look to her...then to another hellhole like that nearby, with a water pump and an outhouse for general use in the backyard, their first home.

Cousin Yossel was a street peddler, and the next day bright and early Elya and Avrem went off with him to meet his supplier, a fellow countryman—*landsman*—and to begin learning the ropes. Bertha and Dora Leah, with Minna acting as guide, spent the time looking for various household items, like a piece of cloth—a *shmate*—to divide their miserable quarters in two, which they bought for next to nothing or *hay kak*.

From that day forward, from the first rays of sunlight to as long as they could stand it, Elya and Avrem were out yelling for candles, shoe laces, matches, and whatever else the *landsman* filled their packs with. And soon after asking around, Bertha and Dora Leah were doing basting for a sweatshop, so that within the year both couples were able to move into places of their own—real apartments with running water and gas stoves and gas jets for light, even if they were on the top floors of tenements on that same Lower East Side.

The packs were next to go, replaced by a pushcart full of lotions and tonics, which Elya and Avrem stationed on the Bowery off Houston, in the hope of attracting actors and actresses on the way from nearby theatrical costumers to the theatres further downtown. The brothers were soon adding other items to their stock like lip-heighteners and hairpieces, which also brought to them prostitutes and fairies—*feygelekh*—from under the El on Allen Street, an embarrassment at first until they realized what a blessing this clientele was for the items that they had too much of.

Just as soon as it could be managed, the two couples were enrolled in a public school at night to learn English, so as to be more in step in this new world and better able to help Josef, now Joey, and the other offspring when they came along. Those English classes became the special joy of Bertha, who was already familiar with some of the reading selections, like "Friends, Romans, and Countrymen," in Yiddish.

Children…for quite some time Bertha had been haunted by a fear that something was wrong with her, but finally that fear was laid to rest.

Thank Heaven, she sighed, after putting two and two together while lying awake beside Elya late one night, and realizing that it was definitely so.

At the beginning of their third year there in America, with a neighborhood midwife and Dora Leah assisting, she gave birth to a fine baby girl…Martha.

A FRIDAY IN THE SPRING OF 1896

Sunlight, morning sunlight, is pouring through the far kitchen window like fresh butter, brightening the wall behind the ice box. All is still except for the tapping of water from the faucet.

Bertha, who is now Mammeh, stands before the sink in a pale lime-green chiffon waist and navy skirt, which is protected from splatter by a silly frilly apron of purple and brown, all three of her creation. With a soapy piece of cheese cloth, she gently rubs the baby's milk glass, which is of the *yortsayt* or memorial variety, two for a penny at a certain synagogue. Waiting to be washed, each in its turn, are the breakfast cereal bowls, plates from the eggs and rolls, and cups and saucers—plain white with a slightly uneven border of light blue flowers.

One, one, one, everything is done and dripping on the drain board. Wiping off each with a dish towel, Mammeh puts them away in the cupboard, then takes up the dishrag again and turns to the table, down the center of the room, to sweep its white oilcloth clean of crumbs.

Four Lives

After this, there's the shopping and cooking, the whole place from the parlor forward having been given its good dusting and scrubbing yesterday. And with a little luck, Mammeh considers, there may be time to get in a few stitches before dinner.

Her gaze shifts to a Singer opposite the ice box, and a small pile of cut fabric on the floor beside it. Of dark grey wool with a thin white stripe, it is to be made into a suit, a business suit, for Abe, as brother-in-law now styles himself. For he and husband, Eli for short, go to business now; yes, they have a store on the same street where the pushcart used to be. The job of stitching together fell to her lot because Dora Leah just gave birth to twin girls, and with Joey, a wild one—a *bandit*—only in school half a day, she is up to her ears in work.

Mammeh smiles wryly—her own Martha, in a nighty and socks, is lying fast asleep on the new suit-to-be.

Rinsing the dishrag and hanging it, wrung tightly out, on the sink's lip, Mammeh steps over to the bread box on top of the ice box, and finds a good hard heel of pumpernickel in it. Then seeking the jar of schmaltz below on the ice, she ekes out a chunk with the big knife and spreads it on the bread's surface.

"*Bobe-leh-eh*," she coos, after adding a few chips of salt to it from the metal shaker. "*Bobe-leh-eh-eh*," she coos again, making for the sleeper on the goods.

The baby's dark brown head stirs...the eyelids with their long lashes part...her eyes, a rich chocolate brown, stare.

"Here"—Mammeh holds the *shtikl* of bread out.

Bobele reaches up for it.

"No, sit," Mammeh says.

The little one obeys and receives.

"So *nu*, don't you haf sometink to say?" Mammeh playfully scolds. "Tank you or sometink?"

"Hn"—*Bobele* is busy scooping up the oniony goo with her tongue.

"Dot's all? Hn only?" Mammeh shakes her head; this matter of the child's not having uttered a word, but not one word yet, has been on her mind for quite a while. Joey was already talking at eighteenth months, and with such expressions—like a regular native. But now is not the time to dwell on it, Mammeh cautions herself. There's too much to do.

Ready on the chair near the door are her pocketbook and two market baskets, from one of which stick out some sheets from yesterday's *Forverts*, everyone's Jewish newspaper, to be used for wrapping. A navy jacket, companion to the skirt, is draped on the chair-back, and a matching gauzy hat with a spray of white flowers, more of her handiwork, sits balanced on it.

Mammeh takes off her apron and drops it on its nail in the cupboard, then slips into the bathroom to tuck in any stray hairs from her bun and put on her hat.

"So, Bertha—Mrs. Ferber," she addresses herself in the large, round mirror opposite the tub.

Her eyes peer back from deep within their sockets, aquamarine with black dots; her cheeks are very full.

"*Oy*," she murmurs at some lines running from the nose to the mouth on either side. She's noticed them before, but now they are very obvious.

Mammeh pulls the skin back at the ears to make them disappear, then lets go. The ugly creases return.

So what's there to do—she shrugs. A person has to smile once in a while, don't they?

Back in the kitchen, there's the child to be seen to, who is too young to be taken along—unable to walk very far—and cannot be left around the corner at Dora Leah's because of the tumult there. Mammeh goes and gets baby's blanket from the next room.

"*Bobe-leh-eh!*" she calls, bustling over with pocketbook and baskets looped on her arm and the blanket under it. "Come, you'll stay by Mrs. Lefkowitz"—a solution that was resorted to last Monday...not the best idea but better by far than tieing the little one to a table or sofa as some mothers do. "I'll be beck in a vile."

The small legs scramble up, the tongue still scouring the heel of bread.

Outside in the hall, Mammeh locks the door with her key, and down they go—step, step, step—to the apartment just below, where she knocks.

"*Kum arayn!*" yells a high squeaky voice, bidding them enter.

As before, the neighbor is in her rocking chair, with a black shawl on her head and a heavy grey blanket covering her legs to the hips.

"It's me again!" Mammeh calls out in Yiddish. "Is it all right? You really don't mind?"

"Mind? Why should I mind?" Mrs. Lefkowitz answers in Yiddish. "What else do I have to do? Besides," she says to the little one in English, "vee like vun anudder, don't vee darlink?"—and spreads her arms to receive a great big hug and a kiss.

Bobele stays put, not keen about the idea, for which one cannot altogether blame her: the old one's face is crisscrossed by many cracks and looks dry like twigs.

Even so, we cannot always have everything in life exactly the way we want it—Mammeh gives the small back a nudge to get the feet going.

The ordeal is quickly over. *Bobele* retires to the other side of the room and plops down on the floor.

"Do you want anything, can I get you something, Mrs. Lefkowitz?" Mammeh asks, after releasing the blanket there.

"No, thank you," the old one answers. Her son will be coming to see her soon, and will take care of anything, whatever it is.

Mammeh waves bye-bye to the baby, who is sleepily gnawing on the hunk of bread.

At least the child eats, she consoles herself, clopping down the stairs. Not all kids do, you know. Take Joey, for instance; he's always been more interested in toys and games than food, and almost has to be sat on sometimes before he'll take something in his mouth.

Now honestly—Mammeh is still hurrying down—if there were a choice, which would you rather have? There's no need to answer.

Still—she's on the ground floor now, with the vestibule and street door directly before her—shouldn't at least something have rubbed off on *Bobele* by now from the two of them playing together, the cousins?...

Outside in the fresh air, it's an extra-fine day, the sky pure blue without so much as a wisp of white anywhere.

Now let's see—Mammeh goes over everything in her mind. There's a carp sitting pretty on the ice upstairs, baked last night with potatoes, carrots, and onions. And other items like noodles are on hand, so actually there's not that much to buy—

"*Oy,*" Mammeh groans, suddenly remembering. There's one thing—it's an old story—she always conveniently forgets about it until the last minute, when necessity calls it to mind. Horrible, horrible—"*Oy,*" Mammeh groans again. All the same, her feet take her down the stoop.

Along Clinton she makes her way, past a solid line of pushcarts heaped with goods galore, over which sellers are bawling and buyers haggling, mostly in Yiddish with Russian, Polish, and Rumanian thrown in. Into Madison her feet lead her, which is quieter, and then into Gouverneur, practically dead.

Finally, there is Gouverneur Slip and her dreaded destination, the pier building at the end of it.

"*Vey iz mir,*" Mammeh wails, full of woe. And just like the other times on reaching this point, she begins picturing to herself what will be.

Inside stand row upon row of long wooden crates stacked on top of one another. All is hushed. A man approaches—in a bloody apron. Things start rustling around uneasily. The man unlatches a wire door. There is a lot of jockeying for place. In goes his hand. Out springs this small chicken-body covered with reddish-brown feathers!

"*NO, NOT ME-E-E!*" *it shrieks with yellow beak wide open, wattles quivering bright red.*

No-o-o, the cry echoes in Mammeh's head, No-o-o! Then some words from a poem they gave her to read in night school pops into it—

Welcome, frequent sights of what is to be borne.

Fine for you to say, Mammeh sniffs, referring to the nature-loving Englishman who wrote it. You, by your lake...

She's at the entrance to the awful place. Within, there is customer-babble punctuated by the barking back and forth of the men working there. So far so good.

Fortunately, Loy, who usually waits on her, is free. He brings what she's there for—with dark blue eyes and pink cheeks darkened by bluish-grey stubble—and holds it for her to test under the wings.

It's the same story every time. "Fine," Mammeh says, after giving a pinch, and as he moves away, she faces round to the window, which opens onto the river.

Some gulls are wheeling there—"Wee! Wee!"...

"Mrs. Ferber?" Loy is back, with his same serious blue look.

Facing that way again, Mammeh dares to lower her gaze to his hands...where the thing, now food to be cooked, is laid out on wax paper flesh-side up, with some little yellow eggs under the ribs.

"Fine," she repeats, all woozy, and hands him her quarter.

There, it's over, a maternal voice inside her tries to soothe, as she stows the package away.

You see, finished, the same voice calms. Her toes steer her out of there...

The way soon becomes lively with people once more, and before long, there is Hester Street or the Khazer Mark—Pig's Market—as people have nicknamed it, but not really, just another place that mixes the bad with the good, as Mammeh's fond of pointing out...where pushcarts overflow with glinting red apples, sunny pears, blackish grapes, and dewy green vegetables, while the gutters beneath trickle with every kind of filth imaginable... where nectary and tangy fragrances vie with the most foul stench.

Mammeh nods hello to an old skull-capped herring dealer with a crinkly salt-and-pepper beard, a dear friend in need on several occasions when the two brothers and sisters-in-law were still having trouble making ends meet. Then there's the widow with the babushka who fixed her up with carpet slippers last fall (one large, one medium, one very small)...who smiles slightly at her smile, perhaps remembering. Half a block away Mammeh walks with head high past a devil with eyebrows who once sold her a pair of tin scissors for steel.

Her next stop is Goldman's Bakery, whose plate glass windows are piled high with orange-brown knobs of challah breads. "Ah, heavenly—a *mekhaye*!"—Mammeh is already inhaling the divine aroma of yeasty dough baking. And now there's a bushy tangle of carrot and parsnip tops, leek ends, parsley, and dill hanging over the edge of one of the baskets and bouncing along in step with her.

Two customers are just leaving, and the narrow aisle inside is miraculously empty.

"*Gut shabes*," Mammeh greets white-faced Mr. Goldman and his white-faced missus behind the mottled white marble counter top.

Portly in their aprons, they remind of Uncle and Tante, and in fact they are near neighbors from back in the Ukraine, which entitles her to a loaf from a special rack...

It's getting late, Mammeh sees outside, after acquiring a few of those luscious-looking yellow pears. The sun is on its afternoon slant now.

But what's this? There's something unusual a little way up the street in front of a butter-and-egg store—a man with a deep tan wearing a turban on his head and a long garment like a housecoat without a collar.

What is he, what's he selling, Mammeh wonders, catching sight of a stand consisting of a plank laid across two barrels. She can't help herself; she has to go and see.

The odd one, who deals in dried fruit, is even odder-looking close-up—with a fat gold ring hanging from each earlobe, traces of a red beard showing on his leathery skin, and bright greenish-blue eyes like turquoises.

Mammeh is beside herself with curiosity. "Are you a Jew—*Bist du a yid?*" she asks in Yiddish.

He lays a finger across his lips and wags his head from side to side—doesn't speak Yiddish, it would seem.

She tries in English: "Are you a Choo?"

That he understands. He nods, Yes.

"Vere you from?"

"From Toikey," he answers in a gravelly voice.

"Toikey?" She ha-ha's, he must be kidding. "Dere are Choos in Toikey?"

The stranger is not to be trifled with—"Dere are Jews all ovah, lady." His eyes begin to cast about.

Mammeh points to his apricots—"How much?" After all, it's only fair…taking up his time.

He tells her, a mere nothing, and does the picking, with fingers that are not the cleanest but clean enough, tossing the orange-colored chunks into a tiny white bag on a brass scale that looks like an ornament from a church.

Now Bertha, please, no more delays, Mammeh lectures herself with the pittance paid…

No sooner said than she is struggling up the stoop with her stuff.

In the vestibule, a delicious spicy sweetness meets her nostrils, someone else's soup. Mm, whoever it is, she didn't linger in the street over foolishness.

Mammeh begins walking up, then all at once remembers the baby and begins to worry—is she alright? Maybe she didn't

doze right off like on Monday. Oh Bertha, you fool you, hurry!
MAYBE SHE WANDERED AWAY SOMEWHERE, WHERE OLD EYES COULDN'T FOLLOW HER! Mammeh begins climbing in earnest, with the baskets.

"There, now—we'll—see," she huffs, on the third floor at last. With her heart in her mouth, she grasps the doorknob and gives a push—"*Gevalt!*"

Mrs. Lefkowitz's old chin is on her chest—she's snoring! And the child?

Is still sitting on the floor, in the same spot.

"Thank God," Mammeh breathes with heaving breast. And you know something, Bertha, consider yourself lucky, and let this be a lesson to you. Next time leave her with Abe and Eli at the store if Dora Leah can't manage it. Insist!

Bobele is on her feet with the blanket gathered, ready to go.

Mammeh digs in one of the baskets for the tiny bag with the apricots, and tiptoeing up to Mrs. Lefkowitz, sets it in her lap.

"Mm-mm," *Bobele* whines in protest.

"Sh-sh," Mammeh warns, and snatching the bag back, takes out two of the ambrosial orange pieces.

"Is it gut, do you like it?" she asks, when they are chewing, on the stairs.

"Mum."

Mammeh blinks and bites her lip—I don't understand, maybe there's something wrong with her. Maybe I should take her to a clinic to be examined.

Upstairs she unlocks the door and leaving her burdens on the table, goes to the window, the one by the fire escape where it is brightest—"*Bobele*, come here to de light."

The socked feet skip over, dark hair flying.

Mammeh gently takes the head in both hands, and ever so gently pushes it back—"Open up, please."

The small mouth forms an "O," and the tongue comes out.

There's only a throat back there. So what is it, what can be the matter, Mammeh puzzles.

An image comes...of the turbaned stranger with the turquoise eyes putting a finger to his lips. Comes...and goes.

The afternoon is mellowing into evening, and soon a few bright stars will be out. On the stove, the soup and pears are slow-cooking, and another pot, with salty water, has just been added for the noodles.

Bobele is napping again on the cloth meant for Uncle Abe's new suit.

From the cupboard, Mammeh has brought a tablecloth, white linen with a white satin floral pattern, to replace the oilcloth, and set out plates, those same white plates with the slightly irregular line of blue flowers, for her, Eli, and the baby. Now she comes with Tante's candlesticks, tall with fresh white candles.

It needs but a napkin to cover her head.

Ready to strike a match, Mammeh becomes aware of a kind of general hush, as if something similar is about to happen in the houses all around...as if in each and every kitchen, a mama like her is about to do the same thing.

The right wick is lighted first. Mammeh murmurs in Hebrew, her hands encouraging the flame to grow—"*Borukh ato...*"

The prayer is finished—"*...ner shel shabas.*" Mammeh's palms form a cup above both flames, waving brightly, and her eyes close.

This is silly, really, a certain part of her remarks, Uncle's rational part. All the same, do it, Tante the practical one insists—another old story.

"*Lieber Got,*" Mammeh begins to God, in Yiddish, "please continue to watch over all of us and ours, including those we left behind."

She pauses a moment to let this sink in Up Above.

"Also," she continues, now very softly, "can you see to it that my husband has it a little easier? He works so hard."

Enough—Mammeh pulls the napkin off...

The little one is up now, sucking on a thumb.

"*Bobele*, are you hungry?" Mammeh asks, and goes to the stove to spoon out a piece of carrot for her from the soup.

The door opens—it's Eli, of course. His cheeks are pale, but there's a little of the old life around the eyes.

Just a minute, he says, wants to wash up...

They're all three at the table now, about to begin on the fish, which was carried from the ice box oh so carefully, so the jelly wouldn't slip over the saucers' sides.

How everything glows—the silver of the candlesticks with their golden lights, the satin in the cloth and knobs of challah reflecting them, even the little china crocks of mustard and horseradish with their tiny spoons.

Mammeh takes up her fork, Eli his—not quite so gloomy in the face anymore.

Bobele has her fork clutched too. Her lips suddenly part, she sings out shrilly, flourishing it—"DE COUNT OF MONTE CRISCO!"—finally some words.

"Heh-heh," Mammeh giggles. "How do you like that," she says in Yiddish.

CHAPTER

2

Martha's chief delights from early on were in the feel of things. She counted as particularly good the softness of Mammeh's face against her own soft face, the sweet roughness of the cloth on which those refreshing daytime naps were sometimes taken, and the prickly-tickliness around Papa's lips when he kissed her goodnight.

On the floor beside Mammeh treadling away on the sewing machine one morning, Martha began tracing one of the linoleum's pink-and-purple rosettes with a finger—and it felt lovely, like the taste of penny candy. Happening to look down, Mammeh noticed her pleasure, and slipping out a while later, brought back a box of crayons—wonderful waxy things to make outlines of and color in anything *Bobele* wanted to, on a torn-open paper bag provided for the purpose of course.

Along about Martha's fifth birthday, there was a fresh delight, when Mammeh, expecting a peddler at any moment for some baby bibs just finished for him, asked her to help take out the basting. Martha picked with a pin so quickly and deftly that Mammeh couldn't get over it, so from then on her *bobele* was lending a hand regularly.

Soon, all too soon, though, those sweet-as-sugar times came to an end. One day in early September, after rocking with the treadle for ever so long, Mammeh called for Martha to leave off with the crayons and come over, saying, "It's for you, *Kreynele*"—and what did the new garment turn out to be but one of those frilly white aprons worn by school girls over their dresses. With the thing looped over her head and tied behind in a bow, Martha became aware that the moment was at hand.

P.S. 13 with its red brick facade was the same school that Mammeh and Papa had gone to with Uncle Abe and Aunt Dora Leah to learn English, she was informed as they wended their way there the next morning. Better yet, when viewing it from the corner, she would find that it had three different towers: a fine, thin one reminding of a fairy castle's, a rectangular one like a fort with slots for shooting out of, and one coming to a fat point like a church's. Best of all, inside, instead of yellow gas hissing from jets, there were bright-as-day bluish electric lights—just like on Broadway! So, difficult as it was to be parted from Mammeh for those three long hours, Martha didn't feel all that unhappy, and in fact once seated at the small round tables with the rest of the children, she was quite content—especially when the teacher, Miss Levinson, with her ready smile, handed out pretty sheets of rose, grey, blue, and violet paper.

But alas, those pleasant times of cutting out circles, squares, and diamonds and pasting them on other pretty sheets were also destined not to last. In first grade the following fall, Martha had Miss Monihan for a teacher, whose cold eyes behind the rimless glasses together with her pinkish skin like pork and the fuzz on her chin struck the class with terror, especially when she screeched for all thirty of them to sit absolutely still while the pupil who had been called on recited. Small wonder then that the time never went fast enough until three o'clock, when *Bobele* could return home to fold, go hunt for, and do whatever else Mammeh required of her.

Second grade, even though under the tamer hand of Miss O'Brien, was worse yet—with H-O-M-E-W-O-R-K assigned all the time, which HAD to be done. Yes, every weekday night after supper, as soon as Papa spread his *Forverts* on the kitchen table, out would have to come the books from *Bobele*'s schoolbag or else Mammeh at the sink was sure to inquire, "She didn't gif you anyting today?"

One night in the middle of the spring term, Martha was going over a new story in her reader, when all of a sudden Mammeh asked if she would read to them a little. Joey, now in sixth grade and making excellent progress, had done it for Uncle Abe and Aunt Dora Leah when he was just starting, Papa pointed out. So there was nothing for it; Martha turned back to the first page and began singsonging, "Once upon a time dere was a liddle goil who was lovt by one 'n all, but mos' of all by her granmudder, who gave huh a priddy red velvet cloak…" And she was quite willing to go on to the scary part about the wolf if they wanted. But no, after a few more sentences, Papa said it was enough and Mammeh thanked her.

The next day after school, surprise of surprises, Mammeh was taking *Bobele* to a school on Second Street for some elocution lessons with, of all people, Miss Levinson from kindergarten—indeed, just as Uncle Abe and Aunt Dora Leah had done with Joey. Fine and good, only no sooner did nice Miss Levinson pronounce her diction much improved than, also like Joey before her, Martha was signed up for Hebrew—which would not have been so bad if the old greybeard of a teacher hadn't insisted that she learn just to sound out each letter with its vowel, never mind what the words meant.

Even so, good times there were too, for instance on Sundays, when after a late, leisurely breakfast of lox-and-bagels washed down by hot tea with oodles of milk and sugar, they would all three board a trolley bound for uptown. There, in the Metropolitan Museum or some other place like that, they would spend the day peering at the pictures and statues, and gawking at the other visitors on the sly, especially the fat, expensively dressed ones, who Mammeh nine out of ten intuited were Jews like themselves, albeit German ones.

Once instead of heading straight for home afterward, they went for a stroll down Fifth Avenue, passing a large hotel with a long line of flags flying outside, which Mammeh said was the Plaza, then some millionaires' mansions, which she claimed looked just like Czars' palaces, and then St. Patrick's Cathedral with its many stained glass windows and stone spires, great and small. As Mr. Flynn or Flint, owner of a saloon close by the store, had bragged that St. Paddy's was a knockout on the inside too, Papa proposed that they go in and have a look, since they were there already. So schlepping up all those stairs to one of the entrances, they tiptoed in, but went no further than the other side of the doorway—to find facing them down the length of that enormous cavern-like place a huge golden cross. After they'd silently taken it all in for a few moments, Papa whispered, "C'mon, let's go," and Mammeh, following with Martha's hand gripped tightly in hers, remarked, "Who vould ever have tought vee'd be in a choich."

There were other good times at night in one of the Yiddish theatres downtown, thanks to the generosity of some of the actors and actresses who patronized the store and had free passes to give away. Since the plays often dealt with adult matters, Martha's eyelids began to grow heavy almost as soon as the curtain went up, and she looked alive only when the whole place burst into an uncontrollable fit of laughter or melted into painful sighs, which it did on occasion. Once, however, during something called *Hamlet* (which she imagined from the program had to do with eggs because the word sounded like "omelet"), she remained sitting straight up in her seat the whole time, with her attention glued on black-bearded David Kessler in a Robin Hood suit, whom everyone had it in for except a school chum and his sweetheart Bertha Kalish, to the extent that she was able. Not only that, when the high point came, with the poor prince, planted before a mist-enshrouded parapet, pointing a dagger at his chest and crying out—

Zayn oder nisht zayn—dos iz di kashe!

Martha, along with Mammeh and Papa, judged it the most affecting thing, while many around them let out wails as if of recognition and an old one next to her tearfully wagged his head, murmuring, "*Ikh veys, ikh veys*—I know, I know."

Later that same evening, they went to a Grand Street cafe as had become their custom after a performance. Thinking to pass the time while waiting for their tea and pound cake to arrive, Mammeh casually mentioned another play they'd seen earlier in the season, which was very similar to this *Hamlet*, involving a poor Talmudic student and his wicked uncle of a rabbi. And then she made the awful mistake of saying how attractive—*azoy sheyn*—Boris Thomashevsky had been in the lead. Well, that was all Papa had to hear. "You should only see what he looks like up close, that Thomashevsky!" he very nearly shouted, with eyes smarting. "Like a big fat bum—*groyser bomeke!*" Papa didn't calm down in a hurry either; Mammeh had to use many soothing words and give him quite a few pats on the arm before that happened.

Some months later, Martha gleaned from certain things said at home that Mammeh was going to have a baby, and not long after, she gave birth to a little girl, Dinah. A year or so later Martha gathered that it was the same story again, and soon she had another new sister, Pauline. Naturally, the house was turned upside down as a result, with Papa staying home to help out and Aunt Dora Leah showing up from time to time with Joey, a big boy now, to bring them groceries—so that Martha, who was going on ten, often felt left out of things and sometimes even in the way.

As no one seemed to mind, she took to playing jacks with some girls from her class after three o'clock—especially freckle-faced Essie, with green eyes and red pigtails, who taught her how. Jacks, jacks, jacks—that was all Martha soon had on her mind, though why, she couldn't for the life of her say at first, since she was not very good at it...cursed with small hands. But in time came the realization that win or lose, each descent of the ball and scooping up of the squiggly metal things brought her a keen sense of "rightness," for lack of a better way to put it. In any event, it wasn't long before she had her own shiny red ones, bought with saved-up pennies, and was practicing with them in bed at night: toss...snatch up...hold tight.

One afternoon as Martha and her crowd were busily bouncing and grabbing, another classmate named Tillie came running up and shouted out that some settlement workers had just opened up a new clubhouse for children a few blocks away on Rivington, where they had a lending "liberry" and swings in the back. "Oh boy!" they all whooped, and rushed right over to join up, which gave them the privilege of borrowing books that day. Martha chose *Little Women*, which she'd already read but wanted to experience again, struck by that noble soul Beth, who always put everyone before herself and never complained to the last gasp.

Having the time of their lives in the backyard playground several days later, Martha and her friends were approached by Miss Nancy Lee Smith, a counselor for the College Settlement House, as it was called, who proposed that they form themselves into a regular club as some other children had done. Feeling shy in front of this gentile lady from the South with her mild blue eyes, complexion like pink-and-white tulips, and auburn hair, they nevertheless saw the advantages to her suggestion, such as being able to go on outings to museums and The Central Park with her, and to do other things like make jello and cocoa in one of the kitchens. And that is how The Damsels came into being, with Martha as the first president, Essie the secretary, and Tillie treasurer.

Every now and then in the midst of all the fun, Martha would begin to feel uneasy about being away from the house so much, and before going off the next time, made it a point of asking Mammeh, who was usually fussing with one or the other of the babies, if she could do something. "No, denk you," Mammeh would always answer in her unruffled way. Papa would be home before long, and in a pinch there was always one of the neighbors if she needed anything. *Bobele* should go on living her life as she had been, and above all, enjoying herself...

Four Lives

One morning some years later—Martha was twelve at the time—she noticed a small cloud of red blood dissolving in the toilet after getting up from it. Immediately she went and privately told Mammeh, who had warned of something like this happening some time ago and taught a good deal else besides. After Papa was gone, Mammeh made *Bobele* come and sit in her lap—"For de lest time, probably"—and gently touched her lips to the new little lady's brow.

A little lady—before turning in that night, Martha spent an extra few moments in the bathroom looking herself over... scrutinizing her eyes, which were Papa's good fudge brown but deeply inset in her cheeks like Mammeh's...the high forehead above them, which was very high indeed...the small, straight nose...mouth like a kitten's.

Yes, a little lady, she confirmed. And one day there'll be a man. Certainly the feeling, as hinted at by Mammeh, was already there, had been for some time...

The Feeling. When it arose, which was always in the dead of night, she knew just how to handle it, having learned gradually—rolling over and arranging herself so the place, newly covered with hairy down, was flat against the mattress, then wriggling and squirming while pressing, until a fine WARMTH *washed over her...and another...and* ANOTHER*...enrapturing her.*

Snaking, she called it, to herself alone of course...

Little Fanny, one more addition to the family, was born the following year, and as soon as she could crawl around, there seemed to be no choice but to put her in the front bedroom with Martha, so that Mammeh and Papa, who slept back in the parlor, could have some peace. "I don't mind at all, really," Martha said, when Mammeh sounded her out. The new *bobele* was very fetching with her eyes like coals, tawny skin, and Mammeh's black mane, and besides, deserving of some special consideration because Dinah and Pauline, aged four and three, were beginning to show themselves resentful.

By then Martha was deep into *Macbeth* and struggling to master long division, to say nothing of spelling demons like "perseverance."

43

In addition, there was a dress to be made for graduation next June, which Mammeh would be helping with, as well as initiating eldest daughter into the mysteries of knitting and other kinds of needlework, if time permitted.

Graduation...there was Martha, all in white among her classmates, filing into the makeshift auditorium in time to "Land of Hope and Glory," fervently rendered by Miss Ferro the music teacher...and there before the podium waiting to dole out the pink-beribboned rolls of parchment with pudgy hands was unsmiling Miss Jackson the principal. And oh what joy afterwards when all of Martha's friends, gathering round, stoutly maintained that except for one other outstanding dress—which didn't really count because the girl's mother worked for a fancy-schmancy modiste—hers with its simple but striking line of ruffles down the front, accented by smaller ones around each wrist, had turned out the best of all.

"I'm so heppy," Mammeh said, and Papa was too, only less so, Martha sensed, very likely disappointed that she hadn't been a winner like Joey and received the gold or silver medal, which had gone to the girl with the swell dress and another goody-goody. But all thoughts except the glorious here-and-now vanished as soon as they walked through the door back home, where amidst an uproar of kids, Uncle Abe and Aunt Dora Leah were good-naturedly unpacking mounds of corned beef and pastrami, and baked beans, sauerkraut, pickles, and mustard from Katz's Delicatessen.

What course of study to pursue at Girls' High that fall and what to do with herself eventually were questions that had already begun plaguing Martha. Now, as of the next day, they became paramount. Papa's wish was that she enroll in the academic program so as to be able to go on to a teachers' training college, thus sort of following in the footsteps of Joey, soon to enter The City College from Clinton and destined for dental school...but she didn't know. The money from teaching was good and teachers had a certain status, but to be like one of those frumps at P.S. 13?...Martha just didn't know. Finally, after fretting over it the whole summer, and more out of desperation than anything else—because a decision had to be made—she decided on the commercial program like Essie. "I'll get a job as a secretary after," she said.

So Papa missed having his way once more, but as Mammeh was quick to point out by way of consoling him—it was, after all, the girl's life.

A FRIDAY AFTERNOON IN MID-NOVEMBER THE FOLLOWING YEAR (1907)

The sky, all winter-white today, is turning grey, and it has grown considerably colder.

Just out of school, Martha is stepping briskly along University Place, feeling smart in a rust-colored coat with a squirrel collar and a matching beanie, both of them Mammeh's handiwork after an original in a second-hand ladies magazine.

Ordinarily there is Essie to make the trip home with, the two of them having wangled similar schedules. But the poor girl is in bed with cramps today, so Martha will be all by her lonesome. But that's alright, I'll manage, she assures herself. In fact, sometimes—like right now—it's a good thing to have a little vacation from that best friend whose chattering—about matters of little consequence—has been grating on her nerves of late.

Arrived at the corner of Fourteenth Street, Martha sets her satchel down, Uncle Abe's now slightly lackluster graduation present. She has mental notes all made of what must be done this evening after the kids are in bed and she has the kitchen table all to herself with Mammeh and Papa as of old—a portion of *Silas Marner*, the future of "sein" and a few other German irregulars, and some algebra problems.

What's coming, her trolley maybe? She does a little keep-warm dance while looking leftward to see.

As usual at this hour, there's a tangle of traffic going back toward Fifth Avenue—mostly horses and wagons with a few hapless automobiles and a tram-top peeping here and there. The mess is presided over by a policeman in white gloves with a whistle, who has his work cut out for him: no one wants to listen; everyone is yelling.

"Finally," Martha breathes, letting out steam. The congestion has broken up somewhat and an Avenue A car has managed to slip through.

It grates to a standstill beside her.

Alleyoop, up and into it she goes, and miracle of miracles, it's not crowded; in fact, she's in for a treat, a vacant double on the left next to a window.

Clang-clang, the trolley has started up again.

Martha darts a glance in passing at Union Square, which Papa has said is the gathering place for all sorts of riff-raff or *khaleryen*, as he calls them, radicals whose sole aim in life, it seems, is to open up a big mouth and make trouble. Nothing much is there as far as she can make out, the same as every other time she's looked—just groups of men in dark bowler hats and topcoats amidst bare black trees...grey smoke from their cigarettes drifting up...

Dead Man's Curve is next—where Union Square meets Broadway—and just ahead will be white Steinway Hall with its stone awning supported by the four columns, where serious musical concerts are held at night for Germans. Luchow's, their restaurant, is somewhat further along across the way.

"Ahem!" A young conductor is before her, very young, with eyes of cold-grey blue, in a uniform slightly too large for him—probably an Irisher like the rest of them, emulating a father or an older brother.

Martha hands him her nickel.

They're passing the Academy of Music now, corner of Irving Place, all reddish brown with a long row of arches for entrances.

Four Lives

What's playing, still the same thing? Yes, *The Old Homestead*, a silly story about some American gentiles—*goyim*—in a small New England town, according to someone Martha knows, Papa very likely.

Now, there's Tammany Hall, the Democratic Party's headquarters, a rich-ripe plum in color except for white around the windows—with its crowning glory way on top, the white statue of an American Indian in full regalia. On the stoops loiter more men in dark bowlers and topcoats, and inside is the office of the chairman, Charles Murphy, who really runs the city, not Mayor McClellan, as everyone is aware...

The huge black metal overhang of the Third Avenue El is coming up, and that's more or less the end of the show. Beyond for a block or two, there'll be one-price clothing stores, gated and padlocked, or about to be, by their bearded owners for *shabes*, the sabbath, and interspersed among them, penny arcades and shooting galleries, where young Irish toughs hang out and shabby *kurves* or street women lurk in the shadows. Then, over to Avenue A and southward, it will be mostly tenements like home.

Time to gather your wits, Martha cues herself. Now what's the matter, what's bothering you? For something has been since the morning, and if the truth be known, for longer, much longer than that.

Is it Papa, she considers. Not really; he doesn't seem to object to what she's doing anymore, thanks to Mammeh. If that's what Martha wants, to sit in an office taking dictation and typing all day, why that's fine with him, he's made it clear on more than one occasion. As for friends, true, The Damsels are no more, but there's still Essie, and lately Ray and Ceil, whom they met at a College Settlement basketball game one Saturday night.

No, it's the schoolwork, that's what it is, Martha finally realizes. Yes, even though she's been doing well, extraordinarily well, if one can believe someone like Miss Liplich in Steno, who is not exactly given to handing out compliments. "I've never seen anyone catch on to Pitman so fast," she recently confessed to Martha.

I don't care, Martha tells herself now. I don't like it, any of it, really. It's not me, it's simply not me, and that's that.

※

But of course, not wanting to be a secretary any longer, and indeed to go on with school, was one thing; recognizing one's true calling, as the saying went, was quite another. So there was no point in Martha's breathing a word about her disillusionment to anyone at home until she had come up with something else.

The best thing to do, she decided after cudgeling her brains for some time, was to take a walk over to the College Settlement after school one day, and see if she could find someone to talk to. By the greatest good fortune, who should be there in the offices upstairs on the particular afternoon she chose but The Damsels' own Nancy Lee Smith.

"Of course I remember you!" Miss Smith immediately piped up in her lilting Southern way, and thankfully this friend-in-need of years gone by had time for a chat.

The next one knew Martha was pouring her heart out…indeed, just like a little kid instead of an almost-grown-up young lady of fifteen.

The only thing is, when she was done, Miss Smith, strangely, just sat there in her swivel chair tapping her pencil. In truth, so long did she remain there, without uttering so much as a syllable, that Martha began to feel uneasy.

Finally, though, Miss Smith did have some words of wisdom to impart—"You know, sometimes looking at someone else's problems helps to put things in perspective, even when that someone else is quite different from us." And with this, she stood up and went over to her bookcase, and plucking a volume from it, handed it to Martha—"The hero of this, for instance." The title was *The Way of All Flesh*.

Martha got started on the book that very night—however, at first had disappointingly found it a little boring: all about the Pontifex family, whose scions, including Ernest the young man, were priests in the English Church. But then, reading on, she came to the part about Ernest's disgrace, from which the "meat" of the story was precipitated—that to lead a truly meaningful life, one had to "kiss the soil."

Yes, that's it, that's what I'd like to do in some form or fashion, Martha saw at once: to return to our basic common human denominator.

To kiss the soil, to kiss the soil—the phrase echoed and re-echoed in her head...even later, when she was lying in bed in the dark beside little Fanny fast asleep.

The next morning, as soon as she opened her eyes, there the exact thing was, indeed as if it had been waiting there in her mind all along. Yes, it was perfectly reasonable: since she had by then learned just about everything there was to know about joining pieces of cloth together at Mammeh's knee, she would go to work in a factory where they made clothing!

All fired up, Martha could hardly contain herself until after her last class that day, when she would see Miss Smith again.

Only curiously, Miss Smith turned out not to share her enthusiasm for the newly discovered vocation-to-be, stammering out something about its being an extremely bold step, not to be undertaken lightly.

It occurred to Martha that maybe this blue-eyed lady had intended to influence her through Ernest's service to the poor to become a counselor herself, as they at the Settlement had done with other former club-members. But no matter; as far as Miss Martha Ferber was concerned, the die was cast. In fact, for reasons that could not be fathomed at the moment, Martha felt more certain than ever that a job in a garment factory was the right course to take...

This will really upset the folks, especially Papa, she anticipated on the way home. So once more it became necessary to make use of her wits.

The most politic approach, it soon came to her, was to tell Mammeh, the more objective one, first. This Martha decided to do the following morning, after Papa had left for school with Dinah and Pauline on his way to the store.

"I don't understand," Mammeh began, once the whole thing was revealed.

The two of them were sitting face-to-face across the table over second cups of coffee. Baby Fanny was playing by herself on the floor beside the Singer.

"You say you vant to voik mit your hands"—well, wasn't that what one did as a secretary basically?

"Yes, it is," Martha had to admit, "but—" She looked searchingly into her mother's eyes, those familiar bluish-green eyes like strange seas—"I'd really prefer—something more direct—like sewing."

Mammeh considered, and came up with a new idea. How about if she were to find work for *Bobele* uptown with a modiste, like the mother of that girl with the extra-fancy dress at graduation?

Martha shook her head, knowing a bit about that life. "You end up being a kind of—of servant."

Mammeh smiled a small smile—"And in a fectory it vould be different?"

"Well, yes—and no," Martha answered, but couldn't explain beyond that. "Just take my word for it."

Mammeh's hand, plump and soft despite all the scrubbing and scouring, swept some crumbs left over from breakfast off the edge of the oil cloth into her other hand.

"Do you realize," she said, on returning from the sink with palms dusted, "dot in dose places dere are people suffering from consumption und udder diseases because of de bad air? Supposing you should get sick like dot too? How do you tink Papa und I vould feel?"

Mammeh was right about that, Martha thought. "Still—"

"Also, in dose places, as you must be avare, dere are udders vit' all kinds of crazy ideas about toining de voild upside down"—which

50

could mean strikes and lockouts, very likely with fists flying and worse.

Her mother had a point there too. "Still—still—" But all Martha could think of to respond with was something about wanting to go back in time and regain something lost, which wouldn't have come out right.

It was getting late. Mammeh agreed that she should be the one to break the news to Papa, and they got up to walk to the door.

Before the kiss, there was one last appeal: Maybe daughter would like to help out in the store like Joey after school? Uncle Abe, who was not keen on having women in the business, probably could be sat on.

Martha's eyes began to fill, and she felt a sob rising in her throat. "No, Mammeh, please—try to see it my way—I have to do this!"

The next day when Papa said good morning to her, his eldest born, he was a shade paler than usual.

I can't help it, Martha agonized inside, I HAVE to!

After he was gone, Mammeh had one small request: Would *Bobele* be good enough to stay in school until she turned sixteen?

AROUND FOUR-THIRTY ONE SATURDAY
A YEAR OR SO LATER (*JANUARY, 1909*)

It's freezing out. Two-day-old snow, tinged with blue in the fading light, covers Washington Square's grassy places and runs along the black tree limbs above.

Swathed in black, with a black bird's nest of a hat on her head, Martha sits huddled on the edge of a bench, having just come from the trolley on Broadway.

The bronze statue of Garibaldi stands poised nearby, its greenness also topped with white.

Martha's next stop is the Asch Building at Number 23 Washington Place, straight ahead on the corner of Greene Street. But it's necessary to wait a few moments until almost closing, so Raphael (pronounced "Rayfeel") Benowitz, the one she's supposed to see and a friend of Mammeh's notions dealer won't be out of pocket too much for himself and his crew, who work by the piece.

Boy, am I nervous, Martha can't help acknowledging to herself. A little discouraged too: not a single soul she knows—not Ray or Ceil, or even Essie with her freckles—liked this scheme of getting to the heart of things and working with her hands in a clothing factory, and Essie was particularly vehement, crying out, "Oh Marth, don't do it! Please!" Martha's knees are pressed together and her toes go tippety-tap as much from the jitters as the iciness.

Even so, it's still what I want and I'm going through with it, she affirms to herself—now! Directly across the way, where Washington Place meets the Square, the windows of the American Book Company have lighted up (in lilac!).

She hops to her feet and crossing over, skims along the block to Number 23's door and lobby, which is small and rather smart-looking in its mottled beige marble facings.

Two young men in dark green uniforms are leaning out of elevator doors, the closer of them a good-looker with lips like pale raspberries. "Where to, sister?" that one asks, as Martha steps in.

"Nine," she says weakly.

He draws the gate shut, gives a tug to the cable, and pushes down on the handle.

Ooh-ooh, Martha goes to herself, as her stomach is left behind. She's been in elevators before with Mammeh in department stores, but can't remember when the last time was...

"Nine, Triangle," the good-looker announces.

Beyond, there's a steady rumbling as if from machinery, a lot of it.

Now get hold of yourself, will you, something inside Martha urges.

The young man pulls open the gate. The door, unbarred, slides back by itself.

The rumbling turns into thundering! There's a stale smell, as of sickness, in the air.

Martha is standing before a large room packed with long tables arranged in horizontal rows. Every inch of space on them seems to be occupied by people bent over sewing machines pounding away.

Now where is he, this Benowitz, Martha wonders, suffering from the noise—her ears! All she knows is that "he's not exactly a spring chicken."

Here and there a pair of eyes darts up, from hands zipping a piece of fabric through. Many of them belong to girls her age, give or take a few years.

Where, where, Martha continues to wonder, casting about.

Ah, there! In the middle of a row two-thirds of the way down, an older man with glasses on the tip of his nose and a mop of white hair is waving for her to come. He's wearing a unionsuit top as a shirt, crossed by red suspenders.

How do I get there, Martha asks with her hands.

To the left and around, he motions—QUICKLY!

A partition has blocked her view that way. Stepping forward toward the lead table, she sees that there's an aisle running to the left wall and down along it, with a desk in the corner where front and side aisles meet.

In a trice she is nodding hello to a pleasant-looking young blonde woman sitting there and an older one with a sallow face standing over her, the checker and forelady Martha has been forewarned. The next moment she's squeezing through old Benowitz's row, face flushed with joy and fear...a little out of breath.

"Let's see vot you can do," he gabbles, when she's there, and gets up, drawing along a flimsy white cotton waist with one sleeve. His eyes are watery blue with bloodshot whites, there's stubble on his cheeks, and from his nostrils protrude curly tobacco-stained hairs.

Martha takes his place, and he hands her a side panel and a back of the same delicate stuff, plucked from a wicker basket below on the floor.

Martha opens her coat, pulls her arms out, and throws it back, conscious that her dress of brownish-orange with white flowers—created by herself on Mammeh's treadle after something in an R.H. Macy window—is slightly out of place. Even so, she carefully puts the seams together, and slipping them under the foot, lowers the lever.

Her right toe feels around for the pedal.

The old blue eyes have been minutely observing—"You evah use a powah machine before?"

"Yes," she answers, "in school, last term"—the truth, but most of her experience comes from Mammeh's treadle.

His chin screws up disparagingly. Then, the pedal found, he leans more closely—"Go very light, and be careful of de tumbs, dot dey're not dregged under."

Her big toe flexes itself—a thin line of sweat has come out on her upper lip.

Reeeng! a bell shrieks out. The motors, which are way over by a line of windows to her left, begin dying away, and with them machines all around her.

Benowitz signs for someone to hold it with the switch for their row. "Go ahead."

Martha touches with her toe—the needle flies away! "Oh!"—the material is bunched up like an accordion.

You didn't do as he said, she lectures herself with head down. Try again, but go really easy this time, for heaven's sake. She lifts the lever and smoothes the puckered place, then securing it, applies her toe once more...

"Let's see," Benowitz says, after she's expertly cut the threads, and raises it close to his eyes. "Not bed." Then giving it back, he reaches down for the other side panel—"Vunce more."

She passes the two edges under—*zoom*!

He inspects again, approvingly.

People all over are on their feet, and there's much loud talking. Martha gets up too, to be eye-to-eye with old Benowitz for his verdict.

"You tink you'll like dis line of voik?" he asks over his glasses.

Like? How could one not like? The power of it! The sheer raw power! "Yes," Martha answers, "I do already," and grins enthusiastically.

Benowitz is pleased and displeased. "Dis is a ver serious place," he says. "No time for fun. Everybody here needs de money."

Martha's head goes down again—he's right. "All I want to do is work," she assures him.

Well then, he'll take her on as a learner at $4 a week. In time, if things work out, he'll put her on pieces, where the sky's the limit, to $10, maybe as high as $15.

Martha nods agreement.

He has to go get his things from the cloakroom, which is within the front partition; then they'll ride down to the street together. A crush has developed in the aisle, what with some coming from there and others like himself just starting out. So it'll take a few minutes, he warns her...

Now then, Martha breathes, waiting by herself, aren't you glad you came? Nothing ventured, nothing gained, as they say.

Very pleased, she lets her eye roam around the room, and it comes to rest on the back partition, which is on the right a few feet behind her row.

The button for that ear-piercing bell is there, and a large, round clock hangs solemnly above it. Under them stands a short, stocky man in a grey shirt and pants with a black belt who—well—must be one of the bosses.

He's just standing there and staring—with perfectly arched eyebrows and straight brown hair parted way over to the side. In his late thirties perhaps.

Probably looking forward to returning home to his family and relaxing, like everyone else, Martha figures...

"Here vee are!" Mr. Benowitz calls from the aisle, in a worn black overcoat. A dusty bowler is in hand.

She goes to join him, and they begin inching their way along with the crowd toward the door—a single door—in the partition back there.

She can call him Benny if she wants, he tells her, in their slow progress. That's the name he's known by here.

In front of the door is a very old man in overalls, Martha notices, in his eighties for sure. He seems to be making each person open up pocketbooks and whatever else they're carrying before they exit.

Checking for stolen merchandise, Benny explains in her ear. The waists are very expensive in the department stores, and here at Triangle you're a *ganef*—a thief—until you're proven innocent.

They've got a lot of nerve, Martha fumes to herself...still, widens her purse when her turn comes.

"That's right, Nat!" a sonorous man's voice rings out behind her. "Look'em over good!"

It's the boss with the perfect eyebrows.

How can someone who seems so nice be so mean-spirited, Martha thinks.

"*Kok im un*," a female voice behind her gravels in Rumanian-flavored Yiddish—verbally heaping excrement on the guy.

"*Halt dayn moyl!*" Benny hisses at her—shut your trap. That one, with a wild look in her eyes, is a member of his crew, it would seem.

"*Bestia!*" an Italian woman nearby mutters.

"Management's gotta right to pertect its property," Benny tries to reason.

"Sonomabeech!" another *Italyeyne* curses...

Outside the partition door, there's a vestibule where a bunch of people are waiting for two freight elevators.

"Who was he?" Martha asks Benny in a low voice, meaning the hated one.

Bernstein the production manager and a brother-in-law of Mr. Blanck, one of the owners, he answers. Poison, to be avoided at all costs.

Too bad, he seems so—nice, Martha can't help repeating to herself.

Her mind turns to other things, and—"Oh boy!"—it suddenly lights on something almost forgotten. She fishes in her purse, finds a small cardboard box, and holds it out to him, old Benowitz, her crew leader—"This is for you, I understand it's customary." Inside is a gold-plated stickpin.

The grizzled chin quickly nods, and he stows it in a coat pocket without looking.

An elevator arrives. Martha piles in with everyone else, and down, down they go, slowly, with creaks...

In the lobby before they part company, Benny asks if she speaks Yiddish by any chance.

"Not really," Martha answers, "only *farshtey*"—understand.

"Hah"—he bobs his head—"a Yenkee."

CHAPTER

3

Jerrold was the kind of "boy" whom every mother would give her right arm to have as a son, according to Fanny telling this tale from her wheelchair.

In some respects, a young man of his rare virtues would have fared better today than in his own day, but in others not.

As a true-blue American, Jerrold was twice blessed, descending from an early Dutch settler named Vanderlynn through his father and being a Livingston, albeit one of the many minor Livingstons, on his mother's side. From his forebears, Jerrold's pa had inherited a small farm outside of Tarrytown, where he raised a little wheat and kept a few head of cattle. But that was not good enough for the likes of Ma's people, and care for her husband though she might, they considered the marriage beneath her.

Jerrold was born in the farmhouse, an old clapboard affair, and there he remained, an only child, until he was five, when quite suddenly, within the space of a week, Pa and Ma both took sick and died. In later years, Jerrold carried with him a fleeting memory of some neighbor-woman fixing something to eat in the kitchen, while an older man and two burly sons, her menfolk, were digging the graves out back in the vegetable garden.

Another memory Jerrold had of that sad time was of himself sitting high up in a buckboard wagon next to a black-suited preacher with a drooping moustache, who praised him for being "a brave boy" and drove him into town—to Aunt Serena, his mother's only sibling, who lived on Franklin Street close by the Post Road. A maiden lady of a certain age, with her hair parted in the middle and two braids wound round, Aunt immediately judged Jerrold to be "the spittin' image" of his pa, but for lack of an alternative, was willing to let him stay on. Likewise remembered by Jerrold was getting up very early the next morning to go have a look in the hall mirror—and observing that he had steady brown eyes, hair like faded straw, and a slightly sallow complexion; also, that his lips were very thin, with no indentation between the upper one and his nose.

Aunt Serena's house, which was of red brick in the boxy Dutch style with a sloping roof and a big front porch, had been left to her, along with a modest annuity, by her father, a lumber dealer, whose Livingston face looked down from above the fireplace in the front parlor. In that house, Aunt lived by herself, with an Irish woman to do the heavy work, who was replaced from time to time, as Jerrold was to become aware, because no one could stand being away from the big city for very long. Aunt occupied her time with this and that, but especially with making clippings from *The Ladies Home Journal* and some other magazines that she subscribed to. Aside from that, she was a regular communicant at Christ Episcopal, in which Jerrold too was soon kneeling down of a Sunday, and every so often she had a circle of single ladies like herself in for tea.

At the first of those gatherings after his arrival, he was dawdling in the parlor doorway when Aunt Serena called for him to come get a piece of fudge, and then as he was going off to the kitchen to eat it, she remarked to her friends with a sigh, "A burden, but what can one do, kin's kin." This made Jerrold all shivery, as if he were in a long, cold, dark tunnel all by himself, but the chocolate's buttery sweetness, savored to the last morsel, soon made the chill go away.

By then, Jerrold had shed his overalls for a pair of salt-and-pepper knickers, and was sleeping in a kind of storeroom off the kitchen, which Aunt had fitted up with a cot and a dresser. On her recommendation, his days were spent at the large mahogany desk in the study, turning the pages of Grandpa Livingston's old books to look for pictures...by the light of a kerosene lamp reminding of the one hanging over the plank table back home. Once, after a week or so of doing this, Jerrold forgot that Pa and Ma were no more, and began wondering—until he caught himself—when they were coming to fetch him.

On Jerrold's turning six, Aunt enrolled him in Cobbs, as the public school in Tarrytown was called, and by the year's end he was dealing pretty well with the alphabet and beginning to get the catechism by heart in Sunday School. In time, two boys were singled out as friends to pal around with—Roger, who had buck teeth and wore glasses, and Peter, whose cheeks of mottled pink and hair with streaks of gold Jerrold rather envied. Their favorite haunt came to be down by the Hudson, Tarrytown's zee, where there were piers to fish from and a little sandy area that passed for a beach, and where in winter they would chase one another around the ice on their skates or else walk across to the opposite bank just to say they did. Roger and Peter came from large families, so their fathers, a grocery clerk and the manager of a livery stable, were constantly hard-put to make ends meet; nevertheless, there was always a place for Jerrold at their tables, which made him feel a little uneasy, conscious of their pity for his orphaned state.

All in all, though, as Jerrold grew, things were not that bad, with Aunt Serena only raising a fuss occasionally about keeping his room neat and orderly, and giving him a fair share of the kinds of birthday and Christmas presents that boys delighted in, like a pen knife. But then came a fierce disappointment, when she absolutely refused to allow a dog in the house, even a small one like Peter's, and turned out to be even more adamant about a nifty tom offered by Roger from his cat's litter, which would "spray all over the place" when it got older and "leave that terrible stench."

Jerrold was twelve at the time and found this objection somewhat puzzling, as something similar had been happening to him of late while he was asleep, a gummy substance with a gamey odor oozing out. Could there be a connection, am I related to cats in some way, do I have cat blood in me, he wondered. However, putting two and two together from recollecting how cats, and dogs too, carried on with one another, he was eventually able to form a rough idea of what the stuff was supposed to be for. A good thing too, because one day not long after, Peter told him about a secret game he'd been playing with some older boys in an abandoned shed, where they all did it deliberately with their hands while sitting in a circle. "Gee, that sounds like fun!" Jerrold said, but unhappily there was no invitation to join them —probably because being scrawny, he still looked like a kid. But that's alright, he assured himself, you don't need them really, you can manage just as well by yourself at home. It was simply a matter of being careful about the sheets, so that Aunt wouldn't find out. Jerrold began that very night, having all the fun he cared to...

By the end of eighth grade, it was more or less decided by Aunt Serena and Jerrold's teachers, since he could add up a column of figures with a fair degree of accuracy and wrote a good hand, that he should be a bookkeeper, which meant staying on at Cobbs for another two years. At the same time, through some connection of Aunt's at Christ Episcopal, he began doing odd jobs after school for the gas company, which was then but a hop, skip, and a jump away from the good old waterfront.

As of this point, with Roger working as a stock boy in the grocery store with his father and Peter destined for a mining college out west, whose entrance exams he had to prepare for, the three boyhood chums understandably began to drift apart. To dispel the gloom, Jerrold took to filling the empty hours with reading, and here he was in luck, for Tarrytown's public library, called the Lyceum, happened to be very well-stocked. Of all the books that he devoured during this period, the Merriwell series were his favorites, for Frank the hero likewise had no parents. Always managing to emerge from his hair-raising escapades with the same purity of heart and high spirits, Merriwell became an ideal, something for Jerrold to shoot for—in the end, better, far better, than friends really, who were here today and gone tomorrow.

At the gas works, Jerrold soon came to the attention of Mr. Stivers, the head bookkeeper, on whom his sterling qualities were not lost. And the result was that on turning sixteen, Jerrold became one of his assistants. A short, trim man with furry eyebrows, Mr. Stivers soon showed himself to be an ideal boss—exacting when it came to keeping the numbers straight in their columns, and the very soul of discretion over ink accidentally spilled and so on. Before long, Stivers and his wife being childless, a kind of friendship developed between him and Jerrold, which as matters were to turn out would also prove fortunate…

One summer day some years later, Mr. Stivers hurried to Jerrold's desk with a message just received: Serena Livingston had been taken seriously ill; her nephew was to go right home. On his feet at once, Jerrold half-ran up Main to Franklin—to find a small crowd of neighbors on the porch surrounding Mabel, Aunt's latest charwoman, who was holding a handkerchief to her face. Seconds later, as he was galloping up the stoop, the doctor, an old white-beard, stepped out from inside with his bag. "I'm sorry, my boy," he gravely said. Aunt had suffered a severe stroke and was gone before he got there. "But don't worry," he added, indicating Selby the Undertaker's wagon just drawing up, "everything's been taken care of."

Jerrold was dumbstruck, for even though he and Aunt Serena had not been exactly what one could call close—certainly not like

Roger and Peter with their female relatives—she was all that he'd had in the world, saving the many distant Livingston cousins. And in a kind of stupor he remained through the wake and funeral, which happily for him were presided over by some of her bosom friends. Then on returning to his old self again, he became filled with foreboding, recalling the doctor's words, "Don't worry, everything's been taken care of." Aunt had never seen fit to confide in her nephew concerning her affairs, and somehow he'd never thought to inquire—until now.

The beginning of an answer came one day, in the form of a letter from a Mr. Louis Collins of Byrne & Collins, a law firm on Main, requesting that he stop by their office at his earliest convenience—which Jerrold lost no time in doing with Mr. Stivers' kind permission. A pudgy man with extra-shiny glasses, Mr. Collins lost no time himself, informing Jerrold as soon as he was seated that Serena Livingston, the deceased, had left her entire estate to the daughter of a cousin on her father's side. Further, upon learning of the windfall, said heiress, who resided in Buffalo, had given instructions that the house, which was the estate's chief asset, be vacated and put up for sale at once. As for him, the nephew—Mr. Collins' eyes, behind the sparkling glasses, sought for compliance from Jerrold, and his manner became ingratiating—things were not as bleak as they might seem. His old auntie had left him a special bequest of $450 to set himself up in life with.

Out in the street, Jerrold, feeling very down, took himself to task for not having had a serious talk with Aunt Serena while it was still possible. Only when, how, he argued with himself. Still, to be turned out of one's home, as much his as hers almost—horrible! And then, where should he go?

Returning to the office, he couldn't help blurting everything out to Mr. Stivers, who was indeed eagerly waiting to hear, and just like that, the immediate problem was solved, with his benefactor suggesting in his soft-spoken way that Jerrold come and rent from him.

Four Lives

"You can have your pick of rooms," Stivers made it clear, and he was certain without even asking (though he would) that Mrs. Stivers, who knew all about Jerrold, would welcome him with open arms.

The next evening found Jerrold going home with that truly feeling individual to meet the missus, a slender woman with eyes that tended to pop a little, who, sure enough, turned out to be as gracious as one could wish. As for the house, a two-story structure of wood, it too proved to Jerrold's liking, looking from its crest of a hill on the corner of Storm and Central straight down to the river and beyond to Nyack on the other side with the Ramapos, true purple mountains, in the distance.

Jerrold moved in with them several days later, and the Stiverses encouraging, he took the right dormer room because of its view and the sense of isolation it gave—for still deeply troubled by the recent turn of events, he desperately needed to feel alone (without actually being so) to think things through. And that is just what he did, climbing way up there to his eagle's nest in the evening after dinner, to lie on his bed and just let his mind roam...with the wide expanse of water and distant land before him fading to deeper and deeper blue.

It took a number of nights spent like that before a thought—The Thought—came: in addition to being Aunt's home, the house belonged to her, and like every other individual, she had a right to do with her property whatever she saw fit. And Jerrold's conclusion? Best to forget about it, just to forget...her... everything.

But that was not the end of his ruminating. Still to be dealt with was what to do with himself now that Aunt was no longer at his back prodding—whether to stay on here at the job and with the Stiverses, or with nothing to keep him here any longer, perhaps to push on to someplace else...

The following Sunday, instead of going to church, which he no longer seemed to have a stomach for, Jerrold decided to take a walk. Striking out eastward along Neperan Road, where for some reason he'd never ventured before, he soon found himself in open country with row-on-row of wheat waving on either hand.

Then all at once, after a certain bend, there was a field that was all overgrown, and beyond on a kind of rise, an old broken-down farmhouse with a caved-in roof—home, his original home.

No Trespass signs were posted along the roadside there, so the State probably took it for taxes, Jerrold surmised. Either that or some private party bought it and just let it go to seed.

All the same, he hiked himself up over the fence and made his way up a rocky weed-strewn lane to the front door. Then, after pausing there for a moment to contemplate a rusty kerosene lamp lying among some weather-beaten planks in the wreckage within, he went slipping and sliding round to the back—to come face-to-face with a patch of wild spinach and lettuce.

Two splintery grey wooden crosses were dimly discernible in the midst of all that vegetable tangle.

Well now, he thought, after staring absently at it all for some time, if you were to make a move, where would you go?

The answer came, but not at once, not until six months later...

It was one of those frosty winter mornings, and everyone in the office had been buzzing with the news the moment the doors opened. At noon that day, two of Tarrytown's summer millionaires were going to have a race on the ice—in a custom-built Maxwell from the nearby factory and a Pierce Arrow.

No great admirer of those wealthy folk, who took little interest in the town's affairs, Mr. Stivers was nevertheless curious to see whether the two gay blades would make fools of themselves or what. "How about it, would you like to come?" he asked Jerrold, stopping by his desk shortly before the time, in a mackinaw and cap with visor and earflaps.

Why not, Jerrold thought, always on the lookout these days for some way to break the monotony, and hurried to don his own cold weather gear.

By the shore, a goodly crowd was gathered, rich people mixed in with locals. Beyond, on the ice, the contenders, in goggles and fur coats, had just brought their spiffy-looking vehicles to a halt before a makeshift starting line.

Suddenly—*crack*!—a pistol went off. And then the air was filled with shrieks as gears ground and tires skidded, and the two autos roared and spun around and roared again!

Oh boy! Jerrold shouted out inside himself. The power of it all! That's what I need...this place has grown too small for me.

EARLY ON A MONDAY AFTERNOON THE NEXT MONTH (*FEBRUARY, 1909*)

All in brand-new brown, including a stylish tweed cap, Jerrold is gently rocking with the train, conscious of how dapper he looks—of how becomingly earth tones blend with his tan skin and wheaten hair.

Tenements have been flying by outside the window. Now all at once the train is speeding through a pitch-black tunnel.

"Grand Central's next!" a conductor bawls.

Brakes are applied. Bright bluish-white lights appear on either hand, like shining needles. The train slows down and comes to a stop with a tiny jerk.

"So here we are," Jerrold murmurs, and jumping up with his tapestried carpetbag firmly in hand, begins shuffling out with the other passengers.

On the platform, he eyes the arched glass roof with its intricate pattern of iron supports high above, and then the adjacent tracks, where as many as five trains are pulling in and out at the same time.

Best not to stare so, he reminds himself, brim full of good advice and dire warnings from everyone down to Mr. Cohen the tailor.

The rest of the way to the gate he keeps his gaze lowered, glancing up only momentarily when he reaches the vastness of the waiting room.

Now for the outside, Forty-Second Street. Jerrold leans his shoulder against the street door.

"Golly, gee!" It's like a splash of cold spring water on a hot summer's day: the trolleys and their clang-clang's, the carriages and wagons with their rattles and rumbles, the honking of the autos! Why that much traffic's not to be seen in Tarrytown for a month of Sundays!

He draws in a deep breath. Ah, the air! Absolutely the cat's meow, honest-to-goodness gasoline fumes!

And look at those buildings! Across the way there are some eight stories high at least, while up a piece to the right is a regular juggernaut, the Manhattan Hotel, that has to be twice that size!

But enough, Jerrold checks himself. It's time for serious business. Now let's see—he has to get down to the West 20's, where decent rooms are to be had at reasonable rates, according to Tarrytown's station master. West, west, which way is west, he wonders, and starts off to the right. If it's not this way, then it'll be the other, he remembers from the map, which is stuck away in his bag.

Fifth Avenue, a street sign two blocks over announces. So, a lucky guess.

But can it be? It's like a Fourth of July parade there, with shiny horse-drawn landaus, victorias, and broughams together with chauffeured limousines four abreast—and wonder of wonders, a doubledecker bus of fire-engine red!

He should hop a cab at this point, so the Stiverses recommended. But I just want to see this one thing, Jerrold insists to himself, and despite the screech of a police whistle, lunges diagonally across to the other side.

Before him is this huge stone structure in-the-making, with dark-skinned, black-haired workmen who remind him of Indians moving around inside. A placard identifies it as The New York Public Library, soon to open.

Now for the cab. But—"Ooh!"—something else has caught Jerrold's eye, a truly gigantic building maybe a mile down. It's the

Fuller, nicknamed Flatiron, he recalls from a picture in the guidebook, also in his bag. I've got to, I've just got to see it!

He rushes away with long strides, passing the Tiffany Building, like an Italian palazzo...the Knickerbocker Trust Company, a Greek temple...the Hotel Waldorf-Astoria, ringed round with electric lamps like sentinels...B. Altman's Department Store, a block long...the Cafe Martin and Holland House, whatever they are...and Brentano's Bookstore, another block long...

"Sure is something," Jerrold sighs, with his head bent way back so as to take in all of the Flatiron's twenty-five stories. Just like the prow of a ghostly ship, as the book says.

Now where are we, he prods himself at long last. The sky's turned very white and it seems to have grown considerably colder. Gonna snow, I reckon, better get going.

But—"Jeezy!"—there's something else way way down that looks like a white cube with a kneehole in it, Washington Arch for sure, sister of the Arc de Triomphe in Paris, France, scene of one of Frank Merriwell's most daring escapades!

The carpetbag becomes light in Jerrold's hand, as he takes off again past...Arnold Constable's...Chickering Hall... Fourteenth Street...brownstones with stoops...the First Presbyterian Church...the Church of the Ascension...the Hotel Brevoort...and more brownstones...

"Boy, oh boy!" he lets out, after passing through the Arch's "hole" and going almost clear over to Washington Square's other side for the best view. "Just perfect!"—meaning the complementary touches of white in the pink townhouses flanking it.

Jerrold's still moving backwards.

"Young man, vatch vhere you're going!" a female voice calls from nearby.

Jerrold looks alive. One more step and he would have gone off a curb onto some trolley tracks. "Thanks, mam, much obliged," he says, with fingers to his cap.

She's a matronly type in a black dress and a bonnet, with a mouth that's done its share of pursing. Her eyes, which are somewhat too close together, study him narrowly—"You vouldn't happen to be lookin' for a room by any chance, vould ya?" She has a trace of an accent.

"Could be," Jerrold answers, mindful of the White Slavers and kindred dangers that his well-wishers back home filled his ears with.

"Well, that's my place over dere"—she points south to Number 61 in the middle of the block, which is pink with white trim in imitation of the finer houses across the way. "Got a honey of a vun in de front on de top floor. Just fell vacant the other day. Care to see?"

Still a little hesitant, Jerrold at the same time feels irresistibly drawn—to the Arch, the trees, and what they must look like from up there. "Sure, if you have a mind to show me"…

"What part of de vorld ya from, somewhere in the north of Europe?" she asks, with his arm firmly grasped as they cross the street.

Jerrold sets her straight, telling her his name.

"Mine's Branchard," she informs him in her turn. "Everyvun calls me Madame Branchard."

Oh, jiminy! Jerrold panics. Mr. Cohen the tailor had something in particular to say respecting women who use that title—namely, to beware of them, they can ruin a young man's life (whatever that means). "Are you French?" he asks.

No, her late husband. She's Swiss, German-Swiss.

Well, the woman certainly sounds on the up-and-up, Jerrold concludes.

They've arrived at the stoop, a steep one. "Say"—Madame Branchard pulls up short—"you don't drink, do ya?"

"Mam?" Jerrold says squeaky-like.

This seems to satisfy the widow-lady. "So vhatcha gonna do here, write a book, a play? Is that vhat you got in the bag dere, a manuscript?" she plies him as they're ascending.

Who? Him? No, of course not. He's going to get the newspapers and find a job, he explains.

On the top step, Madame Branchard opens the door with a twist of the knob—which is how one can get in until midnight, she emphasizes. After that, it is necessary to ring the bell. "But don't make it too late," she adds. "I need my beauty rest."

Inside is a foyer with a table on the right for receiving mail and a mirror above it, illuminated by a single gas jet. On the opposite wall is a long row of paintings in gilt frames, all dark except for what the licking yellow flame chances to bring out here and there—the silver in a cloud, some daisy petals; an elderly gent's bulbous red nose.

"By former tenants," Madame Branchard explains, and leads the way to stairs in the rear, which they begin mounting...

"Look here"—she's stopped short once more—"ya not a lady's man, are ya?"

Jerrold grins and feels his cheeks grow hot—"No, mam." Though a nice girl to share his life with would certainly not be amiss once he's established, he confides to himself.

Madame Branchard's nostrils flare—well, in the event that he experiences a change of heart, let him be forewarned, there's a rule pertaining to THAT too. Under no circumstances—"None, dya hear?"—are visitors of the opposite sex ever allowed in tenants' rooms.

As they near the second floor, a piano strikes up with a tune that swells and swells, and promises to go on at some length.

"My son Emile," Madame Branchard offers. "Yesterday he vas a painter, tomorrow he's gonna drive a team of horses for a brewery, today he's tryin' to be nice to me. De music's from Signor Puccini's *La Bohème*, 'case you don't recognize it"...

The third floor landing is within sight. Jerrold suddenly remembers—Oh gee!—that he didn't ask about the rent. "Say, could you—?"

"Fifteen dollars a month, payable in advance," Madame Branchard says over her shoulder, breathily. "Is dat alright?"

"Quite," Jerrold answers. And it certainly will be once he's employed...

Up there at last, Madame Branchard unlocks one of two major doors with a jangle of keys—"As I said, it's not one of your run-o'-de mill rooms"—and throws it open.

Jerrold remains rooted to the spot—"I'll say."

It's all there—the Arch, the trees, the elegant townhouses, everything!—through three windows, framed by deep-golden draperies with swags.

"Told you," Madame Branchard crows.

Furthermore, she points out, everything is there for him to set up housekeeping with, including a two-burner stove on a stand, a sink, and a small gas refrigerator, all tucked away in an alcove behind.

As for furnishings, he can see for himself, tip top: a divan covered by a Confederate flag along the left wall...a fireplace opposite, with a gas burner in it, a smoky-pink mirror above, and a maroon easy chair before it—

"I'll take it," Jerrold says, and sets the carpet bag down to get his billfold out.

"Dis used to be where Patti stayed ven she vas in town," the Madame chatters.

"Oh?" Jerrold hands over three crisp fivers.

"You know, Adelina Patti, de preemah donnah?"

"Sorry, never heard of her."

The Madame's aghast...and is gone.

"At last!" Jerrold breathes. He's been longing to strip off coat and suit jacket and go sit in one of the windowseats...just sit and look out...

The snow has finally come, and is floating down in plumpish flakes. The streetlights have recently blinked on and are casting violet circles on the ground, which is almost uniformly covered.

Beyond, in the gathering darkness, the Arch is a dim shadow, and the lights in the houses across the way shine hazily, like steely points in a mist.

Jerrold has arisen now and again, once to turn on the gas jets in the fireplace and bring back the colorful flag from the divan to wrap himself in. But essentially he's been there all that time, with knees up and hands clasped around them.

Drowsy now, he'll be going to bed soon—but not before you swear one thing, he prompts himself.

Swear that whatever you do, no matter what happens, this place will remain yours.

※

The next morning Jerrold expected to see white drifts piled up outside, like back home after a heavy snowfall. But no, crazily, on rolling round and raising his head, he found all traces of it gone, with only the street slickly wet and the sky reflecting blue here and there in murky puddles.

"Starving!" he complained to a greyish-pink reflection of himself in the fireplace mirror, and went, with a bulge in his drawers, to get his overcoat hanging on the rack in the alcove.

When did I eat last, he wondered, back from the toilet a few moments later. Slipping shiveringly into his clothes, he recalled a Hershey bar consumed during the walk down from Grand Central yesterday, and before that, breakfast with the Stiverses, a lugubrious affair with his promising to write and so on. Is it possible, nothing down my gullet since then?

"Gotta get some food," he murmured, making for the stairs with cap and coat back on (but minus tie and collar underneath). I'll have to ask somebody where to go...

As he was about to descend the final flight, a door creaked behind him—the landlady's. "Psst!" someone hissed.

Jerrold looked round.

"Hi!" the same person greeted through a crack there.

The door widened a little to reveal a fellow around Jerrold's age, fat of face with a pair of eyes close together from which a large nose depended, underlined by a small tight mouth.

"Name's Emile, but to my friends I'm Chucky." The fellow had on a red flannel shirt and overalls.

"Pleased to meet you," Jerrold said. "I'm—"

"Yeh, I know—Jerry. Mama already told me all about you."

Speaking of the devil, Madame Branchard's voice sounded shrilly from within—"Aim-eel?"

"She's mad, I got up late," Chucky explained in a hangdog fashion.

Seems like a nice sort, Jerrold decided. Might be someone I'd want to pal around with in time once I get settled. But the gut was really rumbling. "Say, do you know where a guy can get something to eat around here?"

"Try Third Street, plenny of places there," Chucky suggested, and rattled off directions.

Inside, Madame Branchard called again, very insistently this time—"Aim—eel!"

"Gotta go," Chucky whispered...

Outside, Jerrold stood for a moment on the doorstep to behold the Arch, positively glowing golden from the sun on it, and the houses on either side a resplendent pink, shrines at which he hadn't worshipped as of yet that morning.

Then he was off...left to the corner, which was Thompson, and O'Reilly's Saloon, with the barn-like light-orange hulk of Judson Church opposite...and left again to the El's black metal overhang on the next cross street, which was it, Third.

Now where? Stores there were indeed on both sides, but what they were Jerrold could not make out, with shoppers thronging the sidewalks and pushcarts lining either curb.

Must be a drugstore or something like that around here. Feeling genuinely queasy now, he strained to see beyond the mounds of purple eggplants, green and red peppers, and blue-tinged broccoli...and noted in passing that the vendors were mostly dark-skinned folk reminiscent of the laborers at the new public library yesterday—all of them EYE-talians, it now occurred to him.

Where? Where? In one of the store windows across the way, there were dozens of salamis dangling over a formidable stack of gilded olive oil cans and a grinning pig's head.

Ah, there! In the middle of the same block was a tiny shop displaying baked goods on trays.

Jerrold crossed over, all wobbly in the knees, and made a little bell on the door tinkle vigorously as he entered.

"*Buon giorno*, gooda morning!" a male voice sang out from somewhere behind the counter, on the right.

Heading for the nearest of four small marble-topped tables, Jerrold sat heavily down on a wire-backed chair with a red leather seat.

A roly-poly man in a white apron, with mustachios and an almost bald crown, materialized—what would the young gentleman's pleasure be?

"Anything, doesn't matter," Jerrold murmured, with head bowed...ready to moan.

The man with the mustachios showed concern—"You sicka?"

"No"—Jerrold told him what was what.

The baker hurried away, and came right back with a powdery jelly doughnut on a piece of waxed paper. In his other hand was a small glass of steamy dark coffee in a silvery metal holder.

Jerrold grabbed the doughnut up and greedily bit into it, and washed the mouthful, half-chewed, down with a gulp.

"Good, eh?" said the man, standing by.

Jerrold nodded, certainly was. In fact, it was downright delicious, the doughnut's cakey part absolutely melting, the jelly silky beyond belief. Finished in a trice, he licked his lips and fingerdotted the crumbs.

"I breeng you another"—Jerrold began to protest. "Don't worry, you no have to pay, thissa one is on me."

A train roared hellishly by on the el-tracks above, setting the floor a-tremble.

"You know, you very skinny," the baker said on his return, when Jerrold was sinking his teeth into the free one. "Not good to be lika that." If one became ill, really ill, there was no flesh to lose—"Easy die." The man thumped at his belly under the apron—"Looka me, no die thin." He broke into a hearty laugh—"Maybe hit by automobile."

Jerrold hahha'd with him—it *was* funny.

"You gotta eat gooda stuff," the baker went on, very seriously.

He's right, Jerrold thought, only how was a person like himself ever to do so who didn't even know how to boil water, as the saying went?

The man heard Jerrold out as he explained this, then with an I-know-just-how-to-fix-that expression, called in Italian to the rear of the shop.

A frizzy-haired woman with many freckles on nose and cheeks and a toothy smile stepped through a curtain back there.

This was Giuseppina, his wife, the baker informed Jerrold; his name was Arturo. Whereupon there was a brief conversation between the couple in their tongue, in which he put a question to her and she responded with a bob of her chin while nervously wiping her fingers on a towel.

"Okay, it's settled," Arturo announced. Jerrold was to go shopping for food with her, Giuseppina. She'd help pick things out and at the same time as they went along, describe how to cook them.

Jerrold was flabbergasted—"Well, I—"

Arturo wagged a finger: no use arguing, wouldn't take no for an answer.

Boy, what a break, Jerrold confided to himself. Why it's—it's like finding the Stiverses all over again!...

Four Lives

On the way home some time later, he paused midway on Thompson to give his arms a rest—from lugging two straw baskets chock full of all kinds of wonderful things to eat, including the makings of a splendid white bean soup with a succulent ham bone.

Somewhere above in the tenements, a man was singing in a deep, rich baritone...a long, weaving melody, foreign-sounding but somehow pleasant.

Something made Jerrold look up—and there overhead was a flock of pigeons on the wing, just taken off from their home on a nearby roof.

It's good here, it really suits me, he decided.

SHORTLY BEFORE EIGHT ON A MONDAY MORNING
A MONTH LATER (MARCH, 1909)

It sure better be my lucky day, Jerrold grimly observes, while inspecting what can be seen of the suit in the mirror. All he's had so far with respect to jobs is one turn-down after another. And why? Because he lacks New York experience, those who interviewed him kept giving as the reason.

Casting back to all the people he's seen in brokerages, publishers, and all sorts of retail establishments great and small, including a one-price clothing store way downtown somewhere, his mind fastens on a middling bank official with a fleshy face, immaculate in a cutaway, who seems to represent the rest.

"But how do I get New York experience?" Jerrold inquired with a catch in his throat.

The banker merely smiled, as if responding, That's for you to figure out, dear fellow. Now good day...

Well, today should be different, is Jerrold's feeling.

The chance has come about through the kind efforts of Arturo and Giuseppina of all people, whom he's visited almost daily since that first time, and taken completely into his confidence. Understanding the urgency of the situation—that Jerrold's little hoard of money is dwindling away—the couple asked around among their neighbors, and lo, it turned out that someone's daughter knew for a certainty that the bookkeeper in the factory where she worked needed someone to assist him. The place belongs to Jews, it appears, and Jews, in Arturo's opinion, are never easy to work for even under the best of circumstances. However, the daughter had no particular complaints about these people, Giuseppina was happy to report.

Well, we'll soon see, won't we, Jerrold concludes, after giving a last tug to his tie, which is brown with a thin blue stripe to match the suit. The only Jew he's ever known has been Mr. Cohen the tailor, who was certainly alright...

Below, on the landlady's floor, all is quiet, with Chucky at work, Mrs. Branchard having patched things up with his new boss; so Jerrold learned from meeting him on the stairs one morning. One of these days, soon as everything's settled, I'm going to stop by after supper and ask if he'd like to do something together, Jerrold vows, not for the first time.

Outside it's just a matter of walking to the second corner on the right, then left to Washington Place, and up it a piece.

With those quick strides of his, Jerrold is there at Number 23 within a few minutes, and stepping into the elevator. "Ten, please," he says.

The operator, who seems too young to have a receding hairline, eyes him suspiciously—"That's Triangle's offices. Yuh have an appointment?"

"Yes," Jerrold answers, lying as the neighbor's daughter recommended. "Yes, I do."

"Ten it is"—up they go...

The elevator door slides open to reveal a large room with several rows of long tables ranged along the far end, where dozens of people are frantically running irons over what look like women's garments, while leftward on the other side of a partition, a man is barking orders over paper cartons being bounced around.

"Can I help ya?" a female voice nasally sings out to Jerrold's right.

Four Lives

"Yes, I'd like to see Mr. Levine," Jerrold tells her, after regaining his presence of mind, lost for a moment at the sight of the ironers flinging their cords about like mad snakes to the accompaniment of the yelling over boxes whack-whacking in the background.

Just then the last of a row of opaque glass doors opens behind her, and out comes a fortyish man in shirtsleeves with a grey-and-white tie and darker suit pants.

"Oh, Mr. Levine?" the receptionist calls.

Luck, I'm in luck again! Jerrold cries to himself, and instantly springs forward—"Sir, I wonder if I could interest you in myself as your assistant?"

Mr. Levine, who has a waxen face with a cleft in his chin, surveys him through pince-nez.

"I mean—could I see you for a moment?" Jerrold winningly pleads.

"Come in," Mr. Levine says in a quiet way that seems habitual with him, and re-enters his office with Jerrold following right behind.

Inside, once Jerrold is seated before the bookkeeper at his desk, the whole story of how he got there comes pouring out.

"You'll never be sorry for taking me on, sir," Jerrold ends by arguing. "I'm a hard worker, and of course I'm quite willing to start at the bottom."

Mr. Levine looks thoughtful.

Bang! suddenly goes something close by, another of the office doors having been yanked unstuck from the sound of it.

"Just a moment"—Mr. Levine gets up to pull his own door wide.

Passing by is a man of around his age with reddish-brown hair, who is also in shirtsleeves with a tie.

The bookkeeper calls him by name—Harris, one of the big cheeses—and both of them begin talking, with Harris casting looks Jerrold's way.

At long last the big boss shrugs—"Alright, he needs a job? Gif him to Boinsteen." Then he shouts to someone coming toward them—"Hey, Sam!"

79

The new guy is short like those two, but hefty, and has a kind of baby face.

Mr. Harris waves to Jerrold—"C'mere, kid!"

Jerrold feels himself tensing up: what's this kid stuff? Is that what I look like? But he goes over there.

"Here," Mr. Harris says to Bernstein, "you vanted anudder floater, here he is," and bids Levine, who now has a sheepish look on his face, walk on with him.

Floater? What's a floater? Jerrold wonders, left alone with this Bernstein, all in grey.

The man fixes him from under sleepy eyelids that are arched over by perfect brows—"I'm going to put you in Shipping today with Mr. Markowitz"—meaning, Jerrold surmises, on the other side of the partition where the man is still shouting over the racket of the boxes.

"Go buy yourself some Levi's or something this evening," Bernstein continues.

Levi's? Jerrold considers with eyes down. So that's it, they're going to make a workman of me.

Bernstein has one final instruction: "Tomorrow you'll report back to me, hear?"

"How—how much?" Jerrold asks.

"Six dollars a week, take it or leave it," Bernstein snaps, through lips that seem to sneer.

CHAPTER

4

Hippolyte was a one-of-a-kind without whom Fanny's tall tale would in no form or fashion be complete. There never was or ever will be anyone quite like him again. Originality of his kind is deserving of a medal. Truly, one could kiss such uniqueness.

Hippolyte's parents, Josef and Anna Havel, came from Borova, which literally means "pine grove," and was one of a dozen or so Bohemian villages that went by that name. Later in life, Josef claimed to be related to the Czech writer and patriot Karel Havlicek, another "Borovan"—which was probably just boastful bragging. Be that as it may, Josef was the schoolmaster in *his* village of Borova, and actually enjoyed a reputation there for being a man of some learning and culture.

Originally from Melnik, long noted for its fine food and choice vintages, he was inordinately fond of a good Sunday dinner, and as the story goes, this was what impelled him at first to dine at Borova's new inn, whose proprietor was a Jew named Shimon Zamenek. At any rate, Josef and Anna, Shimon's twenty-five-year-old daughter, eventually cast amorous glances at one another, and despite misgivings on the innkeeper's part—that the schoolmaster, who was forty and a Roman Catholic, would impose his will on the younger Anna in matters of religion—a match was made.

The story further goes that not long after the marriage ceremony, which took place in 1867, Josef decided for unknown reasons to try his luck in America, and with Papa Zamenek supplying a goodly part of the wherewithal, the newlyweds headed for Praha, the Little Prague of Chicago. There, through some family connections, they became established in a ramshackle house on Taylor Street, where they eked out a bare living from a sausage stand outside their kitchen window while waiting for something better to come along. Hippolyte, their first and only child, was born the following year, and realizing the innkeeper's worst fears, Josef immediately whisked the baby off to St. Wenceslaus Church to be baptized.

The year after, the Great Fire came, and alas, swept away what little the couple had accumulated in worldly goods—indeed, like so many others they escaped from the flames with only the clothes on their backs. However, thanks to the generosity of a Czech building and loan fund, they were soon able to start over, this time with a saloon above which they lived in Little Pilsen. According to the arrangement, Josef handled the marketing and accounts while Anna managed things in the kitchen, with the help of a hireling to serve up her mouth-watering cabbage and potato soups garnished with heaps of freshly-baked rye and black bread.

Anna was small and delicate, with a mass of wavy dark-brown hair; Josef, being tall, thin, and fair himself, used to refer to her as his gypsy. As Hippolyte grew older, he began to resemble Mama more and more, with the same dark flashing eyes, wee fig of a nose, and lips that curled up at the corners at the least provocation. And that is how he came to be Papa's "little gypsy boy."

In Hippolyte's eleventh year, there was a particularly harsh winter, and Anna took sick and died of pneumonia. Her household cares passed into the hands of a big-breasted woman they had working for them at the time, also called Anna, with whom Josef soon struck up a "friendship." Hippolyte found himself needing Mama as never before—to intercede with Papa, who had taken to drink and grown surly.

The saloon, left to run more or less by itself, became the watering place for all sorts of German and Czech radicals, who abounded in Chicago at the time, and curiously it began to flourish. Hippolyte, by then a short, wiry youth with a shrill voice and attending school at St. Procopius, began helping Anna out in the afternoon and soon fell under the spell of all the ferment. And the upshot was, he took to spending every spare moment poring over whatever the experts downstairs judged to be worth reading—from Zola, Ibsen, and Anatole France to Dostoyevsky and Gogol. Not only that, it wasn't long before Hippolyte had his own personal vision of the future, when, as Shelley and Whitman had hinted between the lines, the weary laboring ones of the world would rise up as one man, and beating their ploughshares into swords, put the Dread Oppressor down. Nor was this vision mere idle speculation; on the contrary, out of it evolved the firm belief that one should strive with all one's might to bring it about, regardless of the ethics of the situation or consequences likely to ensue—for as Hippolyte was soon quick to repeat after Bakunin, and Stirner too, if one read him closely as well:

"THE PASSION FOR DESTRUCTION IS ALSO A CREATIVE PASSION!" In short, he had become an anarchist.

Mass he didn't dare stay away from—not as yet—lest the powers-that-be at St. Procopius discover it and expel him, which Papa would have made him pay dearly for with his strap and perhaps even his fists...

One day in the midst of all the excitement, when Papa was off somewhere, came another turning point in Hippolyte's young life. Anna called for him to leave off swabbing down the tables and meet her upstairs, where she had something to show him, and the next one knew, there they were on the bed together with his wiener inside her. "Now run, horsey, run," Anna urged, and it being wonderfully warm and frothy in there, away he raced, stumbling now and then—deliriously!—but rising right up and galloping away again. In time, after more trysts like that, Anna explained what they were doing and taught him other things as well, including this rule that she made him promise to follow for the rest of his life—"Whatever you start with a woman, always see it through to the end."

Eighteen eighty-six, the year of the Haymarket Riot, found Hippolyte finishing up at St. Procopius and looking forward to when he would be free—FREE AT LAST!—to do as he pleased and help make history. But then on returning with his satchel one afternoon, he found Josef waiting with a somewhat shamefaced Anna—and he could hardly believe his ears. It seems that the woman had bought them out lock, stock, and barrel, using her little bit put by over the years. Further, there had been another swain all along, whom she had seen on the sly and was now about to tie the knot with. And so Josef announced that as soon as school was over, he was returning home to Bohemia and taking Hippolyte with him.

How Hippolyte's heart raged. "What do I want to go there for?" he screamed. "This is my home!" And schemes of running away to California or some other place where no one would ever find him flashed through his mind. However, when the time came for boarding the train that was to take them to New York and the trans-Atlantic steamer, there he was going along—for reasons best known to himself.

Their first stop was Borova, where old Grandpa Zamenek and Uncle Stephan, Mama's brother, were civil but distant. So between the awkwardness and plain boredom—there being absolutely nothing to do and no one interesting to consort with around town—Hippolyte was only too glad to depart when his father gave the word.

Josef had thought to go to Prague next, but at the last moment opted for Vienna, with an eye to obtaining a position as a tutor among the rich and powerful there, and at the same time to enrolling

Hippolyte in the University or perhaps a Gymnasium to prepare him for entry. Only no sooner did the two of them arrive than a bunch of supposedly old cronies attached themselves to Josef, and he began spending whole nights with them, and days too, carousing.

What could Hippolyte do but plead and cajole, and when that had no effect, what but to go off by himself to Ottakring, the working class quarter, and see if he could find a political group to join with ideas similar to his own. Happily, thanks to the German drummed into him at St. Procopius, he did manage to do that, and happily the comrades, who operated from a properly grim cellar, were young and full of daring—all except the leader, Wilhelm Körber, who regarded the world through eyes like hard coals and uttered whatever was on his mind curtly through a John Brown beard.

Hippolyte's gaining acceptance among them was another matter, for everyone regarded him a spoiled darling in his still new-looking American clothes. But just as he ferreted them out, so too he wooed and won them, including that Körber. Whereupon there was no holding him back; he was everywhere doing everything...from scribbling articles for the group's newspaper *Jugend* to trying to convert the prostitutes thereabouts, sometimes his bed partners...from marching through the streets shouting slogans with fist pumping to taunting rival groups and even, on occasion, slugging it out with them. And since he was always in the forefront and among the most vocal there, inevitably there were arrests and imprisonment, with beating after beating, and ultimately expulsion to Switzerland...then Berlin...and then Paris.

While there, he received an urgent summons from Josef, who had by then drowned his liver in drink, and deciding to chance it, he returned to Vienna under an assumed name. But somehow word of this reached the ears of the authorities, and he was arrested on the spot. Nor was that all; vehemently denouncing the police for their inhumanity in accosting him at his dying father's bedside, Hippolyte was this time hauled off to a lunatic asylum rather than a jail. And in that awful place he would have stewed forever, had not Körber, his old leader, gotten wind of it and somehow arranged for a young doctor of leftish tendencies to go there and attest to his sanity.

From Vienna, Hippolyte wended his way to London, where now as a grown man with thick-lensed glasses and lots of hair on upper lip and chin, he became a jack-of-all-trades in a cheap boarding house on the East End. Inwardly he was different too...sort of crying or dying. But some months later all that was to change: he would LIVE again as never before...

Well, well, he crowed to himself one day, with a street circular in hand. Autonomie, a German anarchist club, was having a rally that night, at which the featured speaker was to be Emma Goldman. Who hadn't heard of RED EMMA, as the tabloids pegged her? He pictured her dogged expression and lush lips, which, alas for her, had been plastered across their front pages all too often in recent years. Imagine it, the very same individual who tried to sell her body in the streets to pay for the pistol needed by her lover Sasha (Alexander) Berkman to assassinate Henry Clay Frick, millionaire grinder of the faces of the poor, was there in London in the flesh! While inclined to keep to himself of late, Hippolyte felt this was something not to be missed; he absolutely had to go.

Turning up at the hall in good time that night, he took a seat in the back, content just to listen—but fate would not have it so. To his distress, a young fellow sprang up in the middle of the Comrade's speech and insultingly rebuked her for something or other, and while she had no trouble holding her own, Hippolyte decided to seek her out afterward and offer a few commiserating words. As it happened, he was not the only one to be so inspired: Ferdie Schmidt, a regular he-man "with muscles in his shit," as people said, reached the podium at the same time. But whose utterances did the Comrade incline her ear to most, and whose eyes did she peer into more searchingly? His—his, Hippolyte's! And more startling yet, suddenly switching into English, which Ferdie did not understand too well, the illustrious one proposed a rendezvous for dinner the following evening!

The place was Hippolyte's choice, since he "knew" London well, a fish-and-chips joint off Russell Square. And the time was passed agreeably enough, with him telling her all about himself—among other things, that he came by his anarchism naturally, through his mother, who was "a full-blooded gypsy," and how he narrowly escaped rotting away in the Vienna looney bin were it not for the kind offices of "the celebrated Dr. Krafft-Ebing" no less—to all of which she listened attentively. However, when it was time to say goodnight in front of her hotel, leave it to him to make a terrible faux pas. The Comrade gave such a squeeze to his hand, whose redness and rawness from his job he kept concealed in a glove, that he saw stars—and out came, "You sure have a firm grip for a little lady!" That should have been the end of everything between them. But no, she only looked at him severely—and made another date for the next evening to be taken round to see some of London's poor neighborhoods.

Again he and the Comrade seemed to hit it off, but then toward the end, he committed yet another blunder. Thinking to set things straight, he pulled off the glove to show her the sores, which indeed moved her to compassion. However, when he began to complain, she quickly checked him with eyelashes batting angrily, "No vork is degrading." Quite right.

From then on, they were almost inseparable, and Hippolyte soon began to suspect that her interest in him was not strictly professional; in fact, finally, when she invited him for wine and cheese in her room one night, he was sure of it. Well, you're no saint either, he chided himself. Still, there was Sasha to consider, languishing away in a lonely prison cell (for wounding Frick by pumping two bullets into him and stabbing his leg with a supposedly poisoned dagger). And so, Hippolyte persuaded Ferdie Schmidt to come along. But wouldn't you know it, Ferdie stayed only long enough to fill his face—and now I'm in for it I bet, Hippolyte sighed as soon as the guy was gone.

Sure enough, the next moment the Comrade was moving closer to him on the little settee, and planting her mushy lips on his...then slipping her tongue in, mushier yet.

What could he do: he was only human—his pecker turned into ironwood (whatever that was). Still, what about poor Sasha, jerking off or whatever he was doing all by his lonesome in the caboose.

To his question, delicately murmured in her ear, the Comrade had the perfect answer, delivered breathily, with her fingers already creeping into his fly—"De flesh iss de flesh, und ven it calls, it must be answert."

What a feast they had then...with him holding out to pleasure her until his brains almost burst...then, when his member needed a little urging for a second go-round, with her wrapping those puckery lips around it...and then, when he absolutely could not anymore, with her pushing his head down and nose into hers...and finally, when his neck gave out, with her pressing his hand into service (sores and all)!

With the coming of dawn, there they were side-by-side with hips touching and fingers twined, planning a future together. He would quit his job, and they would move into another hotel as man and wife. During the rest of her stay in London, she would take him along to meet old friends like Kropotkin, another muckamuck in the Movement. They would then betake themselves to Paris for an anarchist congress, and then go on to Switzerland, where he would read for a degree in Philosophy and try to bring in a little cash with his pen to supplement an allowance that some rich Americans were giving her to study Medicine.

Those were the plans, but the reality (like all realities) turned out to be otherwise. The friends—principally Kropotkin and Victor Dave in Paris—either ignored Hippolyte and spoke only to her or else, if he dared open his mouth, immediately proceeded to make quick work of his ideas and show him up before her. This led to his drinking a bit too much and saying a few things that perhaps had been better left unsaid. "My bitter pootsy," the Comrade inevitably tried to soothe, with some strokes to his brow. Then as if that weren't bad enough, her sponsors learned of the liaison and without a moment's notice cut her off without a sou. Whereupon she had no choice but to return home to the States, where a reputedly handsome devil named Ben Reitman was ready to step back into her life—to say nothing of Sasha, whose prison term would be up one of these days.

After that, it was only a matter of waiting there in Paris until some other well-wishers sent the passage money. Meanwhile, without the least idea of what he would do after, Hippolyte kept the two of them from being reduced to beggary—by dishing up Eggs Benedict on an alcohol burner for the other comrades at the hotel in the morning, which she, anything but a cuisinière herself, thought simply miraculous. With the arrival of the funds, came a moment of illumination for him, with his suddenly realizing that it was impossible to live without her. And he let it be known that he was willing to remain by her side on no matter what terms.

When they sailed into New York some weeks later (in the year 1900), there was Ben Reitman on the pier, indeed with lechery in his eyes and a fine brush of a mustache framing a dimpled chin. Hippolyte spent the next month fruitlessly trekking hither and yon in search of work, and disgustedly laying his weary bones down in her kitchen on East 12th Street every night—until she took pity and got him a job writing for the *Arbeiter Zeitung* back home in Chicago.

The exile lasted five years, a lackluster time in which he gloomily watched from afar as her magazine *Mother Earth* got under way. Finally, though, with Sasha at last a free man but wanting only to write his prison memoirs, she had need of her Hippolyte in New York again to help keep an eye on things while she and Ben went gallivanting around the country filling lecture engagements.

An easy existence it didn't prove to be, with Hippolyte quite often having to resort to dishwashing and other distasteful occupations just to put a little food in his belly. But he didn't mind—really I don't, he assured himself over and over, back on his cot in the kitchen every night.

Only with respect to loving did he feel a lack, and that too, when she became aware of it, the Comrade took steps to remedy...

It was Mother Earth's first New Year's Eve ball (1907), and the Lyceum, big hall, was packed. There was Hippolyte gadding about as a Spanish conquistador, when all at once this young Dulcinea with shadowy blond hair and pale green eyes slipped through the crowd and put a hand on his shoulder as if she were an old friend.

Her name was Paula Holladay and she came from Evanston of all places, he learned as they danced.

She was a seamstress, but had no great liking for it, she made it clear, shyly but openly. "I'd be only too happy to work at something else, if only someone would show me how," Hippolyte heard additionally.

She also, quietly, had this burning desire to blow up the world...

A few months later, thanks largely to the Comrade's thoughtfulness and generosity, Hippolyte and his new girl had themselves a dandy flat in a charming old house, painted on the outside in their favorite color combination—purple and chartreuse—with a small restaurant in the basement to make a living from.

It was at Number 135 Macdougal Street, just south of Washington Square.

A SUNSHINY THURSDAY IN MAY, 1909

It's getting on toward three o'clock, a bit late for marketing, but there it is, that's how things are; anyway it's done.

Straining under the load of two bulging straw baskets, Hippolyte comes tearing round the corner of West 4th and Macdougal, throws a glance at the Square, which is gloriously in full leaf with the green still new and fresh, and scoots along as quickly as his legs, in black waiter's pants, will carry him.

Reaching the house, he notes that the shutters upstairs are thrown back, and thinks, Ah, she's up and about, my liebling, my Paula. Then in through the wrought iron gate he passes, and descends the crumbly stone stairs.

Jiggle, kick behind him, slamble—he's in the vestibule. Nudge with knee, kick behind him again—he's through that door too and on the inside, which is all in darkness, the white plastered walls blending in with the table cloths.

Straight down to the back, Hippolyte thumps, and the swinging door there, which leads to the kitchen. "Whew!"—he dumps everything onto the butcher's block within, and stands still for a moment to recover from a stitch in his side.

His eyes roam to the porthole over the stove, and with nothing in particular in mind, he takes a look out...at the four small tables ranged along the walls on either hand, and the two long ones flanking the center aisle...at Liebling's counter way up front...at the two windows over it with their view of people's legs between the black metal fence posts when they pass by above on the sidewalk.

The menu is on a child's blackboard, affixed to the left wall:

Corned beef hash	*15 cents*
Roast duck	*25 cents*
Koenigsberger Kloepse	*20 cents*
Paprika Schnitzel	*20 cents*

All orders with fried potatoes or spaetzle & veges du jour
Salad 5 cents extra

Hippolyte darts out, erases the Kloepse with two smears of his fist, and chalks in, Hungarian Goulash.

"Now gotta make it!" he announces back inside, and scooping some onions out of one of the baskets, good hard ones like small cannon balls, he chooses a small knife from a wooden wall rack and begins peeling. *Sniff!*—his eyes smart behind the glasses.

Soon with the nastier job of chopping over, he lifts a large sautéing pan down to the stove from a hook, turns the spigot for the gas, and strikes a match—POOM!

The oil swims hot; he goes and gets the onions.

"Now for the *flaysh!*"—with them dumped in and the pan given a shake. Unearthing a small slab of red beef and part of a pork shoulder from among the other purchases, he trims and cuts. Then setting aside the pork and bone, he hurries to the pan with the beef chunks, drops them in, and vigorously salts and peppers, douses with paprika, and sprinkles with caraway seeds.

"Next case!" Hippolyte calls out, after stirring with a wooden spoon, covering with the lid, and lowering the flame. He steps across to the icebox, finds a bottle of Pilsner inside, pries off the cap with the knife, and takes a swig—*Yoik!*—burps. Then standing it precariously on the edge of the block, he gets busy turning peppers and tomatoes into bright green and red slivers.

Liebling has come into the restaurant he senses, and looks to the porthole—yes, in a cool green silk kimono, which matches her eyes and sets off the gold strands in her hair. She's collecting soiled linen, and swatting crumbs off chairs with a napkin.

Transferring the bottle to beside the stove, Hippolyte puts the pork bone in and the pork chunks after it, then gives more stirs to the meat-and-onion mixture, now grown tangy, while watching her again.

Liebling notices, and he smiles. But she doesn't smile back, her way. One table, two tables more, and she brings in her bundle to be laundered.

"Dearest," Hippolyte greets her, and taking the wash, sets it on a stool. "Good morning." His lips touch hers and touch again. By force of habit, his tongue wriggles in—to find her own, its mate, just within, as if waiting. So. His mind casts back: when was the last time we did it, yesterday, the day before? He can't recall exactly—and what difference does it make really.

"Come," he says, and slipping an arm around her waist, her silky waist, leads her to the stove.

Steam blinds him for a moment when he raises the lid. Then he sees that the onions are soggy and meat is getting there—in a few minutes, after the remaining ingredients are added, they can go away and leave it.

Hippolyte positions her in front of him, so his chin peeks over her right shoulder, and takes up the spoon. He nuzzles the side of her neck and sucks on the skin there, soft and sweet, while stirring.

"Oh," Liebling moans—her head shoots up, shoulder jerks down, she writhes.

"Beloved," Hippolyte murmurs, and parking the spoon, clunked free of stuff, on the edge of the pan, grasps both of her breasts. They are rather small and tend to sag a little in spite of how young she is—but there's a grey mole, like a pearl, on the left one that he'd give anything to tell the world about!

"Oh," Liebling moans again as he caresses, "Oh-h-h."

Time to pour in the beer! But no, she won't let him...has his hand firmly in hers and is dragging it down...down.

"Yes-s-s," she hisses as one of his fingers finds the fleshy piece inside the hair there, like a fat baby's tongue.

Hippolyte is as ready for her, his hardness pressing through his pants against her ass. I'll just tip the Pilsner in, then make a grab for the peppers and tomatoes, he schemes.

"No!" she warns, and clutches!

Foolish, foolish when there's a perfectly decent bed upstairs, he tells himself, but what can one do. His other hand springs from her breast to the stove to turn off the flame—springs back!

Her tonguelet down there has grown fatter, but is not finished yet. Not...quite...yet.

"Oh!" Liebling sighs, and pitches forward.

He keeps her from falling—and now as there's nothing for it, he mashes and mashes against her back!

"Paula!"—her name breaks from him like a sob. "I'm—your—DOG!"

Night has just about fallen; the legs and skirts that pass by the window above are dark against dark, and in the restaurant, candles flicker in their metal holders on a number of the tables.

Out back Hippolyte, now sporting a black bow tie and cummerbund, pulls open the oven door and slides out a pan with three golden-brown duck breasts sizzling in it. "Done, surely"—he stabs one with a long fork. "Ya."

In a trice, the breasts are loaded onto plates, with spaetzle added to one, crusty homefries to the other two, plus a hefty dollop of carrots to each and the crowning touch, a ruby-red crab apple.

"Ahoy!" Hippolyte calls out, speeding toward the door with hands burdened. Charging through, he makes for the table down front, around which sits a trio of young men in shirtsleeves.

A swell girl, Hippolyte thinks, noting Liebling, in pale yellow, behind her counter. She's deep into his essay on the French Revolution in this month's issue of *Mother Earth*, or there'd be a smile for him now, he feels certain.

"Who gets the spaetzle?" he bawls to the threesome. Newcomers here, they're law students at NYU, he's gathered, and from their looks and expensive clothes, sons of wealthy German-Jewish merchants.

"Here," answers one, who has thinning hair and two moles on his right cheek. "I don't care what you say," he continues to the other two. "Aristocrats can never be one hundred per cent for the people"—evidently referring to Byron, about whom they were speaking before.

"That's not so, they can too," counters the one opposite him, who has woolly blond hair, and is the recipient of a duck with homefries. "Look at Tolstoy, look at Kropotkin."

Now if you were to ask *my* opinion, Hippolyte interjects to himself—

"That's different, they're Russians," the one with the moles rejoins.

"I don't see what difference that makes," the woolly blond shoots back.

Well, I wouldn't say that exactly either, Hippolyte argues inwardly, and deposits the last duck before the third, who has black eyes staring from an alabaster face framed by black hair, and seems to be slightly younger than the others.

A vein, like a streak of lightning, bulges on this third one's temple. He can hardly get the words out, he's so wrought up—"Byron was a—a PROFLIGATE!'"

"A profligate?" Blondy cries. "What's that got to do with it?" Two Moles joins in.

"Puppies, they're nothing but a bunch of bourgeois puppies," Hippolyte mutters, turning away...

At the table in the rear sits tender-featured Ida Rauh, another seeker after refuge from uptown German-Jewish stultification, as her protesting dress of sackcloth grey and solitary quarters on the corner, at Number 39½ Washington Square, bear witness. With her is a disgustingly clean-cut WASP named Max Eastman, who teaches something or other at Columbia University, and picks up a bit of cash on the side (quite a bit, it would seem) from lecturing on Women's Suffrage.

Earlier, this Eastman was doing all the talking—about the elusive nature of HER rights—and Miss Rauh was listening in a wistful sort of way with her chin propped in a hand. Now as Hippolyte is about to breeze by, the guy is still at it, on the subject of poetry, with their pickled herring and chopped liver yet to be touched: "It's the property of alert and beating hearts...unconditionally on the side of variety in life...the offspring of a love that has many eyes."

That's the anemic Yankee's way of making love, Hippolyte comments internally—CUMS through his mouth...

A familiar finger is beckoning from one of the large tables along the aisle; it's the Comrade, Emma. Finished with their goulash (the doggy goulash of love!), she and her party are ready for dessert, it seems.

"For me de epple shtrudel," she says, when Hippolyte is beside her. "You'll haf to see about de udders."

His gaze shifts to Ben the Bastard with his snaky eyes and fine moustache guarding cleft in chin—also strudel...then to Sasha with his full lips, in new wire-rimmed specs—as well...and on to Sasha's latest, round-of-face Becky Edelson, all of seventeen, in maroon and brown with strings of glass beads for earrings—the same...and finally to two young couples, friends of hers visiting from out of town—likewise.

The Comrade turns an inquiring look his way—"Do you haf enough?"

Yes, just, Hippolyte figures, and nods.

"Coffee for everyvun, is dot right?"...

"Ho hum, all in a day's work," Hippolyte croons, back in the kitchen, and brings out the tray with the strudel roll, afloat in chicken fat (a secret ingredient), from a drawer in the oven.

He's about to wield the spatula when something prompts him to look out.

Fancy that, the anarchist crowd is playing a game now, a kissing game—with Ben's fine moustache covering the Comrade's pouty mouth...she, Sasha's blubbery lips with hers... Sasha, Becky's...and on around.

"Mm-m-m!" Hippolyte yearns from the porthole, and puckers up to her, his old love...then in his mind, licks the girls' noses.

SO LONG! ADIOS, MUCHACHOS! DON'T FORGET YER BRIEFBAGS!

The barristers-to-be went off, with sweat on brows and cigars in cheeks, destined for the arms of a very accomplished Lola in Madame Someone's house in the Tenderloin.

Four Lives

TA TA! FAREWELL! COME BACK SOON, YA HEAR!

The Comrade and company were next to go, in search of Tom Paine's old digs if they could find it, to show Becky's out-of-town friends.

The restaurant is all in shadows now, with a single candle flickering, and wouldn't you know it, that Eastman is still jawing away—about Margaret Sanger and the blessings of birth control!

With all of his chores done, Hippolyte marks time at the porthole, one of the market baskets, to accompany him out for a breath of air, standing ready on the stovetop.

Oh well, no great matter if I slip away now, he says to himself at length, when there's no sign of a let-up over there. Even so, he leaves the kitchen with head bowed and stealthy tread "like a guilty thing surprised."

Up front in the half-light, Liebling waits, sleepy-eyed.

"Do you mind?" Hippolyte says to her. "I'll only be a while"—then inclines his head toward Eastman and poor sweet Miss Rauh, still applying her ear—"I'll take care of it later, okay?"—meaning the dessert dishes and coffee cups.

Liebling nods, perhaps understanding this desire for space and breath, recently felt by him, but certainly accepting of it, which is the important thing.

I need it, I simply need it now and then, or I don't know what I'd do, Hippolyte tells himself...

Outside on the sidewalk, he inhales deeply of the cool night air and gives a semi-stretch—"Ah, *luft*, LUFT!"—then with the basket slung, heads for the Square and the benches amidst the foliage.

It being a weeknight, no one is about that he can see—only a hooker swinging her purse, and a cop with his billy keeping an eye on her.

Reaching the trees, Hippolyte picks up a path leading to the Arch and the chic red-brick houses with their white doorways on the other side, near which it has been his special pleasure to plant himself of late.

97

Nimbuses of pale violet from the street globes overhead illuminate his way.

Only two of the houses on the row show signs of life, the street level of Number 11, just short of Fifth, where a single bluish light burns, and the parlor floor of Number 8, in the center of the block, which is whitely ablaze. A party must be going on there, Hippolyte decides—both sides of the street are lined with carriages and automobiles.

It so happens that he knows a good deal about the high-and-mighty residents of this quarter, being a frequenter of the same greengrocers and butchers as their servants. For instance, in Number 11 there's an old geezer with bug eyes and a walrus moustache named Tailer, whose forebears were bigshots under the British in Colonial times.

A painful memory comes to stab at Hippolyte's inner being like a sword. On the last walk this way several days ago, he had a run-in with that man, which had it not been for the difference in their ages, might have ended very badly.

Briefly Hippolyte reviews it in his mind, as if trying to justify:

Noting the light on night after night, he finally had to go and see what was what there, and quietly entering in at the gate, tiptoed to the window. Of all things, the guy, swathed in a padded dressing gown, was seated at a table clipping articles out of the Herald and pasting them into a scrapbook. Wondering what anyone could find so interesting in that conservative rag, he got up real close to the glass—and lo, the clippings turned out to be all about fires and mine disasters and famous people who had met infamous deaths, some of them his pals probably...

*But wouldn't you know it, my luck, all of a sudden the codger looks up and notices me with my nose pressed there, and, holy shit, makes a beeline for the door. Boy, did I beat it fast! I can still see him shaking his fist behind me and yelling with his old chest heaving, "*I'LL HAVE THE LAW AFTER YOU!*"...*

Well, we'll just have to give that Tailer a wide berth, won't he, Hippolyte advises himself, now by the fountain, and takes his way further along in the direction of Number 8 and the party.

"Rest!" he decrees, at a bench where he can have a look without being observed.

The windows have been thrown open over there, and one can hear the hum of many voices. Now and then he glimpses men and women in evening dress holding long-stemmed glasses.

This house belongs to a filthy-rich Englishman named Guinness, who is married to the daughter of a real milord and accustomed to rubbing elbows with the like from abroad. But crazily, the man and his missus also pretend to be what they call "advanced thinkers." For instance, last New Year's Eve, they had Delmonico's or Sherry's cater an expensive bash for their help, which was kicked off by the two of them waltzing around with the housekeeper and butler.

Hippolyte smiles ruefully—doesn't make up for the miserable way they treat the slaveys the rest of the year.

The talking across the way dies down, and a sonorous grand piano strikes up, the spieler doubtless some virtuoso who has been engaged especially for the occasion. The piece is full of high trills, by Liszt very likely.

"What do those society fucks know about music," Hippolyte sneers. They just listen, that's all.

Mindful of the basket beside him, he peers around to see if the copper with his stick is lurking somewhere.

No, that keeper of the peace (such as he is) is nowhere in sight, and in fact, all he's aware of are the low voices of some of the drivers passing the time of day in their vehicles parked by the curb just ahead, along with the occasional clop or snuff of a horse.

Wary all the same, Hippolyte gingerly reaches in and brings out a pint of corn, unscrews it, and quickly tilts his head back—"Argh!"

The rippling on the keyboard peters out. There's a burst of applause and some shouts of "Bravo!"

Hippolyte takes another swig...and another.

Gabrilowitsch or whoever the master tinkler is begins on a new Liszt, all rumbles this time.

Okay, let's go, is Hippolyte's thought, and stowing the bottle away, he hoists himself up.

But first it's necessary to uncork a little. His feet propel him to a nearby tree.

The main door over there opens wide—the musical forest murmurings thunder. A liveried servant steps out, and barks: "Viscount Ranleigh's car!"

"That's me! Nice chewin' the cud with yuh, bud," a youthful voice speaks up, not ten feet from Hippolyte on the other side of some bushes.

"Viscount, huh," Hippolyte mutters, and strains to have a look...with his fly open, preparing to trickle.

A tuxedoed man and a woman in a splendid white gown, both in their thirties and handsome in a dark-haired sort of way, have just stepped past the majordomo, and are descending the stoop.

In front of Number 9 next door, the headlights of a shiny black touring car come on, in preparation for the visored chauffeur's starting it up and meeting them at the foot.

"That's all right, Edgar, we can manage," the master calls, with an English accent.

"Can—you—now?" Hippolyte mutters again, and has a sudden fiendish idea.

Climbing over the railing, he begins making for them, trickler in hand.

The couple have just settled in the back seat.

"Piss-s-s," Hippolyte hisses, "piss-s-s"—and wafts a jet at them.

"Ee-ee!" the woman screams. "What the—!" sputters the Viscount. *Eh-eh-eh*, goes the starter.

"Piss-s-s," Hippolyte hisses, still bearing down.

"Ee-ee-ee!" the woman screams again. "For God's sake, Edgar!" the Viscount cries out. "I—I'm trying, sir," the young chauffeur squeaks.

B<small>AROOM</small>! the car booms, and catapults forward.

"H<small>EEHAW</small>! <small>HEEHAW</small>!" Hippolyte hoots after them...ran out of juice anyway.

THE ſTRIKE

CHAPTER 5

The Machine, there's nothing like it. Sit down before one just once, and you feel like the single most powerful person in the world. Go on stitching away until you're in the swing, and you end up becoming one with that mechanism and turning into a new only half-human creature…which is better by far than being made Divine.

To wind the wheel and make the needle rise, to slide the fabric under and then to give a tap to the pedal, with your hands guiding…it's like a dance. And presto, no sooner is that piece done than you're reaching for another…to begin on a new step.

It's all in the touch, your light toe-touch, and in your unfettered mind directing it.

Started on straight seams, as rightly she should have been, Martha fell in with her crew's routine in short order, so it wasn't long before she was craving something more exciting to do, like collars, sleeves, or cuffs, which required a lot of stitching around. However, while acknowledging her rapid progress, old Benny, the crew leader, was not about to hear of any changes so fast; in fact, it took quite a while before he would even consent to her working by the piece, as he'd originally promised, so she could earn more money at least.

From time to time, while fretting over this, Martha wondered whether there might not be some other reason...like Mammeh, for instance, who—with Papa egging her on, naturally—had perhaps communicated with the old one through her notions man, his friend, and persuaded him to make things difficult for her eldest-born so that she would grow discouraged and quit. But I just can't believe that of my mama, Martha quickly countered each time, picturing her mother's clear-shining face—and she was right, of course. The real reason for the delay was revealed when Benny at long last gave in to her wishes. "Here in America, *se brent*, everyvun's in a hurry and vants instant ekshun," he said, after giving a final scrutiny to her work with glasses raised. Whereas in his native Warsaw, one had to go through a lengthy trial period first before being accepted into a trade.

Unlike the job, the place needed a bit of getting used to, as all of them there on Triangle's ninth floor—some two hundred, Martha guessed—were really packed in at those long tables, which seemed to occupy every inch of space except for the front and side aisles. And yet to come was the summer, when in addition to the roaring of the motors and needles pounding over the sneezing and coughing, everyone would be sweating to beat the band—and very likely insisting, even on the very hot days that the windows be kept shut tight as a precaution against catching one's death from a draft.

Closeness was a minor matter, however, compared to the danger of fire from some of the motors throwing off sparks. And on Eight, Martha heard, there were not only more misfiring motors like that but also some cutters who refused to take the regulations seriously and smoked on the sly.

Of course, the building was fireproof, Benny among others was quick to point out, and for minor mishaps, a row of water pails hanging in the vestibule on each floor could be called into service, along with hoses from standpipes on the stairs—as indeed Martha saw happen on several occasions when a pile of cloth began to smolder from sparks embedded in it. But what if the oil in one of the drip cups under the machines somehow caught fire, and it spread to others, attacking tables and chairs and all the cloth lying about, and could not be brought under control by those means, leaders like Jake Kline and Morris Elzufin wondered. Most important of all, would everyone there on Nine be able to get out in time? Those in the rear like themselves had a choice of a single fire escape outside one of the windows on the side aisle, or that narrow opening in the back partition, through which only one person could fit at a time so that old Nat in his overalls could "look'em over" carefully. And for the people working down front, the situation could turn out to be even more treacherous, as the two elevators on that end were small, and the door to the stairs was usually kept locked, with the key sometimes left dangling from the knob by a string but sometimes not, to confuse anyone of a mind to beat it out that way with merchandise.

No question about it, the possibility of a fire flaring up was a real one and something for Martha to be concerned about, which she was. But truth to tell, it was as nothing when it came to her annoyance with Triangle over the many rules you had to follow. For instance, in the morning it was necessary to be in your seat ready to zoom away at eight sharp, when the bell screeched out, and you could take lunch only between twelve and twelve-thirty, at which time you were expected to work straight through to six, or later if there was a rush order. Yes, it was just like being back in public school, except that instead of your receiving a severe bawling-out or being made to stand in a corner, sallow-faced Anna Gullo the forelady or Bernstein, if he happened to be prowling around, shouted out to pretty Mary Leventhal the checker to record a fine against your leader's name. And then as if that weren't bad enough, at the end of the week you saw that amount duly deducted from your share of the crew's take, along with the usual percentage of management's charges for needles, thread, and the like, and The Triangle Benefit Society that it had created.

To what extent the folks at home were aware of all this, Martha had no way of knowing. But one thing was for certain: she didn't dare breathe a word about any of it to them, for fear that the trouble with Papa would start all over again, possibly with Mammeh joining in now. On the other hand, once she had seen what was what at Triangle, Martha did feel a need to talk things over with someone, and who was there really but friend Essie. So she dropped ole freckle-face a note proposing that they meet for ice cream sodas after work one evening.

The only thing is, after everything was poured out, Essie's reaction was much the same as when Martha first mentioned the job, as might have been expected. "Oh Marth," she cried with real alarm in her eyes, "I'd give that place the bum's rush if I were you! Right now!"

What was there to do then but try to set this well-meaning friend's mind at ease. "Well, yes, I plan to do just that," Martha responded. "But not at once"—for to hear people talk, conditions at many other factories left something to be desired too, so she would have to keep her eyes peeled and make some discreet inquiries first.

Later, after she parted from Essie, it was another story, for Martha realized all at once that things at Triangle were not *all that bad*. First and foremost, she was making good money there, even in spite of management's dipping a hand in: nine dollars and change almost every week. And then, foul-smelling as old Benny was most of the time from wearing the same unionsuit top over and over, she had grown rather fond of him—as indeed he had of her in spite of his objections to her youth and inexperience, she now saw. Why, as proof of this, just the other day when she pushed her chair back to let a boy crawl in under her machine to replace the belt, which had snapped, the old one had risked a fine for unnecessary talking by muttering under his breath—"Up, up, ged up!"—to help preserve her back, the first part of a machine operator's body to go.

True, Benny was a left shoe by comparison with other crew leaders, and as Martha had gradually come to realize, none of the others had any use for him, especially the loud mouths behind them, who could be very cruel and cutting. For instance, on their happening to get into the elevator with Jake Kline one evening not long ago, the guy—who was hardly more than a kid, wore round wire-rimmed glasses, and had a nose like a pointing finger—began taunting him, "So, Benny, *vos makhst du*, Benny—what's doing?" whereupon one of his girls jeeringly singsonged, "Ben-ny-ny? Benny Ben-dovah-ah?" while another rapped out, "Ben-ny, bend ov-er and kiss my ass!" But that only endeared the old one to Martha the more.

Benny's crew were of a piece with him, flotsam and jetsam that no one else seemed to want. But Martha didn't mind, accepting them as part of him, just as they in their oddity viewed her apparently.

Closest to her in age were the twins Yetta and Greta, both with glittering eyes and thin, pale faces like dull silver coins, who were also on seams and sat next to her on the left. Benny, on her other side, shook his head and tsuh-tsuh'd concerning them over lunch one day: their papa had recently died of consumption, and now the mama and two little ones were home in bed with the same sickness.

Across the table, opposite the space between Martha and him, was big Olga the collar setter, who had an olive complexion and lips the color of calves liver. At odds with Benny over some matter in the past, Olga rarely spoke to him, and in fact as soon as the lunch-bell sounded, shifted her chair around to the table in front of them to eat with some woman friends of hers there.

The bone of contention between her and Benny was Raiseleh the Rumanian, who sat to Olga's right. Somewhere in her thirties, Raiseleh was very fair of face with dimples in each cheek, and had a wild look in her eye. Every day at lunch, as soon as Olga turned away, she would point her own chair rightward to face the windows overlooking Washington Place where, once her herring-on-pumpernickel was consumed, she would occupy herself with some crocheting, which she was forever undoing to a string of muttered curses. Her problem, people whispered, was that she had gypsy blood in her veins, and everyone kept their distance from her lest something of theirs be found missing or she curse them with *a nehore*—an evil eye. But it so happened that Raiseleh was a first-rate specialty sewer, capable of joining together the flimsiest pieces of cloth with remarkable speed and deftness. So to Benny, all the talk and her *meshugas*—particular forms of craziness—were beside the point. "Just so lonk as she does huh voik and minds huh own business," he explained to Martha...

Lunch, that precious half hour, was clearly the high point of the day for everyone, and so it became for her too, when she would relax with her sandwich of gefilte fish or whatever else Mammeh had on hand and a jar of hot tea with lemon, brought in from the outside by Lem the porter. Benny almost always had the same thing too—salami on thick chunks of rye oozing with mustard, and a hefty sour pickle running with juice—which he munched on in silence for the most part, leaving her free to look around.

At first with eyes roaming, her ears would pick up snatches of conversation here and there, in Yiddish mostly... about a dance a bunch of girls were planning to attend at some hall...a boy someone was nuts about...things like that. But eventually her attention would come to rest on the front table, close by Mary Levenson's desk, where sat a small select group consisting of Bernstein's younger brother Jake, their cousin Morris, and Edie Harris, niece to Isaac Harris, one of the owners.

Rumor had it that Jake, who had a longer, thinner head than big brother's, was stuck on Mary with her blue eyes and blond hair. It was also said that Morris, who was all of nineteen and very sweet in a rosy-lipped way (as well as related by marriage to Mr. Blanck, the other owner, like Jake and Bernstein), had eyes for Edie, who was going on seventeen like Martha and the spittin' image of her Uncle Ike down to the pear-shaped face and reddish-brown hair. And who would not have been fascinated.

The Strike

In time, Martha found herself inventing little stories about one couple or the other—for instance, *How all in tan topped by a snappy straw hat, Jake sallied forth on a rare day in Spring to squire Mary, holding a bouquet of bright yellow nosegays to the bosom of her pale green dress. How after reaching The Central Park and going in a bit, they strayed off the path—but not too far off—in search of a cool, secluded spot. How once they were seated on a bench there, his eyes ardently sought her dainty blues, and his strong hard hand took her delicate yellow-sheathed one and pressed...*

Occasionally solemn-faced Anna Gullo the forelady would join them on a chair dragged in from the cloakroom. And once in a while Bernstein himself would show up with a store-bought sandwich, and then standing with an elbow planted on the desk's ledge, he would cheerily hold forth with sinuous mouth going, until they all burst out laughing.

Imagine, Martha couldn't help marveling the first time, Bernstein the *paskudnyak*—the scoundrel—telling a funny story.

DAY'S END
A SATURDAY IN THE LAST WEEK OF JUNE, 1909

Just parted from Benny, on his way home to Brooklyn via the subway on Astor Place, Martha is standing and waiting on the corner of Broadway and Washington. Her outfit, a waist and skirt combination of pale rose after Lord & Taylor beauties, hangs heavy from the heat, like lids on eyes.

It'll be along any minute now, she tries to reassure herself, of the Broadway trolley to take her downtown. Moist in the armpits, she looks northward past Wanamaker's many arched windows to the grey spires of Grace Church, beyond which there's a bend.

"At last," she sighs. A trolley has come round. Now if only— Yes, the windows are all open, there'll be a breeze.

Stepping up and in as soon as the car grates to a halt, Martha finds it almost empty, and takes a vacant double on the left. Dry goods stores begin flowing by—one-after-the-other-after-the-other—all gated up for *shabes*. Ah, air, cool air.

The conductor is there to collect. She asks for a transfer as usual. Under her arms and in other places, it's almost dry.

Now if only— She takes herself to task with Mammeh's voice—what now, there's always something.

If only there were someone to talk to at the shop, her inner being answers right back—meaning some girl to share thoughts and feelings with, as she and Essie used to do when they were schoolmates.

Not that I haven't looked, I have—whenever an opportunity has presented itself, like in the washroom during the break and waiting for the crowd to get through the partition at closing. However, time after time the girl she singled out either acted very snotty because Martha was new to the business, or else smiled shyly as if to say, What's an American like you want with a greenhorn like me.

Oh well, there's still Essie, Martha consoles herself. In fact, after supper tonight the two of them are going out for a good time together: to the Junior Basketball game at the College Settlement gym, which is to be followed as usual with a Junior Hop.

Not without some amusement, Martha pictures it all: *players racing across the waxy wooden floor with the ball bouncing, back and forth, back and forth. Then finally with the peep of a whistle, it's over, and both teams retire to the locker room to wash up and change. In the meanwhile, the old upright has to be wheeled out, which nice Mr. Kent does in a trice with a few of the younger boys. Now Mrs. Tucker from one of the mother's groups appears, twisting her hands with a slightly agitated look. But then setting herself down on the piano stool, she beholds the keyboard as if about to partake of a sumptuous meal. On one side of the room are the girls, dressed to kill naturally, whispering in little groups. The boys, also in their best, face them from the other side, egging one another on, with nudges. How will it all end? With Mrs. Tucker* STRIKING UP. *Somehow partners find each other.*

The Strike

At the last Junior Hop, Martha's first, a boy with a moon face and sleek yellow-streaked hair came up to ask her to dance right off, and the next thing one knew, she was doing the one-step with him, and then a waltz.

His name was Davey Goldstein, he told her, with a large, wet mouth that seemed a little too eager to kiss. After school (at Stuyvesant), he worked for his father who had a fur salon on Grand Street.

When the waltz was over, he excused himself, and danced a few numbers with someone else. But then he returned to do the Going to Boston with her, which they both thought great fun, strutting down the aisle between the clapping boys and girls.

After that, Essie signaled—alas, from the sidelines, where she'd been most of the evening—that it was time to leave. Whereupon Davey wanted to know if he could walk Martha home.

No, absolutely out of the question, was her reaction. Why she'd just met him, what would he think of her?

Well then, maybe they'd run into one another at the next Hop, he said, not at all discouraged...

Maybe so, Martha thinks, with the trolley now bearing down on Houston, her stop.

Rising to her feet, she heads for the rear, and steps down the moment the car is stationary.

About to go, with transfer in hand, for the one going eastward on Houston, she pauses for a moment, as is her wont sometimes, to gaze down the rest of Broadway.

Amidst the welter of tall buildings, The Singer towers over all, its tippy top like a giant thumb with a pin stuck in it—which reminds her...

The Machine. For months, ever since that first day of trial with Benny, she's hardly been able to sleep at night thinking about it: her toe pressing down...arms moving forward as if to embrace...whole being following through.

And now? Now the hunger is still there, but as before after her first weeks, she longs for there to be something more to it...for it to be a little more complex...

Should I then keep an eye peeled for that Davey tonight, and try and get next to him, Martha considers.

The elder of two sons, with no burning ambition to become a doctor or a lawyer, after graduation he'll probably stay on with his father in the fur establishment, which sooner or later they'll move uptown.

"Oh do it, Marth!" one can just hear Essie, who's had no luck in love at all so far herself. "You'll be rich!"

In Martha's mind, Davey's lips approach hers for a kiss...and she wrinkles her nose...they shine with his spit. Not only that, on your wedding night you'll have to do everything else with him, she reminds herself...and imagines his hand, with a furrier's finicky fingers, lifting the hem of her nightgown.

No, she decides, crossed over and waiting, once again sadly in the heat, it's not for me. What is, remains to be seen, but not that, not with him anyway.

✻

From day to day, week to week, and finally, alas, month to month Mammeh had been hoping against hope that Martha would get sick and tired of Triangle and quit, as any sensible person would have. For according to Mr. Shapiro in the candy store and some other people in the neighborhood, the place was *paskudtsve*, not fit for pigs, let alone human beings, especially such a charming young lady.

So what's going to be, Mammeh wondered, early one morning, on realizing that the summer was half over and there was still no change in sight. Only one thing occurred, and that was to get hold of Benowitz, the girl's crew leader, and sound him out to see if he could be counted on to help and possibly to use his influence with her.

Eli, on waking, pronounced it a capital idea when he heard, as well he might, having been hounding her, poor Bertha, day and night to do something about it from the moment they knew Martha had been hired. "Tell her to invite him for dinner Sunday," Eli said. "His missus too," he added.

And what should I say if the girl wants to know why? Mammeh wondered, moving about in the kitchen.

As if reading her mind, husband, on the way to the bathroom, had the perfect answer: "Say that we want to meet him, that's all"—the logic being that while this was a free country, parents had a right to know whom their children were working for...

Sunday found them in the midst of a terrible heat wave. *Oy, it's hot*, Mammeh moaned to herself, as she gave a final not-too-energetic wipe to the sink with the dishrag.

Even so, the food was ready, table set, Eli, wearing the pants of his salt-and-pepper summer suit with a shirt and tie, was already sitting there, Martha too, and Dinah, Pauline, and Fanny, eight, seven, and four, had been packed off to the parlor with lollipops and strict orders about behaving themselves.

"So where is he?" Mammeh began complaining, when the clock struck three, the appointed time, and the man had not shown up yet. While putting the finishing touches to everything that morning, she had begun entertaining the suspicion that nothing would come of this scheme, no matter how much she and husband might want it to.

"Hello, here I am!" a husky voice called out from the hall.

The door flew open It was indeed he, the man Benowitz, and he was by himself.

"Something for you," he said, handing Mammeh a cloudy jar of sour tomatoes from the wife, who sent her apologies. She took in pieces at home, he explained, and today at the last minute, just as they were about to leave, this order had come that needed to be filled at once.

In any event, it was just as well, Mr. Benowitz went on. "She suffers from vater in de legs and vould never hef been aple to make it up all de stairses."

A fine how-do-you-do, Mammeh thought, already not in love with the ugly yellowish curlicues hanging out of his nostrils.

At Eli's bidding, Mr. Benowitz removed his jacket, of cheap grey muslin, and there was a burn mark from an iron on the back of his shirt, another strike against him.

"Come sit down," Eli said, and motioned to the place, across from Martha.

The old one did so, mopping his brow and neck with a grey rag of a handkerchief.

Mammeh brought *shav* borscht with slices of hard-boiled egg in it, pleasantly cool from the ice, and served it out. The four of them ate in silence, except for the zupping of the old one, which was rather to be expected.

What's next, the watery bloodshot eyes inquired when his spoon was down.

Cold chicken with a tangle of greens, at which he smacked his lips, followed by stewed *floymen*—plums—for dessert, which brought forth an "Mmm" from him.

"So what's new?" Eli casually asked in Yiddish, after they'd shvitzed some from glasses of hot tea with lemon, a sign that the meal had come to an end.

"Nothing much," Mr. Benowitz as casually returned, with a Polish twang. "There's a little strike over at Rosen's? Do you know the place?"

Eli frowned—"Who knows from factories?" He was a shopkeeper. As for trouble of that kind, he'd never had much use for it.

"They're after higher piece rates," Mr. Benowitz continued, disregarding the edge in Eli's voice. "Crazy—*mishuge*—they'll whistle for it."

There was nothing more to be said on that score by any of them.

What now, Mammeh wondered, after listening to the faucet go *drip-drip-drip* behind her for some moments.

The Strike

Martha, who had sat through everything so far with eyes down, shifted uncomfortably in her seat, apparently not too happy with the way things were going either.

Old Benowitz's mouth opened again—"As for the *meydele* here, their girl"—he assumed they wanted to know how she was progressing with him, and proceeded to tick off her various virtues: what a quick learner she was, how obedient and well-behaved besides—

"So what kind of a future do you see for her there at Triangle?" Mammeh put in.

The shaggy old brows shot up, the thick lenses with them. "Future? Who said anything about a future? To meet a nice boy and settle down with him and bear his children, that's a future." He focused on Martha—"Isn't dot right, *Tsatskele?*"—his cutesy.

Martha smiled weakly.

Mammeh, reading between the lines, perked up. Now there's a thought. Maybe the girl has her eye on someone in that awful place? Could that perhaps be why *Kreynele* has stayed on there for so long against all reason? Is it possible? But if it is, why hasn't she said something? True, she's often closed-mouthed about things, that's her way. On the other hand, if this is so, it's a very serious matter.

"Would you care for some more hot water?" Mammeh asked the old one, to set things in motion. He'd served his purpose, and there was no further need of him, as far as she could see.

Thank you, no, he was very grateful, he assured her, and took the hint...

So where does that leave us, Mammeh worried the air after he was gone.

But obviously the matter could not be discussed in front of the child, and Eli, realizing this too, had already buried his nose in the paper.

"Can I help?" Martha softly asked, meaning with the clean-up. The old one had left behind a bit of a mess.

"No, denk you, I can menedge," Mammeh answered, preferring it that way, an old story.

Apple-of-her-eye went and got a book from her room.

"Vat's it about?" Mammeh wanted to know. The title on the spine was *Jane Eyre*.

Always happy to oblige, Martha summed up the story to the point where she'd left off reading. A poor girl is sent to an orphanage by a mean old aunt after committing some trifling offense. Later, when the same girl is all grown up, she lands what seems like a swell job with a certain Mr. Rochester of Thornfield Hall.

"Such a story," Mammeh commented, "to go lif in a house already *af tsoris*—gone to the dogs—with a moody down-at-the-mouth man she hardly knows. It vouldn't heppen to a Jewish goil, not so fest anyvay"—or would it? Mammeh shot a glance at this child of hers, who day by day seemed to be turning into more of a stranger.

The corners of Martha's kitten-mouth turned up; the deep-set dark eyes twinkled.

So much for that at least, Mammeh breathed, and began soaping the glasses.

Something made her look toward Eli, who seemed to be more absorbed than usual in his precious *Forverts*, his eyes, those dancing eyes of old, intent behind his glasses.

What can be so interesting? Mammeh ambled over, noticing as if for the first time that husband's hair was almost all grey.

The piece was one of the *bintl briv*, letters to the editor Abraham Cahan, the writer a woman whose husband was suffering from an incurable illness and wanted to return home to Poltava to die. Their children, who were born here and not quite grown up, had put their filial feet down and were absolutely refusing to go. What should she do?

What indeed? And what does he give as an answer, Cahan, a notorious socialist? Mammeh's eyes skimmed down.

The Strike

No answer really, just that they should all talk it over, and in the process, as the correspondent, would see, one side would give in a little, then the other, then the first again, and so on, until a compromise acceptable to everyone was reached.

Mammeh's heart went out to the woman. She understood, or felt she did, deep down without words, as if she'd intimately known the poor creature caught between husband's wishes and children's need from having seen her every day of their lives.

Only let something like that never happen to me and mine, Mammeh silently prayed.

SEVERAL HOURS LATER

The sky is blue-black, like ink of that color, and has blurry white points that seem to pulsate.

Mammeh is lying on her back with Eli beside her snoring lightly.

Nearby on their mattress, Dinah with her bright blue eyes and curly reddish hair and Pauline the blonde with pea-green eyes sit chattering about the fun they're going to have at summer school tomorrow. Free coloring books are going to be given away!

Martha's voice rises now and then a little further off as she fills a small sleepy-head's ears with a bedtime story. It's all about a poor Jewish damsel who is falsely accused of stealing a ring by a wicked tante, but is saved from being sent to prison at the last minute by the appearance of a handsome stranger.

From a greater distance comes the *tick-tick-tick* of a baby rattle, and a man's voice whining, "C'mon-n-n, just relax-aax, have someting tuh drink-ink." *Shpritz-z-z* fizzes a seltzer bottle...*glug-glug-glug* goes the Welch's grape juice being added.

There's a trace of tar in the air from the sun's harsh beating down all day.

Eli rolls over and throws an arm out, so it lands across Mammeh's midriff.

Oy, for all the world to see. "Eli, please, vee're on de roof," she murmurs in warning.

"*A mise meshune*," he curses, calling down a bad death on everyone, and draws the arm away.

Mammeh can't help smiling: to think that he should desire her now almost like in the beginning. A flush, like warm milk, suffuses her chest: and that the feeling should be likewise on her part.

For safety's sake, so as not to tempt fate, she turns away from husband onto her side.

Old Benowitz comes to mind again, and briefly Mammeh goes over what he said: about *Kreynele*'s future being to marry someone nice and have children with him. The question is, when he looked at the girl after this and asked—"Isn't that right, *Tsatskele*?"—did he mean something by it, and if he did and she is truly interested in someone, again I repeat, how come her mama hasn't heard about it? The only explanation is, finally: there may be a reason I can know nothing of.

Alright, let's suppose, for the sake of argument, that there *is* someone, Mammeh continues. That doesn't mean he's at the factory necessarily, does it? For instance, there was some talk a while back between Martha and the friend Essie about a boy named Davey, whom they met at one of the settlement house dances. True, *Kreynele* was not too enthusiastic about that Davey, or so it seemed from Essie's constantly nagging at her, "Oh c'mon, Marth, keep an open mind." But it could indicate that she already had a liking for someone else she saw there.

Could and could not. Mammeh shifts around uneasily. Who knows what to think. The trouble is that the child has never looked at boys the way other girls do—that is, as far as one can tell.

Mammeh feels the urge to lie on her back again, and begins slowly turning so as not to disturb her man. But no such luck, her elbow digs into his ribs.

"*A vos vilst du fun mir*—what do you want from me?" he grumbles.

The Strike

"*Shah*, go beck to sleep," she directs.

Normal the girl certainly seems to be, with not a blemish on her body anywhere, small, firm breasts, pink nipples, and a nice growth of hair below. And periods she's been getting regularly, ever since the first. But beyond that—longings and so on—is anybody's guess...

It has become very quiet. The children are all cuddled up—Martha with Fanny, Dinah and Pauline—and everyone else is dead to the world too. The only sounds are Eli's zizzing and another man echoing it not far off.

Let's face it, Mammeh continues, the real reason you're worried is that not just any man will do for *Kreynele*. What she needs is someone special to value her talents, or at the very least to tolerate them without making her life miserable. Where would one even begin to look for such a rare individual? Growing on trees, they're not. And you know something, Bertha, the sad truth is that if I were the mother of such a boy, I'm not sure I myself would like to see him connected with a girl who is so different from everyone else.

So where does that leave my best *bobele*?...

You know, for once in your life I believe you could use some advice, it occurs to Mammeh after a while.

The only problem is, whom to seek out for it. Sister-in-law Dora Leah, as always, has her own worries at home, and worse yet, now her home is further away: the family moved to Brooklyn last January. People in the neighborhood? Yes, to look after the baby in a pinch, but they were hardly the ones to discuss such a weighty matter with. Besides, as everyone is fond of pointing out, laugh and the whole world laughs with you.

Desperately, Mammeh, in her mind, reaches out to Tante in Berdichev. But alas, Tante is no more, passed away last year, and Uncle six months after her.

Who else? Mammeh's eyes turn upward—to the dark sky with its wavering white points. But then she shrugs. It's good for making one feel better perhaps, to know that someone or something is there and it's not complete Emptiness—but that's all.

The silence suddenly seems more profound yet, as if everyone up there on the roof were not fast asleep but truly dead (God forbid). The snores, even Eli's, seem to mock her.

Mammeh begins to feel—yes, like the woman with the sick husband and rebellious children who wrote in to the *Forverts*...as if a similar current were dragging her out to the same wide, wide sea.

Shall I wake Eli? Mammeh thinks in a panic. No, let him be, poor man—and then the answer is there. What's sauce for the goose and so on: she too will write a letter to editor Cahan. Yes, I'll sit right down and do it first thing in the morning.

And if the man answers with the same advice, to talk things over? Mammeh questions. Well, that's how it will have to be. But somehow I don't think he will, no two situations being alike.

Now what shall I say? Mammeh's shoulders wriggle deliciously, and bottom follows through, as she becomes lost in thought...

Here's a beginning—

Dear Mr. Editor,
  The world is full of trouble, and I'm thankful that the worst of it has passed over me and my family, which I'm sure you'll agree I should be.
  It's clear from reading your paper, which my husband and I have been doing for many years, that you and your associates do not have much liking for people like us, who own a business, even a little business. Stinking Capitalists you call us, and look forward to the day when the Masses will rise up and put us all down. Okay, but just the same we too are human beings, and we too have the right to speak out.

It's a little on the long-winded side, Mammeh judges. But as with making a suit or a dress, better to have too much; one can always take it in later. Onward...

The Strike

Let me come to the point. My husband and I have four wonderful children. Three of them, the younger three, are just fine. However, the fourth, the eldest—

And then I'll tell him all about everything, sign Yours truly, and—But wait, there's something else I want to add...

P.S. Please be so kind as to keep this letter to yourself without printing it, as I'm not after publicity like some people I could point to. Also, I don't want anyone to recognize me, BECAUSE quite frankly I'm ashamed of complaining when there are so many people who have it worse than we do.

Yes, that's good, just right, Mammeh judges, relieved to the extent that one can be under the circumstances, and her mouth opens to yawn. But then it snaps shut again—and his answer?

Let's see, this is going to be a little more involved, for Abraham Cahan is not exactly a nobody, and on top of it, he's very smart, with enough brains for two ordinary people.

Hm, is it possible that he would take a personal interest in my *kreynele*? Maybe so, but don't go banking on it, someone as busy as him may simply not have the time...

Dear Mrs. Ferber,

In accordance with your wishes, I have kept your letter in strict confidence, though in all honesty, I don't see why you should feel ashamed. As you made clear, you are entitled to voice your particular griefs, and to receive a response just like everyone else—though as you also indicate, and I agree, another's troubles, like not knowing where the next meal is coming from, would be more crucial in terms of survival.

As for your being a despicable Capitalist, forget it, we never meant to include you in that category. In fact, we feel quite confident that when the Glorious Moment arrives, you, who are obviously not insensitive, will be in the forefront with us to take part in the general Tearing Down.

Good Sir, Mammeh interjects, I wouldn't pin my hopes on that if I were you. You'll have to let us know what you and your cronies are going to replace the whole thing with first. Bear in mind that, while not in Chains, we shopkeepers from the other side do have something to lose, something of importance to us, if not to you, that wasn't easily come by...

> Now as to your problem, Mrs. Ferber, there is a solution, but it's not of the best. Nevertheless, I urge you to accept it, for lack of another actually. Here it is:
> *NO SOLUTION.* In other words, wait and see what tomorrow brings.

Wait, again wait? Mammeh considers. Well, if one must...

I hope I've been able to offer you a little comfort and good cheer in your distress, Mrs. Ferber, and I remain, Sincerely yours, etc.

CHAPTER 6

Nothing was quite like early Sunday mornings, Jerrold quickly came to realize. No matter what the season, whether in rain, shine, or snow, then the Square was his to let his eye range round. It gave warmth...like one of those fur coverlets the wealthy folks in Tarrytown were supposed to bundle themselves up in when being chauffeured around the countryside.

This particular Sunday morning in mid-August was no exception. After washing down one of Arturo's melting jelly doughnuts with a mug of aromatic coffee, brewed in two tin cups fitted together according to Giuseppina's directions, there was Jerrold still in his pajamas, of pale mint green, lolling in one of the window seats. A bluish-grey kitten, a gift from that kindly couple, lay asleep in his lap.

"Dusty," Jerrold softly cooed, tickling behind one of the ears. "Dear Dusty."

The slits that were the creature's eyelids parted, to reveal eyes like amber harvest moons. *Pur-r-r*, it went.

Out in the Square, already heating up for the day, the Arch's white marble seemed to be surrounded by an aureole, while around it the trees, sagging under their load of leaves, were sort of sighing in haziness.

Perfect, it was just perfect—that is, except for one thing. In the sky above the more easterly of the fine pink townhouses was a grey stone structure in the shape of a trapezoid, crowned by a small golden dome with two balls on a rod sticking up from it. It was the tower to the recently-completed Metropolitan Life Insurance Building, uptown on Twenty-third Street.

Oh well, what we don't like we don't have to look at, do we, Jerrold rationalized, and shifted his gaze away—alas, in the direction of Number 23 Washington Place.

"Oh jiminy, that God-awful place!" he muttered, of its upper reaches, visible over the tree line—and away flew all the delightful Sunday morning feelings.

When, oh when, am I going get out of there, he brooded, by no means for the first time. It had begun as horrible, and by now become well-nigh unbearable. Why, no one there, including Bernstein apparently, knew his real name, and that was the least of it. That guy with his grim baby face was always finding the stinkingest jobs for Sonny to do—like crawling under the sewing machines with a bucket to collect the used-up oil from the drip cups, which nine times out of ten meant not only getting the black gummy stuff all over his hands, but also on his face and even in his hair.

And if you think Shipping is any better, you're sadly mistaken, Jerrold lectured an invisible audience. It was always HE, Sonny, who had to grab those huge cartons up in his arms and set them down on the dolly, HE who had to wheel the top-heavy thing over to the elevator and ride downstairs with it, and HE who had to grab each and every one up again and bounce it onto the dray! And what, pray, were THEY doing, Mr. Markowitz's assistants Solly and Louie, who should have been helping out alongside him? Why playing cards in a back room somewhere, or else, can you imagine it, supervising him so as to assure that HE was doing a good job!

"Boy!" Jerrold smoldered.

The Strike

And that wasn't the worst of it. There were times when one person would tell him to do one thing, and then, maddeningly, someone else, equally in authority, would come along and tell him to do something else. Like yesterday, for instance, when he was all set to bring up some sorely-needed bundles of cut material from Eight, and Mr. Harris stuck his head out of his office and insisted that he go scrub down the latrines in the men's room. "I don't care vat Boinsteen said, you listen to me!" Harris shouted before Jerrold could fairly open his mouth.

"Boy oh boy!" Jerrold protested again—and jumping up, left Dusty behind to go slump in the maroon cushiness of the easy chair, with his back to the outside.

Just pinned to that nightmarish place, he moped, after reviewing the alternatives yet once more. To take time off "to attend to an important personal matter," one didn't dare. And the same went for playing sick—the reason being that either you worked for those miserable folks or you didn't, and if ever any of the bigshots smelled a rat, which quite often happened, out you'd be thrown without any further ado.

No, you're just going to have to grin and bear it for now, and that's that, was Jerrold's conclusion like the other times, until he had enough money put by to tide him over for a while. And certainly that time was not too distant. Thanks to Giuseppina's sound advice about food and Arturo on other matters like seconds in clothes, he'd been socking it away at the rate of a dollar or two a week for quite some time now, and his goal, the $450 originally left him by Aunt Serena, was nearly reached. On Friday the bank book showed a balance of $398.

I'll tell you what, he made a deal with himself. As of tomorrow, we'll begin buying the papers again every day, and keep an eye peeled on the want ads. Then if something promising turns up in one—like an assistant bookkeepership or even a position as a clerk—we'll take a walk over after work, if we're not too tired, to see what the building looks like.

Okay, so now relax and go enjoy yourself, he softly pleaded, in a voice reminiscent of someone in the past...who knows, perhaps that faceless young woman, his mother, lying beneath one of the old wooden crosses back home in the kitchen garden gone wild...

But it can't be for too long, he reminded himself, taking in the view from the window with kitkat anew, and as confirmation, his eyes momentarily sought the mantel, where a handsome bronze timepiece now stood tall (picked up by him for a song from a Third Avenue pawnshop).

Yes, in a few minutes he'd have to begin getting ready to go to church, of all places—a Roman Catholic Church, that is. He had a date with Arturo and Giuseppina, and their daughter Rosa, to attend mass at St. Anthony of Padua at eleven o'clock.

"Hm," Jerrold went, not exactly pleased at the prospect. For no question about it, something was brewing.

Curiously, it was not until several weeks ago that he discovered his friends actually had a child, and that she was a girl of his age. Sipping on espresso with Arturo one evening, Jerrold got a glimpse of a young someone with frizzy hair, freckles, and a profusion of teeth like Giuseppina, stepping in from the rear of the shop with a tray of fresh cannoli. Then Arturo introducing him, Rosa smiled uncertainly, whereupon quickly depositing those new pastries in the display case behind the counter, she slipped out through the curtain again—to reappear in much the same manner each time Jerrold turned up after that...sometimes to linger for a moment, fidgeting with her hands on a small white towel, as Giuseppina was in the habit of doing.

This past Tuesday, came a fresh development. Leaning his mustachioed round face close to Jerrold, the baker confided that he and his wife had the greatest respect for him; indeed they regarded him almost like a son. Then came the invitation for today.

Taken somewhat by surprise at this turn of events, Jerrold felt hard put to do anything but accept. But once having parted company with the man, he became filled with misgivings—for what else could his old friend have in mind as the outcome than some expression of interest in the girl by Jerrold.

Mind you, I've got nothing against her, Jerrold told himself at the time, as obviously she was a far cry from the machine operators at Triangle, who could be very loud and boisterous, to say nothing of downright fresh. But there was the rub: having yet to exchange more than "Good evening" with Rosa, he didn't rightly know that he truly liked her. And then, he wasn't sure, for lack of experience, whether a girl to whom he might give his heart away should resemble her mother to that extent.

Beyond this, there was also the matter of affordability to consider. Looking to make the Big Move one day soon, did he, Jerrold, at this point even dare think about the bold step that all three of them were very likely envisioning?

Of course, Arturo would give him and the girl a fine send-off, of that Jerrold was sure. And the good man would probably help them out later too, if need be.

Even so, (to repeat) such an arrangement was not to be entered into lightly…

And now, with eyes fixed once more on the Arch and the trees wavering in the filmy light, Jerrold realized that something else about this possible change in his circumstances was troubling him as well…something more elemental within himself that he was at a loss to put his finger on.

CHOOSING

Spiffy is the only way to describe it. In a blue-and-white striped jacket over white trousers, topped off by a creamy straw hat tipped at a jaunty angle, Jerrold looks his very best, as if he were all decked out in spats and swinging a cane.

St. Anthony of Padua, a blockish structure of stone and red brick, is on the other side of Houston, with the usual rose window, and crosses showing on every high point.

Quite a few people are already milling about out front, many of them adults, but shepherding many more little boys and girls.

Halfway across—"Ah!"—Jerrold recognizes his friends amongst the throng, and quickens his pace.

Arturo, all in white from neck to foot, wears a Panama to shade his face, while Giuseppina and Rosa, with freckles freshly scrubbed, have gotten themselves up in matronly dark blue and posy pink.

Jerrold's fidgetiness of this morning returns. Even so, he gives a cheerful hail over the din—"Good morning!"

Giuseppina stands happily by as Arturo, eyes a-glow, slings an arm around him and squeezes his shoulders.

Rosa, grinning too, greets him back, careful of her pronunciation—"Good morn-ing, Jer-rold."

Her hand is demurely tucked in mother's arm.

A pair of neighbors on the look-out for them come over—a swarthy old crone and her not-so-young daughter, both of them dressed completely in black, to the lace shawls enshrouding their heads. The little circle breaks into Italian, with frequent glances his way.

"*Belli*" and "*bambini*," Jerrold's ear picks out. "Rosa and the young American will make beautiful babies," they are probably agreeing. He grows a trifle queasy.

Some of the crowd begins mounting up the stoop, which is a steep one. It has become sultry out, so if everyone is not sweating now, they soon will be. Arturo waves for their party to follow—"*Andiamo!*"

The men climbing ahead of Jerrold are removing their hats, so he does likewise. It suddenly strikes him that he alone is fair-haired in that crowd; at the same instant, there's Arturo's hand, warm and moist, on his back.

Inside, a rare jeweled light of pale blue and lemon filters down from stained glass windows high up in a cupola, making the large space there much brighter than expected. Along either side, from down front clear to the back, runs a line of dark-green marble pillars like moss-covered tree trunks. White gardenias are piled high before the altar.

The pews all seem to be filled except for the last two on the left in the back, where there's just enough room if they split up. Arturo and Jerrold enter the one, Giuseppina and Rosa slip into the other right behind them.

Almost as if he were a boy again, Jerrold imitates Arturo, genuflecting and dropping to his knees with palms together. Jeezy, comes the thought, do you realize that if you marry her, you're probably going to have to do this for the rest of your ever-lovin' life.

Cautiously, his eye roams sideways to the wall. Every so often along it, between tall stained glass windows, is the painted statue of a saint or some other holy one, all of them looking like so many rouged-up, larger-than-life plaster dolls.

*R*ING-*ING-ING*! go some bells resembling sleigh bells. Jerrold gives a start.

From a door beside the altar emerges a young man in a white robe, swinging a golden censer pouring forth grey smoke. Behind him step three more young men, similarly garbed, bearing a gleaming golden cross between flickering candlesticks. Next comes a choir of all men and boys, caroling long phrases in Latin. A priest in white brocade trimmed with gold brings up the rear.

The procession makes its way to the back and around, then starts down the center aisle. In its wake, a sweet-smelling cloud from the censer settles over everything.

Some of it gets into Jerrold's throat, an old story from Christ Episcopal back home. With eyes down, he covers his mouth and discreetly coughs.

The men and boys reach the altar and disperse on either side of it.

"*In nomine Patris, Filii, et Spiritus Sancti*," the priest intones in a loud voice.

"Amen," Jerrold dutifully responds with the rest of the congregation, that Patris phrase being just about all the Latin he knows.

Wood-creaks and bumps sound from all over, as everyone including him rocks back from knees onto seats.

The choir strikes up again, with something more lilting this time.

You can bet your bottom dollar this is not going to be over in a hurry, Jerrold warns himself. Again he gives a look leftward, and his eyes meet those of the statue of a young friar with a womanish face, who is holding an infant in a white dress.

In his mind, Jerrold returns to the matter at hand: courting Rosa, should he be so inclined. As he understands such matters, which like other guys he's sort of picked up along the way while growing up, a young man has to ask a young lady's father for permission to call on her first, and if it is granted, he then has to sit and talk with her for a time, after which if she agrees to let him hold her hand, the next thing to do is to produce a ring, which he must present to her on bended knee, at which point, usually, it is appropriate for him to touch his lips to hers. However, where Rosa is concerned, is it safe to proceed in the same way, considering how differently Italians are known to view personal matters at times?

For instance, after this, Arturo and Giuseppina will very likely invite me to come have something to eat with them at home—Jerrold pictures himself climbing to the floor above the bake shop, where he's never been before. Supposing I agree, should I then walk beside Rosa and try engaging her in conversation, as one would an American girl, or what?

The choir's deep and high voices have tapered off.

The priest's mouth opens, and becomes a bell—"*Dom-in-us vo-bis-cum!*"

Everyone mumbles an answer, and rocks forward onto knees again, Jerrold with them.

The censer-bearer rises and steps over to a lectern, and begins reading something in Latin.

It's from the Bible, Jerrold surmises, and missing the plain English of Christ Episcopal, resumes his deliberations.

The Strike

Supposing that some perfectly natural and normal act of mine turns out to be an utter abomination in Arturo's eyes, what then? Believe you me, a matter like this is not to be taken lightly; Italians are noted for their fierce tempers—as he himself bore witness to one evening not long ago from the bake shop window. As if from out of nowhere, a young guy suddenly came tearing down the middle of the street under the El with a look of sheer terror in his eyes. Hard on his heels ran an older man, outrage personified, with a stiletto in his hand, followed by a pack of other "fathers," equally incensed. A girl Rosa's age hurried along behind them, sobbing her heart out.

The mixed voices of the choir are warbling sweetly now, and the whole place is sitting once more.

But is such a thing possible with Arturo here, Jerrold wonders. Could this friend work himself up into a frenzy like that on my account? No, I think not, he decides after a few moments, for the simple reason that the man seems to want very badly to bring this connection with his daughter about. No, chances are, if I do pull a boner of some kind, he'll find it in his heart to let bygones be bygones, and at the very worst explain how to go about things the right way next time.

The priest attempts new bell-like heights—"*Dom-in-us vo-bis-cum!*"

On his knees, Jerrold hears further praying all around him.

So that's that, now what other problems might come to the surface.

The censer-bearer stands again and goes to another lectern, and begins reading in Latin once more.

Jerrold heaves a sigh. Well, if the truth be known, you have absolutely no experience with women, especially with you-know-what. For never having seen one undressed, as, for instance, his old friends Roger and Peter did their little sisters, he hasn't even the least clue as to what they are like down there.

But surely you're not going to let something like that stand in your way, Jerrold's practical side argues. After all, there are books on the subject, some of which, he seems to remember, one can buy through the mail to save embarrassment.

Yes, but a book doesn't always take everything into account, the other HE points out, like things that might go wrong. For instance, supposing on your wedding night, you're all alone with Rosa in a strange hotel room—Jerrold imagines it—and after getting on top of her in the bed, you can't find the place to put your peter in! What good is a book going to do then? Or else supposing that you manage to and it hurts her and she screams and wakes up the other people in the hotel, and they all come running in their nightshirts to see what the matter is! No book will tell you what to do in that case for sure. Jerrold's upper lip is covered with sweat. WHATEVER WILL YOU SAY?

"*Credo in u-num de-e-um!*" the priest vocalizes.

I can't, I can't go through with it! Jerrold's whole being cries out within him. I don't want it, I don't want *that* with her! I want— What it is, what he would really like, steals sylph-like into his mind, and steals away again.

The men and boys of the choir are singing whisperingly-soft now, like faded flowers.

There's a nudge from Arturo. "Oh"—a collection basket is reaching out toward them on the end of a long pole. Jerrold fumbles in his pocket for change.

The priest is above in his pulpit, ready to begin on his sermon, which will be in Italian, Jerrold guesses.

So it is, and promises to drone on and on...

I must have fallen asleep, Jerrold realizes some time later.

The priest has returned below to his table, and is busy preparing the host and wine.

Much calmer now, Jerrold sees what should be done next: he has to make his position clear to Arturo and Giuseppina at once, so there aren't any hard feelings and they can all go on being friends. I'll attend to it the moment this is over.

The Strike

There's a movement behind him: Rosa shifting on her knees perhaps. Kneeling himself, Jerrold turns to see.

Rosa's eyes register surprise—she smiles slightly. At the same time, her praying hands descend to her sides, and the right seeks to bury itself in the folds of her dress—but not fast enough!

Jerrold has spied a stub of a finger protruding from the pinky, like a twig sprouted from a twig!

So! He's facing the altar again. So! His stomach begins to churn, and something bitter comes up into his mouth. He swallows it with a painful gulp, conscious that Arturo beside him has sensed something is not quite right and is perhaps wondering what it might be.

RING-ING-ING! go the sleigh bells, seeming harsh now.

Jerrold's back hunches over, as does everyone else's.

The priest holds the wafer aloft—the jangling sounds afresh. Now the chalice goes up—there's another rattle from the bells.

Down front, people rise and file to the altar rail. The priest passes along, ministering to them on their knees. As they move away, a new group rises.

Patience, it won't be long, Jerrold lulls himself, and waits, still on his knees, with jaw clamped…

You see—Arturo and the others in his row are on their feet.

Now it's just a matter of the row behind us, Jerrold decrees, as his friend returns.

Giuseppina and Rosa go to the rail, and in no time at all are back…a little paler than before, with lips pressed together.

Giuseppina knows, Rosa must have told her, Jerrold figures. Oh, it's a bad business, and I'm afraid it's going to get worse yet.

The priest opens his bell-like mouth—"*Deo gratias.*"

That's it, the end, Jerrold perceives, and somehow hauls himself up. "See you outside," he murmurs to Arturo before striding away…

Out on the street, with his straw chapeau back on, Jerrold assumes a stance facing the stoop. Once it's done, go home and get back into your pajamas as if you never left, he counsels himself. Then make yourself a cup of coffee BLACK as HELL, and relax.

The doors above open, and everyone begins streaming down.

Jerrold singles out Arturo in his white suit with the Panama.

"Were you sicka?" Arturo asks, when they are face-to-face. "I thought you mighta got sicka."

The man knows too now, he's just pretending, Jerrold concludes. "No—I'm fine."

Giuseppina appears with pretty pink Rosa, both of them evidently having decided to put a good face on things. The hand with the extra stump of finger is firmly tucked in mother's arm.

Arturo's arm encircles Jerrold's shoulders, and he pops the question about going home to dine with them.

Now don't weaken, Jerrold cautions himself. Sorry, he says, and begins offering excuses.

"Plans?" Arturo echoes. But he thought it was understood, and Giuseppina has fixed such a lovely meal, *braccioli*, one of her specialties, a real treat. Can't the plans be put off to some other time?

Giuseppina's chin bobs encouragement, but clearly her heart's not in it. Rosa isn't even up to a smile anymore.

Jerrold makes a further effort to explain.

"Beeziness?" Arturo repeats. Who ever heard of conducting business on a Sunday.

Jerrold feels his patience starting to wear thin, but he brings himself up short. After all, the man's only trying to save face, as anyone else would under the circumstances, and at the same time still hoping to make a match between two young people for the sake of their mutual happiness, as he understands it. Jerrold begins to have second thoughts. Maybe—

But then the scene in the hotel room comes rushing back, with him about to descend on Rosa with his peter.

No-o-o! Jerrold hollers inside of himself. I can't do it! I can't! I can't! Not with her! Or anyone else!

"I'm sorry, really sorry," he says, and raises some fingers to his hat brim.

Home Jerrold went, to be sure, and indeed got right into his pajamas. However, he didn't feel up to the coffee, and instead sank onto the bed and fell fast asleep with puss-puss on the pillow beside him...

No need to look at the clock; one can tell at a glance from the shadows on the walls that it's late afternoon.

Up, up, Jerrold prods himself. Time to think about something to eat, and there's nothing but a hard hunk of Gorgonzola and some stale Italian bread in the icebox.

His legs begin to obey—but then freeze. What'll I do about THEM?

Jerrold's practical side comes to the fore again: just don't bother with them anymore, that's all, or else put in an appearance now and then to show Arturo that everything's alright, so he won't ferret you out here, using his concern about your well-being as an excuse.

And don't worry about getting your fill of baked goods either. There's a place he's heard of over on Cornelia Street, owned by some brothers named Zampieri, that's supposed to have even better stuff at the same low prices. Now you can go and try it out without feeling guilty.

As for friends, obviously you must find others. Only this time let there definitely be more than one, so you won't end up in the bind you are now. Shall we start with someone here in the house? His mind casts about, but all it comes up with is old lady Jones, his next-door neighbor, as there's a lot of moving in and out, and those tenants who stay on seem to keep very much to themselves.

Oh well—Jerrold is breathing a mite easier—something will turn up sooner or later, I have a feeling. Now let's think about this evening's meal.

Some months ago, during one of his rambles around the neighborhood after work, he happened on a nifty French restaurant in the basement of a hotel named Brevoort, up a piece from the Arch on Fifth, and passing by from time to time after that, he made a point of peering through the windows down there. The place, which is reasonably priced, has bare wooden tables where you can sit with just a cup of coffee, if you want. Also, you can have one of the French newspapers, on wooden rollers, brought to you at no extra charge, it would seem. Furthermore, the clientele appears to be just plain folk like himself, guys mostly.

There's only one sore point—and it returns to plague him now, as it has every time he's been of a mind to skip down those stairs and saunter in. Aside from the drugstore in Tarrytown and Arturo's shop, which don't really count, he's never "dined out" before, and isn't quite sure how to handle things.

For instance, the menu (which they keep in a glass case up on the sidewalk) is all in French—only French of such a high caliber that in spite of his two years of it at Cobbs and a dictionary, he's yet to make head or tail out of what such items as *veau à la Marengo* and *mouton à la ravigote* are. So if the help are all French-speaking, which seems likely, the question is: do I dare use such French as is at my command to ask the waiter about the various dishes, or should I simply take potluck and accept his recommendations?

The size of the portions might also present a problem. Supposing that the one the man brings me isn't generous enough. Should I mention this to him or try and get hold of the manager to complain, or should I just quietly send for something else and make it a point of not giving them any further business?

In addition, there's the matter of the tip, which not for all the world would he fail to leave, since that is what is done. However, he hasn't the vaguest idea how much it should be, and is absolutely terrified at the thought of what might happen if he doesn't leave one large enough. For instance, the fellow could raise such a fuss as to make the whole place ring out—and then I'd be so mortified, I'd never so much as go near it again, lest someone recognize me!

The Strike

So what's there to do, how might I get around those impasses, Jerrold ponders. The answer—now that true need has arisen—is soon forthcoming: he should try and learn the ropes in some no-account joint first, where it doesn't seem to matter what one says or does, for example, from the looks of it, a place like Jim's Oyster Saloon under the El on Sixth.

Yes, of course, Jerrold sees at once. And in the meanwhile, you can brush up on the French, so as to be ready for that good place when the time comes.

"Yesirree, now we're talking!" Jerrold's legs swing round, jarring the feline ball of fur, which snoozes on. All you need is a grammar book with exercises to do. I bet that big bookstore on Fifth near the Flatiron—Brentano's, I think it's called—has something of the sort.

In no time flat, he's back in the trousers, jacket, and hat and—"Alleyoop!"—high-stepping it down the stairs...

"Psst!" someone hisses on the landlady's floor.

Well, well, it's that Chucky—to whom Jerrold still hasn't said more than "Hello" and "See yuh" when they pass on the stairs.

"Hey, Chucky! Boy, am I glad to see you!" Jerrold booms, just able to make out the guy's darting eyes and banana nose through the crack in the door. Why didn't I think of him before?

"Sh-sh," Chucky hushes, with a finger to his pinched little mouth. "Mama's asleep."

Meaning Madame Branchard of course, whom Jerrold most assuredly has seen to speak to: the first of every month like clockwork when she comes up to collect her rent, and snoop around for tell-tale signs of dissoluteness. "Sorry," he whispers.

"How about it, you wanna go have a beer?" Chucky sort of whines. He's in his bathrobe.

Beer? "What a swell idea!" Jerrold agrees, who has never so much as had a whiff of the stuff in his nostrils. Boy, you sure are a stick-in-the-mud, he takes himself to task. Here you've been on your own in New York all these months and never once thought to try some.

"Aim-eel?" someone squawks from inside. It's HER, naturally.

"Meet ya outside," Chucky hisses...

This is it, Jerrold tells himself, descending the stairs again. This is the break you were hoping for. Congratulations, you certainly could use a little fun for a change.

Downstairs by the door, a small pile of mail left over from yesterday waits on the table, an old story here at Number 61. Either the person to whom it belongs is away somewhere or, more likely, simply hasn't bothered to pick it up.

With a pang Jerrold suddenly remembers his old friends the Stiverses, to whom a letter is long overdue. For shame, he scolds, after they were so good to you, and vows to set things to rights the first chance he gets.

Out on the stoop, there's the minutest breeze, and the branches across the way, heavy with their leaves, are slightly swaying.

It has recently turned twilight: in the distance the Arch looms, a dark shadow.

"I hope ya don' mind my duds," Chucky says, stepping out a few minutes later, in the red flannel shirt and overalls that he had on the day they met. Everything else's on the line, it seems.

"Not at all," Jerrold assures, and notices that he's a mite taller and much thinner, which somehow makes him feel like the guy's father.

"Is the place on the corner awright?" Chucky asks, as they begin descending to the sidewalk.

O'Reilly's, Jerrold recalls, having passed it often enough on the way to Arturo's. "Sure, whatever you say."

"You're gonna like it, I betcha, I betcha," Chucky puts in, as they walk along.

A twinge of apprehension grips Jerrold: we're going to a place where grown-up men meet to drink and talk.

To enter, you have to get through a pair of carved swinging doors. Chucky leads the way, pushing both in at once with pudgy fists.

The Strike

Inside, extending down the whole length of the room, is a dark-wooden bar with a blue mirror behind it, before which are several formidable pyramids of glasses.

"Hiya, Blacky," Chucky nasals to an unshaven guy standing amidst a cluster of pals at the near end. They're all wearing black suits and bowlers.

Blacky raises a finger of recognition, his mouth still going with a yarn he's spinning.

Chucky steers a middle course. Jerrold is right behind him, treading sawdust under foot like dry grass.

"Hey, Chucky!" someone hails him from way down on the other end, where another group, in less severe colors, is gathered. The guy is slight of build and has slicked-down hair.

Chucky gives a nod, and plunks a foot on the brass rail. Jerrold follows suit, and looks up to find his clean-cut Yankee face topped by the straw hat bluely reflected in the mirror...beneath clouds of grey smoke from cigars and cigarettes swirling around greenish-yellow gas lights.

Blacky's crowd breaks into loud laughter—"Hah! Hah! Hah!"—the punch line to his story apparently having been reached.

Behind the bar, a burly man in shirt sleeves with a big bushy moustache comes padding over.

"O'Reilly the owner," Chucky murmurs to Jerrold, and does the honors—"This here's Jerry. He's rooming with us."

Quickly sizing him up, O'Reilly offers a hand—"Pleased to meet ya."

"Same to you." Shaking with him, Jerrold is conscious of how frail and clammy his own mitt is by comparison.

"A coupla lagers," Chucky orders.

The man goes to draw two light-golden steins, and clumps back with them, slicked off with a stick, then takes their coins—a nickel each—to ring up in a fancy gilt register—*PING!*

"Well"—Chucky grabs his up by the handle—"here's lookin' at ya."

"And to you," Jerrold says with his raised, then takes a small sip—to find the brew a little on the bitter side, but all in all not bad.

Hanging in all its glory above the register is the portrait of an older man surrounded by a wreath of crossed shillelaghs and American flags.

"That's Moiphy, the big boss at Tammany," Chucky explains.

Murphy, who has a double chin and a paunch, and wears rimless glasses, strikes Jerrold as a paternal type in an Irish sort of way.

"Blacky over there's his nephew," Chucky adds, meaningfully.

"That so?" Feeling pretty good, Jerrold imbibes a real mouthful this time, and chases it down with another.

When both steins are nearly empty, Chucky takes the initiative once more—"C'mon, drink up and we'll have another."

Jerrold's agreeable—"Don't mind if I do"—nevertheless mindful that pal here initially said one.

"Say, are ya hungry?" Chucky asks, after O'Reilly with his moustache has brought the new drafts, and gestures behind them.

Jerrold swivels round, and there along the opposite wall—Glory be!—is a counter loaded with crockery heaped with food.

"Help yourself," Chucky invites, "no extra charge."

Jerrold's amazed—"Do you mean it?"

"Some of it's a little on the salty side," Chucky has to admit. "If it don' agree with you, jes dump it"—tilting his head toward a brass spittoon.

Jerrold makes a mental note to go for some baked beans, baloney, pickles, and rye bread after this stein is finished, if there's nothing else doing.

"Everything alright, boys?" O'Reilly inquires, on the way back from doling out more drinks on the far end.

"That it is," Chucky answers, then confides to Jerrold out of the corner of his mouth, "If you hang aroun' long enough, he'll give you a free beer too."

The Strike

Very ni-ice, Jerrold croons inwardly. He's liking this place more and more.

In another trice, at Chucky's bidding, O'Reilly comes with two additional refills.

Is that the third or fourth round, Jerrold wonders. Oh well, what difference.

Meanwhile Blacky over on the left has just finished another ha-ha story, and he and his cronies are now engaged in a friendly argument about a prize fight that took place the other night between Malloy the champion and someone named Dennison.

"Why if only Denny'd been given a square deal, he could've creamed him," Blacky is saying, and goes on to blame the referee, who persisted in looking with blinders on a certain questionable blocking tactic of Malloy's.

"Aw c'mon, get on with ya," a supporter of the champ challenges. Others join in.

Blacky turns all hot under the collar—"Here! Lemme show ya, lemme show ya!"—and dances into the middle of the floor. His eye lights on Jerrold—"Hey, kid, c'mere."

Jerrold's a little fuzzy in the head—Who, me? Does he mean me?

"Go on," Chucky urges under his breath.

Jerrold adjusts his focus and begins moving, as if on high-piled velvet.

"Don' worry, I aint gonna hoit you," Blacky makes it clear.

Coming up, Jerrold sees that the man has round shoulders and a pot belly—in short, is a chip off the old block, Boss Murphy his uncle.

"Now les pretend he's Denny, okay?" Blacky says to the others. "Put up yer dukes," he tells Jerrold.

Anything you say, Jerrold thinks, and clenches his hands into fists before his chest.

"Now aim for here"—Blacky point-points to his nose.

A little unsteady on his pins, Jerrold pokes with his right.

Blacky deftly parries the jab with his elbow—"Yuh see! Yuh see what I mean!"

The point has been made; there's no further cause for discussion. Blacky claps Jerrold on the back—"You're alright, kid"—and inquires after his name.

Jerrold's not thrilled about this part, but what can he do.

"Get a load a dat, Vanderlynn! Hoity toity!"

No sooner has Jerrold returned to Chucky's side than O'Reilly's there with a fresh stein. "On me, Jerry," Blacky calls over. "No hard feelings, 'k?"

"A good kid," Jerrold's ear picks up. "Coulda done a real job on me nose if he wanted ta."

Someone in the crowd makes a crack, causing the rest of them to burst out—"Hahaha!"

"Where, whadya mean!" Blacky cries. "Whadya mean circumcised prick!" He cranes his neck and shifts his head this way and that in the mirror.

Feeling good, really good, Jerrold eases himself round, so his back is resting against the bar. What time is it?...What DAY is it?...Who cares...and Chucky reminds him of a bird. OH BIRD THAT NEVER WERT!

"Hey, ole buddy," Chucky pipes up after a little, "I gotta piss."

"You do?" It's necessary for Jerrold to reflect on this for a moment—"I do too."

"You foist"—Chucky motions to the back on the right.

On the way, Jerrold lurches past a whole lot of blurred pictures of prize fighters and race horses. Boy, I'm really blotto, I think.

Arriving at the place, he gives a yank to the knob. A naked bowl is straight ahead, its porcelain edge encrusted with grey scum.

Pushing the door closed behind him, Jerrold begins unbuttoning—only somehow he's thrown off balance and slams against the wall! "But thass alright, no harm's done," he singsongs, and positioning himself once more, takes out his peter.

The Strike

The pee foams as it hits the water—"It's fun!"

Outside, once he's done, Chucky's leaning with his head down. "We're goin' after this."

Jerrold floats by *on silver skates* in Hans Christian Andersen fashion.

"Did everything come out alright?" a husky voice calls from the bar.

"Yup," Jerrold answers—and looks over there.

It's the slender chap with the pasted-down hair who greeted Chucky before, when they came in. All alone now, the fellow, who is "older," holds out his hand—"Name's Smitty."

"A—a pleasure," Jerrold responds, vaguely alert to the possibility of another new friend in-the-making.

Once handsome perhaps, Smitty's face is weatherbeaten with many lines on it, and the hair is a shade darker than his own wheaten.

Jerrold is all ready to pass the time of day with him. But there's Chucky at his elbow, looking very serious about leaving.

"Who—is—he?" Jerrold wants to know, as they're bumbling along toward the exit.

"No one special, jes hangs out here," Chucky sulkily replies, as if, at some time in the past, that Smitty gave him a good spanking over his knee or something.

Well, he seems alright to me, Jerrold airily decides, so we'll resume from where we left off next time. As I said, the more chums the better.

Outside, it has cooled off quite a bit, and the Square is all in darkness except for the street globes, glowing violet.

For Jerrold, going home is like struggling against a stiff winter wind or wading hip-high through water. But at long last he and the pal make it, and are on the top step of the stoop.

Chucky jiggles the handle without success—"Darn, no help for it!"—and stabs at the bell.

A few minutes elapse before the fanlight brightens. Then the door swings open and there, in a man's silk dressing gown with her head encased in a polka-dotted kerchief, is Madame glaring.

At the sight of them, her eyes widen—"Aim-eel, what have you done!"

Done? Jerrold considers. What does she mean, done? "'Scuse me," he mumbles, and slips by her.

Ole buddy is still catching it behind him as he reaches the staircase—"You wicked boy!"

"I'm sorry, mama, I didn't mean it," the poor guy snivels.

"Bad enough, you go and get yourself soused—"

"Oh, Jerry's awright, honest. Where—where is he? HEY, JERRY!"

Jerrold's already up one flight, and feeling-feeling-feeling like the cat's meow...*with* SUGAR *in his* VEINS!

CHAPTER

7

The oddest thing, just as Martha was on the point of despairing over ever finding someone her age to talk to at Triangle, suddenly there was someone—or so it seemed at first.

The girl's name was Elsie Shuman, and she was a chubby with a big furry mole ugly as a spider on her cheek. To make matters worse, Elsie was an awful slob, whose hair often hung down in greasy strands on a dress soiled with food stains. And to complete the not-too-pretty picture, she was a member of Morris Elzufin's crew, one of the loud-mouthed bunches in the rear. Even so, despite those bad points, Martha was determined to make friends with her from the first moments of their initial encounter—that is, if Elsie felt so inclined.

That meeting took place after work one day in late August, on Broadway and Washington Place, where Martha usually waited for the downtown trolley. Benny had just parted company with her en route to the subway, when along came Elsie, likewise heading for the Lower East Side. "I yooshully take de 4th Street across and den de Avenya A down," she explained, but thought that she would try going this way for a change.

Soon, gliding past all those dry goods stores, they struck up a conversation, and one thing leading to another, Martha learned that

Elsie had lost her father when she was very young, with the result that she'd had to spend every afternoon at home drudging away on piece work with her mother and brothers in order to keep life and limb together—which made Martha feel sorry. The poor girl had missed many a good time that she herself had enjoyed as a member of The Damsels of the College Settlement.

The next day Elsie showed up on the corner again, and this time riding along, the two of them compared notes about boys they'd met, for like the other girls at Triangle, Elsie went to her share of social functions. And by one of those strange coincidences, they found that Martha had been approached for a dance at one of the Junior Hops by the same silly guy who had asked Elsie at some hall on another evening.

"What a riot!" Elsie hollered in her rather shrill voice. The guy was a German or an Austrian, and his way was—before sputtering out, "May I hef—mit you—de dance?"—to make a little bow first.

As for Davey Goldstein, of course Elsie had set eyes on him, as who hadn't. "Lemme tellya," she confided, after hearing of his attentions to Martha, "whoever manages to snag that blond god as a husband can consider huhself a very lucky goil"—an old story.

Pleasing as it was to have this new "friend," Martha was not blind to the possibility that Elsie might be after something, especially since she continued turning up at the trolley stop on succeeding days after Benny was gone, as if she were trying to avoid him—and Martha's suspicion proved only too true. But on her mentioning this possibility to Benny, he was only fearful that the girl was trying to steal his precious *tsatskele*, a regular speed demon, away to go work for that trouble-maker Elzufin—which was not so.

The real reason for Elsie's attentions, which came out when next they went downtown together, was purely and simply this: some friends had invited her to have dinner with them in a restaurant the following week, and wanted her to bring Martha along if she cared to come.

The Strike

"Dinner at a restaurant with strangers?" Martha questioned. "Who are they?"

Oh, just some educated women like the College Settlement counselors, who wanted to help poor working girls improve their lot, Elsie answered. They'd formed an organization called The Women's Trade Union League, and brought into it some older women from the factories. Now they'd expressed an interest in meeting Martha, among other people.

"But who are they?" Martha insisted on knowing.

"Well, dere's Mary Dreier for one and Helen Marot for anudder," Elsie ticked off, and the factory women included Leonora O'Reilly and Rose Schneiderman. "Didje ever hear of dem?"

"Sort of," was Martha's reply, who indeed sort of had. "But how do they know about me?"

"Oh, I told dem. I told dem all about yuh." Then Elsie added yearningly, "I sure hope yuh can make it."

As for the restaurant, it was a cute little place close by the Square—"You'll love it." They could rendezvous there, and then later have each other for company going downtown, just like always.

Naturally, Martha left the matter up in the air, wanting to get Benny's reaction first.

And what did the old one make of it, after the whole tale was told with their heads close together the following day at break time?

Well, first he had to know who those women were, did Martha remember the names?

Yes, of course, she said, and reeled them off: Dreier, Marot, O'Reilly, and Schneiderman.

The old one's runny eyes behind the glasses squinted in concentration: Mary Dreier and Helen Marot were both *goyim*—gentiles—and, as Elsie claimed, rich well-educated women dedicated to serving the poor...Leonora O'Reilly, an Irish firebrand, was to the best of his recollection teaching sewing in a trade school for girls, and had recently adopted an orphan, whom she was bringing up by herself with some assistance from another of those wealthy women…"Schneiderman is vun of ours"—a little one but very scrappy, with red hair, who was known far and wide for the *hegdesh*—tumult—that she'd created among the cap makers not long ago, which resulted in their organizing a union and getting their detestable cockroach Bosses to cough up a contract.

Unions, contracts, bosses—Martha wrinkled her brow. "Will they try to do something like that here, do you think?" she plied him furtively.

Her old friend's shoulders gave a heave. "Try mehbee"—doing was another matter.

"Yes, but look at Rosen's," she argued. "You said that the strikers there would go whistle for their money"—whereas it was almost two months later now, and they were still out. Not only that, rumor had it that old man Rosen had grown so desperate with the busy season coming on that he was about to cave in and give them the whole kitenkeboodle they'd asked for.

"Okay, but let's see foist, let's see him settle foist," Benny shot back at her. And then, even if he did, Rosen was after all one thing, Harris and Blanck, their owners here, were quite another. "Beleef you me, dey vouldn't stand fuh such nonsense, not for a minute, dis vun needah"—meaning Bernstein, who'd just come in through the back partition and was making for the bell. "Specially him"—for as she very well knew, he was in thick with some of the cutters downstairs, big hulking fellas ready to do his bidding, whatever that was, at a moment's notice, with no questions asked.

Lowering his voice, the old one reminded her of a fracas that had taken place there before her time, which she'd already heard mentioned in passing—how one day Kline and Elzufin started making noises about the company benevolent society that Harris had cooked up to squeeze yet more blood out of them in the form of dues…and how they were accosted by two of those *shtarkers*—bullies—who beat them up and kicked them the hell out for a week.

The Strike

Is it possible that someone with such a mild look to him should be capable of such baseness, Martha considered, with her eyes now on Bernstein, about to ring in the second half of the day.

In her mind, she sketched his perfectly arched eyebrows, sleepy lids, and twisty mouth, and put in two furrows above the bridge of his nose. No, it can't be, I simply can't believe it, they're all exaggerating—she rubbed the creases out.

I bet that wouldn't be so with Mr. Harris, though. Let's see—to Harris's pear-shaped face, framed by the reddish-brown hair, she added similar anger marks, and while she was at it molded the mouth into a disagreeable "O." Yes, quite right, they belong, she saw, in fact they rather made the picture complete.

"So what do you think, should I go meet those women or what?" Martha asked Benny at long last.

Her good old friend tilted his head to one side—"*Nu*, so, talk is cheap"...

That being that, it was only a matter of Martha's letting Elsie know that she'd be at the place at the appointed hour, which was duly taken care of on the way home that day.

The next step, which was to break the news to them at home, she looked forward to with dread. Yes indeed, this is not going to be easy by any means, she saw, for in addition to Papa's continued opposition to daughter's laboring away in a factory, he had this unreasoning antipathy to labor actions, and Mammeh shared his feelings to a certain extent.

Deciding on the tried-and-true approach of telling her mother first, Martha waited until the kids went to bed that night, and giving as an excuse that she wanted to discuss some "women's matters," led Mammeh to the bathroom.

"So here vee are," her mama announced with her shy smile, when they sat facing one another on the toilet seat and lip of tub—her nice way of saying, I trust that the world isn't coming to an end.

Martha's heart beat wildly as she began.

"Vell, I kent say dot I'm heppy about it," was Mammeh's reaction when the thing was out.

Martha felt the tears coming—"But it's only a dinner."

Mammeh sadly shook her head. No, there's more to it than that, her eyes seemed to say, those familiar blue-green eyes. Dinner with strangers, with *goyim*, and partaking of unkosher food (even though they weren't that strict at home) signified that this child of hers, so unlike the others, was about to drift further away.

And she's got a point there, Martha was willing to concede...

Outside in the kitchen, Papa gave a yawn over his *Forverts*.

Mammeh's chin sank. "I kent promise anytink mit him dis time"—meaning that if he raised the roof again at yet another step in the wrong direction, there was no telling how it might end.

"But why? What am I doing that's so different now?"

Mammeh was quick to respond: "Nottink. He's just older, dot's all."

Older? What's that got to do with it! Martha protested inside, and from the depths of her being she wrenched herself violently away from him. Let me go! Let me be!...

So now we'll see what we'll see, she brooded a while later, lying beside little Fanny in the darkness.

It had been quiet so far back in their room, with only Mammeh's sensible voice audible from time to time. Now suddenly there was Papa shouting out—"*Vos nokh!*"—what next.

Now came an outpouring from him, in which Benny figured, certainly no favorite of either of them. "*Vos nokh!*" Papa shouted out again—what next.

Almost against her will, Martha began to imagine.

Next, Nokh: *A haggard, wretchedly-clad young woman is stepping along beside an office building in a heavy downpour, one of many with signs across their chests. Someone begins to chant, and the rest take it up, she among them*—"O*N STRIKE!* O*N STRIKE!*"

Next, Nokh: *The same girl, in black-and-white stripes, is on her hands and knees with a scrub brush. A grim-looking matron comes,*

152

The Strike

and ushers her to a waiting room full of other gaunt-faced girls in prison garb, each in the midst of a little group of whispering relatives.

Papa, whose hair has turned all white, cries out at the forlorn one just brought in—"Vos nokh!"

Back in the parlor, Mammeh had the floor again, and was speaking calmly but firmly.

She's probably using the same old argument, Martha figured—this is a free country, and the girl has a right to live her own life. I'm sure my mama'll manage it somehow in spite of the misgivings—Martha closed her eyes.

But then she opened them right up again, as a fresh scene arose in her mind: the one of protest against Triangle's fake benevolent society that Benny mentioned the other day.

It's mid-morning, and on the Ninth floor the machines are pounding away as usual.

Suddenly Jake Kline, with his gold-rimmed glasses and pointing finger of a nose, jumps up, and makes a mad dash for the bell button, which he presses down on HARD.

The rapid-fire stitching dies away, leaving only the motors... like empty hands.

Waxen-faced Morris Elzufin with his yappy mouth comes to stand boldly beside him.

"Peeple! Voikers!" Kline calls out.

There's a rush of feet outside the partition, and two snarling thugs come charging in with fists flying—"Sonofabitch! Bastard! I'll get you! I'll fix you!"

Knees are pumping. Elzufin's shirt gets ripped down the back. KER-RACK! *go Kline's specs, ground underfoot.*

But somehow the pointy nose manages to break away—"Peeple, voikers, look vat dey are doing to us!"

One of the brutes jumps Kline from behind. The awful pummeling begins all over again.

Yes, Martha realized, let those wealthy women set things in motion with their league, and as Benny said, that's what those rabble-rousers will have to look forward to once more.

That—and worse. She pictured the old one, scrawny Yetta and Greta, dark Olga, Raiseleh the crazy Rumanian, and herself all cringing to ward off more bone-shattering blows from those goons! Martha shuddered, close to tears—it must never come to that.

But now came an entirely new idea—and Bernstein, where would he be in all of that?

He's down front by Mary Leventhal's desk, leaning against the ledge with an elbow on it.

And how would he be feeling about it all?

Who knows, it's anybody's guess. *His head is a blank circle.*

MEETINGS

Just listen and see what they have to say, is Benny's final piece of advice.

Outside Number 23's back door on Greene Street, there's a slight edge to the air, hinting of autumn. Picture-perfect in a straw sailor hat with two navy ribbons hanging down and her own exclusive creation of Scotch plaid, pinched in at the waist and set off by cream-colored lace at the throat, Martha turns away from him.

Round the corner onto Washington Place she briskly goes, anticipating that ahead in the Square, the green of the trees will be dull and dryish, and that, who knows, a few sprays may already be lying on the street with their leaves crinkled up.

But what's this? Someone familiar—in a pale lime-green suit and a hat of sunflower yellow—has just stepped out of Number 23's front door. Why it's Sonny the helper (whose real name is Gerald or something like that).

Boy, Martha marvels, where does he get the money for such snappy-looking clothes? Can't come out of the pittance they pay him at Triangle, that's for sure.

The Strike

Having taken giant steps, Sonny is about to cross over to the Square's asphalt path beside the trees, while she's only halfway down the block, passing the entrance to the NYU building.

Maybe a woman, some older woman, is keeping him, it occurs to her. That's how many American *sheygetses*—gentile boys—get their start in life, they say. But it's also possible that he's simply a smart shopper like some other people, including yours truly, Martha reminds herself.

On the same course that she intends to follow—along Washington Square East to its south side—Sonny has outdistanced her by far now.

What's the rush anyway, is he going to see his woman, is that it, Martha wonders. Oh well, it's none of my business really. But possibly he simply lives far out somewhere and is running to catch the El on Sixth and get there fast, so he can spend the rest of the evening taking it easy.

Walking by the trees herself now, she spies the statue of Garibaldi further in, and the bench where she waited to go see Benny about the job that time—when was it, a year and a half ago. How silly I was then, to sit there tapping my toes in the freezing cold...like another person...

"Now howdya like that!" Martha exclaims, on turning into Washington Square South.

Sonny the Sheygets—in his bright yellow and light green—is standing on the top stair of a stoop a block or so down.

What can he be doing there, is that where his woman lives? If so, why doesn't he go in, why's he loitering there? No one home? And if that's the case, how come he hasn't got a key? Don't tell me she doesn't trust him.

Having made some headway, Martha is now coming up to the place, one of a number of slightly run-down three-story houses in a row.

And now she sees that he's paused there by the door—with his brown eyes, straight nose, and thin lips under the hat brim—simply to take in the view.

"Hello," she greets him, more shyly than she expected. "Is this where you hang your hat?"

Sonny smiles back, as shyly, it seems—"Yeah"—and motions upward to the top floor.

Martha also takes pleasure in the white presence of the Arch flanked by the fancy pink townhouses across the way for a moment. "It must be really beautiful from up there," she ventures at long last, meaning his place.

"Yes," he answers.

"Well, so long," she tells him, there seeming to be nothing further to say.

He nods, likewise.

There's an Irish saloon on the corner, with wilted green paper shamrocks in the window left over from St. Patrick's Day. Martha can't help looking back.

Still in the same place, Sonny feels her eyes on him, and smiles again.

Too bad, he just misses being handsome, she decides, moving on. The mouth should be fuller, and the upper lip needs an indentation. Also, the hair, which is wheaten as she recalls, ought to be a shade darker with that tan complexion.

Be that as it may, he's better-looking than Davey Goldstein any day—she pictures the settlement house boy puckering up his lips with the spit on them.

Of course—this seems to come from out of the blue—someone with a pair of sleepy eyes outlined by perfect eyebrows is another matter.

Martha's breath comes short. She stands stock still.

Well, now I've heard everything. Really, Martha, you can't be serious. You're stuck on a louse like that? On HIM? On Bernstein?

Please, Martha, say it isn't so. Why he's at least twice your age, and married too...with children...and a wife who's supposed to be very pretty, and almost as young as you are.

The Strike

I beg of you, Martha, anything but that. Say this is some kind of—

No, it's not, a soft voice insists deep down within her. It's not a joke.

A hop, skip, and a jump, and there Martha is, on the corner where Washington Square South turns into West Fourth.

Just as Elsie said, the restaurant is a few doors down on Macdougal, in the basement of a plum-colored building trimmed with chartreuse.

Once through the wrought-iron gate, Martha descends the crumbly stairs one by one with a fistful of Scotch plaid skirt clutched.

"Ooh!" A window has afforded a glimpse of candles flickering on tables, and people sitting quietly around them—which is a far cry from the brilliantly-lighted Rumanian eatery on Second Avenue that her folks like to go to, where loud exchanges of insults between the customers and the waiters are the rule.

"Martha, over here!" Elsie calls from her fatness and mole, as she steps in.

Her friend, in pink-and-blue, is at a table straight ahead with five older women, all smiling with creases round their noses and inquisitive eyes.

At a gesture from a young blonde at the counter, Martha removes her hat and receives a check for it.

"Come sit here," Elsie says, tapping the chair next to her, and begins making the introductions.

On the side opposite them sit Mary Dreier and Helen Marot…Miss Dreier with piercing blue eyes, honey-colored hair, and a granite chin…Miss Marot notable for steel-rimmed specs and a man's shirt and tie.

To the right, blinking good-naturedly, is the scrappy little redhead Rose Schneiderman…and beside her, Leonora O'Reilly, who is indeed handsome in a Gaelic sort of way, as Benny intimated.

Alone on the left is Miss Cora Black, remarkable for her green satin dress set off by sparkling diamonds in comparison to everyone else's bland summer colors and lack of glitter.

Martha hardly has a chance to get her bearings before this peculiar-looking chap, who seems to be all hair from head to chin, is before them with a pad and pencil.

Elsie jabs her with an elbow—"Whadya wanna drink? We've ordered gin fizzes."

What'll I do, Martha considers. The only alcoholic beverage she's ever imbibed has been Passover wine, doled out in sensible paternal doses.

The guy is ogling her through his glasses, and has a smirk on his face as if he were enjoying her discomfort.

"Water'll be fine," she says.

With all due apologies, a discussion begun before Martha arrived is resumed, and Miss Schneiderman, who had the floor, takes it again. "As I'm sure you've hoid me say, in de future I vould like to see vun big vomen's union"—which would include female workers from all over the world without regard to their level of skill. Only then could all their individual needs be seen to.

"I agree," Miss Marot, the one with the specs and tie pipes up, "only I'm still of the opinion that it should include men as well. We can't simply exclude them because they've excluded, and continue to exclude, us from their organizations. Look at it this way"—Miss Marot appeals to them all—"too much is at stake in the long run."

Miss Schneiderman turns to pretty Miss O'Reilly beside her—"Vat do you tink?"

Miss O'Reilly has to meditate on it for a moment. "I said I don't know before, and I really don't," she answers finally. Devoted to the cause of labor all her life long, time and again she has found herself being forced to agree with male workers when they say that women make poor union members—"for the simple reason that most of those I've known want to stay on the job only until

The Strike

they get married, and then all they're interested in is having babies and keeping house." With a snide smile, Miss O'Reilly tosses this last out in brogue: "It's sa deep, there's nah gittin' to the bottom of it."

"Hahahaha!" Miss Schneiderman lets out, with her little red head thrown back.

Martha is positively enthralled with the conversation, hardly able to believe her ears. It's wonderful—WONDERFUL! Intelligent talk by like-minded females of differing opinions is just what the doctor ordered, it seems.

Everyone looks to Miss Dreier now, she of the blue eyes, honey hair, and grim determination in her jaw. "Actually it doesn't make any difference vat form de ultimate organization takes," she begins, revealing a slight German accent. To her way of thinking—and she too has said this before—the main point of such a body would be that it provide workers, both male and female, with an opportunity for self-expression and to develop leadership abilities. "Be dot as it may"—the man is coming with the drinks, so she has to make haste—"vee must seize de moment ven and vhere it presents itself, and such a vun is now at hand."

So, something is definitely brewing, Martha cues herself.

"GIN FIZZ!" the hairy guy bellows, and smartly sets the tumblers down before each of them in turn. "Water."

"Now ladies"—it's Miss Dreier again, with the "waiter" hovering—"our liddle sisters have families vaiting for dem, so let's send for de food now, yes?"

They all know what they want, and tell the man one after the other.

Quickly scanning the blackboard on the wall, Martha's eye thankfully lights on roast chicken.

The odd fellow having gone off with his pad, Miss Dreier raises her glass—"Let's trink to our success, shall vee?"

"Hear, hear," Miss Marot seconds.

Elsie elbows Martha again—"Didje hear about old man Rosen?" Word has it that he threw in the towel this morning, and that the strikers are indeed going to get everything they demanded—"higher piece rates, union shop, de woiks."

That's really swell, Martha joys to herself, genuinely delighted. Wait till Benny hears.

Miss Dreier levels those blue eyes at her—"How vould you feel if de same ting vere to happen at Triangle?"

"Me?" Martha says, and falls to searching for an answer.

Miss Marot, who was lending an ear to Miss Black, murmuring something about how much her Papa, a broker, might be persuaded to contribute, adds her bespectacled eyes—"We understand that your father and uncle are in business for themselves, and that what you earn at the shop is pin money, whereas as you know, everyone else—"

Miss Schneiderman and Miss O'Reilly, who have been chatting together, quiet down.

Even the waiter or owner or whatever, who has come to collect the empty drinks, seems to be holding his breath.

"Well," Martha begins—and seeks within herself anew, probing a chasm, wide and deep…until a dim echo from the past arises like the refrain from a half-forgotten song, One must kiss the soil.

"Well," she begins again—and now her newly-discovered *feeling* for Bernstein flutters away, along with thoughts of safety for Benny and the crew. "If it ever comes to that, if it really does, I think that I could be counted on to help."

It's a revelation to her as well as to them—and the waiter as well, whose eyes are absolutely popping.

Whatever is the matter with the guy, Martha worries. I do hope I'm not gonna have trouble with his HANDS or something, when he serves me.

"Well, Hippolyte," Miss Marot sort of sneers, obviously annoyed with his dawdling there too, "are you going to bring us our dinner, or do we have to go marching into your kitchen and bring it out ourselves!"

The man clicks his heels and bows stiffly from the waist like a Prussian—"Your wish is my command, Madam."

He certainly is different, Martha confides to herself. I don't believe I've ever beheld anyone quite like him.

To pass the time, Miss Dreier asks after Miss O'Reilly's adopted little girl, Alice, who seems to have been feeling poorly of late.

Martha is disappointed—is that it, is that the end of serious conversation? So what did they want of me? Just that, an admission like that?

"WHO GETS THE SCHNITZEL?" It's the dippy one, with three plates.

Nora's "big sister," Miss Perkins, is the next topic to be covered, Miss Marot wanting to know how *she* is.

Yes, I guess it is the end, Martha's forced to admit, feeling robbed of her secret, like a nut of its kernel. And what's going on, what are they up to?

Back with the last two dishes, the man gives Martha's an extra wipe with his side-towel before setting it down.

"*Bon appétit,*" Miss Dreier pronounces, and they all fall to.

"Mm, the veal is good," Miss O'Reilly says. "Try some, Helen"—and cutting off a piece, she reaches over to deposit it on Miss Marot's plate.

"Thank you," Helen gulps, in the middle of a swallow, and passes her a slice of duck in exchange.

"May I offer you a liddle stuffed peppah?" Miss Schneiderman hopefully inquires of Martha.

"Much obliged, but I'd rather not," Martha replies, trying not to be unkind. Fowl that's been slaughtered without the blood being drawn from it is quite enough for one evening, and lurking in the stuffing may be some *khazer*—pigmeat—which has yet to soil her lips.

Miss Schneiderman seems to comprehend in her smiley way...

Miss Black is the first to put her cutlery down—"I'm not very hungry, had a late lunch"—and her hand brings out from the purse in her lap a slim gold case, from which she extracts a cigarette with a special look to it.

The waiter, happening by, produces a match, and strikes it alight with his thumbnail.

Miss Black nods, sucking in her cheeks, then waves off a blue cloud, exhaling.

Martha tries hard not to stare: a woman at the same table as her smoking. What would Papa say? Why he'd be fit to be tied.

Miss Black, who has a small round face like an apple, with several folds to her eyelids, notices, and returns the stare. Then her expression becomes mushy, like Davey Goldstein's when he's about to kiss—and she drawls, "It must be aw-aw-ful having to drudge away in a factory all day."

Martha feels the blood rise to her cheeks—she's got a lot of nerve. Who does she think she is, in her shiny green dress with the bluish diamonds in such bad taste.

The maniacal waiter-chap stays for the outcome, with Miss Black's left-overs balanced on a palm in mid-air.

Martha looks pointedly at Miss Rich-Bitch. At the same time something else rises up in her, and again it is something lost that has been found—"I can only speak for myself. I *like* what I do. I *don't* consider it drudgery."

Everyone begins talking at once to cover awkwardness.

Grinning like a hyena, the Meshugener ecstatically twirls the plate round on his fingertips.

❦

The party of women and girls are finished with dessert, and everyone else is gone.

Marking time from his peephole in the kitchen, Hippolyte focuses on the outspoken one in her Scotch plaid with the lace collar, who is

The Strike

spooning custard into her sweet little mouth. To think that such profound words should issue from the likes of her, after all nothing but a bourgeoise. Imagine it—"I *like* what I do. I *don't* consider it drudgery." Why he could have swept the pussy cat up in his arms and given her a great big hug when she uttered them! "Oh-oh!"—he still can.

As for the Protagonist—his gaze shifts to the woman in green satin.

Having taken leave of the others, she's approaching Liebling at her counter—with a wad of bills in a silver money clip.

"That's right, pay," he mutters. "That's all you're good for, cunt."

At the door waits her chauffeur, tall and pasty-faced, in a visored cap and form-fitting tunic with balloon pants.

"Bye, Mary, Helen!" she calls. "See you soon!"

"Go already," Hippolyte growls. "Get your shitty ass outta here."

The chauffeur reaches out to grasp the woman's arm, which is slender to the point of seeming frail.

We'll fix you one day, Hippolyte broods, you and your kind. Yes, one day soon when things are different, THE LEAST, THE VERY LEAST YOU'LL DO IS GET UP STAIRS BY YOURSELF!

"Meanwhile, go screw with him," Hippolyte mutters—and lets his imagination run rampant on the subject—

Intent on doing his job, the chauffeur turns the key in her limousine's ignition, and steers a course for home, her father's stately mansion in Westchester.

The only thing is, when they pull up at the front door, she directs him to continue on along the driveway to a lane leading into an apple orchard.

"Stop!" she cries, when they are well in among the trees and away from prying eyes.

He obeys, and dims the lights.

"Come here!" she barks.

He clumps out into the darkness, lushly perfumed by ripening apples, and opening the door to the back, slips in beside her onto cushioned velvet.

"Take it out," she orders.

His fingers work at his fly buttons—his hand brings forth the thing she means, flabby like rolled pastry dough.

"Is that the best you can do!" she demands. "Is that really it!"

He tries pumping on it. But in vain: it remains a lumpen lump.

"Disgusting," she scolds, and working to get the saliva together, she spits at it—POOH!...

The real chauffeur and his dam are above on the sidewalk—the Little Bourgeoise with the fresh mouth is the next to leave, together with her tubby sidekick.

Farewell for now, my chickadee, Hippolyte bids her in his mind, as they're saying goodbyes. We'll meet again one day, I assure you. Yes, on that same better day, when you and I will rise up with all the others who have come to like conclusions, and reveal ourselves, as if by some grand design...

The two girls gone, it's the turn of Rosey the Redhead and Nora Nice now.

Ta ta, ha ha—they're out the door.

Now what—Hippolyte narrows his eyes.

On their feet, the big cheeses Mary Blue Eyes and Helen Specs-and-Tie are having a few last words together.

What the hell are they up to, Hippolyte puzzles. Some kind of action at the girls' place of employ obviously, but what exactly, and when?

Not that it really matters, doomed as it is from the start, as any such stratagem would be that's based on relatively minor matters like wages, health care, and working conditions, instead of the Real Issues. Still, I should strive to keep the Comrade and Sasha informed about their moves because—well, simply because we ought to know.

Liebling is about to go over to the table to begin the clean-up.

The Strike

No, let me, Hippolyte waves her off.

"Our Nora's looking vell, don't you tink?" Mary is saying as he nears them.

"Yes, that she is," Helen agrees, "only I do wish she'd begin forming a few opinions of her own, and take a stand now and then for a change."

Hippolyte shakes out a soiled napkin, and drapes it over his arm, like a dead fish.

Mary snickers—"Dot Cora's some handful. I don't tink anyvun liked her."

"Well, handful or not, they better get used to her, and the others too," Helen warns. "We need the publicity those women'll bring us, to say nothing of the cash, and the sooner everyone realizes this—"

C'mon already, what's going on, Hippolyte nags to himself, as he gathers the dessert dishes.

"So how do you feel about de girl?" Mary inquires.

"Well, she certainly is the right type—"

"But?"

"But let's face it, she's a little too independent for our purposes, as I told you I rather imagined she'd be, and you just now heard yourself."

Ja, ja, Hippolyte echoes internally, those union-lovin' folks never have been ones for recognizing true talent when they see it.

Blue Eyes and Specs-and-Tie have begun ambling toward Liebling for their hats.

"How's Caroline?"—it's Mary again. "And ven are you both gonna come have dinner with Fran and me?"...

And that's that, Hippolyte sighs.

There's just these dishes to do, and that's it—he's back in the kitchen with the load from their table.

But what's this? A new party has just come down into the restaurant—a broad-chested older woman wearing a purple-plumed Merry Widow hat, and a mulatto girl with ginger hair in pink frills.

Hippolyte bustles out—"Evenin', ladies"—and leads them to a clean table close by the kitchen.

Purple Feather squints up at the menu—"We'll have—the peppers."

"Right." Hippolyte hurries inside and gets busy transferring two orders of the luscious green things from their baking pan to a small pot.

"All in a day's work," he croons, lighting the stove. Something makes him look up.

Liebling has left her counter, and is heading his way.

The sauce from the peppers begins to show a little life. He takes a spoon and stirs.

Liebling slinks in, and comes to stand beside him. Her head finds the soft spot between his shoulder and chest, and nestles there.

Some ballad or lullaby drifts into his mind, something from long ago that his mother or the other Anna, his stepmother and first love, used to sing...and he hums.

"HEY!" a voice like a boy's voice shrills out, making the crockery almost ring.

It's Purple Feather, glaring at him two-fistedly from the doorway.

She opens her mouth again—"Hey, what is this, a restaurant or a house of assignation?"

Hippolyte gets all on fire. What, ASSIGNATION! She's calling my love a whore? BUT HOW DARE SHE! Setting Liebling aside, he grabs up a cooking fork and levels it at the intruder—"Out! Outta here! GET OUT OF MY KITCHEN!"

"Okay-ay, okay-ay!" Purple squeals, fending off the pointy prongs from her copious bosoms with a beefy hand. "We jes want our grub, that's all."

The Strike

"And you'll get it," Hippolyte snaps. "Just keep your shirt on and a civil tongue in your mouth."

"A coconut," Purple grumbles, back in her seat, and pats her young companion's arm consolingly.

"Inverts," Hippolyte mumbles. What goes on here tonight anyway, we've had one batch of them after another. He clunks the spoon after giving the peppers another stir.

Well, one really shouldn't fault them so severely—his rage is passing. As the Comrade has pointed out on more than one occasion, inverts can't help being the way they are, and since their problems, if such they be, baffle even the experts, they're more to be pitied than anything else.

He slides an arm round Liebling's waist, ivory-hued silk oh so smooth. The peppers are fully alive now.

"Dearest," he murmurs, "go thou upstairs and prepare thyself for my coming...and thine."

CHAPTER 8

"Har! Har! Har!" Benny roared out, after Martha told him about everything the next day at lunch. "Dot's de vay dey are, de socialisten and deir friends," he explained, referring to the long faces that everyone pulled when she gave that disgusting Miss Black her comeuppance. "Dey alvays vant you should hate de job foist, so den later you'll loin to luv it."

"Well, one thing's for sure, I didn't exactly make a hit with those league women," Martha gave it as her opinion—the ride downtown after with Elsie certainly seeming to confirm it. Not her usual chatterbox self, the girl had said simply that she would see Martha around when they parted company, meaning in all likelihood not to look for her on the corner anymore.

"Don't let it bodder you, *Tsatskele*," the old one offered, with a little pat. Those ladies were clearly a bunch of amateurs, and the result was going to be lots and lots of bungling with much good money poured down the drain and maybe even a few heads unnecessarily broken.

"And Rosen?" Martha reminded him teasingly.

Not at all in a joking mood, Benny shrugged—"Rosen is Rosen." But to repeat, if those women and their associates tried to get something like that started here, it would be an entirely different matter.

Why Harris and Blanck would eat the *drek* from their own behinds first—Martha should pardon his expression—before yielding to pressure of any kind, but most especially if it came from a bunch of meddling socialist-inspired outsiders.

Bernstein stepped through the door—that oft-complained-about opening in the partition, his invention apparently, through which only one person could pass at a time.

Martha watched as he squeezed through the aisle, narrow down there because of the partition jutting out, and made for the bell button, movements so familiar that she could just about follow them with her eyes closed.

It still seems incredible, she thought, beholding the sleepy lids, arched brows, and sinuous mouth, now dear to her. How could he be on THEIR side?

Benny had just washed down with hot tea the last bite of his salami on mustard-drenched rye.

"Not that it matters, but what do you suppose those women wanted with me?" she asked.

Her good old friend's shoulders rose and fell again—"*Ver veyst*"—who knows...

Several days later, just after the break began, came a piece of news that was truly electrifying—the operators at Leiserson's on Seventeenth Street had gone out! This from the girl behind Martha, who told her to pass the word along.

"So? *Nu?*" Martha taunted Benny. Now what did her fine-feathered-friend have to say about that?

His runny blue eyes with their red-and-yellow whites regarded her with disdain—Louie Leiserson was second only to Harris and Blanck when it came to being a toughie and holding out against demands. "Beleef you me"—he had to shout to be heard over the yackety-yack of the Kline and Elzufin crowd in the rear—"DOSE PEOPLE VILL MARCH MIT DEIR SIGNS TILL DEIR FEET FALL OFF!"

The Strike

Once again Martha had a vision of shadowy female figures parading up and down beside a dark office building with the rain falling in bucketsful...and she shivered as if her own thin soles were sodden with the wet and cold.

From that day forward, the air at the shop was constantly charged with a kind of New Year's Eve euphoria, a war about to break out at any moment, it would seem.

Benny felt it as well as Martha, and it wasn't long before she sensed that he was considering some step of his own.

Finally, after closing on Saturday, he proposed that they stop off at a drug store on Broadway before going home, so he could discuss something with her in private.

"You know, you're like mine own child," he began, when they were perched on stools at the fountain and sipping on tall, foaming ice cream sodas.

Since he'd lost three children to diphtheria at an early age, it wasn't difficult now, given such a prelude, to guess what was coming.

Sure enough—"Me, I'm an old man with mehbee a few more years left," but she, Martha, had her whole life before her. And now that it really looked as if there were going to be trouble at Triangle, wouldn't it be better if she took those *goldne hentelekh* of hers—golden hands—and went to work somewhere else for a while.

It happened that his wife had some connections in white goods—underwear—he continued, and all he had to do was say the word and she'd put out feelers, which would almost for a certainty result in something suitable turning up.

"Don't enser now, only tink about it," Benny tried to pacify. And his look added: I'm sure your folks would want it—who knows, they might even end up thinking better of me for it.

"I'll do that," Martha agreed. But already at the trolley stop, with his back receding before her, she was saying to herself, Not on your life, dear friend. Why, to go now would be tantamount to walking out on you and leaving you to face everything without me—which on no account could she do. Another thing, she'd be missing any new developments—yes, and the chance to become involved, which I do believe I would, as I told those league ladies.

There was, of course, another reason. But that one she didn't care to go into just yet...

Back at the shop the next day and for quite a few thereafter, everyone kept saying that it was just a matter of time. However, while the picket line at Leiserson's showed no signs of weakening and Louie the *Shmegege*—jackass—was beginning to tear his few remaining hairs out, a week passed and then another with it all quiet at Triangle.

Finally, though, the time came. It was Saturday, September 25th, and Anna Gullo the forelady had just pressed the bell for quitting when there was Jake Kline's voice ringing out as the machines died away—"Say, Mistah Boinsteen!"

Everyone in the place lowered their voices. Those who were on their feet sort of froze there. All eyes shifted to Bernstein, who'd come to stand beside Anna.

"*Nu*, dere we are," Benny muttered to himself, with a shake of his shaggy head.

"What can I do for yuh, Jake?" Bernstein called back, as if the two of them were standing on opposing mountain peaks.

Kline threw down the gauntlet—"Vhat can you do? I'll tell you vhat you can do, Mistah Boinsteen. You can call a meeting of de employee benevolent association."

"A meeting of the association?" Bernstein countered, with seeming good nature and a slightly lofty tone. "Jake, whatever dya want a meeting for?"

Kline's nose between the specs seemed pointier than ever, and the trace of a smile played on his lips—"Vell, being dat ya been taking dues outta de pay envelopes for a quite a vile now, vee vant to know

The Strike

how much's in de till, and undeh vhat conditions a poisson can draw from it."

Only Bernstein's mouth moved—"The association is Mr. Harris's department. I'll have to refer the matter to him, and he'll come and speak to you about it, okay?"

"Fair enough, vee'll be vaiting," Kline responded, there being nothing else to say under the circumstances.

Martha caught a glimpse of Elzufin gloating, and of Elsie nearby him, with her mole all scrunched up, grinning.

"It's a bed business, a BED business," Benny murmured, and his old head wagged as if he had the palsy.

And him, Bernstein? Martha wondered.

Oblivious to the loud discussions going on all around and people beginning to leave, she looked to him, still there beside the bell, staring into space as usual—and suddenly she realized a thing or two. Even though his brother Jake and cousin Morris enjoyed a certain privileged status as operators, Bernstein, as an in-law of Mr. Blanck's, had to feel caught in between...was a man divided.

Martha was very sorry—I wouldn't want to be in his shoes for anything!

An urge arose to pass her hand across his brow to smooth it...

Who could sleep that night and the next. Coming in the following Monday, Martha felt like Rip van Winkle, with little recollection of how she had spent the past two days.

As soon as the bell sounded at eight sharp, there were Mr. Harris and Bernstein stepping off one of the passenger elevators down front. Striding briskly past the cloakroom and along the side aisle, they resembled birds in formation, except for big boss Harris's being resplendent in a light brown suit with a peach shirt and green tie while Bernstein wore only his usual greys.

The two of them ending, with a little extra maneuvering, on either side of the bell button, Harris's eyes picked out Kline in his seat—"Jake, I understend dot you ver inqviring about our benefit association."

"Dot's right," Kline answered, and sprang up.

There was a general holding of breath—only audible was a buzzing whisper from someone translating into Italian.

Mr. Harris smiled, which somehow made his ears stick out. "Vell, Jake, I don't see dot it's any of your affair really, seeing as how you don't belonk to de association."

"I'm esking for my goils," Kline shot right back.

"Me too," Elzufin made himself heard from his seat.

"*Ikh oykh*," an old one down front added his voice—he as well.

Mr. Harris's eyes sought the ceiling for recollection. "Ven I lest looked, dere vas a liddle ovah tree hundred dollahs. Mr. Levine can gif yuh an exact figah if yuh vant it." According to the rules, when a person died, a certain amount was allotted to his family for burial expenses, provided that the person was a member in good standing of the association at the time of his death.

Kline straightened up to his full height—"De members vant to change de rules." With the High Holy Days almost upon them, some operators, normally hard-up because of the small amount of money they made there, were finding it especially difficult. "Vee vould like it to be dot in a case of extreme hardship, a poisson can hef ten dollahs if he esks fuh it."

"Dot's out of de qvestion," Mr. Harris quickly responded. "If anybody is so short of kesh, he can borrow from us."

"Borrow?" a voice full of emotion rang out from somewhere. "A loan? He vants us to take out a loan mit him?" another echoed him, equally choked up.

"So dey can be in hock to you fuh de rest of deir lives?" Kline took up the cry. "So you can take out more yet from de envelope?"

Angry lines appeared on Mr. Harris brow, indeed more or less as Martha had sketched them that time—"Take it or leave it." He folded his arms purposefully—"And now I consider de matteh closed." If anyone cared to discuss it further, they could do it later, on their own time—"I'M R-R-RUNNING A BUSINESS HEAH!"

Bland as ever, Bernstein gave a high sign—the motors roared into being.

"*Oy vey*, from bed to voise," Benny moaned, rocking back and forth.

What next, Martha caught herself wondering (like Papa!). What?—feeling a little empty from being left out of everything.

Later on at closing time, she and Benny found themselves riding down on the same elevator as Kline and some of his people, along with Raiseleh the Rumanian, who pushed in behind them.

"So, Benny, some doinks, hah," Kline teased in his best mocking tone.

"Ben-ny Ben-do-vah," singsonged one of his girls, a very small one, who looked to be under age.

"*Shah*," Kline told her—keep quiet—and growing serious, he informed Benny, in Yiddish, that a meeting was going to take place later at a certain union hall downtown. "How 'bout it, vould you come?"—meaning with his crew, of course.

"No, denks," Benny curtly replied.

Now I don't know about that, Martha thought. While annoyed at Kline's incivility, she felt that the old one ought to have asked her opinion at least before declining such an invitation.

"Look, it's important," Kline argued. This was no time for petty annoyance over a little harmless fun. "Everybody in de shop vill be dere"—except maybe some of the *'Talyene*.

"No"—Benny's mind was made up—"denks again."

Martha was really irked now—after all, what if *I* wanted to go? But just as she was about to say something, there was the same singsonging Kline-girl glaring at her.

"Goody-goody," that one sneered, and gave her a sharp bump with her hips.

Caught by surprise, Martha could only touch the hurt spot—but Raiseleh, beside her, saw this as a truly hostile act not to be taken lightly.

"Vat you do!" she cried out, and made a rush for the Kline-girl. "I KEEL YOU!"—they became locked in a fierce struggle of shoves and kicks.

"Fight! Fight!" people called, as they would have "fire." "Stop! Stop it!" Kline yelled—he and Benny together wrenched the pair of them apart, going at it tooth and nail.

"SHE'S CRAZY!" the Kline-girl sobbed, clutching her throat.

Kline put a protective arm around her. "You vanna fight?" he barked at Raiseleh, whom Benny and Martha had a firm hold on. "Go fight in de ring fuh money—or bettah, klobber dose bloodsuckas, de bosses!"

So, another reality, Martha sighed, quite shaken by it all, including this final injustice of Kline's blaming her "champion" solely for the fracas.

"Thank you," she whispered in Raiseleh's ear at a certain point, as they continued on down to the street.

Raiseleh gave a show of dimples. "Schmenk you," she mimicked disparagingly, probably unaccustomed to expressions of gratitude.

THE DAY

Something is different, Martha senses, riding back up to the shop the next morning. Even when it's early like this, one usually sees a few others from Triangle on the elevator, but curiously today there are just people from the factories on the lower floors.

Inside, once she's there on Nine, the feeling of differentness changes into a kind of emptiness—and for good reason. The only operators present besides herself are a sprinkling of babushka'd Italian women and girls down front, uneasily waiting for the rest of their groups to arrive.

The Strike

It certainly is odd, Martha acknowledges, not without a certain strange elation, and heads for her machine...the Machine whose every nick and scratch she knows like the back of her hand.

But where is everyone? The clock above the bell button is going to strike eight at any moment.

Ah—the old one just trotted in from the vestibule, and hard on his heels is Raiseleh, chomping on a hard pretzel, followed by Yetta and Greta, with their pale, thin cheeks also working.

"Any idea what's going on?" Martha asks in a low voice, when he's beside her.

"Soich me," he answers. Then stowing away his lunch in its paper bag, he reaches below to the wicker basket for a sleeve-setting left unfinished yesterday.

From somewhere outside comes a sort of rhythmic murmur.

Martha gets up, and slipping past the twins, goes to see what it is from the windows on that side, which look onto Washington Place. Benny is right behind her, with the same idea.

I know, I just know what it is, she tells herself, raising the sash. Yes indeed—in comes a chorus of voices chanting, "On Strike! On Strike!" She bends over the motor casing in front of the sill and puts her head out—yes oh yes. There's a line of people marching with signs beside the building—"On Strike! On Strike!"

They must have voted for it at the meeting last night, Martha figures, a little disgruntled at not having been there.

But there's no sense crying over spilt milk, she quickly cautions. For very urgently a decision has to be made now as to what they're going to do.

Martha looks to Benny, who has been taking it all in with more shakes of the head and "tsuh-tsuh's" from the next window.

For a moment, while the two of them stand there facing one another, he becomes in her eyes the doddering old butt of Kline's cruel teasing, whom she towers head and shoulders over. But the next instant he is her good friend again, and more than that,

Raphael ("Rayfeel") Benowitz, crew leader par excellence, who hired her against his will and didn't live to regret it.

"Vee kent stay here," he says simply.

Martha's heart gives a leap—he's echoed her sentiments exactly. Come what may, they must throw in their lot with Kline and his bunch, there's no other choice.

"De only ting is, vee'll hef to be very careful," the old one warns. Bernstein is probably downstairs with his *shtarkers*—goons—and in all likelihood they're guarding the back door on Greene Street to prevent anyone from sneaking in to do mischief, to say nothing of sneaking out like themselves. So the best plan, it seems to Benny, is to try leaving by the front door, opening onto Washington Place, which for a variety of reasons might yet be unwatched.

As for getting there, the men operating the elevators to the lobby aren't likely to cooperate, so the only possibility is the adjacent stairway. But the question is, can one get through to those stairs, whose door is sometimes locked?

Benny beckons to Raiseleh—"*Kum aher*"—and sends her to see what's what.

Raiseleh is back in a trice—alas, the door's locked, and the key, usually left hanging by a string from the knob, is missing.

"*A khalerye zol zey trefn!*" Benny curses, reminding Martha of Papa when he heaps cholera on people. "But we're not finisht yet," the old one assures her, and puts his thinking cap back on.

"Yuh," he says after a little. They'll go down to Eight by way of the Greene Street stairs and try there for those leading down to the lobby.

"*Kum!*"—he waves. And off they all scurry—he in the lead, Raiseleh following, Yetta and Greta behind her, and Martha, with her skirt clutched like them, bringing up the rear.

Through the partition door each passes in turn, Martha giving a last look at the *'Talyene*, very gloomy now with their eyes down.

It's only a matter of the stair door next to the elevators, and down they all go, four pairs of ladies' heels clicking.

The Strike

Martha catches up with them in Eight's vestibule, as the old one is instructing Raiseleh before dispatching her again: to wit, if Miss Lipshitz the checker should be at her desk, just tell her that the toilet upstairs is broken and you *darf geyn pishn*—have to go pee.

Raiseleh comes back with good news this time: the door is open, and Lipshitz is nowhere to be seen.

Now comes the really hard part: for all five of them to get safely past a few cutters, who, according to Raiseleh, are standing with their backs turned at the windows overlooking Greene Street.

"Okay," Benny directs, "you foist dis time"—meaning Raiseleh, which is only fair, she having taken the risks as scout. Martha, Greta, and Yetta would follow, with him last. They'd meet on the first landing, and then go together the rest of the way down.

Martha gives Raiseleh a running start, then after starting off down the side aisle herself, takes a fast peek at the Greene Street windows, where a handful of men are leaning out with their fat *tokheses*—behinds—sticking up, which makes her hurry along the more.

Rounding the corner by Miss Lipshitz's desk, she recalls the select group that used to gather for lunch around the same spot upstairs—Bernstein's brother Jake and cousin Morris, and little Edie Harris the niece. Most likely they're home "sick" today, or else hiding among the muckamucks, their protectors, on Ten.

Raiseleh is waiting on the other side of the stair door, and then there's Greta and Yetta coming up right behind, both of them giggling and all out of breath.

"*Kum, shnel,*" Benny hisses the next moment, and takes the lead once more.

Down, down they go, with heels tick-ticking again...to Seven, Six, Five, Four...and finally the lobby.

"*Shnel, shnel!*" Benny urges over his shoulder, as he scampers through it.

Greta holds the door for Martha—and that's it, they're all on the outside, huffing and puffing with eyes ready to start from their heads.

The last few people on the picket line have just passed by. "Ho!" one of them calls out, happening to notice the newcomers.

Others turn their heads, and then the rest—and then with a resounding whoop, the whole pack takes off for them.

Smack on Martha's cheek goes a pair of fat lips flanked by a furry mole, Elsie of course. "You did it after all! You did it!" Kline is screaming to Benny with tears in his eyes.

"BECK IN DE LINE!" booms a man, presumably a union man with a megaphone, from somewhere. "GET BECK IN DE LINE!"

Still jubilant, they're all about to re-form themselves when suddenly a fresh cry is heard—"Hey look, de *Talyene*! De 'Talyene've come out too!"—who indeed have, and are huddled just outside the door smiling shyly from their babushkas.

"Now howdya like that," Martha murmurs, as everyone goes running to hug and kiss them now.

"PEOPLE PLEEEZE!" the official voice pleads.

Somehow the line takes shape again—and then *slap slap slap*, all feet hammer on the pavement—"ON STRIKE! ON STRIKE!" everyone hollers out.

Stepping along with Benny, Martha is absolutely ecstatic. This is the life! This is what real living's all about!

Approaching the corner of Greene, those in the lead all at once come to a standstill, causing everyone behind them to pull up short.

The reason is Bernstein, Martha perceives, who has apparently just come from the back door.

Bernstein's eyes, those usually sleepy eyes, are wide, as if to say, What did I do to you all to deserve this, how could you have walked out on me like this?

Reading the look too, the crowd explodes into laughter—"Yahahahaha!" And rising above it all is a voice, clear and shrill—"PIZDA MATI!"—Raiseleh cursing his mother's secret parts in choice Rumanian.

Oh, the hurt, Martha sees. The circle of a face that she was at a loss to fill in once—Bernstein's face in her mind—is blank no more.

The Strike

When the big day was over, Martha was once more faced with the problem of making the folks understand, especially since things could very well take a turn for the worse in days to come, with summonses issued and arrests made, a regular occurrence at Leiserson's for some time now. Mulling it over on the way home, she decided to tell her mother first as of old, leaving Mammeh to accomplish the impossible with her father again.

Papa was still at the store and sisters Dinah and Pauline at their settlement house clubs when she walked through the door, so Martha thought it best to strike while the iron was hot, while the maternal hand was giving the final touches to a heavenly-smelling mushroom-and-barley soup.

"Vell, I kent say dot I'm altogedder surprisedt," Mammeh confessed when the new truth was out, having been kept abreast of what was happening at Rosen's and Leiserson's, as well as Triangle, by Benny's old friend, her notions man. "De qvestion is, are you sure dot's vhat you vant?"

Their eyes met, and for a long moment Mammeh's familiar aquamarine pupils with the black dots looked deeply into hers.

Martha spoke up at last—"Yes, I am, Mammeh."

Later that night, listening in the dark beside little Fanny, she heard only low murmuring back in the parlor—indicating that either my good old mama's really a wizard, or Papa has at last truly thrown up his hands.

The next day found him his usual self, a little distant but cordial enough.

So that's it. Martha breathed her habitual sigh of relief— however it was managed, I'm free.

On Washington Place that morning, strike leader Jake Kline made it clear to all assembled that everything would be on the fair and square, with everyone doing their share of the *shver arbet*—picket duty—each day, and spending the rest of the time helping out with this and that at a rented hall on St. Mark's Place.

Nodding at every other word close by him was Abe Baroff of the Waistmakers' union, whose rimless glasses and crinkly blond hair together with the suit, shirt, and tie made him look just like a Yankee banker. Anyway, so Olga, their collar setter, jokingly remarked to Martha and Benny when they ran into her.

In the days that followed, this Baroff became a familiar figure on the curbside, where he was forever haranguing one and all parading by him "to get it over with and join up already." Such a step seemed much to be desired by Martha, who felt that membership in the union's larger body would bring them all a certain measure of security. But she turned out to be the only one in favor of the idea, everybody else, including Benny, regarding their differences with Harris and Blanck as a family argument to be settled exclusively by the parties involved.

Another daily sight on Washington Place was a deluxe white touring car, parked on the other side of the street. Usually to be found in it, besides the tall and stately Inez Milholland, the owner, were representatives of the Women's Trade Union League, especially Helen Marot, who was constantly engaged in dictating news releases and the like to a public stenographer.

Joining them from time to time were other "observers" on the order of that dreadful Miss Black, who never seemed to get their fill of staring at the doings across the way from behind the car's closed windows. Now and then one of those members of the Mink Brigade plucked up the courage to come over and march up and down a few times with a sign—just to brag about it to friends later, Martha and Benny supposed. Once the numbers on the line were augmented by a gorgeous *goy* named Max Eastman, who was a minister's son and very sweet on Miss Milholland, it was bruited about.

The Strike

The police, of course, were also in evidence, with a pair of them stationed almost from the beginning at the two doors, so as to assure Mr. Harris's and Mr. Blanck's unmolested arrival and departure in their chauffeured limousines. However, it wasn't long before one of those black paddy wagons was also on the scene, ready to whisk away some hapless individual hand-picked by one of Bernstein's goons, which was soon happening at least once every day. That is, sauntering out the building, the guy would suddenly lurch into his intended prey on the line and begin complaining loud and long about his right to go peacefully about his business on God's free sidewalk. Whereupon the officers in the wagon would apprehend the poor victim, who was nine-times-out-of-ten a girl, and haul her off to the Jefferson Market Courthouse, where she'd be thrown into a jail cell, full of shady ladies, to await trial—unless she were able to post bail, of course.

Happily, things seldom came to that pass, for right behind the Black Maria would zoom the white touring car, expertly handled by Greek goddess Milholland, with Helen Specs-and-tie hurriedly counting out the "ransom money" into honey-haired Mary's capable hands.

Noticing that the *shtarkers* usually singled out poorly-clad girls, Martha took to dressing with more than deliberate care, and in that way, she figured, managed to escape that fate, as did Raiseleh and the twins, onto whose less promising clothes she sewed little decorative doodads.

Bernstein. Every so often of a morning on turning the corner from Greene with the line, she spied *him* walking up Washington Place from the Square and probably the Sixth Avenue El beyond. Nearer and nearer *he* came—usually in summer blue, with a straw hat on—as she, pace-for-pace beside the old one, advanced in *his* direction. But each time on *his* closer approach, it was to pass everyone by as if *he* didn't want anything further to do with them—herself included, alas.

BOBE MAYSE *A Tale of Washington Square*

In bed at night, she yearned to touch her lips to those eyes so obstinately refusing to look.

MID-OCTOBER, END OF THE THIRD WEEK

There's a faint chill in the air that softly fans the cheeks as one heads toward the Square.

The shift will soon be over for Martha and Benny, moving along now with the same breeze at their backs.

Both sides of Washington Place are all in shadow, while up ahead the tall, slender buildings peculiar to Broadway are bright gold from the sun's last rays.

"How're you doing?" Martha inquires, all too conscious that he's not been up to snuff today.

"Fine, just fine," Benny assures. "Mine tootsies hoit, dot's all"—and when a man's foot aches, so fares the rest of him.

"You going home afterward?"

That he certainly is—the missus has plans for him, he's supposed to work on the pieces with her. And how about her, *Tsatskele*?

"Well, there's nothing doing at the hall"—so Martha guesses she'll stop in at the union and see if that nice Miss Schneiderman or whoever's on duty from the League needs a hand with something.

He's all admiration—"I gotta hend it to yuh, *keyn eyn hore*, you're a strong goil"—and he follows it up by spitting, *Pooh-pooh*, to chase the evil eye away.

As they near the corner, spots of sunlit sidewalk take on a diamond-like glitter, and the rows of glass blocks running alongside the building, which allow light into the basement, shine a dull mother-of-pearl.

"So how do you feel about everything now?" Martha asks at long last—that is, about their chances of winning here at Triangle, now that they've all held out for so long.

"Vin?" Her old friend's cheeks with the stubble wrinkle up in a wry smile. "Doink isn't enough? You vanta vin too?"

The Strike

Martha's quite serious—"But of course." After all, why else have they undertaken all this except to win?

Well then, if that's her position, he doesn't know what to say because— The idea seems to strike him for the first time—because to him there isn't any such thing as winning really.

"You see—" But his command of English just isn't adequate and he has to finish what he's trying to bring out in Yiddish…

"Winning is like beauty," Martha translates, disappointed but marveling. "It's in the eyes of the beholder."

❦

No one could have been more surprised than Mammeh at Eli's reaction to Martha's becoming involved in the strike, which was indeed mild as mild could be.

But of all things, on their waking one morning a month or so later it turned out that husband had actually been terribly shaken by the news and had just not let on, keeping it all bottled up inside himself.

Not only that, just now, with Martha and the girls gone off, he had prevailed upon Mammeh to put little Fanny in the back with something to keep her busy so they could have a long, serious talk together.

"*Oy Got,*" Mammeh groaned, with a faint glimmering of what was in the offing.

When she re-joined him in the kitchen, this man with the extra-shiny glasses and hair now completely grey, whom she'd lived with for so many years, looked at her from across the table like a perfect stranger—another stranger like *Kreynele*!

He came right to the point, in Yiddish—"I want you to make her give it up."

"Make?" It being the last thing one would have expected, Mammeh didn't know what to say. Since when did either of them try and make anyone do anything?

"Yes, make," he repeated. "I insist—that—you do it"—his hand beating out the time.

The only thing to do, it seemed, was to plead with him to be reasonable.

"Reasonable?" He grew very pale—and scraped back his chair to get up. "That's what she should be! Tell it to *her!*"

"Eli, please!"—what if he should make himself sick over this?

"Why does she do it, what's there to be gained from it?" he complained.

But it's all so simple, Mammeh thought. Why oh why can't he get it through his head? "She wants to help poor girls earn a decent living—daughters of people like ourselves who haven't been as fortunate." That much Mammeh herself understood, aware of there being more that she didn't.

Eli simply wouldn't accept that—"They don't need her help. They've got all kinds of loudmouths to help them"—and then in the end if the strikers won out, would those same poor girls appreciate the effort she'd made? "Not on your life," he scoffed. "They'd only laugh—they'd have a good LAUGH at her expense."

Mammeh decided to try the old argument.

But husband, having heard it so often before, knew just where the weak point was. "Yes, of course it's the girl's life. But tell me, if someone put their head in the oven and turned on the gas, wouldn't you turn it off, or try and pull that person out?"

"And how would you, the mother, feel," Eli went on when she remained silent, "if daughter were taken into custody and dragged off to that stinking hole, Blackwell's Island?"

He positively glowered—"How?"

No, Mammeh answered in her head, no, it won't happen. No, not to my child!

"Look," he began arguing, with his hands, "we came here to this country with just the clothes on our backs practically. My brother and I were out selling, first with the packs, then with the pushcart,

The Strike

from morning to night, seven days a week, in all kinds of weather. Why—?" Husband's voice broke and his eyes blinked hard.

Mammeh looked away, embarrassed.

"—why should our child have to go down to the same pit?" Eli sprang up, and grabbed jacket and hat—"THE SAME HELL!" Three steps, and he was out the door, slamming it behind him…

Now what's going to be, what's going to be now, Mammeh brooded, still at the table. And as if that weren't enough, there was little Fanny staring in the doorway, apparently having heard Papa shouting and then the door banging.

"It's alright, *Bobele*," Mammeh soothed with mustered cheerfulness. "Go beck an' finish coloring."

Then after a little she tried working in like fashion on her own shattered nerves. He'll be okay. As soon as he reaches the store and the first customer shows up, he'll forget, and later he'll wonder what all the fuss was about.

But then, ready to begin the breakfast clean-up, Mammeh had second thoughts. Never before had husband gone off in such a state. "*Oy!*" she moaned—and her mind fell to imagining.

With hat and jacket on, and face adjusted for the street, Eli makes his way along Rivington to the Bowery and two plate glass windows, in which colorful cosmetics boxes are tastefully arranged among impeccably-bewigged heads.

Brother Abe with his square jaw looks up wonderingly from the desk in the back when the little bell atop the door tinkles more loudly than usual.

Eli comes to stand before him. "Take me in," he pleads with features all contorted. "I can't go home anymore"…

At day's end, the two of them board a train for a certain stop in Brooklyn, and then switch to a trolley. Pretty soon, as the sky is fading, they're striding together down quiet, tree-lined Forbell Street with its many high-stooped brownstones, until they reach the one on the corner of Mason.

BOBE MAYSE *A Tale of Washington Square*

Sister-in-law Dora Leah opens the door as they come through the gate, and at the sight of them, her lips above her knobby chin part— "Eli! What a pleasant surprise! All alone?"

And don't think it couldn't happen, Mammeh sniffs. That, or it could be worse yet, far worse. Her imagination went to work again.

Looking the proper gentleman in his salt-and-pepper suit topped by the black bowler, Eli pauses on the corner of Rivington and Allen, still very upset deep down.

Across the way under the El, a coarse-looking woman, heavily made up, with a bow the color of deep red roses in her henna-dyed hair, is leaning out of the second-story window of a small red-brick building that looks like an old-time schoolhouse.

She shows her teeth and waves for him to come up.

He crosses over and steps through the entrance to the stairs within.

"*Oy*, terrible! TERRIBLE!" Everything that was sure to follow in that sleazy room was like an icy dagger: their whispers of endearment...hugs and kisses...touches in secret places.

Mammeh cast her eyes about, not knowing where to turn.

Enough already, Bertha, she said to herself a while later. You've had a good cry, now get to work on something and stop worrying. Husband'll come home again the same as always, you'll see.

Mammeh recalled a length of flannel that she'd picked up cheap some time ago and laid away in her hamper. That's what I'll do, she thought, I'll make drawers for the children to wear under their dresses when the weather turns cold. There was only one problem: the color was an ugly yellowish-brown. Oh well.

LATER THAT SAME DAY, AND LATER STILL

It's getting on toward four o'clock and all's well.

The Strike

Dinah and Pauline are at their clubs, after stopping in briefly for milk and cookies. Little Fanny is playing in the back with a friend from the second floor.

Two pairs of yellowish-brown pantlets are finished, and only the very small one is left to be done.

But what's this? Mammeh stops rocking with the treadle, and listens. Someone is coming up the stairs...or actually two people...a female and a male...laughing.

They just went past the landing below and are headed for up here definitely. Who can it be? It's much too early for Him!

The door flies open. Of all things, it's Martha, and behind her, *oy vey*, that old guy Benowitz—the girl shining-eyed, he grinning with rotten teeth.

"Say, do you have a *bisele* tea for us?" *Kreynele* asks, all excited, after the exchange of kisses.

"Soitenly." Mammeh hurries to put the kettle on.

"Mammeh, look what we've got!" Martha cries, holding out something that resembles a business card.

"Vhat is it?" Taking it from her, Mammeh sees that it has "Waistmakers' Local 25, ILGWU" stamped on it, and "Martha Ferber" printed in by hand.

An explanation follows: Mary Dreier was arrested while walking with them on the line this morning, but even though the judge released her as soon as he found out who she was, everyone is fighting mad and people are signing up left and right—"So we thought we would too."

"Dot's very nice"—Mammeh snaps the card down on the oil cloth. "Only if it's alright mit you, vee von't tell anyvun just yet," she adds meaningfully.

The water is boiling—it's time to get the glasses.

"Gee, I feel swell," Martha is confiding to her Benny. "How 'bout you? How're your tootsies? Hahahahaha!"

Look how happy she is, Mammeh nudges herself. Now don't go and spoil it—see what you can do with that piece of not-so-fresh sponge cake in the bread box.

"And Mammeh, guess what else happened?" *Kreynele* chatters on. The cutters have also gone out, all except the goons...

"*Na*"—here. Mammeh sets down a platter of yellow cake-sandwiches with a strawberry jam filling.

Kreynele's voice is shrill as she and the old one pounce on them—"Boy, am I hungry!"

"*Es, es*"—Mammeh pushes the dandy-looking sweet things closer. My dear one is going to need her strength more than ever it looks like. The *alter kaker* too.

One, two, three, and the girl and her "friend" are back on their feet.

Mammeh is all confused. It's almost five. Where are they off to now?

There's no time for lengthy explanations. A special meeting's been called...a straw vote's going to be taken.

On their way out, Mammeh manages to catch Benowitz's eye. You better watch out for her, you, she warns him with a look.

The old head seems to understand—he nods.

It's a quarter to six, and the pot with the pea soup left over from yesterday is slow-steaming.

Once again there are footsteps on the stairs, and once again it's more than a single pair, with voices.

Mammeh draws in her breath as they arrive at the top step and the door knob turns.

Surprise! It's her very own Eli—and with him are the girls, both of them giggling at something he's said in his sly Papa's way. They must have met going along Rivington.

He has a smile for Mammeh too.

CHAPTER

9

Like any casual reader of newspapers, Jerrold was no stranger to labor disputes with their often fearful bomb throwings, clubbings by police and Pinkerton agents, fire bombings, and the wrecking of machinery. But for himself to be involved in anything of the kind was beyond his most fanciful imaginings. And yet, there it was—that's what had happened.

The first day had been the most distressing of all. Showing up early as was his wont, Jerrold had found it quiet on Ten as usual, the pressers and people from Shipping having yet to arrive, and the big bosses, if they had, closeted in their offices. But on emerging in his overalls from the locker room a few moments later, what did he behold but the place in an absolute uproar, with the chief and others rushing wildly around yelling and screaming.

Aware that something was brewing for some time now, as any fool with eyes and ears would have been, Jerrold had immediately realized that the Strike was on. However, as Bernstein was nowhere in sight and no one else seemed to care, the question had been, what should he do. Noticing nice Miss Leventhal waiting at the pressing table by the windows, along with Bernstein's brother and some other connections of the bosses, he had thought to go sound her out. But just then Mr. Markowitz of Shipping had come along—a likeable enough guy with wrinkly brow and bags under his eyes, even if he did bark awfully at times—and Markowitz had simply said for Sonny to "stick around." Bernstein, who was downstairs "trying to deal with those people," would be up before long, and then a floater would most likely have his work cut out for him.

Feeling less at a loss after that, Jerrold had taken a seat by the locker room, well out of the way of things, and contented himself with watching as a semblance of order began to manifest itself, culminating in the various big and little cheeses going to meet in Mr. Blanck's office. Then not long after, Mr. Harris came out to tell Miss Leventhal and the relations, who were beginning to look rather down, that he'd soon have something very important for them to "sink their teeth into"—which turned out to be paperwork of some kind.

Around noon, the two wise-guy shipping clerks, Louie and Solly, materialized from somewhere, and got up a game of pinochle with some cutters from Eight, using a pile of cartons as a table. Then as the afternoon began to wane, Bernstein appeared, and after exchanging a few words with Harris, beckoned for Sonny to go lend a hand at the pressing table—that is, at a little distance from the others because he didn't belong to their set. Whereupon Jerrold discovered that they were writing letters to Congressmen and other influential people urging their assistance in bringing "to a speedy termination" the disagreeable business outside that was "so in violation of free enterprise, both in act and spirit"—which chore Sonny the floater had no real objection to if that was what those who paid him wanted.

But then had come quitting time, when Jerrold had to pass by the line of marchers, many of whom he recognized from seeing them bent over their machines in feverish concentration—and that part he didn't care for at all. How angry they'd all seemed at him. Why, not only had they flung curses after him in their various foreign languages, but some had gone so far as to denounce him as a scab!

The Strike

The next day had been much of a muchness, with a fresh barrage of invective from them in the morning and another at night. And so it had continued during all of October, until Mr. Harris's *shraybers* upstairs had exhausted the list of muckamucks to write to, and begun on a new campaign to inform other shirtwaist manufacturers about the founding of a protective association, which it would be to their advantage to join even if their people weren't out on strike.

Now here at the beginning of the first week in November with the trees in the Square all orange, yellow, and red, and with the picketers still shuffling up and down out there—a fresh duty had been thrust upon Jerrold, for which he was donning his good brown suit that morning.

On Saturday before closing, bald-of-bean and round-faced Mr. Blanck had called for the whole staff to gather round the pressing table and announced that Triangle would be going into full-scale production again on Monday with a new crew of hands just hired. Further, as a gesture of good will—Mr. Blanck had raised his voice to drown out everyone's resounding cry of "Yea!"—the company was going to throw a welcoming shindig for the newcomers during the break that first day, to which each and every one of them was invited, "especially de single young bucks." And here Blanck had given them all a knowing look and a wink.

On the way down in the elevator a while later, Louie and Solly nearby kept poking one another and whispering things back and forth about the coming affair, and once both of them burst out into a loud haw-haw.

Well, if Blanck's idea is for us to have a little fun with those new girls, it's alright with me I guess—Jerrold was putting the final touches to a new tie of bold emerald stripes on gold satin in the smoky-pink mirror over the mantle. But if he expects us to court them or get involved with them in some other way, that'd be asking too much. A fellow has to draw the line someplace.

"Wouldn't you say?" he projected to puss-puss Dusty, looking up with amber eyes from the cushy comfort of the easy chair...

Going downstairs in cap and coat, Jerrold gave thought to Chucky, whom he had seen only a few times in passing since that slightly rowdy night-on-the-town in O'Reilly's. The want ads and his savings had been uppermost in Jerrold's mind.

Wonder what ole buddy's been up to? We should get together again one of these days, I expect.

As for Madam, his ma, except for pursing her lips in an extra pronounced way when up to collect last week, she didn't seem to harbor any ill feelings over their staggering in so late that time. So she probably wouldn't make any fuss about their having another evening out.

THE LESSON

Lunch has just been rung in, and after bustling about for Bernstein all morning, Jerrold is back in his suit set off by emerald on gold, woodenly descending the Washington Place stairs from Ten.

Directly ahead of him are Louie and Solly with their steel-rimmed glasses and bushy moustaches, sporting bright red bow ties and black elastic bands on their shirtsleeves... while in the lead are half a dozen new pressers in freshly-washed overalls with plastered-down hair, who give the impression of being Bowery bums that someone has been at pains to make appear presentable.

"Look alive, boys!" Bernstein sings out almost in Jerrold's ear.

Beltboys Mickey and Danny are bumping along behind him, lugging a gramophone and a stack of phonograph records in paper covers.

Opening the door on Nine, the lead presser lets out, "Holy Hannah!" and the rest of the pressers bunch up, craning their necks to see.

"Cripes," Louie mutters to Solly, "Blanck musta scraped de bottom of de herring barrel on Allen Street, so help me"—to which Jerrold adds, "Amen," after getting a look himself.

The Strike

The side aisle all the way down to the partition is thronging with older women, all of them heavily rouged-up and absolutely stuffed into flashy dresses overlaid by cheap jewelry.

"Okay, goils," Mr. Blanck pipes up from the thick of things. "Vee promist you a good time, und here it is!"

Mickey plunks the gramophone down on Miss Leventhal's desk. Bernstein selects a record from the pile, and gives the crank a few hard turns before setting the needle on it. Music wheezes uncertainly out of the horn, then swells into *The Blue Danube Waltz*.

Sleek in a navy suit, Mr. Blanck motions to Jerrold's group, and waves in some cutters coming through the partition—"Now den, boys, greb yuhselves a partneh!"

The "bucks" comply—except for Jerrold—and all around, couples start swaying with hips ungracefully swinging.

"Hey, Sonny, how 'bout you?" Mr. Blanck calls, over by Bernstein.

Jerrold approaches them uncertainly. "I—uh—don't know how," he has to confess—which is the truth, never having had the opportunity to learn. But of course, the greater truth is that he never had any interest in it, and still doesn't.

Mr. Blanck is flabbergasted, or does a good job of pretending—"Vhat! A hendsome blade like you! I don't beleef it!" Then he makes, or seems to, a sudden decision—"Yuh know vhat? I'm gonna loin ya!"—and grabbing Jerrold's hand, drags him onto the floor.

"Gif us a liddle elbow room, vill ya?"—Jerrold feels his waist being clutched by a surprisingly strong arm.

One of the "girls" notices what's up and alerts the others in a hoarse voice—"Hey, get a load a dat!"

Everyone stops waltzing, and eager to be in on the fun, moves back to the wall or slips into one of the rows with the machines.

Mr. Blanck, whose dark hair surrounding the baldness smells of brilliantine, applies steady pressure to Jerrold's forward shin.

Sweat begins to build under Jerrold's shirt—he jerkily pulls the leg back.

"Hahahahaha!" everyone breaks out.

Flushing with embarrassment, Jerrold unsticks the other leg to keep from losing his balance.

"Hahahahaha!" they all break out again.

Really raring to do his stuff now, Mr. Blanck takes three quick, light steps, and tilts Jerrold backwards into a dip.

Jerrold gets all fuzzy in the head, like that time when he tied one on at O'Reilly's, fearful that Blanck will let him go.

"Ooh, hot stuff!" someone squeals.

Forehead all shiny, Mr. Blanck pulls Jerrold up again—"Dere, you're loint, now go do yuh stuff"—and gives him a shove toward a number of women standing about, as yet unspoken for.

A short one bulging out of blazing purple, with a headful of greasy ringlets, sidles up to him—"Hiya, sweetie."

Conscious of many eyes staring and lips wet with anticipation, Jerrold swallows hard.

"Don' be 'fraid," she coos.

Jerrold gingerly extends his right hand, and awkwardly places his left on her fleshy back—they begin bobbing around. The sweat is positively running under his shirt now, and he can feel it on his upper lip too.

Out of consideration perhaps, Bernstein puts on something livelier, a one-step, and everyone, losing interest in Jerrold and his "mate," trots onto the floor again.

"Fine, yer doin' jes fine," the floozy murmurs through red-smeared lips.

Oh, this is awful, Jerrold silently groans, his nostrils offended in the extreme by her garlicky breath mixed with the overly sweet perfume.

"Gonna show ya something new, 'k?" she whispers.

Jerrold's heart gives a kick—NEW? What? What now?

The Strike

Snuggling up to him, she shifts sideways so her crotch is in line with his right thigh, and then falls to rubbing it there.

Oh God! Jerrold screams inside, and looks desperately around. I must—! How do I—?

"Now watch," the slut hisses—she has another trick up her sleeve—and shifts again, so that her split, with a certain hardness in between, is pressing right against his peter!

God, God, it's just like that time in church with Arturo when he discovered Rosa's extra twig of a finger! Only this is worse, much worse!

"Oh!"—the woman gives a little shiver. "Be right back"—and breaking away, she goes charging through the crowd toward the cloakroom.

Jerrold backs up to the edge of a table, and resting against it, slides a moist palm over his crotch. As soon as it goes down, he schemes, I'll sneak upstairs and hide somewhere till the party's over...

The disgusting tart has returned. "Guess what I did?" she twitters, and ogles him with glittering eyes.

Pfuie! Jerrold turns his head away, full of loathing.

A new one-step is playing. "Like to do it again?" she asks.

Jerrold stays as he is. Let her go...just go!

※

In a matter of a few days, once Jerrold regained his composure—no easy task, by any means—everything settled down to normal, at least as far as the work was concerned, with his doing Bernstein's every bidding from morning to night as of old. Indeed, he was soon even taking the taunting of the pickets in his stride.

Only one chore—a new one—did he come to regard with loathing, and that was when he had to help out replacing the belts on Nine, which for some mysterious reason took to snapping with greater frequency than before the Strike. Purely and simply, the problem had to do with those wretched new "girls," many of whom were given to rubbing a leg up and down his back whenever he was wedged in under a machine, while uttering lewd remarks like, "I bet ya can hold it real nice after ya do it the first time." But in time, even these indignities became a matter of course to him.

ANOTHER LESSON

With all of the cheeses at another meeting in Mr. Blanck's office since before lunch and a promised batch of finished waists not yet sent up from downstairs, it's been a quiet afternoon on Ten.

Jerrold has been resting on his chair by the locker room, after spending the whole morning helping Miss Leventhal count boxes of needles and thread.

Louie and Solly have been indulging in a friendly little game of casino with two of the new guys, while the rest of the pressers have been passing the time of day at their tables.

Now suddenly, when it's just about two, voices are sounding over the scraping of chairs inside Blanck's office, signs that the powwow is breaking up. Sure enough, the door comes unstuck with a clattering of the glass pane, and out everyone pours, except for Mr. Big himself.

Passing by the card players on the way to the toilet, Mr. Harris, with Markowitz, Levine the bookkeeper, and Bernstein in tow, pauses to announce some good news: the Shirtwaist Employers' Protective Association is about to become a fact. That is, to date they at Triangle have received some two hundred positive responses to that letter they sent out, and now it's just a matter of everyone's getting together to firm things up.

Louie throws down his cards—"Hey, dat's great!" Solly follows suit—"Vunderbar!" The two pressers take the hint—"Good going! That's showing 'em!"

Jerrold almost chimes in too, but refrains because he's a little too far away and it would look funny.

The Strike

Pleased at this fine show of support, Mr. Harris says he's going to treat them all to coffee by way of celebration. "Vere's de shvartser?" he inquires, meaning Lem the colored porter.

He's scrubbing down the washrooms on Eight, it seems. So who's left? Harris spies Jerrold on his chair—"How 'bout it, kid?"

"Sure thing, Mr. Harris," Jerrold answers right back, and steps inside to slip his suit jacket over the overalls.

Emerging a moment later, he's thinking, I don't like toting all that hot spilly stuff down the street from Mrs. Goldman's. But what can one do?

Louie hands him a sheet from the score pad with everyone's order jotted down, and Mr. Harris peels off a fiver from a wad in his front trouser pocket.

"Don't forget the change!" Bernstein yells after him, as he makes a beeline for the Washington Place elevators.

"Hah!" the whole bunch of them roars. "Dat's a hot one!" Louie adds.

"Very funny," Jerrold grumbles...

Outside, there are no coppers on either side of the door for some reason—just the line, wending its way on Washington to Greene.

No one pays him any mind for a change, so Jerrold, headed around the corner and up Greene to Waverly, begins moving along shoulder-to-shoulder with them all.

Everyone seems rather dispirited today. He considers and notes that none of those society ladies who cheer them on appear to be present. Indeed, curiously, the snazzy white vehicle usually serving as their headquarters isn't in its customary place across the way. Or perhaps not so curiously: the black paddy wagon is not around either, meaning that everyone may be over at the courthouse.

Ah, there's the girl who stopped to admire the view in front of his house last summer. Martha, I believe she's called.

The girl's deep-set eyes, shaded by a rare wide-brimmed hat with feathers, widen at the sight of him, and her face brightens.

Jerrold nods in acknowledgment, less coolly than he would have to the old one beside her and the rest, after all, her cohorts, and pushes on, leaving them all behind...

Over at the luncheonette, chubby little Mrs. Goldman goes right about her business with his list, and has him on his way again in a trice, with a large box-lid full of glass jars sealed with paper and powdery doughnuts folded in wax paper—and above all, with the change, in bills and coins, nestled on a napkin.

Now easy does it, Jerrold cautions himself out on the street. One false move and—

Up ahead on Greene, the column of marchers is coming round once more from Washington—their garb different shades of grey and brown with a trace of black on the lighter grey pavement.

Considering their measured pace and his present slow crawl, those in the lead should reach the back entrance around the same time as he.

No sooner said—

"Hey lookit, he's bringing dem tings!" a girl up front hollers, seeing him carefully managing with the lid full of jars.

"No fair, he can't do dat!" echoes another girl, with a mean look.

Best to duck in here and take the freight elevator, Jerrold advises himself, just a step or two away from the back door.

"How dare you bring dem coffee and not us!" a third one barks, and spitefully reaches out to grab.

Jerrold swerves to avoid her—which causes one of the coffees to topple over and the paper top to come off!

"Ow-ow!" he yowls, the scalding liquid having splashed onto his hands.

"Gimme dat!" another girl demands, and tearing the whole kitenkeboodle away, dashes it, swimming and steaming, into the gutter.

Oh boy, oh boy! Jerrold whimpers inwardly, and begins backing up.

The Strike

"GET HIM!" several voices yell at the same time.

He turns to run. Someone gets hold of him by the jacket collar, and a small, hard fist lands on his ear with a thud.

A whole pack makes for him with screaming faces—"Get him! Fix him! Ass kisser! Boss's pet!"

Somewhere in the middle of everything, there's that nice girl Martha in her classy hat with the feathers—aghast, with fingers to her mouth.

Jerrold somehow manages to squirm away, and pries the door open enough to slip in.

From a distance comes the *yeep!* of a police whistle.

"Oh-oh! Oh-oh!" Jerrold staggers into the elevator, aching all over. And his hands! They're red and raw!

The operator, a hulking Czech, gets them going up and away from there without comment...

My hands, my hands, Jerrold agonizes, released on Ten. They're hot now, red-hot, and all puffed up.

"Bastards, all of 'em," he tearfully mutters about Harris, Bernstein, and the others, who don't even look up from hovering over the card players as he lurches past them.

Inside the locker room, he bends over the sink, and the contents of his stomach come up and spill bitterly into it.

"My hands, what am I going to do, my hands are burnt!" he wails.

Someone's in the doorway. "Are you okay?" the person asks in a concerned way.

It's waxen-faced Levine the bookkeeper with his pince-nez and cleft in the chin—the guy who long long ago interviewed Jerrold for a job as his assistant, and then stood by without lifting a finger when Harris handed him over to that slave-driver Bernstein.

"My hands!" Jerrold sobs, showing them.

"Ah, I can fix that"—Levine goes away and is back the next moment with half a roll from a sandwich, whose buttery side he begins applying to Jerrold's right. "Left over from lunch," he explains, "my missus always packs too much for me"—and takes up Jerrold's left. "How's that? Better, no?"

"A little, yes," Jerrold agrees. The burning has subsided some.

Levine tosses the roll in the trash. "Listen, kid," he says, of a mind to offer some advice, "you have a little money put by, don't you?"

Jerrold nods.

"Well, why don't you go on home and stay there till this thing blows over," Levine quietly tells him. It would only be a matter of a week or two at the most. "We'll telephone your landlady and leave a message for you as soon as it's official, how's that?"

Jerrold sniffs—sounds good.

Levine further advises that if Jerrold wasn't up to facing that lousy bunch of riff-raff again, the porter could be enlisted to give him a hand up to the roof and over to the adjacent NYU building, so he could leave by one of their exits.

Now there's a decent soul, Jerrold decides through a few more silent tears. The only one hereabouts, THAT'S FOR SURE—except maybe that girl Martha in her hat.

No sooner did Jerrold arrive home than he sank onto the Confederate flag-covered divan and fell into a deep sleep, which lasted until twilight.

"Glory be," he murmured, after yawning widely and having himself a good stretch. Not only did he feel like a new man, but his hands, thankfully, were much improved, with just a trace of redness remaining and the swelling down to almost nothing.

Added to that, you're free, do you realize it? Yes, through a fluke, a miracle, he was free at last to go look for a decent job. And happily, there would still be that awful one to fall back on if things didn't pan out.

The Strike

Jerrold got up with his usual zest, and strode over to one of the window seats.

"Oh!" He hadn't noticed before: outside in the Square only a few leaves were left on the branches, dangling here and there like old red-and-yellow paint rags.

In a few days, with the first shivery weather, they'll be gone too, he sadly reflected...

Kit-kat hopped into his lap.

So—Jerrold began to plan—tonight you'll pick up the newspapers as usual. Then tomorrow, out you go first thing, with the ads marked and a regular itinerary—provided, of course, that the hands are alright, which I'm sure they will be.

But supposing no one wants to hire you again and the Strike drags on and on in spite of Levine's prediction, what then?

What? Well, in that case, obviously you'll have to pull in your belt but good. Meaning, for one thing, that he'd have to replace his current fare of fried cutlets and potatoes with the soups of his first days here. Also, he might have to try getting around on foot as much as possible, and as an added measure, to do so lightly for the sake of conserving shoe leather.

So much for that—Jerrold gave Dusty's blue-grey coat a few rough strokes. Now what about this evening? A little fun is in order, I believe.

Yes, but first there's a bit of unfinished business that needs attending to, he reminded himself. It was something that he'd been intending to do but kept on putting off all these months for some reason—to go over to Brentano's bookstore and get hold of a French primer. And you'll begin doing the lessons at once, so if and when a job does turn up, you'll be all ready to celebrate, in comfort, at that nifty basement restaurant in the Brevoort. Yes, today's the day to get that grammar, absolutely.

Not only that, while you're at it, why don't you—yes, why didn't he head a little further up Fifth to a certain church that he'd noted in passing on a number of occasions, and find out about their Sunday service. For something had been gnawing at Jerrold of late to take part in a religious ceremony, specifically at some Dutch Reformed church like that one, called Marble Collegiate. Different though the ritual would be from Christ Episcopal's, he had this hankering to worship among people of his own kind—that is, on the Vanderlynn side—and see whether he could fit in, especially now with Thanksgiving and Christmas coming, whose loneliness he had felt very keenly last year.

ECSTASY!

Boy, it sure turned winter in a hurry, Jerrold is remarking, as he breathily hurries along under Fifth Avenue's lavender-tinged globes an hour or so later.

Even so, he has the book in its pretty Brentano's wrapping secure under his arm, together with the evening editions. And ten-thirty on Sunday is fixed in his memory as the time to show up at Marble Collegiate—which now, on closer inspection, looks like a miniature version of St. Patrick's.

So whadya feel like doing tonight, he plies, cutting across the Square past the Arch and lily pond with tingling cheeks.

Arturo comes to mind, whom Jerrold, true to his word, has seen only now and then since that fateful day of the finger last summer. I could stop by the shop and bring him up to date with the latest.

But no, that wouldn't be much fun, Jerrold decides, coming up to Number 61. At least, it's not the kind of thing likely to take away the bad taste of today's nightmare. And then you're liable to talk too much and somehow set the whole thing with Rosa in motion again, which would be a fine kettle of fish.

Well, there's Chucky, maybe you can do something with him, Jerrold considers, beginning up the stairs inside—which somehow doesn't seem like such a good idea anymore, now that it's a real possibility.

The Strike

But it would just be for the sake of company. And if you go to O'Reilly's or someplace like that, you could insist on both of you sticking to a single beer this time.

Okay, let's see how we make out. On their landing, he gives a knock.

Inside there is a creak of floorboards—Madam Branchard opens, in her black bonnet and coat, as if she has just come home herself.

" 'Evening, mam," Jerrold greets her, with some fingers to his visor.

Madam's eyes, those eyes too close together like ole buddy's, grow sharp. "Emile's having his dinner."

From over her shoulder, Chucky grins sheepishly, his mouth ringed with grease.

Outside on the stoop moments later, after leaving the book and papers upstairs, Jerrold pauses. It's become colder yet, or perhaps damper—so maybe I should just forget about the whole thing and call it a day.

But then there's O'Reilly's, only a hop-skip-and-jump away. You could go there all by your lonesome.

Yeah, sure, but—but—what do I say?

Aw c'mon, just walk in there and say you want a beer, that's all.

Jerrold begins stepping down, still uncertain.

Honestly, you're going to have to stop being so pussy-footed about everything, or you're never going to get anywhere—at anything.

More confident now, Jerrold turns left on the sidewalk, and with a dozen quick strides is there.

Is this me, he marvels, pushing through the swingers. I can't believe it.

Inside, there's a small group in dark suits and bowlers down front, minus Blacky, the Tammany boss's nephew, and two guys with their heads together on the far end.

Jerrold gives a nod one way, then the other, and makes for the center, where he and Chucky stood before. The sawdust under foot is comforting, but not the angry swirls of cigarette smoke round the row of flaming yellow lights overhead.

Mr. O'Reilly, that big man with moustache, comes clumping from Blacky's crowd with a slight smile—"How ya been? Ain't seen yah around in a while."

Does he recognize me, Jerrold wonders, or is this the way he treats every familiar-looking stranger? Well, no matter. "I'm—I'm fine. Been workin' hard."

"What'll you have, a lager?"

"Yes-es. Thank you."

Marking time till it comes, Jerrold looks straight ahead over the pyramids of glasses and line of whiskey bottles into the blue-tinged mirror.

This really splendid-looking young man looks back, with cap on perfectly straight, and every hair under it in place.

"There"—an icy, slicked-off stein is now before him on a cardboard coaster, and his nickel is gone, slid off the bar's shiny dark surface by O'Reilly's agile finger.

Now go easy, will you, Jerrold warns himself, and getting a firm hold on the slippery handle, brings the tall, heavy glass up for a small sip.

What now, what should I do now? Noting himself in the mirror again, he realizes what the trouble is—let's face it, you don't belong in a dive like this.

Well, just get to work with that book, and you'll soon be ready for one better place at least—which is the honest-to-goodness truth. *Dr. Masson's French Primer*, he ascertained in the store, contains twenty-six lessons, and he already knows *Mon oncle a un ami*, *Qui est à la porte*, and other namby-pamby stuff like that in the first two—so you're way ahead even before you start...

The Strike

Something has changed at the bar's far end: only one man is there now, his companion having gone off while Jerrold was woolgathering apparently.

"Hiya, Jerry!" the loner sings out, in a rather pleasant though somewhat gravelly voice. "Remember me?"

Jerrold vaguely places the man's face in the same spot—a lined face with a greyish cast, topped by slick-backed sandy hair. "Oh yes"—it's the fellow that Chucky had something against—"you're Smitty, isn't that right?"

The guy's cheeks crease more heavily as his lips curl—"Say, you got some memory, considering—er"—meaning Jerrold's state of inebriation that time. But this Smitty is not at all non-plussed—"Whyn't you come over and chew the fat a while?"

A swell idea. Now you see how easy it is to meet people if you want to. All you have to do is relax—and persevere.

"Care for a smoke?" Smitty asks, when Jerrold's beside him on a stool, and offers from his pack.

"Much obliged but don't indulge," Jerrold is forced to admit—though you should, yet another item of good living he's neglected.

Smitty is curious—"I guess ya live aroun' here."

Yes indeed, and somehow unable to control himself, Jerrold pours everything out, including the best part, which he saves for last—how each time one looks out of his windows, whether it be day or night, the Square takes on a new unforgettable magical aura!

"Is that so?" Smitty says, having received it all with seemingly the same degree of enthusiasm.

"I'll be glad to show you some time if you like," Jerrold adds in all sincerity.

"Why that's mighty nice," Smitty responds. "Don't be surprised if I take you up on it"—looking perhaps a little too intently into Jerrold's eyes. But right now, why don't they drink up and he'd buy them another.

207

How do you like that, the guy's got the makings of a regular scout.

"What line o' work yuh in?" Smitty questions, when the new round is before them.

Oh that. Jerrold sighs—and tries to paint as pretty a picture as possible, omitting recent horrors, of course.

New pal is not taken in. "You can do better," he sums it up, with a certain admiration...

That round is consumed a little more quickly than the last. "My treat now," Jerrold announces.

Smitty's hand stays him—"No hard feelings, Jerry, but some other time, okay? Hang on to yer dough till somethin's comin' in again."

A piece of sound advice if ever I heard it, and the guy looks to have a heart of gold, Jerrold registers internally.

When the fresh steins come, Smitty forks over the two nickels, then hikes himself up—"Gotta go"—to the toilet, naturally. Jerry can use it after him if he cares to.

Well, he's a little old for a friend, Jerrold appraises, eyeing Smitty's retreating back. But all in all, there's something comfortable about him. Yes, he'll do just fine as a start. So what's the next step? Should I make a date and have him up some time, or what?

Sliding back onto his stool minutes later, Smitty practically takes the words out of his mouth—"Hey Jerry, how 'bout we go have a look at that view of yours?"

"Now?" Jerrold blurts out, really taken by surprise.

Smitty breaks into a broad grin—"What better time, what else is there to do?"

True, very true, Jerrold acknowledges, and happening to observe their chiseled features topped by their blondish hair in the mirror, realizes that they could pass for older and younger brothers, or with a slight stretch of the imagination, a father and his son.

"So, how 'bout it?" Smitty presses, all of his lines still showing.

The Strike

On his feet after one more for the road and a quick trip to the back, Jerrold feels only slightly woozy. Guess I'm getting used to it, haha.

When new buddy gets up too, after stubbing out a cigarette, Jerrold notes in the mirror that they're both around the same height, and that Smitty likewise favors the color brown in his dress.

"'Bye, see ya!" O'Reilly calls, as they're pushing through the swingers together.

On the street, the two of them move along side-by-side like a pair of rowers in a swell—it's that much brisker out—until they reach the top of the stoop, where the door comes open with a twist.

As they're climbing past the first landing, Madam's voice calls feebly from within—"Don't break up de furniture, boys."

What! Jerrold is indignant. What's she talking about! Then suddenly, with Smitty following close behind, he grows afraid. Maybe the guy's fixing to rob me!

But the next moment, he's discounting this as unlikely because of his self-proclaimed poverty.

Smitty's breath is coming hard, and somehow Jerrold's heart quickens at the thought of something else about to happen…a dark new idea, vague and unformed.

Upstairs at last, Jerrold unlocks the door and breezes in. "It's more dramatic with the lights out. Lookit!"—his arm sweeps to the windows.

Outside, there's the line of bright bluish street globes, and beyond, the trees and Arch are starkly black in sharp outlines against the sky's dark-blueness.

With a closer approach, the sky will darken and the silhouettes fade, and stars will shine like icy points…

Smitty has remained by the door. "Sure is something," he murmurs.

A soft plucking sound, as of buttons being undone, issues from there. "Jerry, dere's somethin' "—pal's voice is husky. "I got somethin' for yuh."

What can it be, Jerrold puzzles, and strains to see.

SMITTY HAS HIS PETER OUT!

"Come here," pal softly commands.

"I—" Jerrold's legs begin to move as if of themselves. What's going on? Is it bad?

"It's yours," Smitty says, more huskily, and grasps Jerrold's hand to bring it there. "It's all for you, if yuh want it."

The thing is silky smooth to Jerrold's touch, like rose petals, and rigid.

Smitty rings Jerrold round with his arms, and pal's lips, hedged by tiny hair-prickles, find Jerrold's dry ones.

"Oh-oh!"—Jerrold grows all trembly.

Smitty's firm hand in the small of Jerrold's back guides him to the divan...

How did I get here, Jerrold wonders, face down on the pillow, without a stitch on.

The tip of pal's tongue is running down the length of his spine. Down, down, it goes, all the way down—then IN—it glides INSIDE HIM!

"OH-OH!" How does the man know to do this?

Smitty, also minus his clothes, reaches into his pants, discarded on the floor, and fumbles to squeeze out some salve from a tube.

Then slipping onto Jerrold's back again, he enters, little by little—"All for you, Jerry"—and PLUNGES IN—"Oh, Jer-ry!"

Jerrold follows, plummeting HEAD-FIRST, down into a deep sweet well.

Someone seems to be speaking, then stops—Jerrold sits up! It's still night out, and he's alone.

The Strike

Peering round the room, he spies a sheet of paper on the mantle—and can't get to it fast enough!

By the light from the street, he makes out:

Dear Jerry,
You came good. I'm glad. See you again soon.

                              Best regards,
                              S.

Everything that happened returns in a rush. Some people (like Louie and Solly, for instance) have an ugly word for it.

But I don't care and I'm not sorry, Jerrold tells the darkness.

CHAPTER 10

"We should thank our lucky stars it isn't raining," everyone on the line kept repeating. But alas, with that cruel wind lashing them in the face at every turn or else buffeting their backs, it wasn't long before they were all feeling truly miserable, Martha as much as anyone else, bundled up though she was, with fingers stuffed in Mammeh's welcome gift of a fur muff.

And this is only the beginning, Martha warned herself one midmorning in the third week of November. Real winter was yet to come, and guaranteed to bring with it not only frigid temperatures, but snow and ice under foot. And when it did, what wretchedness there would be if they were still marching up and down out there?

Closer to home—the closest!—how would her dear Benny fare, who had problems enough as it was. Besides the constantly sore tootsies, some cracks had recently opened on his hands, and refused to heal despite his wife's schmearing them with ointment night and day and some cotton liners that Mammeh sent to wear under his wool gloves.

"Why don't you go wait by Mrs. Goldman's," Martha urged him, the next time the two of them were coming round onto Greene. Only a short while remained before they would all begin taking turns going for lunch, and no one would say anything probably.

Certain individuals in better shape—like Raiseleh, for instance—had already simply walked off without anybody's appearing to mind.

Benny, with eyes more watery than usual, silently agreed—a bad sign.

Maybe I should speak to Kline or someone, and try to get him off permanently, Martha considered, watching him trot painfully away. But then she had second thoughts: some wise guy in the union might use it as an excuse to deprive poor Benny of the few bucks they doled out to him in benefits...

Turning onto Washington, she gave yet another glance at the white touring car, in whose rear seat Miss Marot was dictating away as usual, while Miss Dreier leaned wearily back on the cushions beside her. Appearances to the contrary, it can't be too comfy for them either, was Martha's feeling—though, of course, the interior of that plush vehicle was as nothing compared to the open air...

Coming up now was the lobby entrance, through which *he*, Bernstein, continued to arrive and depart every day. And now that her shift of picketing was almost over, Martha allowed herself the luxury of a little rumination about him, as was her wont.

During her mornings on duty over the past several weeks, she had scarcely seen him, favored only with a glimpse at a distance now and again, when he was beginning to make his way up the block after leaving the Square behind. She had recognized him by the fine dark blue of his coat and hat, and his special way of hurrying along, in rapid short-legged strides.

Well, maybe with a little luck, we'll cross paths again tomorrow—like that one time.

In bed at night, no sooner was she staring into the dark than there were his eyes with that hurt look rising up before her.

What could one do but roll over and, face down on the mattress, plant her lips on his twisty ones...moving ever so slightly so as not to wake little sister...

The Strike

"Look at that," Martha let out, having turned onto Greene again.

Benny, in his shabby old overcoat and bowler, was coming toward her.

"Did you have a good nap?" she kidded, as he fell into step beside her.

"Foist rate," he kidded back, always one to rise to the occasion.

At noon, which was announced by a resounding chorus of lunch bells and whistles going off in the buildings all around, Miss Dreier climbed out of the car, muffled to the teeth, and came to stand a few feet out in the street. She had a sheaf of circulars in hand.

"Good morning, sisters and brudders," she called, in her customary good spirits, and surveyed them all with shining blue eyes.

The line slowed way down, so that everyone was just about marking time.

"A liddle on de nippy side dis morning."

"This is going to be good," Martha murmured, as eager as the next person to hear what was up, but at the same time a little hurt that Miss Dreier gave no sign of recognizing her, no more today than on other occasions when they were a few feet apart.

"Yuh, yuh," went Benny, who now regarded this orange-haired gentile lady as the clever deviser of, among other things, that arrest of hers, which as he saw it, was all for the sake of getting more publicity for the Strike.

Miss Dreier grinned like a naughty little girl—"Vell, here's something to varm you up, I think"—and quickly stepping forward, thrust the circulars into someone's hands.

"Oh boy!" Martha cried to the old one, as she took two and passed the rest.

This was what a lot of them had been waiting for: a meeting of the union's whole rank and file, at which a vote was going to be taken, so rumor had it, for all the waistmakers in the city to go out!

"And guess who's going to be there!" Martha shouted, meaning at the celebrated Great Hall of Cooper Union, where the meeting was to be held—Mr. Union himself, Samuel Gompers!

Yes, of course Benny will go with his *tsatskele*, if she wants.

MONDAY, NOVEMBER 22ND

It's seven-thirty, the appointed hour, and a blue-jacketed union man has just told the large crowd milling around Peter Cooper's statue that there's no more room inside, they should go to one of several halls nearby that are intended to accommodate the overflow.

Deeply disappointed, Martha is on the point of sounding Benny out as to which one would be the best to try, when she spies someone with a mole elbowing her way to the door—old friend Elsie!—and takes off after her.

"Oh hello," Elsie says, with a cool look. A member of the Kline-Elzufin gang, she has her dignity now.

But what does Martha care about such things. Can Elsie help the two of them get in, she asks, almost pleading.

It's worth a try, Elsie responds, perhaps for old time's sake. However, it should be clearly understood that the places they're likely to end up with won't exactly be the Ritz.

Past the doorkeeper and through a thronging lobby, Elsie leads them, to another blue jacket before a door downstairs, who after exchanging a few words with her, nods and beckons for Martha and Benny to follow him.

Inside, the Hall is indeed crowded to the rafters, and between stout pillars, Martha catches sight of good old Elsie chubbily squeezing in to take a last remaining seat some rows down.

The usher shows them to a bench against the back wall, which is already quite full, and makes room on the end by telling everyone to shove over a little.

The noise is almost deafening in there, one and all, mostly female and young, having something to say.

The Strike

"Look!" Benny points to the aisle on the far right, down which a procession has just started, consisting of a small group of dark-suited men and Miss Dreier, in sober black.

In the lead, they recognize Baroff, head of their own Local 25, resembling a Yankee financier as much as ever.

Among the others, Benny singles out labor lawyer Meyer London, with sensitive features like a poet, and his coarser-looking colleague Jacob Panken, another familiar figure from the pages of the *Forverts*.

Bringing up the rear is the meeting's chairman, Benjamin Feigenbaum of Workmen's Circle fame, a baldy with a big brush under his nose—and before him struts everyone's precious prize, Gompers, somehow with the face of a fish, who has thick-lensed glasses and is wearing, of all things, a balloon-like cantor's yarmulke.

"What's he going to do, say a prayer?" Martha jokes, Gompers' indifference to religion being pretty well known.

"*Ver veyst*"—it's anybody's guess. Benny adds one of his shrugs—maybe the guy catches cold easily and wants to keep out the drafts.

Baroff is on the stage now, where in the midst of several packed rows of honored guests, stands a semi-circle of chairs with a lectern in the center.

What about Dyche, isn't Dyche in the approaching party, Martha questions.

Benny scrutinizes the men coming after Baroff—no, he doesn't believe so.

What, the president of the whole shebang, the ILG itself, not there? How come?

A spiteful-looking girl in front of Martha flings the answer over her shoulder—"It's because he doesn't tink goils can vin, dot's how come!"

The dignitaries, from lawyers London and Panken to Gompers, have ascended to the stage and taken seats in the semi-circle—Feigenbaum has procceded to the lectern.

Bang-bang, he goes with the gavel. "LADIES UND GENTLEMEN!" his voice rings out. "IN BEHEF OF LOCAL TVENTY-FIFE OF DE INTERNASHUNAL LADIES GARMENT VOIKERS OF AMERICA, I CALL DIS MEETING TO ORDEH!"

The whole place, including Martha and Benny, jumps to its feet—"YEA!"

Feigenbaum bobs his chin this way and that, as if the cheer were meant for him personally—until it dies down. "OUR FEATURT SPEAKEH TONIGHT NEEDS NO INTRODUCSHUN TO YOU." Gompers rises and steps forward.

Everyone bursts out afresh—"YEA!"

The two men shake hands, Feigenbaum steps away, and there's a general rumbling as the whole place sits down again—quiet.

Gompers opens his fish-mouth, and out comes a kind of English accent—"WHEN I WAS ASKED TO ADDRESS YOU THIS EVENING, I SAID TO MYSELF, I DON'T KNOW WHETHER THE COURTS WILL ALLOW IT OR NOT, BUT IF THEY DO, I'LL BE THERE!"

Pandemonium breaks loose—"YEA-EA-EA-EA!" Boom! goes a photographer's bulb. "EEE!" some girls shriek.

The fish-mouth smiles—"THAT WAS THE FIRST BOMB, AND HERE'S HOPING IT'S THE LAST."

There are nervous titters everywhere.

Mr. Union picks up the thread—"THE NEWSPAPERS HAVE BEEN REFERRING TO MEE-EE AS GOMPERS THE STRIKE MAKER, CLAIMING THAT GOM-PERS IS GOING TO CALL A STRIKE HERE TONIGHT. FOR THEIR INFORMATION, GOMPERS HAS NEVER CALLED A STRIKE IN HIS LIFE!"

How forceful he is, Martha marvels. What power he has.

Benny doesn't seem as enthusiastic for some reason, which is also cause for wonder.

"THE CONDITIONS IN THE CLOTHING TRADE"—Gompers emphasizes with his hand—"ARE A BLOT ON MODERN CIVILIZATION."

Everyone applauds.

The Strike

"It breaks the spirit of men and women"—the hand turns into a fist—"and makes children prematurely old."

Again they all appreciate.

"Now a decision to strike"—Gompers' voice grows softer—"is a serious matter."

There's a mass holding of breath.

"But once all other means are exhausted, and there's no other way, then I say, go ahead. And when you do, let Mr. Shirtwaistmaker know it—loud and clear!"

The whole place is on its feet again, and the roof is ready to come off—"Yea-ea-ea-ea!"

A truly extraordinary person, Martha sums it up, hollering out herself.

Benny is standing too, but just that.

"What's the matter?" she yells in his ear, as the ovation continues.

The grizzled chin gives a show of disparagement—"He's given dis speech before, *Tsatskele*." That is, this is one of many nights on the lecture platform for him.

"Mind you, dere's nutting wronk mit it," Benny tries to justify, as everything begins to calm down. Just so long as one is aware of the truth of the situation.

It's something to think about...

Gompers has returned to his seat, and Feigenbaum has brought on Miss Dreier, who greets them all more nervously than one would have expected—"Sisters and brudders, how vunderful to see you all"—then takes up where Gompers left off, about the step many are contemplating this evening being a grave one.

Talking breaks out here and there in snatches.

Martha finds her mind wandering too. "Will it come to a vote tonight, do you think?" she murmurs to Benny.

The old one replies in his usual vein—how should he know, hasn't got a crystal ball.

Miss Dreier finally brings things to a head—"So vun should be vell aware that it is a difficult decision to make and I'm sure after due deliberation, you vill come up vit de right vun."

Everyone gives her a hand.

Feigenbaum steps up to introduce a tall, thin fellow from some other union, who wants to say a few words.

"*Nu*, so ven is it going to heppen already?" the outspoken girl in front of Martha complains.

"I hope dey didn't pay for all dis chitchat outta our dues," a companion on the right pipes up…

"The key to de whole ting is not to ect hastily," Martha hears coming from the new speaker. "Vun must gif it all careful considerashun, veighink de pro's mit de con's."

Talking breaks out again, a steady hum this time.

Feigenbaum hurries over to wield the gavel—*pock pock*. "Ordeh, please, ordeh. Sh-sh-sh. Show some respect."

The unknown speaker makes a fresh effort, but the talking, which did not entirely let up, only becomes louder.

"*Gevalt*, ven is he goink to finish already!" cries the moaner-and-groaner in front of Martha, with her arms raised to Heaven.

At long last he does, and now Feigenbaum beckons for the unpoetic-looking lawyer Panken, who appears to have several pages of notes.

From somewhere in the audience comes a girl's shrill voice—"Excuse me! Excuse me!" She rises, a small thing in a white waist. "I vant to say sometink!"

"Go on!" someone urges. "Go up dere!" another seconds. "Do it! Go!" others join in.

The little miss quickly slips through her row to the right aisle, and rushes down to the stage with her skirt clutched. Feigenbaum gives her a hand up.

"Speak! Speak!" voices cry out, as she, round of cheek, with jowls emphasized by her high, tight collar, waits for things to be sorted out with Panken.

The Strike

Martha recognizes her as Clara Lemlich, an operator on strike at Leiserson's who has become a great favorite with Miss Dreier and the other League ladies.

"Mr. Panken has agreet to yielt de floor," Feigenbaum advises, and as he and Panken withdraw from the lectern, Miss Lemlich steps up, and swallows noticeably with panicky eyes.

It grows quiet.

"You'll forgif me if I speak in Yiddish," Lemlich begins, not up to it in English. Her look turns to one of pleading—"I am one of those who has suffered from the poor pay and bad conditions that everyone has been talking about, and I am tired of listening to the same thing over and over again."

"Good going, Clara!" a chorus encourages. "That's right, that's telling 'em!" others echo.

"As I see it, there's no reason to delay any longer." Lemlich holds out both arms as if to give a blessing—"I move that we do it already!"

The whole house explodes—"Yea-ea-ea-ea! Do it! Do it! Strike!" Handkerchiefs, hats, and even umbrellas are waving!

"Yes!" Martha adds her voice, misty-eyed. "Let's do it! Everyone!"

Feigenbaum, now beside Lemlich, follows her lead and switches to Yiddish—"There's a motion on the floor, do I hear a second?"

"Aye-aye!" everyone agrees.

"Do you mean to keep faith?"

"Aye-aye-aye!" they all roar back.

"Well then, repeat after me." He holds up his right hand—"If I turn traitor to the cause I now pledge, may this hand wither from its arm."

A great multitude shouts it out, their fists beating the time.

Everyone around Martha is jumping up and down or hugging and kissing.

"It's wonderful! Wonderful!" she nearly sobs, utterly enthralled by it all: that in one instant all of them together should give utterance to the same thing like this, fraught as it is with more heartache and possibly even greater danger!

Benny alone remains unmoved, his face completely devoid of emotion.

Only too familiar with how his mind works, Martha is able to second-guess what is passing through it: that the whole thing was a put-up job; Miss Dreier and Miss Marot, possibly with the connivance of Baroff, had influenced Lemlich to go up there and do what she did.

Maybe so, she answers in her own mind, feeling the blood rise as it has with Papa sometimes. But even if the thing was faked, I don't care, so be it. How everything comes out is all that matters—and that goes for Gompers too, now that I think of it.

The whole place is still carrying on, and now Miss Dreier has joined her protégé Lemlich at the lectern, where both are smiling with their arms around each other.

Maybe this Lemlich has what Dreier and her associates were looking for in me, it occurs to Martha, remembering back to that night of cross-questioning in the restaurant on Macdougal Street.

Does it matter? Not in the least. Do I mean it? Yes, yes, a thousand times yes!

※

The next day, the weather cooperating with a less fierce wind, everybody going up and down in front of Number 23, including Martha, felt as they would have after a *khasene*—big wedding—bleary-eyed and a little foggy in the head, but positively jubilant, and they all moved along with the old spring in their step.

The only person with a displeased expression on his face was Benny, who scarcely uttered a word.

For the first time Martha found herself wishing for more stimulating company—but not for long. Soon, with her friend continuing to remain silent, she became wrapped up in her own thoughts, and eventually, as the excitement of last night waned, she turned them to Bernstein, whom she'd yet once more missed seeing that day.

If only he could be won over to our side, was her final wish, which, of course, was downright foolish, she recognized the next instant.

The following morning, as she was making her first turn onto Washington, lo, as if in answer to a prayer, there *he* was halfway down the block, just leaving the entrance to the NYU building behind. Not only that, comparing his pace with theirs on the line, she felt her heart give a leap.

Yes, barring the unforseen, today was the day that she in her rich brown coat with the black fur collar and hat and muff to match—a little lady indeed—was going to come face-to-face with him again, or just about. It would happen just like that other time, a few steps before he veered left to go in the lobby door and she swiveled round with the line to head for Greene.

It's a miracle! Martha thrilled. An absolute miracle!...

But how pale *he* is, it struck her, as they came closer. Could he be sick, or is it just the dark winter blue of his over garments that make him seem so?

No, the man is truly white in the face, she perceived when the distance between them had shortened some more. Let's only hope that all's well with him, and the wanness is just from worrying about business and so on...

The question now is, will he look my way, Martha debated, when they were about ten feet apart. He was going by the others marching ahead of her, already looking away as usual.

Five steps more, and another miracle occurred! Suddenly, for no accountable reason, his gaze shifted in their direction, and he nodded curtly to Benny—then touched the brim of his hat to her!

So there we are, he knows me, Martha thrilled again. Fancy that, he knows me from Adam.

But did he notice anything? Oh, dear God, let it not be. He must never find out about my feelings—never!

Friday, December 3rd

It's a little past noon and overcast with a light wind playing, and Martha, in her brown and black, minus the muff, is on her way via the Houston Street line to more big union doings.

There's going to be a rally at Lipzin's Theatre on the Bowery, to be followed by a march downtown to the City Hall with a petition for Mayor McClellan protesting the often brutal police treatment of strikers.

Benny won't be coming along this time, but not for lack of her pestering him. Yes, twice the other day she asked him if he'd care to, and each time he declined—claiming that he wanted to use the break in routine to give his hands an extra chance to heal and his feet a rest. But in reality, from various things that he let slip after the call came, she knew better—that he considered the march pointless. And why? Because with the Strike likely to continue, he probably felt that they should concentrate their efforts on the newly-elected mayor, Judge Gaynor, rather than McClellan, who would be stepping down from office in a few weeks.

Well, everyone's entitled to their opinion, Martha felt on surmising this, though deep down she was hard-put to see any real reason for the march herself. Now, however, she simply misses her good friend sorely and is only sorry that she didn't manage to talk him into coming after all.

All around her in the trolley, feathers are bobbing on home-made broad-brimmed hats like hers, as girls in small groups gab away. And as if being by herself like this weren't bad enough, an old white-beard next to her is keeping up a steady patter with himself, begun when he plopped down three stops ago.

The Strike

Oh well, Martha sighs, there's always *him* to think about—but even there she has no luck.

All week long it's been TERRIBLE, those serious steel-blue eyes and his bloodless cheeks coming to haunt her as soon as her head touched the pillow every night.

She's been absolutely beside herself, for nothing that she's tried, but NOTHING, has proved of any avail.

Last night, finally, after squirming around on the mattress for ever so long, she slipped her tongue between his lips...to find his own tongue-tip JUST INSIDE, like a belly button...

Ping! goes the bell for getting off, one of the girls bound for the meeting having pulled the cord. The black hulk of the Third Avenue El is looming outside; yes, it's time.

Other girls stand up too—*Ping! Ping!*—and now just about the whole car is on its feet, ready to go.

No need to rush, Martha assures herself, as they pile out in a pack and take off down the street ahead of her.

Then the funniest thing—she suddenly realizes, trotting along, that the shop she's going by, whose windows are full of oddly bewigged heads surrounded by the prettiest cosmetics boxes, is Papa's.

Who's there, she wonders—as if she doesn't know—and presses her nose against the glass to have a look.

Papa is just inside, passing the time of day with a stout gentleman in a fur-collared coat and homburg with a cane, some actor no doubt.

Martha gives a wave—dear Papa with his shopkeeper's shiny glasses and every crinkly white hair in place.

Noticing her out of the corner of his eye, he smiles his Papa's smile and diddles back.

Does he have any idea where I'm off to? Most likely he does—Mammeh must be keeping him abreast of things, in her politic way, of course. Does he care anymore? One wouldn't know it to see it: he seems to have eyes only for sisters Dinah and Pauline these days.

And Uncle Abe? Martha peers more closely, but he's nowhere to be found. Must be in the back with cousin Joey, his pride and joy—who's just decided on a career in Dentistry.

Supposing you'd been born a boy, would you have followed along the same course, Martha poses, pushing on. Yes, more or less, I guess—that is, provided I'd made it into a decent high school like him, which I probably would have, and then into The City College, also for men only. And my marks would've been just as good, I bet.

But boys don't always fare better, she argues. For instance—

Well, there's Sonny the Sheygets—whose real name evidently is Jerrold.

Look at how those girls beat him almost to a pulp after grabbing the coffee away from him that day. And what for? He never did anything to them, he's only another slavey.

Martha pictures good-looker Sonny as she saw him then, his face contorted by shock and pain, shaking—"Poor guy."

A line has formed outside the Lipzin, with its marquee and assorted bric-a-brac, and more people are arriving every moment to add themselves to it.

"Okay, goils, have yuh membership cards ready!" a union chap bawls, as Martha comes up.

The line promises to be a crawler, so with an almost professional eye, she scans the billboards to see what's playing there at the Lipzin this evening.

It's *Di Yidishe Kenigin Lear—The Yiddish Queen Lear*—with Keni Lipzin. Martha remembers going to see it as a child with her parents: Madame Lipzin portrays Mirele the mama, who, somewhat like Shakespeare's king, unflinchingly endures all kinds of indignities.

"No shovin', plenty of room inside!"—it's the blue jacket again, just behind her, creeping up to the entrance.

The Strike

In Mammeh's opinion, the story was rather overdone, and Papa tended to agree...

"At last," Martha breathes, hastening down the aisle finally toward the first vacant seat, which happens to be in the center.

Benny would have done things differently, of course—either gone further down in order to see better, or else slipped in somewhere in the back, where it would be easy to slip out and away if he desired.

Oh well, it's done, and that's that. In the few minutes that it took to remove her coat, the place just about filled up. Conscious of the usual loud chatter, Martha looks to the stage.

Miss Dreier, Miss Marot, and three strangers, obviously belonging to their set, are consorting together on one end of a long table, while on the other end, a trio of factory girls sit side-by-side staring into space, doubtless the recent victims of police nightstick and boot mentioned in the circular advertising the rally.

Miss Dreier gets up, revealing herself to be dressed becomingly in green. "SISTERS AND BRUDDERS," she begins, and flashing one of her sunny smiles, waits for quiet. "I HOPE YOU HAVE YOUR VALKING SHOES ON."

"Hooray, Mary!" a girl yells out. "Yea!" others cheer. There's an enthusiastic round of applause for her.

I'll take her over Feigenbaum and his pals any day, Martha acknowledges, even if I'm not *her* cup of tea.

By way of starting things off, Miss Dreier has asked her dear friend Miss Rose Pastor Stokes to say a few words.

One of the three strangers at the table arises—a woman in a black south-of-the border outfit, including a Mexican cowboy hat.

"MY FRIENDS," she begins, and she too pauses, but for effect. "I THINK WHAT YOU'RE DOING IS SIMPLY SPLENDID, AN EXAMPLE OF LABOR AGAINST CAPITAL IN ITS FINEST TRADITION."

"*Oy vey*," Martha groans, as this Stokes woman continues in the same vein. If only Benny were here, just for this, I can hear him now—Yuh, yuh, dot's de socialisten for yuh. Foist dey vant you to tink dey know better, den later dey try to make you beleef you tought vhatever it vas up all by yuhself.

Happily, the leftish pep talk is soon over. And now Miss Dreier introduces Mrs. Theresa Malkiel to review the procedure with them—one of the other unknowns at the table, in a black fur-collared coat and fancy hat with an obvious store-bought look to them.

"Gir-r-rls!" Mrs. Malkiel's voice echoes, and with her smear of a mouth, she loses no time.

They'll be going straight downtown via the Bowery and Park Row, six abreast, carrying banners while the supply lasts, after that with arms linked.

At the walkway leading to the City Hall, Miss Dreier, Miss Marot, the league's counsel Miss Rauh, and the three girls will separate themselves from the main body.

Everyone else will begin circling the City Hall Park, and keep on doing so until the delegation comes out again.

"Now remember, girls," Miss Malkiel practically shrieks in conclusion, "This is no laughing matter—there's to be no, but absolutely no, kidding around!"

Martha warmly applauds with everyone else. This Malkiel is okay too.

Miss Dreier's face takes on a playful expression—"De next speaker vill be vell known to some of you"—meaning lawyer Ida Rauh, who will explain about security and the like.

Martha sees at once that there's something different about this one, the last of the three strangers to get up—she has a delicate look, and is simply clad in a worn brown tweed suit.

There'll be a police escort on horseback to deal with any hooliganism, Miss Rauh advises, in a voice that is mellow with a certain strength. In addition, foot patrolmen will be stationed at every major intersection for the sake of controlling cross traffic. Are there any questions?

The Strike

Benny would like her too, Martha gauges, as the woman stuffs papers into an old briefcase amidst polite applause.

"So everyvun"—Miss Dreier is on her feet again. "Are you ready?"—she holds up a diploma-like roll of paper tied with a pink ribbon, the petition.

"Yes-es-es-es-es!" the whole house lets out, including Martha to the depths of her being.

Making a beeline for the aisle, she immediately finds herself queued up again, and slowly coming to the back, encounters Baroff there, who sizes her up in his Yankee banker's way—"You alone, cutesy?"—and without further ado, puts her together with a foursome and another single.

"*Nah!*"—the crowning touch, he slaps in Martha's hands a folded piece of cloth. She should make sure that her group keeps in step so that spectators can read it.

Darting away, Martha notes from a label that the banner will say: Peaceful picketing is the right of every woman. Yessirree, that's my view exactly.

Outside on Rivington, there's a huge assemblage of neighborhood folk waiting behind police barricades.

"Hooray! We're with you! Give 'em hell!" reaches Martha's ears in English, Yiddish, and God knows what else.

A union man waves from under the El, where the column of marchers is being formed—"C'mon! *Shnel!*"

What would Benny think now, Martha wonders, scurrying along with her people in tow, and tells her name to one of the foursome, a dreadfully scrawny girl with deeply pockmarked cheeks.

"Now howdya like dat!" this possibly new chum, who's called Brinah, exclaims when Martha adds that she's on strike at Triangle. The four of them and their co-workers walked out of Diamond a few weeks ago when it was discovered that the boss was taking in work for Harris and Blanck! Brinah can't get over it—"Why you and us is like family, *landsmen!*"

After they're tacked on to the column, Martha pays out the banner till it's spread across to Maria, the other loner, on her end.

"Hey, get a load a dat!" Brinah yells out, something having made her look back toward the Lipzin.

Baroff and his men are quickly and deftly taking people from the crowd and turning them into additional squads of marchers!

The blue jackets are still maneuvering folks around with much pleading when Miss Dreier and her delegation, now in place at the column's head, leads them all forth...

Coming up on the left is the richly ornamented People's Theatre, where Mammeh's one-time idol Boris Thomashevsky holds sway, singing for all he's worth about his own mama...and where, oddly, Papa's favorite, Jacob Adler, can be heard on occasion, magnificently doing his all in the real *Lear*.

Now there's the Miner's Theatre, home of vaudeville for the Irish, which Papa claims is little better than smut...and across the way, the Occidental Hotel, where as everybody knows, Tammany bigwig Tim Sullivan hangs his hat.

Lining the curb on either side are hangers-on from the many saloons and other sleazy establishments—unshaven, in black bowlers, with stale cigars—who take note of the procession as they would of racehorses parading to the starting gate, or else look on glassy-eyed.

"*Shickers*," Brinah sneers, referring to their futile lust for hard drink. "Don't pay no attention to dem."

A train comes roaring by on the tracks overhead, making the ground under foot rumble.

"*Oy*, it gives me such a headick," the girl next to Brinah complains.

All grist for the mill, is Martha's feeling, with Lear on the Heath somehow in mind.

Soon, on the left, is the many-columned gateway to the Manhattan Bridge, like a setting for a Roman triumph...and then the Wind-

The Strike

sor, another Yiddish theatre, but offering only *shund* or trash, Papa says...while opposite is the Thalia, where once long ago Martha heard a black-bearded Hamlet in a Robin Hood suit cry out with his whole heart and soul—"*Zayn oder nisht zayn, dos iz di kashe!*"

The end is in sight: beyond Park Row's thousand-and-one pawn shops and old-clothes stores, where the El is no more...

There, they've made it: they're out in the open, as on a brooding plain, and up ahead waiting for them is a sprinkling of editors, reporters, and curiosity seekers in front of...the World Building, thirteen stories high...tiny Sun, five...and the giant Tribune, nineteen.

Finally, there's the pale pastel-green statue of Ben Franklin with his famous spectacles on, and to the right, the City Hall, crowned by its little clock tower and Lady Justice with her sword and scales—where Miss Dreier and company break away.

Setting off again with the column, Martha—not quite as naive as Benny has made her out to be—falls to imagining, in her best wry manner, what will transpire after the party schlepps up all those stone steps:

How a gentlemanly-like policeman will open from inside, and holding the door for them, bid them enter and be seated, alas, on two hard wooden benches. Then how, after absenting himself for a trice, he will reappear to announce, with all due apologies, that His Honor is still at lunch, but will be with them shortly—which was a development not at all figured on. Leave it to a power-grubber like him to serve us with a trick like this, Helen Specs-and-Tie will convey to Mary Blue-Eyes with a knowing look. But what's there to do, they'll have to wait the booby out.

Ten minutes will pass according to the grandfather clock with its devilish tick-tock. Then all at once the door to the real inside will swing wide as if in a sou'wester, and there he will be, the Man—tall, robust, and were it not for a certain minuscule roll of flesh under his chin, handsome. And once more apologies will be extended, Sorry, ladies, you know how it is being a responsible public servant etc. Whereupon, with the six of them standing, he will press each leader's hand as warmly as he dare, and proffer a few skittish fingers to the girls.

Now it will be time to get down to cases—namely, for Miss Dreier to unburden herself of her pink-beribboned document, which she will accomplish with her usual flare. And now Yetta Raffy, designated speaker among the victims, will take the floor to spiel about the dreadful encounter that she had with one or more of New York's Finest.

"Well, I'm—I'm certainly shocked!" His Honor will self-righteously declare, after giving heed, with cocked ear, to Yetta's every well-rehearsed syllable. To think that such things should happen under his very nose! The Police Commissioner shall certainly hear about it and any other irregularities of a like nature—the Ladies can be sure of that...

Yes, dear friend, that's how it will be, Martha tells the Benny in her mind, a sham like that for sure. And yes, nothing will come of it probably, nothing much anyway.

But now that I've had a chance to consider everything with more care, again that's neither here nor there as far as I'm concerned.

What matters is that we are all here today striving toward something together...something fervently desired that we all heartily believe in, even if the outcome isn't always as one would wish.

CHAPTER

11

Now the truly punishing part of winter came on and not a day passed without Mammeh's raising distraught hands to her breast at the thought of Martha walking up and down in front of that building on Washington Place.

How will it all end, she worried again over her treadle one day, a week or so after the bitter cold began.

Outside it was dark almost like night, and it was not yet three o'clock. For sure, it would begin snowing before very long.

Who's there to talk to, to pour one's heart out to? She gave a look at little Fanny, busy scratching with her crayons at the table. What does she know, a child.

The picture of *Kreynele* chilled to the bone out there finally became too much to bear, and Mammeh rose to go look out the window.

The girl will catch her death, and so will the others…never eating right on top of everything else. And that will be a fine how-do-you-do. It's enough already, the strikers made their point. Now the two sides should sit down together and settle their differences. Everyone is saying so…

Downstairs on the street, people were bustling along all bundled up, with hats pulled low over brows and noses buried in scarves.

Mammeh's eye lighted on a poor soul, weighed down by market baskets, making for the corner.

"*Got in him!*"—a strong gust of wind nearly bowled the *bobe* over.

MILK AND COOKIES

Dinah and Pauline are home from school, and it is even bleaker looking outside, with white flakes threatening to descend at any moment.

The children are at the table: Dinah, eight, with her reddish-brown hair...seven-year-old Pauline, the green-eyed blonde... and Fanny, going on four, with her olive complexion and black mane.

Here comes Mammeh with a platter of everyone's favorite butter cookies topped by walnuts, baked fresh today and still a little warm from the oven. "Don't be beshful," she jokes, and takes her customary place on the far end.

Little Fanny raises her glass of milk with both hands, and draws in a goodly amount with a *zup*—which leaves a foamy moustache under her nose.

Dinah, of the bright blue eyes, points a finger—"What a pig!"

"Come here, please," Mammeh says, and the dribbles are wiped away with the dish towel one-two-three.

"Piggy-wiggy," Dinah sneers, never knowing when to let it rest.

Fanny's face wrinkles up, and she leans toward Mammeh's breast—"Nah-ah!"

"You shouldn't say tings like dot to her," Mammeh gently reprimands. "You see how sensitive she is."

The corners of the Dinah and Pauline mouths turn down.

Mammeh isn't too pleased with how she's handled this either—everything I do seems to be wrong these days.

It's too cold to go out and the two older girls decide to play house in the parlor instead—by themselves, of course...

So when is she coming home, my *kreynele*, Mammeh broods, bending over the machine once more. Don't tell me they're going to keep her out there in the freezing cold to the very last minute like any other day?

Bad enough my precious had to go to work at that Triangle place. Now since the Strike, she doesn't seem to have time for anything else—the Settlement House dances for instance, or even old friends like Essie, who has written several times and dropped by once, unfortunately when Martha wasn't home.

Mammeh's heart cries out in spite of herself—what kind of a life is this for her? Who's she going to meet there on the street and in the union hall!

It's a quarter past four, and Mammeh, in her usual painstaking way, is putting the finishing touches to a bluish-grey skirt, which is to go with a chic rose chiffon waist, a new outfit for *Peysekh*—Passover.

Something makes her glance at the window again. "Oh!" she gasps.

The snow has finally come. Heavy flakes are tumbling down, whitish clumps like pieces of mattress stuffing...

The door flies open without warning—"Mammeh, I'm home!"—it's Martha.

Mammeh is ecstatic—"Velcome, strenger!"—and rushes over to kiss and be kissed, then to the sink to fill the kettle.

"They let everyone go early because of the weather," *Kreynele* says to her back. "There's supposed to be a big storm tonight."

The water for the tea on, needed now is some light from the gas jet overhead with its yellow glow and familiar, comforting hiss, which requires just a quarter in the slot and a turn of the spigot.

Just returned from leaving coat and hat to dry in the bathroom, *Kreynele* is sitting at the table with chin uplifted, as if for an inspection. Close beside her is the little one, and hovering too are Dinah and Pauline, who abandoned their play to come see what all the excitement was about.

Mammeh notes that eldest born's eyes appear to be deeper in their sockets and her cheekbones are more pronounced, meaning that she's lost more weight. But there's a bright side to the picture: the *meydele*'s color is good, and her spirits are still high.

"So vhat's doing mit Mr. Benowitz? Is he alright?" Mammeh asks, just to be sociable.

Kreynele grows serious—"No, he didn't come today. He's got a bad cough. His wife called from a candy store and left a message by Mrs. Goldman."

"Vell, I'm sorry to hear dot," Mammeh says, half-meaning it. And chances are he is laid up, an old one like that, not in such good shape to begin with, staying out in all kinds of weather for long periods of time.

Kreynele is starving—"What's for dinner, ma?"

Oy!—Mammeh is embarrassed for having to be reminded. "Chicken fricassee," she announces, made yesterday, and hurries to get the pot out of the ice box—signal for Dinah and Pauline to fetch cutlery and dishes from the pantry, and the little one to clear the table of her things.

By the time it heats up, Eli will be here, Mammeh figures, giving a preliminary stir...

"You goin' out again?" she hears Dinah inquire of older sister.

Martha adopts their papa's teasing tone—"What's it to you, nosey?"

Outside, it's completely dark now, and the fat white flakes are still hurling themselves down.

"Ah c'mon, are you or aren't you?" relentless Dinah nags, but echoing a mother's sentiment exactly.

Coming with the tea, Mammeh bites her lip, hopefully for the last time today.

"Well, not that it's any of your business, but I'm not," Martha answers. "I'm stayin' home-sweet-home tonight."

The Strike

With many of the Strike's principal events unfolding just a stone's throw away across the Square, it was difficult not to get caught up in it, even if such matters were normally none of one's affair. And here we are yet once more, Hippolyte acknowledged, beholding that sorry lot from Triangle from his usual vantage point by Garibaldi's statue one cool, cloudy morning in late December. These trudgers-along in all kinds of weather, misguided though they had been by those do-gooding union-lovers Dreier and Marot, were of one spiritual flesh with him.

Happily, though, this day was not just for sizing up the Triangle situation from under the brim of his crushed green fedora with the wilted feather. No, he had something very special to do, and in fact it was specifically to attend to it that he had roused himself at such an early hour, quietly pulling on his pants in the half-light so as not to deprive Liebling Paula of her customary long rest.

In a word, he was about to go over to the *Mother Earth* office on East Thirteenth Street and see Sasha, who had been left in charge while Comrade Emma and boyfriend were off on another lecture tour. And he had as his aim to try and persuade that "old friend" of the Comrade's to give a show of support for the Strike, which they in the Anarchist camp had refrained from doing as of yet except in a minor way.

Why should such a gesture be made now after all these agonizing months? Well, yesterday the long drawn-out negotiations to end the Strike came to a complete halt when the bosses, who had agreed to everything else, absolutely put their foot down about a union shop. And now Hippolyte was only afraid that the mink-clad backers of Marot and Dreier would give all these poor women and girls the heave-ho because of their equally adamant refusal to accept the material advantage of higher piece rates and let it go at that.

The point Hippolyte intended to drive home to Sasha was that should such a turn of events occur, the stalwart ones should realize that there were other people around who cared, most importantly as fellow humans.

And how was Sasha likely to react to this idea? Well, there was the rub. Had it simply been a matter of dealing with Emma, there would very likely have been no problem: if nothing else, she would have gone along with it as a favor to Hippolyte for old time's sake. But Sasha, still not quite right in the head after his twenty-two years in the lock-up, was another proposition entirely, especially with his girl Becky there to egg him on. Hippolyte grimaced—I can just imagine.

Lingering in the muddy light as the picketers yet once more wheeled around and began up Washington toward Greene, he gave a scratch to his goatee, and did just that, imagined what would happen:

Along University Place he'll wend his way, mindful of giving a wide berth to more lines of marchers, until he reaches his turn-off at Thirteenth Street.

But first, there'll be an old ritual to repeat in front of the portals of the New York Society Library, caterer to the rich and ruthless, whose shelves are lined with everything that is noteworthy according to those supposedly in-the-know on The Times and Trib—works with titles like "Laid Up in Lavender," "Old Indian Days," "Yolande of Idle Isle," and most recently, "Lonely House" by A. Streckfuss.

*"*Drekfus!*"—Shit Foot!—he'll shout in passing—and if some old fart member of the Society happens to be coming out at the moment, so much the better. He'll shout it again, and give him The Finger!...*

Tickled by the fun, eastward he'll steer, to go past tenement on tenement, until a few paces down from Third Avenue, there'll be that old familiar one faced with stone on the street-level, whose dark, dank hallway is always redolent of cabbage soup in the Russian-Jewish style, with tomatoes, vinegar, and oodles of sugar.

Up the narrow stairway he'll begin, his way lighted by open yellow flames, flaring like Blake's Tyger.

Up, up, to the top he'll mount, aerie of exile, where as any fool knows, only the truly significant in our world lay their heads these days.

The Strike

"Courage," he'll murmur, all out of breath, to brace himself—meetings with Sasha are seldom anything to write home about.

There's no need to knock or wait to be let in, the door's open, whoever comes is welcome—the Comrade's idea...

In the few minutes of Hippolyte's standing beside Garibaldi drawing out his sword, the sky had grown sullen, and now the line of Triangle picketers was like so many deep-dark shadows on dull grey.

He looked away to get a clearer picture of the rest of his vision.

Good old Sasha with his steel-rimmed specs and smeary lips is relaxing in his golden oak swivel amidst the usual clutter of books and papers—reminding of Wilhelm Körber in Vienna and other Movement leaders I've had to do with elsewhere, who each ruled over their cells like petty despots, regardless of the rank-and-file's proud boasts of utter egalitarianism among them.

Perched close by on the Comrade's desk, with sandal-footed legs dangling, is big-chested Becky Edelson, who could pass for a younger sister of those potentates' sweethearts.

There's only one glaring difference between these two and the others: a sneaking suspicion I've been harboring for some time past that, as a result of Sasha's long imprisonment, very little, if anything, goes on between them back there in the bedroom.

Sasha: (Clunking forward in his chair at the sight of me.) Hippolyte! Vat brings you here at dis ungodly hour? (Throwing a twinkle of amusement Becky's way.) I tought de love boids never got up before de sun goes down.

I: (To myself, painfully conscious of having been his replacement with the Comrade, along with Gorgeous Ben). Alright, let him have his little joke, he's entitled. (Then to him.) Look, Sasha— (And I begin.)

Sasha leans back in his chair again and closes his eyes, so as to lead me to believe he's giving whatever it is his most careful consideration, while Becky plops herself in the Comrade's chair to regard me from there...

I: (After making quick work of it.) In other words, I'd just like to see those strikers get a break for a change, that's all.

Sasha: (Picking up on this last, with his eyes still closed.) A break, Hippolyte? Who doesn't need a break? Vee all need a break. (His eyelids widen, and he falls to tapping with a pencil.)

I: (To myself, bitterly.) So, the Greater Russian Slav, or Slob actually because he's also a Jew, is expecting the Lesser Once-Removed Bohemian Slob to begin kissing his ass. (To him, with élan.) What's the problem, Sasha? What possible reason could you have—?

Sasha: (Giving me a ferocious look—but not really, because as the Comrade and I are both aware, this would-be assassin, who pumped three bullets into Henry Clay Frick and stabbed him with a poisoned dagger and still didn't finish the job, is incapable of harming a fly...would be hard-put even to put himself out of his misery, should occasion arise.) Possible reason? All de reason in de voild. You know our policy. (Making the next point with the pencil.) Vee never gif support—to anytink—dot's not initiated by our people. (Flaring his nostrils.) You tink de darlinks need more kind voids said in deir behef? (He motions imperiously to the door.) Go to de Socialisten! Dey'll gif you all de kind voids you vant! (His eyes bulge behind the steel rims.) GO TO DEM FOR GOOD FOR ALL I CARE!

Becky folds her arms and smirks, enjoying the scene immensely.

I: (Also putting my foot down.) Oh no you don't, Sasha! You're not going to get rid of me that easily! (The Comrade warned me about this sort of thing long ago, when he first got out of the clink: "Take care, Hippolyte, or he'll drive everyvun avay from us.") Word is going around that the society ladies are bankrolling those women and girls only for the sake of the attention the poor things are attracting, to help them all get the Vote, and that once they've outlived their usefulness—

Sasha: (Flinging the pencil away, at last.) I don't care, Hippolyte! For de last time, I VON'T DO IT!

Becky's hand goes to her nose—she wriggles the pinky into her nostril...

A light rain had begun to fall, and now among the line of plodders over on Washington Place, black umbrellas were up.

The Strike

Hippolyte's mood was especially grim. If that's how things are likely to turn out with Sasha, I might as well save my breath.

But then—and this was not for the first time—the girl with the high forehead and deep-set eyes came to mind...the one he'd nicknamed the Little Bourgeoise, who had put the Dreier and Marot noses out of joint that night at the dinner party in his place by answering the Rich Bitch back, "I like what I do. I don't consider it drudgery."

And just like those other times, Hippolyte imagined her among the marchers, and indeed thought he made out her slight form clinging close to another under one of the umbrellas.

Eh, go on over to that devil Sasha, and give it a try at least.

LATER: END OF THE DAY

Things have been rather slow in the restaurant all evening, and now as the closing approaches, candles are burning low at three tables, with only a last remaining dessert to be served to a college boy and his date.

Be good to get out for a breath of air, Hippolyte glumly acknowledges at his peep hole. He needs it after the ordeal he's been through at Sasha's hands.

Yes indeed, you certainly had it figured out wrong where that guy was concerned. For the interview turned out worse, far worse, than his imagining, the superior Russky cleaving the half-assed Bohemian in two with one incisive stroke as soon as the proposal was laid on the table:

"Listen, Hippolyte, vy don't you do us all a favor und go home und mind your business"...

Imagine, treating me like that, like a misbehaving child, after all we've been through together! I flew into a rage—"WHAT DO YOU MEAN, MIND MY BUSINESS? IT IS MY BUSINESS! MINE AS MUCH AS YOURS!"

Sasha, for his part, kept on an even keel. "I—say—no," he laid it down, with help from a finger. "Leave de policy making to us, und stick to vhat you know und do best."

Only wanting to throttle him, I couldn't restrain myself—"AND WHAT MIGHT THAT BE, BOOK REVIEWS?"

The Slob answered with a look—that's all, just a look.

Sidekick Becky was beside herself with glee...

You never should have bothered, Hippolyte analyzes now. It was an utter waste of time.

From the corner of his eye, he notices the college boy casting about, and scoots out the kitchen swinger—"Yes?"

The fellow, who looks like a fourteen-year-old but isn't, has acne and wears a cravat. His sweetheart is simply a pleasant-looking girl, also going to school apparently. They'll both have strudel.

When Hippolyte comes back, they're engaged in a soulful duet about Life, in which Kant and Hegel figure considerably.

"Bull," he murmurs, after leaving the crusty apple delights behind. You know what the two of you ought to do, he lectures internally. You ought to stop leeching off your folks, and go out and do an honest day's work.

By the time he brings the coffee, the boy, who is enrolled in NYU's School of Pedagogy, has gotten onto the subject of training teachers.

Foolish, is Hippolyte's private reaction. Teachers are generally born, not made; if they learn at all, it's by example, not rote...

Now just have a look and see if the others are alright, then you can vamoose.

Ida Rauh, who is still tops in his book despite her involvement with Dreier and friends, is at her table in the back, in her old grey dress.

With her is a Dutchman named Piet Vlag, who operates an eatery of sorts in the basement of the Rand School of Social Something or Other, where he divides his time between concocting delicacies like *Hutspot met Klapstock*—alias, a sad *shtikl* of beef swimming in a mess of greasy vegetables—and trying to interest patrons in the idea of cooperatives.

"Cooperative fiddlesticks, cooperative fucks," Hippolyte mutters as he heads over to them.

The two of them look up—the man, light of skin and black-haired, but alas, sadly deficient in chin.

"Can I get you something else?" Hippolyte inquires, directing the question to her, since she in all probability will be asking for the check.

"A liddle soda vater," Vlag says huskily.

Hippolyte whisks his cup and saucer away—"One seltzer coming up!"...

Down front, dressed to the teeth in fur-trimmed grey tweed, is Inez Milholland, who has evidently come straight from Washington Place—the white touring car is parked outside. One of her bosom pals, Violet Pike, sits cozily beside her, a schoolmarm by comparison.

"We'll be leaving shortly," Miss Milholland informs Hippolyte, in a deep, rich voice, when he bends close.

They've been jawing away tête-à-tête ever since they met here by appointment some time ago, and as soon as he is out of earshot, they'll be at it again.

Hippolyte smiles, guessing what's so deliciously hush-hush: Pike the Pickle Puss was arrested the other day while taking a turn on a line somewhere, and is filling Miss Elegance in with all the gory details.

His smile becomes sneaky—that's the best thing about being hauled in by the coppers: beating your gums up about it later. After all, who knows this better than yours truly.

Okeedoke, all set to go, Hippolyte announces to himself, minus the tie and cummerbund, and exits from the kitchen, shouldering his basket.

Liebling Paula, who is privy to nothing about the business with Sasha except that he went to meet with Mr. High-and-Mighty this morning, is smoking thoughtfully at the counter.

Hippolyte's eyes find hers—"Be back in a while, okay?"

She has no objection; in fact, she'll even attend to his share of the tidying up if he's willing.

"Ah, dear one, may things never change," he sighs, donning his overcoat in the vestibule. But I fear, I fear that they will, yes, that one fine day you'll get good and tired of my wandering ways, and find someone who's more clinging, or has something else to offer that's more to your liking...

Outside, the air hangs heavy with mist and it's curiously warm.

"Ach!"—Hippolyte takes in his customary deep breath, and decides to strike out in a new direction, up the Square South for a change.

Blue dance the streetlights as he moves along...reflecting blue in this morning's puddles. His footsteps echo soddenly...

"Well, well," he lets out, after stepping off the curb by Judson Church.

Across the way, a man has just lurched out of O'Reilly's Saloon, and is standing weavingly on the sidewalk.

Why it's only a kid, Hippolyte sees, as he comes closer. Nice-looking too in a Nordic way, and well-dressed into the bargain, he notes in passing.

"SMITTY, WHERE ARE YOU? WHERE DID YOU GO TO?" the young man cries.

Hippolyte turns—the guy's in agony. Too bad, that Smitty must have died on him or something.

"Oh," the young man moans with his head hanging. "Oh-oh."

Feeling the boy's pain, Hippolyte sniffs—but there's nothing to be done, a loss is a loss...

At the next corner, he crosses over to the tree side, and makes for his daily viewing place of these last several months.

"There," he declares, approaching Garibaldi, frozen in revolutionary fervor, and from habit looks up Washington Place, now in blue-black darkness.

Everything of this morning slowly begins to return—how he stood there watching as that sad lot of women and girls went up and down, finally under umbrellas in the rain, with the Little Bourgeoise perhaps among them...how he side-stepped one small company after another like that on his way up University Place.

Hippolyte's mind gallops crosstown on Thirteenth Street to that hallway reeking of sweet-and-sour cabbage soup, and vaults up the stairs, lighted by spurts of Tygerish flame.

Sasha's face is full of cruel amusement—"Hippolyte, vy don't you do us all a favor und go home und mind your business."

Zaftik Becky grins like a gargoyle.

"SASHA!" Hippolyte bawls out, and clenches his fists. "SASHA, YOU BASTARD YOU!"

He sits heavily down on his bench. But surprise—the seat is sopping wet!

"Very funny," Hippolyte quavers, between tears.

The Fire

CHAPTER

12

Regardless of how everyone including herself suffered out there on Washington Place, Martha never flagged in her conviction about the absolute necessity for the Union. So when, in the final days of December, the rank and file of Local 25 was asked once more to say yea or nay to an offer from Management, which again did not contain a provision for a closed shop, she promptly cast her ballot in the negative.

To her way of thinking, they now had to be more adamant than ever about the issue, even if the great John Mitchell himself had taken precious time off from the United Mine Workers to represent them at the bargaining table. As she explained to Benny afterwards over glasses of hot tea in Katz's, now more than ever operators had to present a united front through a union in order to counter the employers' protective association, which had grown by leaps and bounds.

"Yuh, yuh, *Tsatskele*," Benny agreed without much enthusiasm.

Could he have voted the other way, for a settlement, Martha wondered. Anything was possible, and if he had, one could well understand and even sympathize. For besides the constantly festering hands and aching feet, the poor guy was now plagued with a dry, hacking cough, and his motive may simply have been to get back inside where it was warm and dry.

The next day, when they were walking up and down again, Miss Dreier carefully picked her way over the icy road, and announced with her usual cheeriness that this latest offer of the bosses had also been rejected.

"Good, *gut azoy!*" Martha said out loud. "Let those cockroaches know that we're far from licked yet!"

Others close by voiced their agreement, but not the old one, who simply trotted silently along. Nor was that all: the following morning he failed to appear, and didn't even call and leave a message at Goldman's or the candy store back home, and it was the same on succeeding days, meaning as Martha interpreted it that he wanted to be left alone. So from then on she picketed either all by her lonesome or else with one of the twins or Olga if they also had no one, and sometimes with crazy Raiseleh, when the spirit moved that one to turn up.

The harsh weather continuing, it wasn't long before people began coming down with the grippe and worse, which caused a considerable reduction in their ranks. But that's alright, as long as we're making some kind of showing, Martha buoyed herself.

Then the impossible happened. Arriving home feeling unusually energetic one evening, she did all manner of crazy things, like wash and dry the whole sinkful of supper dishes by herself, and then woke the next morning feeling extremely listless...strangely without even the will to get up and wash her face and hands.

Happily Mammeh, who always had a nose for trouble, came and pressed her lips to *Kreynele*'s forehead, and immediately ordered her back to bed. "But don't vorry, darlink, you'll soon be as guht as noo again," she assured, bringing a pot of hot tea with honey and lemon after Papa and the girls were under way.

The only problem was, the sickness had to run its course first, as they both well knew. So that night Martha alternately burned with fever and shook with chills under a heap of blankets and winter coats, and for the next several days she lay limp as a dishrag.

The Fire

In the meanwhile, as a precaution against the illness spreading, Dinah and Pauline had been packed off to Uncle Abe's in Brooklyn. However, to no avail: no sooner did Martha's head clear and she begin "hocking up" those nasty-tasting globs of dark-green phlegm than little Fanny, shifted to the girls' room at night, became flushed and started vomiting, and then it was Papa's turn, followed by Mammeh, who thankfully had to take to her bed for only a single day.

Once life returned to normal, Martha somehow had no inclination to go out on the line again, and remained at home regaining her strength, as well as wondering from time to time what old Benny was up to. Finally came a day in mid-January when she absolutely had to have more news about the Strike than the dribs and drabs reported in Papa's *Forverts*. So betaking herself to the union hall, she learned that quite a few companies had yielded individually with respect to the closed shop and settled by themselves with their people, and that others were following their lead daily.

Now that's news, Martha rejoiced, and went to put a call through to Benny's candy store.

And oh what a blessing when the two of them were together again, facing one another across a table at Katz's. Except for the cough, which persisted, her good old friend hasn't changed a bit.

So could Martha remember which firms had thrown in the towel, Benny questioned on their getting down to business.

She reeled off what names she could, and immediately his chin wrinkled up—the companies were all very small.

So what was wrong with that?

Well, as he saw it, now with the busy season upon them, those outfits either had to give in and put an end to the Strike at their place, or face the almost certain fate of going under. And that being the case, very likely they were willing to do whatever else was necessary to stay afloat, including take in work from larger companies like Triangle, who had yet to kiss and make up with their help. Benny shook an admonishing finger—"You mark my voids, *Tsatskele*, dot's vhat's going to heppen." And when it did, the Strike would simply peter out.

Yes, I guess he's right, Martha sadly reflected after she and he went their separate ways. The next we'll hear, I suppose, Shop Steward Jake Kline is sounding out Harris and Blanck about taking us all back, which, our luck, will probably be on the same footing as before.

So what should the old one and I do, switch to another line like white goods? Well, while there's no way of knowing for sure without asking, I rather doubt that he'd want to, not having been so inclined when he suggested it for me that time just before the Strike began. And as for yours truly, in all honesty I couldn't bear to be parted from him again.

There was also Bernstein, of course, a continuous living presence in her mind, though she had not set eyes on him in ever so long.

The future thus spelled out, it only remained for Martha to find something to fill the empty hours until the call would go out to return to the shop.

One day soon after, while stopping off at the notions store with Mammeh on their way home from shopping, she picked up a pattern book to thumb through and there it was: crocheting. So to her mother's purchase of some dandy red leather buttons for a certain little someone's new Spring coat were added four spools of heavy thread—in white and several shades of blue.

"Vhat are you goink to make?" Mammeh inquired, as the two of them, Fanny skipping between, schlepped along with their bundles.

"I don't know yet," Martha answered—which happened to be the truth. She'd just have to let it take shape by itself.

Upstairs, as soon as the groceries were stowed, she began plying with the hook at once, using perhaps the same one she had learned

The Fire

with that last year in public school. And before a person could fairly say Jack Robinson, she had turned out a splendid navy flower, both delicate and intricate.

Shall I make some more, she asked the air. Why not, what do I have to lose, haha.

Going at it again after supper, in the midst of Mammeh darning socks, the girls doing their homework, and Papa delving in his *Forverts*, she had quite a few of those dark blue flowers done by the end of the evening, and indeed felt very pleased, as if she had accomplished something.

However, no sooner was she in bed with the lights out than second thoughts came—what's the matter with you, why did you use only one color?

The next morning found her unraveling everything and starting afresh, this time with the light and medium blues as well as the dark.

That's more like it, was her sense of things when the first flower materialized. Of the same design in variegated blue highlighted by white, it looked electrifyingly alive, as if it had recently sprung into being...on another world.

Martha surveyed a pile of a pile of those "living" flowers on the table that night—so what do I do now?

Why make another of a different design, came the answer, what else...

Several days later that flower and its mates were done, as evanescent and complex as the first, and once more the question was, what next.

Two additional series of blue-and-white flowers, each more daring in conception yet, followed within the week.

Now something entirely different is needed, it struck Martha after more deliberation, something to bring all the floral motifs together.

An oval suggested itself, in which would be featured a tangle of trees and shrubbery with all kinds of animals peeking in between, including some creatures no one had ever seen before.

Back to the notions store she went for more thread—red, purple, orange, and yellow now, as well as green-green-green.

Then in no time at all it seemed, that part was finished too, and it was only a matter of surrounding the riotous jungle with the various blue-and-white flowers.

"Have you decided what it's going to be yet?" little Fanny whispered on the day when the job of assembly began.

Mammeh, having paused at the treadle, listened with her cat's eyes.

"No, not yet," Martha whispered back conspiratorially. But obviously it was high time that she did. "Supposing I decide now, okay? It's going to be…"

The words rose from deep within her…"A tablecloth for our new house in Brooklyn, when we move in one day."

LATER THAT NIGHT: IN THE PARLOR

Eli is zizzing in the middle of the bed, and Mammeh is enduring it on her side close to the edge, an old story grown more acute through the years as she put on more flesh.

Her thoughts have been all of Martha of course, dear *Kreynele* whose needlework is every bit as good as her own, if not better. Even so, it seems to her that the girl should no more be hanging around the house diddling with a crochet hook than walking up and down with a sign in the street. AND SHE SHOULDN'T BE GOING BACK TO THAT HELL HOLE TRIANGLE EITHER, WHEN THE THING IS SETTLED!

What should her darling eldest-born be doing then? Well, all I know is that whatever it is, at night after work she should be going out to club-meetings, parties, and dances like before, to have a good time and also to improve her chances of meeting someone, the right one…

Mammeh's side has begun to bother her. The question is, can she turn over onto her back without disturbing him, her beloved. It needs all of her concentration…

The Fire

So, Bertha, it sounds to me as if you're about to take matters into your own hands. Fancy that, after all your fine words these last few years about the girl's having the right to do as she pleases. Mammeh blinks angrily, as if another person were really accusing her—wouldn't you be doing the same thing by this time if you were in my shoes?

Now let's see, where to begin? Ah yes, for one thing, I ought to get after husband here, as well as brother-in-law, to ask around among the suppliers and other business people coming to the store, and see if anyone has a son who is a little unusual or knows of one. Maybe that'll do the trick, but maybe it won't—it isn't like back in Berdichev where everybody knows everybody—so what else?

Well, one can always seek the services of a *shatkhn*, marriage broker, I suppose, like other people who have "difficult" single girls on their hands. But Mammeh has heard that those professional putters-together can be witches, worse than poison! So no, on second thought, that's not for a child of mine...

Not happy on her back anymore, she shifts to her other side, so her rump is against Eli's...

A new idea dawns, the best! We could send *Kreynele* away somewhere, like to a school out of town. The German Jews do it with their children, including the daughters if they're willing to go, so why shouldn't we with ours? And even if my precious one doesn't find a nice boy there, the change in surroundings could work miracles on her. Why it would be like packing a consumptive off to a farm in the country for a while to take some clean, fresh air into their lungs and put a little meat on their bones from the rich, nourishing food!

Mammeh is ecstatic, but then it grows dark before her eyes—those schools cost money, where is it going to come from? Savings they have of course, but that's for the house in Brooklyn, and it wouldn't be fair to take from it for Martha and prolong the move for the rest of the children.

A glimmer of hope arises: maybe there's a way to finagle with the fees. That's what the German Jews do with other things, people say;

they almost never pay the full price for anything. I must get some advice—now who is there?

What about the people at the settlement house? Mammeh doesn't much like them, *goyim* meddling in things they only half understand. But they're the best ones around for the job when you come down to it.

Mammeh rolls onto her back again. They'll know which is the right school, and be only too glad to help fill out the forms, I'm sure.

Also, not to forget the hardest part: *Kreynele* will have to be won over. And who is there better than someone from that place to try and accomplish it!...

Eli has stopped zizzing; that last move did it. "What are you doing up still?" he murmurs in Yiddish. "Do you have a *boykh veytik*"—belly ache—"or something?"

For shame, Mammeh scolds herself, the man needs his rest. "Nothing, it's nothing," she answers him, also in Yiddish. "Go back to sleep."

But husband is awake, and that's that. "Don't treat me like a child," he snaps. "What's the matter, what's bothering you?"

Mammeh tells him briefly, as much as she dares: how worried she is about Martha.

"Mm"—he can well understand. "If there's anything I can do"—his tone is unwavering.

Nu, there's a real human being for you! Brimming with gratitude, Mammeh leans over to plant a big kiss on his mouth.

Receiving it in the same spirit, Eli nevertheless holds her there.

Azoy—so. Mammeh's blood begins to heat up, and her hand reaches for his cheek, always surprisingly soft beneath the stubble.

A pang of fear grips her, another old story—what if one of the little ones hears and comes barging through the door to investigate? Never mind, it'll be alright, she assures herself as she's long been accustomed to.

The Fire

Eli's face is buried in her breasts. Her fingers sift through his hair, and passing over his shoulder, slip down his back. My man, Mammeh realizes yet once more, my one and only man.

Her nightgown is up, raised by herself. I'll tell him the whole story—what I have in mind for the girl—tomorrow.

※

First thing the next morning before anyone was up, there was Martha in the kitchen putting the finishing touches by candlelight to that first crocheted creation of hers.

A truly vital thing, she judged it, after spreading it across the long, rectangular table. Each blue-and-white flower was separate and distinct, and at the same time all the rows of those blooms together radiated contrastingly toward and away from the jungle-like center with its foxes, elephants, lions, and God knows what else.

Not long after, her mother came through from the back in her kimono, followed by Papa in his dressing gown, who gave a quick nod before ducking into the bathroom.

"Ver' nice," Mammeh offered after standing before the handiwork for some few moments.

Martha couldn't believe her ears—is that all, it's just nice? "It's for you, Mammeh. I made it just for you."

"Yes? Denk you."

Could it be that my mama doesn't like it, Martha considered. Maybe I overdid it, maybe I should have stuck to a single subject in one or two colors as the book in Mr. Abrams' store suggested.

"Sveetheart, Papa und I vant to talk to you efter breakfast," Mammeh added in her gentle voice.

Martha was relieved—my mother has something else on her mind, that's all.

Dinah and Pauline scuffed in with tousled mops. "Hurry up, Papa!" Dinah yelled at the bathroom door. "We gotta go!" Her eyes lighted on the table with its new covering—"Hey, some *shmate*!"—rag.

Mammeh immediately rose to the defense—"Vadda you mean *shmate*!" Her tone turned playful—"I'll give you a *patsh in tokhes*!"—smack on the bottom.

It really is good then, Martha surmised, and noting now with a certain satisfaction that the hurly-burly oval together with the radiating rows of blue-and-white flowers had the aura of a painting, went to put on some clothes.

"Hey, *bandit*!" she called to Fanny still snuggled under the covers. "You gonna sleep the day away?"

"Okay-ay!" the little one piped up.

Sifting among her dresses, arranged on hangers along the wall before the bed, Martha chose the Scotch plaid with the creamy lace collar, which somehow seemed appropriate for today.

Back in the kitchen she found Mammeh presiding over the stove, where oatmeal was steaming, water for the eggs was rumbling, and the coffee was chugging.

Covering the table now was the white oil cloth of every day, laden with plates, cups and saucers, cutlery, and glasses, the "fancy" new cloth having been laid away.

Boy, it sure is crowded around here, Martha couldn't help noticing, as Papa reappeared from the back in his vest, with Dinah and Pauline hard on his heels in aprons over school dresses, and Fanny galloping—"Giddy yap!"—with nighty flying.

As soon as things sort themselves out at the shop, maybe I should try and pitch in and—

THE NEXT MOMENT

"Is anyvun hommm?" a familiar old man's voice husks out.

"*Oy, a shvarts yor*"—a black year—Mammeh groans, as the door bursts open.

It's that Benowitz with a red muffler festively wound round the frayed collar of his overcoat.

Mammeh's Martha has jumped to her feet—"It's over! It's over!"

The Fire

"Yuh, yuh," old Benny agrees, not yet recovered from the climb, and begs Mammeh's pardon in Yiddish for turning up without warning like this.

"Tink nutting of it," Mammeh tells him in English. "I'd invite you to join us but—" As he can see, there's not an inch to spare.

Kreynele has managed to squeeze through to him—"When can we start? WHEN?"

"Tomorra," he answers, and goes on to explain that the Union officially declared the Strike over yesterday, February 15th, and that at the same time a sign went up at Triangle's back entrance inviting one and all to return with no hard feelings.

Eli's look has become noncommittal once more, only a slight flaring of his nostrils betraying his true feelings.

Mammeh is impressed by this. And you know something, Bertha, if you had any sense, you'd follow his example.

Benowitz is still yacking away—about how Bernstein got hold of him a while ago through the candy store and told him to spread the word. The terms on which Triangle's old hands would resume employment, including and especially the piece rates, were to be the same as before. However, Mr. Blanck and Mr. Harris were graciously leaving the door open to dispensing with the crews and letting everyone work for himself at some time in the future.

Martha's eyes are on fire—"OH BOY! I CAN HARDLY WAIT!"

It was *bashert*—fated—that's all, Mammeh can only conclude, biting her lip with a slight shake of the head in spite of herself.

※ ※

Without the least notion as to where Smitty hung his hat or even what his real name was, Jerrold had no other recourse than to go to O'Reilly's the night after that memorable one of mutual ecstasy to speak with him there. However, as luck would have it, the saloon was empty that evening, everyone being at a wake according to Mr. O'Reilly. So there was nothing for it except to drink up and try again on the morrow.

With business back to normal then, there was a goodly crowd at the bar, including Blacky the Tammany boss's nephew—but, alas, his friend's slick, sandy head was nowhere to be seen. Afraid of spilling the beans concerning the two of them, Jerrold had simply nursed a few lagers the whole time while keeping a sharp eye on the door through the mirror—only to be disappointed yet once more after seeing this and that individual breeze in, but no Smitty.

What could one do but return the following day, and when there was still no sign of him, on the next and so on. At the end of his tether finally by the end of the week, Jerrold ventured to tell Mr. O'Reilly that he wanted to repay a couple of bucks borrowed from Smitty and wondered if he knew where to get hold of the guy—which led to one piece of information being forthcoming at least. Blacky showed genuine surprise at the news: "Smitty musta taken quite a shine ta ya, kid. Bookies are de biggest tightwads in de woild an' don' go for spit normally."

After that, it was a matter of sticking it out from one night to the next in the hope that the man would appear sooner or later.

He has to, he simply has to, Jerrold yearned at the end of the first week—with all ambition gone save that.

FEBRUARY 15TH TO FEBRUARY 16TH

What time is it? What day is today? Where am I? "You have only to open your eyes to see," *a fatherly voice advises.*

He has: it's mid-afternoon and indifferent out. The day? What difference does it make, it's any day.

"Boy, I sure feel bad," Jerrold complains to the ceiling. His eyes are funny, mouth tastes like the inside of a garbage can, and gut hurts.

He eases himself up to sit—I must have put away a barrel last night. But that was not the worst—his head begins to throb. When he got home, Madame the Landlady let it be known, on opening to his pounding, that she was reaching her limit, and if he kept on like this, it was curtains, she'd have to ask him to vacate.

The Fire

But that mustn't be—Jerrold is uncertainly on his feet now. You mustn't lose this place, anything but that. Remember, you promised...

Back from the toilet in his overcoat, he pauses at the fireplace to have a look at himself in the smoky pink mirror—"Boy, oh boy"—gaunt, grey, with dark circles under the eyes.

"Me-aw!" comes from below him on the floor, and encircles his shin with a furry tickle.

"Oh Jerrold, how could you," he murmurs. Bad enough you don't take care of yourself, but a poor dumb animal? For shame!

Wonder if there *is* anything—he lurches for the ice box, and miraculously finds a half-empty can of evaporated milk inside.

"I must get my bearings," he announces after seeing to kit-kat, and makes for the windows.

Outside the Arch is a grey block amidst feathery grey trees, flanked by the pink townhouses, all lackluster, above which pokes the grey Metropolitan Life Tower with its cup-like dome topped by two balls on a rod...

What happened to you, he reproves himself. You just let everything go: looking for the job, boning up on the French, dining in that snazzy basement restaurant, trying out the Sunday service at the Dutch church. And for what, a will-o'-the-wisp.

That Smitty didn't care for you, really he didn't. Why if he had, he would have gotten in touch with you himself long ago.

A phrase comes floating into his head—if fate will have me king, then let fate crown me...something like that, from Macbeth.

Jerrold heaves a sigh—that's the attitude you should have adopted, and can still now...

Downstairs the street seems deserted, which is curious. Usually there's someone around in daytime, if not a workman, then a nanny with a baby carriage.

Ah, here comes somebody—a lone man across the way, heading west.

Wouldn't it be funny if it were HIM, Jerrold muses, observing that the guy is dressed all in brown.

Jerrold is about to turn away, when he sees—"Well, I'll be"— THAT IT IS HIM!

His hands fumble at the window sash! "HEY, SMITTY!" he calls out.

The guy stops and searches upward from under a tweed cap. Ah!—his cheeks crease into a smile—"How ya been, Jerry?" The rich, ripe voice has a new nasal quality, which makes it more becoming yet.

"I've—I've been hoping to run into you." Jerrold motions toward O'Reilly's—"Don't you go there anymore?"

Smitty scans Jerrold's face—"Been out of town on business."

His friend seems a shade paler than Jerrold remembers him. Is it possible he's been sick or even in jail? That certainly would explain things.

"Tell you what," Smitty proposes, "see you there tonight, okay?"

Jerrold can hardly breathe for joy. But is it real, is it really happening? "What—what time?"

"Six."

The two of them seem to be speaking with more than their mouths, Jerrold feels. "I'll be there."

The man gives a wave, and pushes on.

Sleep was the order of the day...a long, deep, sound sleep nourished by a handful of crackers left over from the Year One and the rest of the canned milk.

Now after a warm bath, Jerrold is just about ready, but there are two things that he's still not happy with: a dark-blue vein that won't go away on his left temple, and his tie, basically red to go with the brown, which simply hasn't knotted right.

The Fire

Well, it'll have to do. It's a few minutes to six...

Below on the first floor, all is quiet behind Chucky's door, ole buddy (hardly ever seen these days) about to sit down to his dinner probably.

Continuing on to the foyer, Jerrold smilingly thinks back to the night the two of them went out together...*and then all at once recalls how in the end, after he staggered out of the washroom, Smitty was all for getting very chummy, and would have had it not been for Chucky, who couldn't drag him away fast enough.*

"Who was that?" *I asked.*

"No one in particular," *Chucky answered.* "Jes hangs out here."

I wonder, is it possible, did Smitty...with him too? Jerrold pictures Chucky's banana nose, eyes too close together like a bird's, sweet little mouth, and beefy body in the red flannel shirt and overalls—with him, and with me? Could it be?...

Well—Jerrold is outside and down on the pavement now—I don't care. Moving along with quick strides, his soles beat out the time—I don't, I don't.

Only let Smitty be here, that's all, he prays, shouldering in the right swinger.

Well? Jerrold's eye flits among the crowd up front. Well? It darts down the bar to the back. No, he's not. "Darn," he mutters under his breath, and his stomach begins to churn.

Ah c'mon, take it easy, his better self interposes, it's early yet, maybe he's held up somewhere.

Reaching his place in the center at the same time as Mr. O'Reilly, Jerrold orders his usual.

But strangely the proprietor doesn't jump to it. "Listen, kid," he says in a confidential tone, "me and the boys've been talking things over. You've been tying one on a bit too much lately. How 'bout laying off for tonight?"

Jerrold staggers inwardly as if from a blow. Does he mean it? Should I go then? But what about Smitty? He might come by any minute, and I must see him—I MUST! "I'll just have one, 'kay?" he hears himself saying. "Smitty'll be here before long. Just wanna settle up with him."

O'Reilly nods coolly.

Jerrold's knees are all a-tremble, and sweat has broken out on his forehead.

You know, you could do with something to eat, his better self warns. Go on over and help yourself at the free lunch counter, that's what it's there for.

Jerrold moves uncertainly toward it, and in a trice is back with some slices of muenster and onion on a slab of pumpernickel.

Now get it all down, every bit of it—Jerrold takes a bite, chews it up, and moistens the wad with a swallow of beer. Good, good food—something urges him to do it again...

Now look here, he tells himself when the last morsel is gone and the stein drained, it's got to be seven at least, and if Smitty were going to show up, he would have by now. So let's call it a night, okay?...

Jerrold imagines himself outside, plodding along the street to the house, then having mounted up the stoop, somehow managing it up the stairs...all those stairs.

There, you've done it, you're home at last, back at your one-and-only home on high. And now his coat falls away, and the cap and jacket—and now the bed rises to meet him, face-to-face, like Mother Ocean...

"'Bye, Jerry!" Mr. O'Reilly calls out behind him. "See ya around!" someone echoes, Blacky very likely.

At the swingers, Jerrold gestures without answering. Oh, the hurt.

Is this a dream, he wonders. The gasjet by the door is yellow-flaming. Now did I turn it on or not?

The Fire

It can't be a dream: someone is here. Is it Smitty? No, another man, all in black with a foreign-looking hat in hand like at a funeral. He's speaking very seriously. Listen—

"Whatsa matter you no come aroun' like before?"

Why it's Arturo, the roly-poly baker with his mustachios and few hairs plastered across his noggin.

"You no like us no more? Giuseppina and me, we do some-a-ting to you?"

The man's right in a way, Jerrold is willing to concede. So let him babble on and get it out of his system if he wants to.

"I hear you hangin' aroun' an Irish saloon with a buncha bums. You shoulda be shame, a nice-a boy like you."

The yellow flame, which burns upward over the man's shoulder, is punishingly severe. Jerrold shades his eyes to follow him the better.

"Whatsa matter, you too drunk to talk?"

That's all ole Arturo has to say and he's ready to leave now, but first the young man, if he's truly feeling contrite, must promise something...

"I promise," Jerrold solemnly intones.

Was it a dream, he wonders with a new day begun and the sun streaming in. Rather not, I think. The yellow gaslight beside the door is still spurting upward and it wasn't he who struck the match to get it going, that's for sure.

Then it *was* Arturo. He *was* here.

What did he want? What else but the same thing that he's wanted all along, for me to take Rosa with her extra finger off their hands.

Guess I'll have to go over there to the bakery, or perhaps, write him and his wife a letter, and scotch those hopes of theirs now and forever.

The question is, what shall I say? Not in any mood really, Jerrold falls to considering with his arms behind his head.

If only—

Almost as if by some magical force, his eye is drawn to the floor in front of the door. A folded slip of paper is lying there!

"Smitty!" Jerrold shouts out, and lunges for it. What? What? He can hardly hold it steady to read.

Only it's not from him, not from his friend. Rather:

Dear Jerry,
My ma sayes I mustent talk to you. A guy named Solly called from your shop. He sayed you'd know what for.
Your freind,
Chucky

So, there you are. Jerrold shakes his head in a knowing way. Tomorrow, willy-nilly, the Triangle grind begins again.

His heart almost beats in expectation.

❧ ❧ ❧

TOMORROW

One couldn't have chosen a better day, is Martha's thought as she waits for the Houston Street car in cold brilliant sunshine.

Bleary-eyed from lack of sleep, at the same time she is keenly alert—I can't wait, I can't wait.

Already her fingers are guiding the silky-smooth cloth under the needle, she can almost feel it. Already her big toe is bearing down on the power pedal, like the answer to a question.

And then there's Bernstein, ever in her being though a stranger to her thoughts this past month.

Really, I don't see that you have any other choice, Jerrold keeps insisting to himself as he hurries along toward Washington Square East. You made your bed, as they say.

And truly that's how things stand. With scarcely two hundred dollars left in the bank, he doesn't dare do what he would really like

The Fire

to: spend the day making a last-ditch effort to find that other position and delay coming in until tomorrow. There's too much of a chance that Bernstein will take on all the floaters he needs today, and then should the position not materialize, there won't be even that.

Beating a path to Washington Place, Jerrold fights a sinking feeling—what difference does it make...

Now there's a pleasant sight. Up the block at Number 23, the line of marchers is gone and people are entering freely, including Speaking-of-the-Devil himself.

Having just descended from the Broadway car, Martha pauses to gaze down the length of Washington Place before forging ahead on foot.

The way is faced by tan buildings flanked by grey pavements on either side...with the roadbed, all charcoal grey, running straight down the center.

Beyond in Washington Square, tree limbs shine black as crow against a rich blue sky.

Joe the elevator boy with his ugly hook nose is giving a long speech about how the lobby elevators are only for front office personnel now.

"Okay, okay," Jerrold cuts him short—and heads for Greene to take one of the freight carriers.

Crossing over is a face he recognizes: the girl named Martha, who was the horrified witness to his shame that day when the hot coffee got knocked over and the angry mob of strikers came at him.

"'Morning," Jerrold says as they meet, and dutifully raises a few fingers to his cap.

"How are you," the girl sweetly returns, from under her broad-brimmed hat with feathers.

The two of them move quietly along side-by-side.

"Seems like ages," she adds after a little.

"Yes, it does," Jerrold agrees...grateful for her discretion.

"See you," Martha tells Sonny the Sheygets as she steps off on Nine.

It's early and hardly anyone is about as yet, which is how she's been hoping it would be.

First things first, before bustling over to the cloakroom to get rid of her coat and hat, she finds the row and slips straight across, past a dozen or so chairs, to stand before it, Her Machine—one among many ranged along the table, yet clearly hers.

Yes, there are the familiar wear-marks on the wheel showing yellow through the chrome.

It's like revisiting the scene of a crime, Jerrold chooses to think, beholding the grey work shirt and overalls hanging in his locker. Yes, even though in his agony over his hands he neglected to lock it, there they are just as he left them—down to the coffee stains.

I'll shake them out good somewhere for now, he schemes. Then Saturday I'll take them home and give them a thorough scrubbing.

"Hey, Sonny!" someone hails from the doorway.

There's no need to look: Jerrold would know the voice anywhere, in his sleep even. But he does all the same.

"When you're done, c'mon out here," Bernstein says with his customary grimness. "Got something for ya ta attend ta right away."

Nine is pretty well full now, and everyone is busily gabbing away—as if it's summertime and the whole lot of them has just gotten off the train from the Catskills.

The Fire

Martha is sitting pretty amidst a clean-shaven Benny in a new union-suit top, Yetta and Greta with pink bows brightening up their pale faces, and the enemies to the death, Raiseleh with her loony look and dark Olga.

The only one in the room not enjoying himself is poor Sonny, who is furiously raising a cloud of dust with a broom down front.

The girl in the chair behind Martha taps her on the shoulder. "Someone should tell de *sheygets* to wet de bristles in de terlet," she says in a low voice. "Udderwise we'll all be esphyxilated here."

The relayed message ultimately comes from Jake Kline and his bunch in the back, who are putting on a brave show...talking it up like losers at cards.

Glad to oblige, Martha leans across the table to Olga, and watches as the word is passed along from row to row, ending with Bernstein's brother Jake, who is whispering sweet nothings to blonde Mary Leventhal at her checker's desk.

Sweeping away for all he's worth, Jerrold has been deep in thought about Levine the bookkeeper, the only one who seemed to care that time when he wrested himself away from those mad girls and ran upstairs with scalded hands.

Now what if you were to try and see him sometime?

Jerrold pictures Levine's waxen face with its tendency to sweat behind the pince-nez.

You know, it's altogether possible that if the guy were approached in the right way (and at the right time, of course), he might—he just might give you a little something to do. Even a couple of hours a week would be better than nothing.

The gabbing has grown louder yet, and one can't help picking up snatches...how thanks to a sister's getting married, someone now sleeps in a bed by herself...how someone else with a face like a dog, poor thing, had a baby as pretty as a picture...

Any moment now, Martha tells herself, as the clock hand moves a notch away from eight.

Yes, there! Bernstein has stepped through the partition door. She follows his progress to the bell button, where sallow Anna Gullo the forelady is already waiting.

Wonderful, just wonderful! Everything about him is exactly the same, down to the perfectly arched brows, sleepy grey eyes, and sinuous mouth.

And now, having perceived this, Martha is overflowing with good feeling and wants TO DO SOMETHING! Something, something—but what?

The very thing comes! "Say, that reminds me," she says to Benny, with a touch to his arm, "if they ever decide to let us work each for ourselves, how 'bout we go partners?"

The old one is quite amazed and searches her eyes—"You mean it?"—that a speed demon like her would be willing to team up with someone like himself, who is not what he once was? "Now dot's a true friend!"—and grabbing her forehead, he plants his lips on it, *Smack!*

Bernstein has noticed, as have a good many others. "HEY, YAH ALTER COCKER, WHAT'RE YOU DOIN' FOOLIN' AROUND WITH THE GIRLS?" he yells kiddingly. "IS THAT WHAT A FEW MONTHS OFF DOES FOR YOU?"

Everyone bursts out laughing.

Martha's cheeks are burning, but oh, she's happy. Sam Bernstein...my Sam.

CHAPTER

13

1910 has passed, and a new year is under way.

For Martha, things at the Triangle Shirtwaist Company have run along the same course, with her continuing to be enthralled by the work of stitching up, and to be enamored of Samuel Bernstein, production manager, who is still unaware of her feelings—as well he should be, considering her extreme reserve.

Mammeh, still harboring a faint hope of seeing her eldest-born established in "better circumstances," did make it her business to stop in at the College Settlement House one day, and by the greatest good fortune got to see the head person herself, Miss Elizabeth Williams, the most gentile-looking of gentile ladies, who after hearing her out, including how talented Martha was, agreed that the girl should go away to a school out of town. In fact, Miss Williams said that she was sending off a letter to her own dear Smith College that very day, asking them to accept Martha on a trial basis.

Kreynele, however, put her foot down when she learned of the plan, and remained adamant in spite of all efforts to persuade her, including a last-minute attempt by her old counselor Miss Smith, who came to the house expressly for that purpose. And Mammeh in turn, mumbling something about not wanting to live off her children, "especially under *these conditions," flatly rejected Martha's offer to contribute her savings of a hundred odd dollars, plus a small sum monthly, toward the purchase of the new house in Brooklyn.*

Jerrold in the meanwhile did indeed go knocking on Mr. Levine's door "at a certain point," and managed to talk the bookkeeper into taking him on as a "learner" one day a week, provided of course that Mr. Bernstein approved of it, which happily he did. Other than that, Jerrold has strictly followed the straight-and-narrow, going directly home after work every night and staying there—except for one instance when he strolled over to Third Street to assure himself with a peek in the tiny bakery window that a letter he had sent to his old friends Arturo and Giuseppina advising them that he had "met someone" at a Protestant church social had produced no dire effect.

Little need be added where Hippolyte, arch "kitchen anarchist," is concerned, except to say that his life, ever a matter of mediating between the need to love and be loved by liebling Paula, and to commune alone among the trees in Washington Square at night, has simply continued to bumble along in its usual fashion.

As for the greater world, 1910 saw two notable events occur, which everyone in the Square's environs, both among those issuing the orders and those in receipt of them, would have done well to pay more heed to:

—On March 19th, a fire broke out in Henry George Allen's hat factory on the corner of Waverly and Mercer Streets, and thick black smoke forced five hundred people working in the ten-story building to flee for their lives—which was no easy matter as it turned out. Quite a few found the doors to halls locked and elevators deserted, and had to resort to narrow ill-lighted stairways and rickety fire escapes to make good their escape. Among the casualties were a thirteen-year-old boy and three girls, one of whom, aged fifteen, died following a leap from a window.

—On November 25th, a commercial building across the river in Newark caught fire and became almost entirely engulfed in flames, and this time there were twenty-five fatalities, nineteen of whom fell or jumped to their deaths.

The Fire

MARCH 25, 1911

It's always rather hectic at home on Saturday mornings, and this one is no exception, Martha sees. The whole family, except Papa of course, is going shopping for new shoes for *Peysekh* today, and Mammeh, looking very business-like in street clothes, is trying to turn Fanny's fine black hair into braids that will stay, while keeping after Dinah and Pauline to finish their cereal and put the bowls in the sink.

It being payday, Martha too wants to do something special. After work, she has in mind going over to Fleischmann's Viennese Bakery on Broadway and Tenth, where for some time now she has been stopping off to buy schnecken for the family's Sunday breakfast, and to treat herself to a dish of ices in the ritzy little restaurant with the peppermint-stick awnings.

Only needed is to slip on her coat, black and skimpy at the waist with epaulets, over the striking lavender waist and crisp black skirt she has chosen just for the occasion, and she's all set—that is, except for the "crowning" touch, lovingly fashioned after the last word in Wanamaker's French Millinery Salon, for which the bathroom mirror is a must.

"My turn next!" she calls, as Papa steps out, still fussing with collar and tie.

No sooner in than she's out again, crowned indeed by it—a black felt bowl piled high with every manner of colorful doodad.

"What dya think, Ma?" she asks. Having worked on it until late last night, she's not sure what to make of it herself yet. Perhaps in her enthusiasm she overdid it with the ornaments, another old story.

"*Oy*, it's beyootiful!" Mammeh exclaims with hands clasped and moist eyes.

"It is? Do you really think so?"—and Martha is dying to go look again. Only there's no time, the clock over the sink announces! Grabbing coat and purse, she blows a kiss—"Bye!"...

If only there were someone to go to that fancy Viennese cafe with, she longs, picturing women sitting there together in their glad rags as she's klopping down the stairs.

But there isn't, not from the shop anyway, no other girl having shown an interest in forming a friendship since the short-lived "affair" with fat Elsie the unionizer. And friends from school, like Essie with her red hair and freckles, whom she ran into on the street not long ago, haven't exactly been sitting on ice waiting for her to become aware of their existence again. Seeming very grown up, Essie was on her way to a new stenographer's job downtown in the financial district, and only had time to shout the news that she's keeping company with a corset-fitter who's looking to go into business for himself very soon.

Oh well, it's nothing new, this being alone, Martha reminds herself. You'll survive...

In the broad open space of Houston now, she beholds the sky, all pale blue with pink-tinged puffs—it's going to be a lovely day.

A car glides up as she reaches the stop. Stepping on, she rejects a place next to an unshaven old one who is bound to smell bad, and grabs a seat by herself.

Clang, clang! There goes the still-familiar red-brick facade of P.S. 13 with its three different towers: one like a fairy's castle, the other a fort, and the third coming to a fat church point. So Mammeh was at pains to point out to her eldest-born *bobele* when taking her there for the first time, Martha recalls.

Coming up is the College Settlement gym, scene of those few junior basketball games and hops she attended. Ray, another girl from the past whom she happened on recently, told her that blond Davey Goldstein with his mushy lips is now seeing a lot of a doctor's daughter he met there.

Suddenly aware that she's eighteen, a terrible age, Martha heaves a sigh—life seems to be passing her by...

Having arrived at Broadway, she must now concentrate on the vexing business of crossing over in heavy traffic to the uptown stop.

The Fire

Fresh possibilities proposed by Mammeh range themselves in her mind: to return to Girls' High and finish the Commercial Program...to work under an uptown modiste for a while and learn the ropes so as to be able to name her price with another, and eventually to open her own establishment.

"The world is all before you," Miss Williams wrote the other day, urging that she give careful consideration to those new suggestions. "You have only to choose a direction."

Yes, but that's just it, Martha answers in her mind, *I have—I have chosen*. Yes, she reaffirms now, as long as there are pieces for me to zip through under the needle, and I get to sun myself in Bernstein's being every day, even if it's just for a few moments...

And now settled as best as can be expected next to a fat lady on the Broadway car, she dismisses it—enough, let's turn to matters more immediately to hand.

Benny, who has been out for the past several days with his cough, which never really went away, isn't coming in again today. So she learned from speaking with him over the candy store telephone last night.

Since the crew is in the middle of a job that should last through Monday and everyone knows what to do, there was only one problem that he foresaw—their crew's take for the week—and he was depending on her, *Tsatskele*, to see him through. What he wanted her to do was sign for the money pouch that forelady Anna Gullo would hand over later in the afternoon, and portion out the bills and change into the small envelopes to be found in the bottom of his work basket—so much to each of the twins and so on. Martha should only be careful that Raiseleh did not see what Olga got and "vicey voisa," otherwise there'd be hell to pay.

As for his share, which would be "fifteen dollahs fair und sqvare" (the same as hers), she was to hold onto it until Monday, when he was absolutely sure to return.

Washington Place is in sight: it's time to get up and pull the cord.

Martha has one of her bright ideas and breaks into a grin—I'll go him one better. I'll bring the *gelt* to him tomorrow in Brooklyn with a box of candy!

Jerrold was up late last night bearing down on the French and overslept this morning. But this is not the first time it has happened, so he knows just what to do to cut corners. Thankfully, there's something to spur him on—he'll be working under Mr. Levine today.

"There, all ready!" he huffs, and standing tiptoe, strains to see what he can in the smoky-pink mirror of the new grey pinstripe suit, recent handiwork of Mr. Rosenzweig of Avenue A, a leading authority on what a young man should wear out into the business world according to a pushcart peddler supposedly in-the-know.

"*Et maintenant mon chapeau*"—Jerrold gingerly transfers a black bowler from a wooden head by his elbow to his own.

"*Mon cha-peau*, pretty good, huh?" he chirps to kit-kat, curled up on the easy chair.

The French primer's entire twenty-six lessons he's painstakingly gone through, and now he's stolen a march on the extra conversational exercises in the back—"*De où vient sa tante?*" Yesirree, before very long, you're going to be chattering away like a native and ready to take on a battery of smart-aleck French waiters.

Before rushing off, Jerrold can't resist taking a peek out the window.

"Golly gee!" The Arch, the townhouses, and even the Metropolitan Life Tower are all fiercely golden, and every twig of every tree is full of little puckered green lips.

Next on the agenda is for you to go to that Marble Collegiate, he meditates, heading for the door—that is, to switch over for one Sunday from the Episcopal church called Ascension, where he's been a regular communicant for some time now, to the Dutch one to see what it's like.

The Fire

And last but not least—he's skipping down the stairs—in another couple of months, just as soon as the bank account is up to snuff again, you're going to bid those miserable slave-drivers at Triangle a fond "adieu" once and for all.

And boy oh boy, is that ever going to put a few noses out of joint! He's passing Chucky's door.

"Psst! Hey, Jerry!" Chucky hisses through the crack. The tip of the guy's nose is rosy red, and he's all bundled up in a heavy flannel robe. "Got a co'd," he croaks.

So what's it to me, Jerrold sneers inwardly, still rankled by ole buddy's note of many moons ago in which he said, "Sorry, buster, my mom says we're through."

"Hey, I hear you're on the wagon, that true?"

"Sure is," Jerrold tells him—not that it's any of his business.

Chucky's forehead creases meaningfully—"Like to play some checkers later?"

Jerrold jumps at it—now there's a thought! But not so fast, his better self cautions, let the guy stew for a while. "Got an engagement this evening," he says, "maybe some other time, okay?"...

Passing the mail table downstairs, he recalls the Stiverses back in Tarrytown, to whom he has recently written.

You sure didn't do as well here for friends, he chides himself, remembering yet once more how the kindly couple took him in when he practically found himself out on the street after learning the contents of Aunt's will.

Everybody made a first-class chump out of you, if the truth be known—Jerrold has stepped out onto the stoop. And that Smitty, who had only one thing on his mind, led the pack.

Well, you're a little smarter now and hopefully won't be taken in so easily the next time someone approaches you for something.

The ninth floor is positively a-bubble with chatter this morning. There's going to be a gala dance at the Lyceum tonight, and just about everybody, except Jake Kline and his people, figures on attending.

I sure wish Benny were here, Martha yearns, feeling utterly left out of it all. Even the prospect of filling in for him at sleeve-setting doesn't hold much excitement for her. This being her fourth day at it, the novelty has begun to wear off.

"Uh oh, something's up," Jerrold murmurs with sinking heart, on getting off the elevator upstairs.

Bernstein is waiting for him—that is, the man, in his usual greys, is standing in the doorway to Levine's office passing the time of day with him inside, and why else would he be doing that?

Whatever is on his mind, rest assured it's not going to be good.

"Listen kid," Bernstein begins as soon as Jerrold is within earshot. It seems that Danny, the belt boy on Eight, is out sick today and they're swamped with orders down there—"So would you mind? I just can't spare anybody else."

All disappointment, Jerrold heads for the locker room. And what are Mr. Levine's feelings about the matter? I can just imagine, he scorns inwardly, picturing the bookkeeper's lips outlined in sweat.

Try and think of something else to get your mind off it, he tells himself, blinking hard...something really pleasant...

One day, just as the magic number is about to register in the ole bank book, I'll pick up a copy of The Times and there staring me in the face will be this ad seeking someone who first-and-foremost possesses sterling qualities of character.

Instantly taking pen in hand, I'll use all my talents to the utmost, and three days later will arrive this note requesting that Mr. Vanderlynn appear for an interview on a certain day at a certain time, or by appointment when it is convenient for him.

The Fire

The signatory will be—well—a man of a certain age named Donald Sanders, who wears his white hair rigidly parted on one side, and comes to work every morning in a dark grey frock coat and a wing collar with a black tie.

After telephoning the shop that day and telling them I can't make it because of an awful pain in the gut, down there to the brokerage on Wall Street I'll hie, where I'll immediately be ushered into Mr. Sanders' office and made to feel utterly at home.

Whereupon he'll proceed to review my work history so as to be sure that he has it right:

—one year of practical bookkeeping experience with Mr. Levine, preceded by a long stint of feeling my way around in the company.

—prior to that, an extensive introduction to the field under the exacting guidance of Mr. Stivers at the gas works back home.

"Well, everything seems to be in order," the good man will pronounce at long last. "However"—a stray thought will cause his usually placid brow to wrinkle up—"I wonder if after laboring away for Mr. Levine in such an—an exciting atmosphere, you wouldn't find our humble establishment a little too—"

*"*Oh no, sir! I certainly wouldn't, not for the world!*" I'll shout (but not really).*

"Well then, we'd be most honored to have you join us," Mr. Sanders will say, after breathing a sigh of relief...

Yes, indeed, it won't be long now, Jerrold buoys himself, as he carefully hangs the new suit up in place of the work duds. And don't think that something like that won't happen either.

Breezing out of the locker room the next moment, he practically walks into Bernstein's arms, as if the man were coming to bawl him out for taking so long.

"I—" Jerrold begins fishing for an excuse.

But curiously Bernstein isn't the least bit worked-up. On the contrary, there's an expression of concern, genuine concern, on his face— "Look here, kid, you seem to have made quite a hit with Mr. Levine—"

All confused, Jerrold looks, simply looks, into the half-moon eyes.

Bernstein lays a hand on his shoulder and rocks it—"C'mon, chin up. I'll never ask you to do anything like this again, okay?"

You know, maybe I misjudged the guy, Jerrold can only think, walking off toward the stairs. Maybe he's not such a bad egg after all.

※ ※

It's break time, and on Nine, excited chatter has broken out again about the dance tonight.

Picking at salami on pumpernickel, Benny's old standby and her own favorite combination for the past few weeks, Martha is glad now that no one is paying any attention to her because it allows her to concentrate on things of greater moment.

Down front, Sam Bernstein, her Sam, is standing and leaning against the ledge of Mary Leventhal's desk, surrounded as usual by blond Mary, pale Anna Gullo, young Morris Bernstein of the very red lips, and little Edie Harris—everyone in their little crowd except Sam's brother Jake, who is upstairs saying hello to two nieces, Mr. Blanck's children, visiting with their governess.

Sam is in the midst of telling them one of his funny stories. Martha knows this for a certainty because of his lips, which have a tendency to develop an extra twist to them on such occasions.

He's just paused to pick up a store-bought sandwich from its wrappers and bite into it, and with both cheeks going, to gulp from a jar of hot tea, bag in, which he does with pinky stretched out…

Sam's fingers, including that one, are stubby, indeed almost repulsively so. They are the one feature about him that now after such a long time of observing him from afar like this—how long has it been?—she finds distinctly distasteful…

The others have left off in their eating to await the story's punch line. Martha holds still too.

There—"Hahaha!" they all let out.

The Fire

Morris and Edie smile fondly at one another…it needs only Jake, still up on Ten, to exchange an endearing look with Mary.

One trouble begets another. Only concerned with being on time this morning, Jerrold was forced not only to skip breakfast but also forgot to take along the lunch he packed last night. So when the noon bell rang, down he had to go to Mrs. Goldman's to buy himself something. But first before that, he had to borrow some kerosene from Mr. Brown the machinist to get the oil smudges off his cheeks, residue from the wells under the machines, which as usual, with everyone's being so busy, are near to overflowing.

Oh well, all grist for the mill and soon over, Jerrold consoles himself, back in his old place on Ten—and sets his jar of rich creamy coffee, lid off, down on the floor beside him.

Nearby, Louie has suddenly gotten very lucky at cards with Solly and two cutters…over by the Greene Street windows, some pressers are quietly turning the pages of newspapers and munching…while off to the right, the door to Mr. Blanck's office keeps opening as people come to pay cooing and kissing respects to his kids…

Boy, I could eat a whale—Jerrold removes a large buttered roll from the paper bag in his lap, a sort of breakfast and lunch combined when opting for it instead of the pickled herring that Mrs. Goldman was trying to tempt him with.

The break nearly over, it's time for Martha to take a trip to the washroom.

Bernstein is always gone by this point, but today for some reason he's still there with his little group—which means that in passing, she'll be coming the closest to him she's ever been.

Already her heart is in her mouth as she squeezes through her row, where the people at her table and the ones behind are all sitting with their chairs out. By the time she reaches the aisle, her knees are ready to cave in, she's so fidgety.

Sam is in the midst of pointing something out to brother Jake, just returned, as she comes up—but then suddenly his eyes light on her!

"Say, where's your boyfriend these days?" he asks, in Yiddish—referring to Benny, of course. "Haven't seen him around of late."

"He—uh—" Hardly able to breathe, Martha stammers out the explanation, in English.

Bernstein's brows, those perfect arches, rise in puzzlement—"You mean to say you don't speak Yiddish?"

"No, only a few words," she hears herself answer—and pushes on, feeling very light-headed indeed.

"Now howdya like that," he says to the others. "And here all along I thought she was from the old country."

There's nothing that can be done to remedy the matter, Jerrold sees.

Part of Mrs. Goldman's crusty pale brown roll in hand, he has been thinking very seriously about the past and the bad things that happened to him since coming to New York, especially how easily he was taken advantage of by everyone.

Until today he's considered that he had only himself to blame, but now suddenly it has dawned on him that the real culprit was the bum-start he got in life—the fact that he was brought up from an early age by Aunt, whose knowledge of the world was derived almost exclusively from the gossip at Christ Episcopal and the pages of *The Ladies Home Journal*.

Be that as it may, there's nothing that can be done about it now, Jerrold repeats. What's lost is lost forever.

As if to emphasize this, he separates the remainder of the roll into its halves.

It's like getting up late in the morning and missing breakfast...

The Fire

Bringing one of the halves to his mouth, he scoops out a furrow of the silky-smooth butter with his tongue—"Lovely."

Breakfast is breakfast, and try as one might, one can never make up with lunch for missing it...

The butter having dissolved down his throat, Jerrold craves coffee, and reaches for the jar, cooling at his feet.

Ah, guzzling sweet—as requested.

Martha is frantic in the washroom. I can't face Him again! What'll I do? What'll I say, she worries, stepping out into the front aisle.

Happily, it's a moot point; in a trice she's there at Mary's desk and passing him with nary a word—just a nod, for which she receives a nod back.

"A gooda girl, one of our besta workers," she hears Anna Gullo tell him.

"Now let it be, don't look over there," Martha murmurs, as she hurries along the side aisle. Don't, I mean it, she repeats, beginning the long push through her row. PLEASE! But she can't help herself, and finally in her seat, she peeks.

Oblivious, thankfully, he's dusting his palms of bread crumbs.

In her mind, Martha grasps one of the hands...*and somehow it comes to rest on her cheek...then slides down to her neck...and then her chest.*

Oh, Martha, you're awful, you really are. All the same, his hand, that same hand in her mind, seeks her midriff.

Now, Martha, stop it, that's enough. *The hand continues downward to her belly. And then—* Oh! *The stubbiest of his short, stubby fingers enters between the hairs to the sweet flesh within—*Oh!...

What's he—the real Sam—doing now? Martha darts another look—and her eyes meet his! He's looking back!

She takes her eyes away as fast as she can—OH GOD! HE KNOWS, HE'S GUESSED!

BOBE MAYSE *A Tale of Washington Square*

❧ ❧ ❧

It's four-forty, and there's just a short while to go. Another of the blessings of Saturday besides being paid, they get to go home early.

C'mon, don't be a fool, he doesn't really know anything, Martha is trying to drum it into herself—after slipping the edges of a fresh bodice and sleeve under her machine's foot. A mind-reader Sam is not, no more than anyone else. He simply glanced your way, that's all.

Her toe touches the pedal, and the material, a very flimsy silk, slides along, her fingers carefully guiding it. Chances are, he wasn't even thinking of you—just looking, without seeing, as you've observed him do countless times when he was standing by the bell. So just forget about it, or else you'll end up driving yourself good and crazy...

The circle of stitching complete, she snips the spool and bobbin threads with her scissors, then turns the bodice around and reaches for the second sleeve.

Soon as you're through here, straight to that snazzy afternoon eatery you'll go. Martha pictures herself strutting up Washington Place to Broadway, absolutely the cat's meow in her sensational hat with all the stuff on it.

Which flavor should I choose, raspberry or lemon? Oh, why not a bit of both?...

"There you are, Madame," *a waiter intones through his nose, as his tuxedo stoops slightly to set a dainty china plate with a lace paper doily before her.*

Next from his tray comes The Thing Itself—a frosty silver goblet, in which reposes a large fluffy snowball, half pink, half pale yellow.

Taking in hand a long, slender spoon, she scoops up a trifle of that icy sweetness-with-the-sour and brings it to her lips, poised to receive it—

R*EENG*! goes the bell.

Martha quickly turns her head—Anna Gullo is alone by the button. Then mindful of work stopping all over, she bears down a little harder on the pedal to get the last few stitches in—done!

The Fire

Chairs are scraping all over, and Martha's ear again picks up chatter about the dance at the Lyceum.

You know, it comes to her, still sitting, you've really got to begin thinking about doing something with yourself. Honestly, you can't go on like this, pining away for a man who, even if he had an inkling and were interested, couldn't do a thing about it because he already has a wife and family...

There's some movement to her left: Greta with Yetta behind her, both of them with very shiny eyes and a pink spot on each cheek from excitement—"Can you let us by, please?" They're in a hurry to get home and do whatever is necessary for their consumptive mama, so as not to miss any of the fun at the big affair later...

Yes, Martha continues, you must begin taking yourself in hand. Meaning that you ought to go to some shindigs like this one tonight, and try to find someone to latch on to. It doesn't matter who really, just so long as he's decent and hard-working. Then when children come, you'd have that at least if things didn't work out between you...

On her feet now, with everything put away and her purse in hand, she waits for the congestion in her row to loosen up.

The side aisle is already packed with people headed one way or the other—to the cloakroom or the partition. Yetta's and Greta's heads are bobbing in the midst of it all.

Raiseleh, across the table, wrinkles her nose—"Sometink's boining"—and thinks to get ahead of Olga.

The dark collar-setter grows sullen. "*Ver geharget!*"—drop dead—she growls. "Vait your toin!"

Martha sniffs—yes, she can smell something too. She sniffs again—now it's gone. Probably a few rags caught fire downstairs, she figures. Such things still happen quite often around the shop, especially on Eight, what with some of the motors given to throwing off sparks, like a few of those on Nine, to say nothing of a couple of cutters persisting in smoking on the sly in spite of the bosses' threats to terminate them on the spot if caught.

"Hey, vere's de smoke comink from?" a shrill voice in the back calls.

"Below has to be," someone behind Martha says.

Raiseleh's wild eyes roll—"I'm gettink outa here!"—and with one mighty effort, she shoves past Olga and the rest of their row, and begins squirming through the crowd toward the door...that infernal door in the partition, which allows only one person through at a time.

No need to panic, Martha assures herself. Sam, my Sam, is there in all likelihood, and he'll see to it, as he always does.

The quitting bell has just rung, and in the Men's Room on Eight, Jerrold is quickly and deftly working to remove the worst of the oil smudges from his face and hair before the place is mobbed with cutters coming to "wash their hands."

There, that'll do. Now it's only a matter of going upstairs to change into the suit, and then Home, James, where he'll give his head a really good scrubbing under the tap.

Out in the room, he can't help hearing all the excited talk—everybody and his brother seems to be doing something tonight—and he's seized by that lonely feeling he gets sometimes...

A woman calls out from the middle of things, her voice full of urgency—"OH, MR. BOINSTEEN?" It's Eva Harris, the boss's sister—"MR. BOINSTEEN, DERE'S A FI-AH!"

Jerrold looks over to the far end of the room by the Greene Street windows where her finger is pointing. Some smoke is rising from the cutting table there.

Bernstein, who has been chatting with Miss Lipschitz at her checker's desk, takes off at a run, opting for the faster secondary aisle that separates specialty sewers from cutters.

Familiar with small emergencies like this, Jerrold trots along after him so as to be on hand in case the man should want him to do something.

The Fire

Halfway there, Jerrold sees what the trouble is: the paper patterns used as cutting guides at that table and kept draped on a wire above it have somehow ignited.

He gets there just as a cutter is emerging from the crush in the side aisle, lugging a pail of water from the row hanging in the vestibule.

Bernstein takes it and tosses it over the line of little yellow flames. Crazily—*Whoop!*—a single large sizzler leaps up!

"Jeezy!"—Jerrold thinks he's seeing things.

"Fire!" someone calls out fearfully behind him. "Fire! Fire!" others repeat.

Bernstein, now standing on the table adjacent to that one, heaves another pail, handed up to him by a second cutter.

The dousing makes no difference whatsoever—the wood has caught. "Keep the water coming!" Bernstein hollers.

"Is—is there anything I can do, sir?" Jerrold asks, very concerned.

"Nothing, just stay out of the way," Bernstein answers, and flings two additional pails, brought by Solly and Louie.

The big lug of a Czech freight elevator operator is plowing through with more water. The flames shift this way and that, fanned by a draft from somewhere—Jerrold pictures the open elevator door on the other side of the partition.

"Louie, Solly, get the hose!" Bernstein yells. The guys go charging ahead with their arms out, like blind men—"Gangway! Let us through!"

It's unbearably hot where Bernstein is now, so slipping down, he moves to the next table—not a minute too soon, the flames have spread to that second one.

Fresh pails arrive, but alas, half empty now from being jogged by everyone, anxious to get out.

If only Bernstein would give me something to do, Jerrold wishes. I'd go anywhere, do anything, if only the man would tell me!

"What took you so long?" Bernstein snaps, as Louie turns up, dragging the hose. "Gimme!"—he reaches down and yanks the thing out of his hands. "Is the valve open?" He points the nozzle and presses.

Nothing happens, nothing comes out! "WHAT THE HELL!" He shakes the nozzle and gives the trigger a good hard squeeze this time. Still there's nothing, not a drop.

"What's the matter? What's going on?" Bernstein demands. Plenty scared behind his glasses, Louie says he'll go and see.

In a trice, someone new bearing a pail is there to say that the valve is stuck, Solly is working on it. Jerrold can make out Louie struggling along not far behind with another pail.

"DAMN!" Bernstein curses, and his eyes, very red now, light on Jerrold—"Sonny, go give Solly a hand."

"Yes, sir!" Jerrold squeaks at the ready, and plunges into the crowd, all coughing with handkerchiefs held to their noses.

Across the room, a bunch of people are wedged in before the door—the forbidden one to the stairs leading down to the lobby.

Behind him, Jerrold hears Bernstein ordering Mr. Brown the machinist to go and get it open—"I DON'T CARE IF YA HAVE TO HACK IT TO PIECES!"

That Bernstein's wonderful, just wonderful! A real human being!

From the street, distantly, Jerrold's ear picks up bells clanging and whistles peeping—firemen coming!

BANG! goes something to his left like a pistol shot...one of the Washington Place windows exploding from the heat!

"VY DON'T DEY DO SOMETING!" someone cries.

"VEE'LL NEVER GET OUT, VEE'LL ALL BE ROASTED ALIVE HERE!" someone else echoes.

BANG! BANG! go two more windows.

Two girls, in their terror, somehow climb up onto one of the windowless ledges. One teeters for a moment—and falls out! "HELP! SAVE ME!" the other screams, and holding her nose, jumps scissor-fashion!

The Fire

Jerrold stands stock-still. Is it possible? Are they gone? Really gone? It's eight flights down. His feet carry him forward the rest of the way...

The vestibule is seething with people, all clamoring to get on one of the two elevators, whose door has just opened.

"Goils foist!" barks a tall Italian in overalls. A man tries to sneak by. The juggernaut Czech elevator operator stops the coward cold and holds him writhing in his arms—"No, ME, ME-E-E!" The Italian resumes marshaling girls in.

Jerrold pushes through to the stair door, and looks up to the next landing, where the valve is, expecting to find Solly there—but he's not!

Must have gone in search of a crowbar or something, is Jerrold's thought, and sidestepping a handful of girls clattering down from Nine, presto he's there, trying with all his might to turn the wheel—trying—trying—until finally the thing is winding loosely in his hands, its threads gone!

I've got to tell him, Jerrold agonizes, meaning Bernstein battling away inside on Eight.

He runs back down the stairs, hoping by hook or crook to squeeze through the partition once more. But it's impossible—men and girls are frantically wrenching themselves out of that small opening in two's and three's.

Up on Ten then! Somebody, anybody in charge! They'll know what to do!

Without meaning to, Martha has let everyone in her row get ahead of her, and now there are only empty chairs and the Washington Place windows to her rear.

But there's no cause for alarm as she sees it. The smoke has disappeared, except for a trace once in a while, and the few shouts that one heard not long ago are also a thing of the past now. In short, the problem on Eight, whatever it was, has been taken care of, as she said it would be.

Ho-hum, Martha looks toward the cloakroom, where three girls bound for the good time tonight have just emerged, singing at the tops of their lungs.

I'm happy for them, I really am, she tells herself, as they kick their legs out together with their arms around one another.

But then her breath comes short—FLAMES, there are FLAMES outside the windows by Mary Leventhal's desk!

"EEEEEE!" the three bosom pals shriek.

"FIRE! FIRE!" others call out.

Martha can't for the life of her figure it out—below those windows is an alley where probably some trash ignited, but how could flames from such a puny thing shoot up so high?

She alone seems to be mystified by this, though: everyone else just wants to get out of there.

"LOOK!" cries somebody to her right, pointing. There are FLAMES outside the Greene Street windows too!

Has to be from Eight, it now dawns on Martha. Then fear grips her at the thought of the possible enormity of it all down there—

To say nothing of what might yet happen here, should the FLAMES get in...and take hold...and reach any of the wells under the machines, which are all about to run over!

Everyone in the aisle is getting frantic, and urging on those close to the partition—"C'MON, LET'S GET OUT OF HERE! WHAT'S HOLDING THINGS UP? FASTER!"

Should I sit down again, Martha considers, feeling very weak. No, don't, something warns her. Whatever you do, don't do that...anything but that, stay on your feet.

What a piece of luck! Jerrold has just reached the top step of Nine, and there, just descended from above, is Mr. Markowitz of Ship-

The Fire

ping, who can be very nice though sometimes very loud.

"Sir—!"

"Listen, boy"—Mr. Markowitz maneuvers Jerrold out of the way of a girl bolting from Nine's vestibule with eyes wide and hair standing on end. "I've got a coupla jobs for yuh."

"But, sir, the valve—"

Mr. Markowitz cuts him short—"We know all about it, and it'll be taken care of." The man's eyes, replete with worry lines and bags, take Jerrold in very seriously—"Now look here, ya know de fire escape in dere?"—meaning inside Nine.

Jerrold is still thinking of getting word about the broken valve through to Bernstein, but yes, it so happens that he is familiar with the fire escape: it's behind the steel shutter of the third window on the right.

Well, needed is for Sonny to go and get that shutter open, so people can leave by that means if necessary. Then when that task is done, he should hot-foot-it upstairs to give Mr. Levine a hand carrying the books over the roof to NYU. Mr. Harris just freed the skylight, cutting his arm very badly in the process, and they've already evacuated Mr. Blanck's kids, bawling their heads off.

Markowitz walks Jerrold, who is now pretty much convinced, to the vestibule. "Okay, everyone!" he yells through the partition, as an Italian mother wrestles her way out dragging a daughter. "Let Sonny in, official business!"

"I'll do my best, sir," Jerrold assures him in parting...

Inside, beyond the pushing, surging crowd, he finds two slight girls hammering on the shutter to the fire escape with their fists—*boom-boom, boom-boom*.

"Here, let me," he says, and yanks out the pin that holds the two parts together, then raises the window with a grating rattle.

The girls hoist themselves up and step out onto safety, with others anxiously following.

Pleased with this small accomplishment, Jerrold looks around to see if there's anything else he can do.

Yes, the door to the Washington Place stairs, mate to the locked one below, where people are also jammed in, while a tall, heavy-set woman pounds away at the wired-glass top section with a sewing machine head—*Whack! Whack! Whack!*

There's a fire axe in the cloakroom that might do the job better, Jerrold recalls—but does he dare go over there? The partition by the Greene Street windows has just caught fire, and before long it will be spreading and block the exit. Worse yet, in the vestibule there's a large drum that's used to empty old machine oil into—which is full to the brim. One lick of flame there, and they'd all be sent to kingdom come!

Maybe I should just—

One of the girls by the door being whacked breaks despairingly away, runs sobbing to the windows overlooking Washington Place, flings up a sash, and scrambling onto the sill, skips out.

That does it—Jerrold decides to take a chance. One-two-three he is across the aisle, still seething with people, and in a row by himself. Now for the easy part, climbing over the tables—

Pfft! something goes behind his back. Whoom! something explodes.

Jerrold whirls around—it was that drum of oil! The whole partition is ablaze, and people are lying dead or dying, and burning, all over the floor there—

Except for one person, Anna Gullo the forelady, who is miraculously left standing—and who now, on a sudden whim, throws her skirt up over her head and dashes straight through the flames.

If you had any sense, you'd do the same, Jerrold warns himself, and begins pulling his shirt out from inside his overalls to use as a cover.

Something metallic rips outside the unshuttered window—the fire escape, with all those people on it, tearing away from the building! *Clang-lang!* it hits and re-hits the ground!

"I don't believe it," Jerrold says out loud. "I don't believe it"—in a daze...

The Fire

The partition is a solid sheet of flame now, and any minute the adjacent tables are going to catch fire.

Vaguely from the street comes shouting—the firefighters with their scaling ladders and nets, for sure—and a chugging as from several water pumpers.

Two girls with dark complexions who look to be sisters are in the row to Jerrold's left, and there's another on his right alone—the decent one with the deep-set eyes named Martha.

"Back!" he orders them, in a voice he hardly recognizes. "Move back!"—motioning behind to the Washington Place windows.

Best to do as Sonny says, Martha advises herself, and begins to edge backwards, feeling her way with the heels of her shoes.

The two sisters on his other side, whose odd combination of olive skin and dirty-blond hair she seems to recall from the picket line, are also pulling back...with hunched shoulders.

If only things had turned out differently. But it's too late to be troubled by such matters now, and too hot.

The big-bosomed woman down front has yet to make any headway with the locked door despite all of her battering. Among those in the little crowd around her, Martha makes out Mary Leventhal and the sweethearts Morris and Edie.

Sam's brother Jake, there too until a moment ago, is now going along his row frantically rummaging in one work-table drawer after another...probably searching for something sharp, like a pair of strong shears, to use on that stubborn door.

And Sam, my Sam, where is he, what has happened to him, Martha wonders.

Way in the back, union *makher* Jake Kline, standing in one of the Greene Street windows, is giving a hand up to one of his girls, while others belonging to him wait their turn.

No, old friend Elsie is not among them.

Jerrold's retreating right calf touches a motor casing, and a slight breeze thankfully fans his back from the window, which is wide open. He shifts round and hops onto the ledge.

Below in the street, there's a long firetruck and three water pumpers, like giant potbellied stoves, amidst many crisscrossing hoses.

From the truck, a ladder is slowly rising, cranked up by a team of black-helmeted firemen, whom it's possible he knows from O'Reilly's, where some from the local companies used to stop in now and then. Fine fellows they are, Irish most of them...

Up, up, up, the ladder reaches—but then stops two floors down.

That's it, that's as high as it'll go apparently, Jerrold sees with a sickish feeling.

If only it weren't so hot, Martha sighs, and where oh where is he, my Sam? Why isn't he here to help us?

The partition is rumbling with fire and the first tables are catching.

If I could get up on the ledge with Sonny, there'd be some fresh air. But what after that, God knows.

Hoping for a sign of something, Martha peers into the flames toward what used to be the vestibule.

Oddly, a man is there, who seems to have just come up the stairs. It's he, Sam, she knows it, she just knows it—IT HAS TO BE!

The individual makes a pleading gesture, as if to say, What can I do? If I knew what to do, I'd do it.

That's alright, she wants to answer, as long as you cared enough to come and see.

The fire, ever advancing, drives the man back with hands over his eyes...and he's gone.

The Fire

How can I help these girls? Jerrold is aware that every single table along the partition is in flames.

Only one thing, and he makes up his mind to start with the sisters, leaving Martha for last.

"Come," he gently says to the younger, and reaches down to her.

Trembling slightly, she seems to understand, and allows him to pull her up beside him.

Oh Jesus, Mary, and Joseph, if there is any other way, show it to me now, he silently prays, and waits a long moment—then grasping her by the waist, holds her out over the empty air and lets go.

"Your turn now," he says to the older sister, and carefully brings her up to him.

Her knees are wobbly, but she's ready.

"Dear God, forgive me," he murmurs.

Martha realizes there's no other choice—I don't see what else one can do.

The buxom woman with the sewing machine head has sunk down before the still-locked door, and so too Mary Leventhal, Morris, Edie, and the rest of the hopefuls. The only one left of that crowd is Sam's brother Jake, who is running wildly around with a brutally red face wherever it's not burning.

In the rear, Jake Kline finally has all of his people up on the ledge with him.

Martha stretches out her hand to Sonny.

The Greene Street windows explode, blowing Kline and his bunch into the sky!

I didn't want it to be this way, is Jerrold's thought. But there it is, that's how it turned out.

Martha can't look down, afraid that she'll get dizzy—Mammeh and Papa will be very unhappy when they hear what happened, Benny too, and I'm sorry. As for him, Sam—

She puts her arms around Sonny's neck and brings his face close to hers.

Jerrold chooses to go along with it and folds his own arms around her.

Her lips seek his…and find them. He presses lightly back. She rests her cheek on his chest—"Sam, my Sam."

CHAPTER

14

Mammeh first heard of the fire from a neighbor in her building whom she hardly knew. The woman happened to be in the candy store downstairs when a telephone call came from someone who had the news firsthand, and Mrs. Shapiro the proprietor, remembering that Martha worked at Triangle, prevailed upon the neighbor woman to go up the extra flights and tell the Ferbers on the way home.

Mammeh, who was in the midst of heating up yesterday's chicken soup, immediately turned off the stove, and sat heavily down at the table. Eli, home early from the store as usual on Saturdays, quietly joined her, and Dinah, Pauline, and Fanny, when they came in from playing a while later, took their places without a word, having heard in the street about the terrible event.

There they all remained until six o'clock, when full of foreboding at Martha's failure to appear, Mammeh decided to go up to Number 23 Washington Place to see if anything could be learned. Should Martha yet come home, Eli was to send word down to Mrs. Shapiro's, where Mammeh would make it her business to telephone from time to time.

Out on the stoop, she had the choice of walking up to Houston Street and waiting for the car, which might not be so fast in coming at that hour, or of beginning the long trek west and north by foot, hansoms and taxis seldom if ever venturing down to the Lower East Side. Fortunately, a better idea soon presented itself in the form of an old-clothes dealer named Moyshe, whom she came upon sitting half asleep under the line of goatbells in his wagon. Having lost his whole family to the dreaded cholera back home in Kovno, Moyshe could well understand her situation and insisted on giving Mammeh a free ride uptown.

The rest of the story of what happened that night she related to Eli, in Yiddish, in better days, when everything had quieted down and she herself had her bearings again somewhat:

> Getting his nag going with me up on the seat beside him, Moyshe agreed that we should follow along on *Kreynele*'s trolley route, so I could spot her in case she'd been delayed for some reason and might yet be on her way.
>
> By the time we reached Fourth Street on Broadway, where we'd thought to turn in toward Washington Square, it was almost dark, and our luck, the street was roped off with a policeman standing in front of it to keep traffic out. On Washington Place, the next block up, the situation was the same, except that here the way was blocked for very good reasons—every inch of space by Number 23 was taken up by fire trucks and other vehicles.
>
> I told the policeman what our intention was, and he, an older man with a red nose, an Irisher no doubt like so many of them, said that other parents of missing girls were waiting for some word straight ahead on the Square, and that if I cared to join them, we could get through on Ninth Street. However, his advice was to return home and wait it out there, and then if *Kreynele* still hadn't shown up by the morning, to go inquire at the various hospitals, and at the Morgue, which was on East Twenty-sixth Street over by the river.
>
> "And you?" I said, looking him straight in the eye. "Would you do that, go home and stay there if one of your children were involved?"
>
> To this he had no answer, and gave a salute with his white glove.

The Fire

Ninth Street turned out to be clear, as the policeman said, but University Place was so teeming with people that Moyshe thought it best not to go any closer, and squeezing horse and wagon into an open spot by the curb, said he would either be there or somewhere in the area if I needed him.

On Washington Square I found a large crowd, maybe twenty deep, all behind wooden barricades with a line of police in front. Up the block on Washington Place, they had water playing on Number 23 in one big gush and two smaller ones, and from above, a little white smoke was coming out.

Quite a few of those around me were indeed like myself relatives of someone not yet accounted for—I can still hear a woman calling out from somewhere over the throb of the pumping engines, "Sadie, what have they done with you, Sadie?" But there were also others who had no business being there: idle curiosity seekers who either stared and stared at the trickle of smoke up there, like a man in a black bowler hat I remember, who chewed on a cigar the whole time, or else they nudged one another and whispered stupid things back and forth.

There was one thing that had me puzzled: some strange dark areas alongside Number 23. What could they be?

I asked a tall, thin workman in a janitor's cap, who was standing and smoking a pipe nearby me, and the man, a German, obliged by giving this reply. Before the fire, there were rows of glass blocks there for letting light into the cellar; deadlights they're called. When the people from Triangle fell or jumped—he showed me with his hand—some of them landed there and crashed straight through, thus creating those dark areas, which were holes.

The man must have worked with boilers or something—he knew the exact weight of the bodies when they came down, so many hundreds or thousands of pounds, I forget—and assuming that I had a personal interest in everything, pointed with his pipe to around the corner on Greene Street, where he said the police and ambulance workers had many of the dead all wrapped up and ready to be hauled away.

However, they were not going to be taken to the Morgue, he added, that place being absolutely too small to hold them all.

Rather, to a pier building nearby—just like the victims of the *General Slocum*, the Sunday School excursion boat that caught fire on the river and sank six years ago, did I remember it?

How many managed to get out, did he know, I asked, meaning from here, Number 23?

Oh, that was anybody's guess, he answered. Why even the authorities probably weren't too certain at this point. He was there watching almost from the very beginning, and during the fire's early stages at least, people from upstairs kept pouring out the front and back doors, with the police grabbing the injured and loading them into ambulances as fast as they were able to. He reckoned that between the smoke, flames, jumps, and falls maybe as many as two hundred had perished. A goodly number to be sure, but clearly a far cry from the thousand-odd lost on the *Slocum*, which included small children as well as women and girls.

Then he went on to begin some other unfavorable comparison between the two nightmares.

Listen, Bertha, this you don't need, I told myself, and thanking him, I moved off to another spot.

Not long after, a bunch of relatives got all stirred up about something and pushed their way past the barricades to the other side of the street—only to go slipping and stumbling among the hoses and fallen debris until the police rounded them up and brought them back.

Soon after, Croker the Fire Chief and some other bigshots from the Department drove up to the entrance in one of their buggies, and the party trudged inside. On coming out a while later, they were all looking good and miserable, and Croker was wiping tears away with a handkerchief.

What can I tell you—seeing this, all the mamas and papas in the crowd burst out crying too, and a Rumanian with a black beard reminded everyone, in a broken voice, that only several months ago Chief Croker had warned in the newspapers that a disaster like this could happen because the buildings in the area were all so unsafe, but of course no one had paid any attention to him.

By that time it was completely dark out, and I was beginning to think about going to find Moyshe and the wagon.

The Fire

But then, suddenly, a spotlight came on from one of the fire trucks, and they raised it up to Number 23's roof, where some firemen had started lowering a long, black bundle at the end of a heavy rope, one of a number of trussed-up "packages" like that they had up there it seemed—and everybody broke down again.

So where is she, my child, is she gone then, I wondered, with my own tears running. It was just hard to believe.

Mammeh returned home in the wee hours of the morning after going in vain from bed to bed in the emergency wards of St. Vincent's and Bellevue and a few other infirmaries where victims of the fire had been taken. Only remaining to be covered was the pier-building, that make-shift annex to the Morgue, but it was not scheduled to open until six, she and Moyshe learned from a sign when they rode by.

Dead-tired after the climb back up to her floor on top of everything else, she found Eli sitting at the table where she had left him, half-asleep with his head on his arms. And Dinah, Pauline, and the baby? Gone, whisked off to Brooklyn to be out of the way by Abe and Dora Leah, who had come as soon as they could after word of the tragedy reached them.

So had anything else happened? Taking a drink of water from the tap, Mammeh learned with her back to Eli that, yes, there had been another visitor later—that man Benowitz.

What did he want, Mammeh vaguely asked, not really caring.

Husband mumbled something—and it wasn't until much later that he gave her the full account, in Yiddish:

> I was just getting used to it being so quiet here in the house, when all of a sudden there he was pushing open the door without any warning, just like that other time when he came to tell us the Strike was over.
>
> WHERE IS SHE, he demanded, breathing hard and looking wildly around.
>
> As you only too well know, he was never one of my favorite people to begin with, so you can imagine what my feelings were. My daughter hasn't come home yet, I told him, and at the mo-

ment we have no idea where she is. I was hoping that this would satisfy him, and that he would then turn around and go away, and leave me in peace again.

Only what did he do but plop himself down beside me and begin rocking in the chair as if he were praying. Let her only be alright, he pleaded. That's all I ask.

Still of a mind to be rid of him, I responded that one had to be patient and hope for the best.

Well, now his face wrinkled up and those watery eyes began to overflow. If only he'd been there, he wailed. He would've seen to it—I had to believe him—he would've seen that she, my loved one, got right out at the first sign of trouble. Yes, if it had been up to him, her crew leader and good old friend, she'd be home now reading a book. Yes, he would have led her to safety—just like when the Strike began and he took her with the other girls, his *meydelekh*, down to the street unharmed past Bernstein's goons.

The man presented such a pitiful sight with the tears rolling down his old cheeks that in spite of myself, I began to feel sorry and said something to try and soothe him, and then when that had no effect, asked if I could perhaps make him a little tea—*a bisele tey*.

What, tea! He waved it away as if it were poison. How COULD ANYONE THINK OF SUCH A THING AT A TIME LIKE THIS! Then he began rocking again, mumbling, She was such a lovely girl, just like his own child—I should pardon him. And so talented, with such a wonderful pair of hands—*goldne hentelekh*. Why one had only to say the word and anything one put into them, no matter how intricate, was done, fast and neat!

Well, I was beginning to grow impatient again—enough is enough already. And that last remark of his about her being just like his child really unsettled me.

But then, just as I was about to open my mouth and tell him a thing or two, he left off, and putting a hand on my arm, began urging me to cheer up, things might not be as bad as they seemed. Maybe she went home with somebody else for some reason, he speculated, or maybe she was wandering around the streets in a daze after her horrendous experiences up there in the fire—in which case, it was just a matter of some kind person or a cop noticing and taking pity—*rakhmones*—and seeing her to the door here.

The Fire

On and on the man raved, suggesting other possibilities even more far-fetched—until I was ready to take him by the shoulders and give him a good shaking.

But once more, just as I was about to do something—if nothing else, point out that he was only making things worse for me, the real father, with his foolishness—he shut up.

For a whole minute there was silence. Then all at once he threw his hands in the air and banged at it with his fists. IF ANYTHING HAS HAPPENED TO HER, he shouted, I'LL NEVER FORGIVE MYSELF! NEVER!

And what was the result of all that carrying on? He got himself into a real state, in fact so sick—*azoy krank*—did he become with quivering blue lips, that I began to be afraid for him.

Would you like me to go find a doctor, I asked after a while.

No, he answered in a hoarse voice with dead-like eyes, it wasn't necessary.

And then, just like that, he got up and shuffled out.

※

Hippolyte had lamb fricassee on his mind when word came of the terrible thing unfolding at Triangle. That is, he'd just gotten a pot of it bubbling on the stove and was about to dip a spoon in for a taste when the doors to the restaurant flew open and of all people, the dike with the purple-feathered hat stuck her head in.

The whole place is one big inferno! she cried out in her shrill boy's voice. Those girls, those poo-oor girls!

Instantly his hands jumped to turn off the gas and fling away his apron, and he was off at a run, up the stairs, through the gate, and out onto the street.

What happened next and thereafter would remain a part of him, like a living presence, for the rest of his life. From time to time on his nights under the stars, he would recount it to an invisible party:

Stopping short at the corner of West Fourth and Macdougal to let some vehicle by, I looked right—to find the whole of the tree-side of Washington Square South lined with those deep-chested horses they use to drag the ladder trucks and water pumpers, while across the way, where the houses are, every stoop had its little group of spectators and there was someone hanging out of every window, with a goodly crowd gathered in front of O'Reilly's too.

As I tore along, straight through the Square, a blot of grey appeared in the sky above the factory building, with more smoke billowing up from it, and now and then a flash of bright reddish orange.

Crossing over the open space past the Arch and lily pond, I saw something large and long go sailing out of one of the upper stories, which left a trail of golden sparks as it fell, and then another like that and another, which I took to be bolts of cloth on fire. But then realizing what they really were, fool that I was, I reached out with my arms to try and stop them...keep them from coming down!

Two more of those young women in skirts—these with their arms around one another—skipped into the air as I pulled up at Garibaldi's statue and the crowd there.

Oh God! God! I cried, and flopping down onto my knees, began blubbering.

Nearby, a classy-looking dame with a red fox skin wound round her neck turned to a friend of the same ilk and whispered that I must have a close relative inside to be making such a fuss, and the friend whispered back that perhaps they ought to go in search of a policeman to assist me.

Go fuck yourself, you whores! I sobbed. Did they ever slink away!

Upstairs, two more girls were getting ready to jump.

People started shouting at them—No, wait! Don't do it yet!

A ladder was being cranked up from one of the trucks—you could hear the winch squeaking. Up, up, it rose...then stopped... two floors down.

Higher, make it go higher! you could hear coming from all over.

But that was it, there the ladder stayed.

Still gasping on my knees, I grew absolutely furious. All the dough in this town, and that's the best they can do! I screamed. For shame!

The girls up there held on for several moments more, until the heat became too much for them, and then fell...straight down like the others.

The Fire

And the firemen with their nets? I wondered. Also useless it seems: the bodies hit with such force that either they bounced in the air and landed elsewhere, or the nets split apart and they went through.

I pounded the ground—OH GOD! OH GOD!

Suddenly it was very still, and I looked up to see why.

A young guy was up on one of the window ledges now, twenty years of age or so I guessed, a good-looker in an American sort of way, and familiar somehow, though I couldn't place him. Maybe he stopped by my joint once to eat.

He'd been standing there for some time of course, but now everyone was first noticing him.

Look, ma, it's Jerry! someone next to me said, a short, dumpy fellow in a red flannel shirt and overalls, the spittin' image of this old witch who was with him, in a black dress and bonnet. Then his face scrunched up and he cried out, OH NO, JERRY, DON'T DO IT!

I looked back at Jerry. A girl was with him, whom he'd taken hold of.

No, JERRY, NO! the fellow with his dam hollered. IT'S A SIN!

Jerry followed through as he'd intended, and down the girl went...all the way down.

Atta boy, I said aloud, though really to myself. There's nothing to be ashamed of, you did exactly as anyone else would in your situation...any other feeling person.

Jerry lost no time in getting another girl up there with him, this one a little older.

Mama's Boy got all worked up again. IT'S A SIN, JERRY! A MORTAL SIN! he cried, his voice cracking through tears.

Lucky for him that his ma dragged him away then, or I would've clobbered him, so help me...

Next...next with Jerry was a dark-haired girl with deep-set eyes whom I recognized at once as the charmer who was so outspoken about her job that time in my place, the one who answered back the rich-bitch in her green satin dress surrounded by her pals, those fawning unionizer frumps. Yes, beyond a shadow of a doubt, it was she, the Little Bourgeoise.

Facing Jerry, she put her arms around him, and he embraced her, and their faces came together, mouth on mouth.

Now there's a good thing, I thought. Maybe they were sweethearts...but maybe not...

A long moment the kiss lasted, and then a roaring wave of flaming red washed over them, and they fell...one...one...all fiery.

SUNDAY, THE NEXT DAY

It's past six and drearily misty out, with a promise of rain soon, and Mammeh is one of many in dark coats and hats on a line that stretches several blocks down First Avenue.

When the alarm clock went off earlier, Eli spoke of coming along, but she dissuaded him, insisting that there was no need for the two of them to go through such an ordeal and the thing really belonged to her to do. Now she's a little sorry because everyone there seems to have someone else to lean on, if not a spouse, then an older son or daughter.

Oh well, it's done. She closes her eyes and inwardly tries to compose herself in her mama's voice—Don't worry, it'll be alright.

"Step up, please!" a policeman calls.

That's the signal for the next twenty-odd people, which includes herself, to go around the corner and speak to a nurse in a navy cape and a white cap who is sitting at an old kitchen table with a notebook and pen.

In a few minutes it'll all be over, Mammeh tries to soothe herself. But it's not easy: filing by are some of those who have just been in the long grey shed down at the end of the block, all of them holding one another and weeping, or else sort of staggering along with their heads down.

"Who are you looking for?" the nurse softly inquires, when Mammeh is there before her. She has blue eyes and blond hair, a *shikse*—gentile—for sure, and is young.

Mammeh tells her briefly: a daughter, eighteen, short, slim, with brown eyes and brown hair. How many times today has this stranger, who is not much older, heard that description?

The Fire

The nurse nods, and smiles slightly, as if to encourage.

Another nice one, like the older red-nosed policeman who pointed out the way and saluted yesterday, Mammeh judges. Yes, when they're good, the *goyim*, they're very very good.

"Next!" the policeman on duty calls. He is standing by the entrance to the shed, where the group before hers is now exiting.

Mammeh floats toward him all light in the head...not knowing which way to turn...

Inside, there's a center aisle with a row of fresh pine coffins on either side; you can smell the wood. In each of those up front lies a still figure with a sheet pulled to its chin and its head resting on a kind of pillow; those further down appear to contain the very badly burned.

Sniffles and snuffles begin to echo as Mammeh and her group move along. She opens her purse and takes out her handkerchief too...

So there we are, no luck—she has come without finding anything to the first of the boxes of charred bones. Now, Bertha, no need to continue, just get out of here, she urges herself. *Kreynele*'s gone, and that's that.

Let's get away, good and away, she decides moments later, heading back along First Avenue.

The viewing-line has grown by leaps and bounds, and now stretches far down. There can't be that many relatives, she realizes, so some of those waiting must be there for ghoulish fun or to gloat at everyone's misery, like last night on the Square.

She crosses over to the other side of First, then thinking to walk a little and let things settle down inside, turns into Twenty-fifth, the first side-street.

It's lined with trees and full of brownstone houses with little fenced-in plots of grass. The shades in the parlor windows are all drawn, which is not surprising considering that it's Sunday and still early.

But what's this! Voices, there are voices behind her, more than two it seems. She looks round—yes, a small group of young workmen are striding up the street, talking loudly.

How come they're awake at this hour, Mammeh wonders. Maybe they never went to sleep, maybe they've been up all night having a good time and are just now going home.

"Hey you!" one of them calls out, amidst their clumping boots.

Mammeh's heart gives a leap—I hope they don't mean to cause trouble—she speeds up a little. What shall I do? It's so very quiet there in Twenty-fifth Street.

"Hey you!" the same one calls again, from closer, they too having put on some steam.

Vaguely Mammeh guesses that they may have spied her leaving the area of the shed and followed. What do they want with me, what'll they do to me, should I go knock on some door? To the next corner, Second Avenue, she would never make it now, even if she picked up her skirts and ran.

Mammeh turns toward them and waits.

There are four of them, all lean and straight like grown men, but with Irish-looking baby faces. Toughs, Americans call them, stout fellows who spend whatever spare time and money they have hanging around saloons and acting like bigshots.

"Hey, I toldja it was a Jew lady," the leader squawks as they come up—he's the cleanest cut of the lot, with straight features and fine hair that stands up a little in the back.

Mammeh stays put, now with a definite pain in her chest.

"Whatsa matter, Jew lady, someone o' yours get burned up in de fia-ah?" he taunts, then murmurs something to his cronies.

"Rah-iia-ha!" they all shout out.

Mammeh snorts: where do they learn to say such ugly things? Not from their mamas surely. What mother would teach a child

The Fire

such hatred? No, it has to come from somewhere else, maybe from their priests—she recalls the ones back home in the Ukraine who used to lead the people on to burn and pillage in the Jewish quarters for no good reason.

"How 'bout it, Jew lady, cat got yer tongue?"

The cronies grin with their hands on their hips.

What's there to say, she should say something. Ah! Mammeh has just the thing. Then let them beat me black and blue if they care to, if that's what'll make them happy.

She looks hard at them, very hard—"Got vill punish you."

The creases round their noses fade.

※

A bass drum is booming—*bum buh-bum bum*—and a trumpet is blaring over it—*wa, wa WA- WA, wa wa-wa.*

Lying flat on his back with hard-wooden bench slats sticking him, Hippolyte gropes for the name of the tune, which is on the tip of his tongue but won't come. Oh, to hell with it—he opens his eyes.

Overhead are many branches with new green buds on them, birds hopping about in their midst, and a grey sky peeping through.

Yee, yee YEE-YEE, yee yee-yee, a high female voice sings in place of the trumpet, the drum still keeping time.

Ja, now he has it, the tune is "Rock of Ages." It's coming from two Salvation Army Band men and a woman, who are planted in front of Garibaldi, a few feet away.

Hippolyte thinks to sit up, but is stopped by something else hard grinding him in the ribs—a pint of corn, or what remains of it, that he went and got in a saloon sometime or other during the night.

People are hovering all around on the grass, talking in low voices. He notes especially a spiffy young clerkly type in a straw hat with a girl, all in ruffles, on his arm. It must be getting on toward eleven, church time, he figures.

Oh boy! Liebling Paula is suddenly there in his mind, and he feels a pang in the gut. Was it busy in the restaurant last night? How did she manage by herself? He pictures her, poor thing, with a strand of her fine golden hair slipping over her brow, looking very gloomy and woebegone.

Nothing for it, we'll have to face the music. "Alleyoop!"—he swings his legs around.

But then his eye lights on Number 23 Washington Place, upstairs there—where now the windows have no glass and there are black burn marks on the brickwork surrounding them.

And now yesterday returns in a rush—the Little Bourgeoise on one of those ledges with her arms around that boy Jerry, her mouth pressed to his, and then the fall, the flaming fall—

Hippolyte's eyelashes bat furiously. "I DON'T WANT TO GO HOME ANYMORE!" he chokes out to anyone who'll listen.

"Disgusting," he mutters, after getting unsteadily under way.

Everywhere one looks on the Square, the paths are strewn with vendors, hawking everything from salted pretzels and roasted chestnuts to jelly apples and hot corn-on-the-cob. The next thing you know, some enterprising soul will be jingling for people to come buy bracelets, locks of hair, and other "souvenirs" from up there.

At the Arch, with no particular destination in mind, he ambles desultorily toward his old stamping ground, the elite north side.

The big cheeses here should be coming out any minute to do their Sunday duty, is his thought as he hobbles along the row of fine townhouses. Leave it to them, they'll probably offer up prayers for the "souls of the unfortunate victims."

The front door to Number 8 opens. "Look here, Ben," a woman warbles in a clipped English way, "if you don't mind, I'd really rather not go."

Hippolyte darts behind a bush to listen.

The Fire

Above on the stoop, well-stuffed in a rich brown frock coat with a top hat, has to be Englishman Benjamin Guinness, and just carefully handed over the doorstep by him would be his missus, a devilishly handsome woman with velvety black eyes set in skin like soft pearl, who is done up from head to foot in bright purple. They're the givers of those lavish fetes for the upper crust, to say nothing of the eccentric one where the two of them waltzed around with their help.

"I just know there'll be a big to-do," the wife adds, "and I'd just as soon not be a part of it."

"Very well then, my dear, I shan't go either," Guinness says.

"Blessings on you both," Hippolyte murmurs with tears in his voice, and vows that henceforth he'll never trouble them or theirs again.

Pushing on, he's quite broken up until Number 4, when he pauses to look back to where he came from and sees that a fair number of people have indeed emerged from other houses, including—yes, that old geezer Tailer with his bug eyes and walrus moustache, who one night gave chase in his dressing gown to a certain peeping Tom caught *in flagrante*.

"'Morning Charlie!" a man sings out from the top of Number 5's stoop.

"Good morning, Robert," another nasals back, on Number 7's.

They are Robert DeForest and Charles Gould, both prominent attorneys, and both soberly attired in black.

Hippolyte slips behind another bush.

"Some business yesterday," offers DeForest, who, besides a hefty paunch, has bushy eyebrows peeping over pince-nez and a moustache trailing off into a Vandyke.

"Mm-mm," agrees Gould, a lanky type with rimless glasses.

They step down their separate stairs to the pavement and begin walking along together.

"Where were you when it happened?"—it's legal-eagle DeForest again. In addition to being connected with the Metropolitan Museum in a big buck way, he's a glutton for sitting on the boards of charities.

"At my club," Gould, another "art lover," answers. "And you?"

"Shameful," Hippolyte derides in a low voice, and mindlessly sets out after them.

So many well-heeled ones have left their houses all along the north side that by the time he reaches Fifth Avenue there's a regular procession up it.

Crossed over now and sort of part of the crowd, he decides to go as far as the first church—Ascension he thinks it's called, brownstone with a rectangular bell tower—and then retrace his steps.

Everyone seems to leave him behind pretty fast, and he hangs back even more to scratch his ass, but before long he has arrived.

"Now look at that," he says out loud, before the glassed-in sign in its box.

The subject of today's sermon—in fact, its very title—is Socialism and Christianity.

Though it shouldn't be all that surprising. Percy Stickney Grant the rector, he recalls, is a frequenter of the Liberal Club, haven of daring ideas...in principle.

Turning it over in his mind, Hippolyte realizes that the fellow has a lot of gall mixing apples with oranges like that—yes, and I've got a good mind to go in there and tell him so! *Yes, do it*, a devil in his gut echoes. *Shame him but good in front of all those la-dee-da parishioners of his who keep him in the chips.*

By force of old habit, he ducks his head as he passes through Ascension's portals, as if something were going to pounce on him or grab him from behind by the scruff of the neck.

Inside, the whole congregation is giving forth with a hymn, to the thundering accompaniment of the organ—

Holy, holy, holy...

The Fire

Now where is he, the do-gooding jackass, Hippolyte wonders from way in the rear, and begins scanning down front, where the choir is ranged.

High above the altar—and impossible to miss—is a huge painting of Jesus up in the air, surrounded by a flock of angels, with his disciples looking up from the ground in amazement.

Hippolyte tsuh-tush's as he would at any waste of time and talent, and goes on with the search.

"A-ME-EN!" the congregation bawls out amidst organ crashes, and in the shiny mahogany pews all over there's a general plunking down.

Ah, there he is, the reverend—Hippolyte has found him. Comrade-Grant-in-theory, in a voluminous robe of gold-tinged white, is surveying them all from the pulpit, where he has just extended his priestly arms.

If you're going to do something, now's the time, Hippolyte's devil prods him, and he begins moving forward down the center aisle.

Grant, who wears his hair parted in the middle and has a cleft in his chin, spies him and lets his arms fall again—which causes everyone to turn around, the women in some very fancy headgear.

All at once conscious of his day-old beard and slept-in shirt and trousers, Hippolyte begins to drag his feet. *SO WHAT, WHAT'S IT TO THEM, GO ON WITH IT*, the demon inside him commands.

Footsteps sound behind him. Someone comes up and touches his shoulder. "Please, sir, this is no place for you," the person says in a voice that is at once grave and mellow.

Hippolyte spins round—to come face-to-face with old Tailer in rich grey with a white carnation in his lapel, he of the mad chase through the Square!

And wouldn't you know it, there's a glint of recognition in the old guy's bulgy eyes. Nevertheless the hand remains—"Just step this way, sir. I'm sure we can—"

Hippolyte pushes the "well-meaning" paw away and turns to go—to hell with him, to hell with all of them!

Outside, a fine spring rain is falling, and clearly he's had enough of this wandering life—at least for the moment. Yes, all he can think of now is his dear one, who may be worried sick about him, and the restaurant, his pride and joy, with its familiar white table cloths and peephole in the kitchen.

C'mon, get a move on—he begins heading back along Fifth, now deserted, as probably the Square will be...due to the cleansing power of rain.

Ah, too soon spoken—behind him on the road comes the clipclop of hooves and whirring of carriage wheels.

"Hoa-ah!" someone calls, and a shiny black landaulette pulls up with its horse, dark to match, daintily throwing its legs out.

"Say, buddy, which way's de building?" yells the driver, who is all gussied up in rose-colored livery.

Building? Hippolyte considers.

"Yuh know, de one dat burned?"

Behind him in the glass-enclosed cab, a young matron and her little girl, both with cameos at the throats of high-collared waists, peer hopefully through the silvery raindrops for the answer.

THE BUILDING THAT BURNED!—Hippolyte can hardly believe his ears. What's the matter with them? Are they crazy? It's the limit, the absolute limit!

"Building? I'll show you building!" he cries out, and hopping up on the driver's step, makes a grab for the whip.

There's a lot of hollering inside—no matter. "You see this?" he says, back on the ground, and brandishes the whip at them.

Mother and child clutch one another behind the glass; the driver is holding an eye.

The Fire

"If I ever catch you coming down here again, this is what you'll get!"—Hippolyte raises his knee and breaks the thing over his thigh, Crack!

The rose-colored clown quickly wheels the horse around, and gives it a boot in the butt.

"Don't come back, dya hear!" Hippolyte shouts after them, racing wetly away.

"Bitches! Bastards!" The pieces of whip flung to the wind, he stretches out his rain-soaked arms before the Arch—"I could kill them all!"

ically applies to large pharmaceutical companies since the larger pharmaceutical companies tend to have more drugs on the market that could theoretically # EPILOGUE

EPILOGUE

The aftermath of the Triangle Shirtwaist Fire is a matter of record:

On April 5th, another rainy day, seven hearses strewn with orchids and roses transported the remains of those victims who had been left unidentified from the pier building on East Twenty-sixth Street to a city-owned plot in Brooklyn's Evergreen Cemetery, where they were interred after a brief interdenominational ceremony. Around the same time from Washington Arch, an empty flower-bedecked hearse, drawn by six white horses in crepe, led off a silent procession one hundred thousand strong up Fifth Avenue; conspicuous among the mourners, naturally, were Mary Dreier, Helen Marot, and Rose Schneiderman of the Women's Trade Union League.

The following December, Triangle owners Max Blanck and Isaac Harris were brought to trial on a charge of manslaughter in the first degree, but to the public's shock and horror got off scot-free when the prosecution failed to prove that they were aware of any doors being locked on that fateful day, the criterion for responsibility established by the court. When giving his account of things at the trial, production manager and in-law Sam Bernstein (who was earlier caught trying to put the fix on a number of witnesses) broke down and wept bitter tears over the loss of his brother and so many other dear people on the Ninth floor, and at his *powerlessness to do anything to help them, as he had so heroically done for those seeking escape from the ever-encroaching flames on Eight.*

And here ends the tale or, if you will, *bobe mayse*—old wive's tale—that Fanny, my late mother, spun for me from her wheelchair, putting her final months to their best use.

As Martha and Jerrold, and Benny too, were creatures straight out of her imagination, it remains for me only to add a few words about Mammeh and her Eli, and, of course, Hippolyte, who strictly speaking were not.

The real-life Bertha and Elias, my grandma and grandpa Ferber, did in time move from the Lower East Side to a house in Brooklyn, and it was there in the "better air" that Fanny and her sisters Dinah and Pauline—her only sisters—finished their growing up.

Hippolyte probably came to her attention in some form or fashion in the 1920s, when she, a factory sewing machine operator, and my father, a dress cutter, were both active in Dubinsky's very vocal ILGWU. I like to think of them wending their way to the little basement restaurant off the Square on Macdougal Street of an evening and dining amidst the many "swells" of advanced ideas consorting there—but who knows. Whenever pressed for an explanation, Fanny always responded in her coy way with, "Ask me no questions…"

Alas, the true Hippolyte, who was not exactly as she painted him, fell on exceedingly hard times after the period of this story, losing his liebling Paula, who did eventually give up on him and find another, or actually others. I imagine him being further struck to the quick in 1919, when his beloved comrade Emma was kicked out of this country, along with Sasha, and deported to Revolutionary Russia. As that truly extraordinary human being Emma Goldman was never allowed to return to us, save once briefly, despite her almost instantaneous dislike for the Bolsheviks and their ways, I see the Hippolyte of reality as growing more and more morose through the

Epilogue

years, perhaps feeling that he had been abandoned and left to uphold the Anarchist cause here all alone. In any event, he, Hippolyte-in-the-flesh, drifted into deeper and deeper alcoholism, and ended his days at the age of eighty in a hospital for the incurably insane.

ACKNOWLEDGMENTS

The author wishes to give special thanks to Raymond Donnell for his invaluable editorial assistance.

Thanks are also due to Dina Abramowitz and the staff of YIVO; Paul Avrich; Gene Berger; Thomas Dunning and the staff of the New-York Historical Society; Arthur Gelb; Peter Gulewich; Irving Howe; George Jochnowitz; Patricia and Harry Katz; Regina Kellerman and the staff of the Greenwich Village Society for Historical Preservation; Bob Lazaar of the ILGWU; Alfred Levine; Mark Piel of The Society Library; Olga Miller; Martin Plotkin; Eva Rensky; Sophie Schulman; Leon Stein; Bayrd Still; Dorothy Swanson and the staff of the Tamiment Collection; Alex Zamenek; Dorothy and Samuel Zucker; the staffs of the Board of Education Archives at Columbia University; the Church of the Ascencion; the Educational Alliance; the Jewish Division of the New York Public Library; the Jewish Museum; the Labadie Collection; the Lincoln Center Public Library; the Manhattan Borough President's Office; the Municipal Archives; the Museum of the City of New York; the New York City Fire Department Archives; Number 6 Washington Square North; St. Anthony's Church; the Tarrytown Historical Society; the Tenement Museum; the University Settlement House; and the Workmen's Circle.

A Note on the Production

This book was designed by Caroline Hagen and set in type electronically by Robert Leuze of SuperScript, New York, New York, using Ventura Publisher 4.1 and WordPerfect 5.1. The type is Old Caslon 337 of the Lanston Type Company, Vancouver, B.C. Linotronic camera-ready copy was supplied by Southern California Printcorp, Altadena, California, and the printer and binder was McNaughton & Gunn, Inc., Saline, Michigan. Felix Kramer of Kramer Communications, New York, New York, provided production advice.